Level Best Crime Fiction Anthology

Busted! Arresting Stories from the Beat (2017)

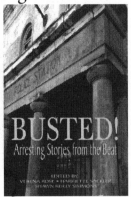

The Best New England Crime Stories Anthologies:

Snowbound (2017)

Windward (2016)

Red Dawn (2015)
Rogue Wave (2014)
Stone Cold (2013)
Blood Moon (2012)
Dead Calm (2011)
Thin Ice (2010)
Quarry (2009)

Deadfall (2008)
Still Waters (2007)
Seasmoke (2006)
Windchill (2005)
Undertow (2005)
Riptide (2004)

NOIR
AT THE
SALAD BAR

CULINARY TALES WITH A BITE

An Anthology

Edited by
Verena Rose, Harriette Sackler
& Shawn Reilly Simmons

The Dames of Detection
d/b/a Level Best Books
18100 Windsor Hill Dr.
Olney, MD 20832
www.levelbestbooks.com

Trade Paperback
ISBN-13: 978-0692938447
ISBN-10: 0692938443
Manufactured & Printed in the United States of America
2017

TABLE OF CONTENTS

Introduction

Food and drink have always been popular elements in crime fiction, from Inspector Maigret's mussels in cream, to Spenser's oyster stew, to Nero Wolfe's private chef Fritz whipping together shad roe for the thoughtful, corpulent detective. Nick and Nora Charles drank martinis, Phillip Marlowe popularized the gimlet in the 1950s, and over thirty characters were poisoned, many times during tea, in the books of Agatha Christie. Crime fiction has long been entwined with gastronomy, and we're excited to join the tradition with this anthology.

When the call went out for culinary crime tales with a darker bent, we were overwhelmed by the response, and by the wide variety of stories we received. The editors considered over one hundred and twenty submissions for the project, which were read blindly. The result is this pot luck collection of stories which is as varied and original as the authors who wrote them, all with food and drink being a main element of the story. In addition to American contributors from all over the country, this anthology features three authors from England, one from France, and one from Israel, to complete our most international anthology to date.

The title *Noir at the Salad Bar* was inspired by the Noir at the Bar phenomenon, where crime writers gather at a (preferably dark) bar and read stories over a few drinks. Conceived by Peter Rozovsky in 2008 in Philadelphia, to date Noir at the Bar events have occurred in cities all over the U.S. and the U.K.

Noir at the Salad Bar, Culinary Tales with a Bite features stories set in many different time periods. The expanding railroad in the American west is the backdrop for "Harvey House Homicide" by Joyce Ann Brown, in which a young waitress hopes to find the truth about the murder of a chef and the disappearance of her coworker. Karen Cantwell's "The Hearts of Men" takes place during WWII, and features a woman who is an expert pickler. "Death at the Hands of Le Fee Verte" by Verena Rose brings us to New Orleans in 1900, and the restaurant where Oysters Rockefeller was created. "Ragbones and the Case of the Christmas Goose" by Rima Perlstein Riedel and "The Case of the Apertured Apiculturist" by Larry Lefkowitz each present new cases for Sherlock Holmes, one involving a missing holiday dinner and the other a suspicious death, apparently by a swarm of bees.

Revenge is a dish served piping hot in Sharon Daynard's "Black Coffee in Bed," which is also the only recipe the main character feels the need to master. Or it can be dished up cold, as in Sheila Connolly's "Cole Slaughter," featuring the world's worst neighbor, who has a long list of complaints about the people living in her quiet suburb.

Breaking bread can be a pleasant experience, or one fraught with tension. In "Consuming Passion" by Martin Edwards, two old college mates get together for a unique meal, and to discuss their grievances. Holiday dinners are often trying experiences, as in John R. Clark's "With Great Relish," a Thanksgiving story featuring a family at odds over who will inherit the farm.

Included also are several gritty contemporary stories, including "The Lobster Tank" by E.A. Aymar, which takes place at the bar in a Red Lobster, and stars a world-weary hit man. Frank Collia's "The Buena Vista Sandwich Club" is set on a food truck where a cook with a dark past is attempting a new life while making the best Cuban sandwiches on the beach. A greasy spoon on the verge of a violent attack is the setting of "Petunia at the Tip Top" by Jenny Drummey, and Michael Bracken's "Smoked" tells the story of a quiet man in a small town whose barbeque is good enough to draw unwanted attention from dangerous people from his past. Two friends who share a happier past find themselves in danger in John M. Floyd's "The Sandman" when one of them reaches out for help from the wrong person.

It seems the farthest thing from reality is Reality TV, as is the case in Alan Orloff's "Togas and Toques." As chefs battle it out on "Caligula's Cooking Coliseum," one contestant falls victim to a bit of *un*healthy competition. And in order to eliminate her own competition, a successful blintz maker in lower Manhattan, who is less than pleased when a new bakery sets up shop across the street, takes matters into her own hands in Harriette Sackler's "Family Business."

A beautiful setting can't hide an ugly crime in Michael Allan Mallory's "A Murder in Montreux," when a man in his pajamas is found dead near the *Quai des Fleurs* in Switzerland. Another unique setting is a big game restaurant in Mara Buck's "A Murder of Crows," where wild animals end up on the menu and people with questionable taste come to dine. New York City in an upscale eatery is the setting of Gerald Ellas's "Sleeping Beauty," where a man witnesses an incident, then runs into the perpetrator again years later, who reveals a hidden past.

In A.B. Polomski's "Grab-N-Go," an ambitious woman transforms the local quick mart into an upscale grocery store, which doesn't sit right with folks, some of whom aren't afraid to do something about it. And in Elaine Togneri's "Playing Games" we experience what life is like in the kitchen for an immigrant worker who was expecting a very different life in America when she left her homeland.

A team of British detectives investigate who killed a wealthy woman hosting her friends, and some foes, at her estate in Lorraine Sharma Nelson's "Antipastdead." And an amateur sleuth in New England goes digging for clues when her bridge partner's daughter falls under the spell of a questionable suitor in Barbara Ross's "Jane Darrowfield, Professional Busybody."

A kitchen worker in a nursing home thinks he can find a way to better his station in life by getting to know the residents a little better in "Deadly Dinner" by LD Masterson. In "Bases Looted" by Jason Half, a lot more than hot dogs and cotton candy are served in the VIP skybox to the visiting bigwigs. But when an expensive trophy disappears, suspicion falls on the food vendors, who have to solve the crime to save their bacon.

A couple of the stories have a touch of fantasy in them, beginning with E.L. Johnson's "Beef Stew," the story of a young ogre who uncharacteristically enjoys human food. And "Candy" by Isobel Horsburgh, features a well-meaning dog walker working for employers who to the outside world are devout vegetarians, but at home are ravenous carnivores, a secret that could ruin them if it got out.

Women who have had enough are featured in three of our stories. "Fed Up" by Louise Taylor stars a woman whose porcine-like husband, who provides everything in life except fun and excitement, has drained all patience from his wife. In "My Life in Killer Recipes" by Leslie Wheeler, one woman highlights various instances in her lifetime when those who've done her wrong ended up paying the price via her very specific culinary chops. And serving up dessert is a woman in Shawn Reilly Simmons's "Humble Pie," who never seems to win, no matter how many times she enters the town's pie contest.

Noir at the Salad Bar, Culinary Tales with a Bite has something for every fan of crime fiction, especially those who enjoy a good meal. So pour yourself a glass of wine, or a cup of tea, or mix up a cocktail and tuck in. We hope you enjoy these excellent stories as much as we do.

Verena Rose
Harriette Sackler
Shawn Reilly Simmons

The Dames of Detection
Editors at Level Best Books

COLE SLAUGHTER

BY SHEILA CONNOLLY

I've always loved farmers' markets, especially now that so many small farms in my part of Massachusetts have gotten into growing interesting, often heirloom varieties of fruits and vegetables. It's so nice to bring home a squash or a bag of apples that you know were picked just that morning. But our season is short, and by October there's lots of squash and root vegetables—and more apples, of course—but no more leafy greens or delicate berries. That's one of the prices you pay for living in New England, but it makes the arrival of spring all the sweeter.

Today was the last market of the year, and it was well attended, because it was one of those perfect autumn days with blue, blue sky and blazing orange and yellow leaves. I was filling my basket with carrots and potatoes when I spied my neighbor Marjorie on the other side of the Town Hall lawn where the market was held. Marjorie and I had been next-door neighbors going on thirty years now. We'd watched our children grow up, playing together. We saw one husband die (mine) and one demand a divorce (hers) and leave. We'd untangled our wrangling pets (my cat, her dog) more times than I could count. Maybe we'd started out cordially enough, when we were both new to the neighborhood, but now we barely spoke. Unless, of course, we met in public, in which case Marjorie went all sticky sweet on me— she'd been raised in the South. Robert Frost once said "good fences make good neighbors," and sometimes I wondered whether a six-foot fence would improve my life now.

True to form, Marjorie had seen me and was now waving vigorously. "Yoo-hoo! Nancy?" she yelled, loud enough to wake the dead in the cemetery down the street. I summoned up a smile and a weak wave in return. But that wasn't enough for Marjorie, and she marched right over to where I was standing.

"Hey, Nancy, I haven't seen you outside for a while. How've you been?" She showed her teeth, but I wouldn't call it a smile.

"Just fine, Margie," I told her. *I've been avoiding you and it's done wonders for my blood pressure.* "What've you been up to?"

"Oh, visiting with the grandkids, cleaning up the garden for winter, that kind of thing. Listen, I've decided to have an end-of-season barbecue in the back yard next weekend. Saturday if the weather cooperates, Sunday if it doesn't. I hope you can come!"

Translation: it would look kind of odd if her next-door neighbor didn't show up for this thing, and people would ask why. "Sure, I guess. Can I bring something?"

"Oh, don't worry about it. I'll have plenty. But if you've got something special that you want to share, that's fine too."

"Okay. What time?"

"I figure around three, maybe? It's getting dark early these days. Well, I'd better stock up on goodies! See you on Saturday!"

"Bye," I said. She hadn't noticed my lack of enthusiasm. I added a stop at the liquor store to my list of errands, because I was pretty sure I wouldn't make it through Marjorie's party without a drink or three.

I could have moved when my husband died, I suppose, but I didn't want to give Marjorie the satisfaction. Our decades-long relationship was complicated, with a couple of major secrets. The big one was that I knew that she'd had an affair with my late husband Harold. But she didn't know that I knew. Neither had my husband known that I knew. He was kind of clueless in general, and he was lousy at sneaking around. He didn't need to tell me about the affair, because he couldn't hide the tell-tale signs—the averted glances when the four of us were together, and longing gazes when he thought nobody was watching, the false heartiness when he laughed at Marjorie's lame jokes. Actually he got along pretty well with Marjorie's husband Bob, who was as clueless as he was.

And that was pretty clueless: I knew that Bob wasn't the father of Marjorie's youngest child. My husband was. He looked just like Harold, which was pretty clear when you saw them side

2

by side. I thought about finding a way to get a DNA test, but in the end it wasn't worth it. I knew, and that was enough. I never told any of them that I knew—it was my little secret, and it made me feel good to know that I had something on them. Hey, nobody ever accused me of being a nice person. Marjorie had staked out that role years ago. I could live with that.

I might have kind of hinted to Bob that she'd been carrying on with Harold. Maybe Bob wasn't so dumb after all—it wasn't long before he filed for divorce. The kids decided to go with him. I'll give Marjorie credit, though—she really did seem upset when my husband died. Maybe he was her back-up plan, but I wasn't going to let that happen.

The neighbors ate it all up. Life was kind of dull in our cookie-cutter 1950s part of town, with its tree-lined streets and tidy sidewalks. Our mess was much more entertaining than anything on the television. I could see the looks people exchanged when one or the other of us walked by. I always smiled and waved, playing dumb. But then one would lean toward the other and put her hand over her mouth and make some comment she didn't want to be heard. I could imagine what they were saying anyway. At least I could provide the bi...ddies with entertainment.

Problem was, now Marjorie and I were stuck in that neighborhood. It was nice enough, I suppose, and it didn't even change much in all the time we lived there. But we couldn't get away from all those prying eyes, the syrupy questions, "How *are* you, dear? How are you managing?" Just fine, thank you very much—living with Harold had been more work than he was worth. Too bad he hadn't left a lot of money, which is why I was still living in the old house we'd shared. I assumed Marjorie was in the same boat. Funny thing—none of our kids wanted to take us in. Not that I blamed them. They had their own lives to lead, and they didn't need to be stuck with a crotchety parent. I hated to ask for anything. I could get by just fine, as long as I didn't worry about the peeling paint and that drip in the corner of the roof. When it came time to get rid of the house, the kids could worry about paint and shingles.

And that's how we all went along, year after year. My fifties slid by, and then my sixties hit. No fun at all. Bits and pieces of my body started giving out, like my teeth. Those things are expensive to fix! And then my blood pressure went up, and so did the cholesterol, and I got a pinched nerve in my back that was painful, although it gave me a great excuse to get out of doing the yard work, or shoveling snow in the winter. And then the cat started piddling on the living room rug. And I needed new glasses again because I couldn't see to read. And something inside the car gave out and the auto place wanted a lot of money to fix it. Don't let anybody give you any crap about The Golden Years. How about The Rust Years?

And now here was Marjorie going all chirpy on me and inviting me to a party. I knew she didn't want me there. Probably she invited me because she figured I'd call the cops and complain about the noise if she didn't. I probably would have.

Why the heck had I volunteered to make a dish for the meal? Because all the other women would, while the guys who were still breathing and walking without help would go all manly and cook hamburgers on the grill and swill beer and talk about sports. And all the other women would huddle together and complain about their medical problems and how their plumbing didn't work anymore. Or their husband's didn't. A real fun party. But I'd said I'd go, and if I didn't show up somebody would notice and comment about it. So I'd go. And I'd said I would make a dish, and by God, I'd make a dish for the crowd. That was what nice people did. I could pretend I was nice for as long as one party lasted, couldn't I?

I had a week to plan my dish and get the ingredients together. I didn't much like chopping any more, since my arthritis started acting up and my knife kept slipping. I hated to turn on a burner to boil something, because there'd been a time or two lately I'd forgotten to turn it off and burnt the pan. I decided I'd make cole slaw. Everybody liked cole slaw, or at least they ate it at picnics because they thought they had to. I had my German grandmother's recipe, didn't I? So I'd make cole slaw for Marjorie's last summer party.

I went back to rambling around the farmers' market and picked up a hefty head of leafy cabbage—not the tidy little volleyball the supermarket called cabbage. I tossed in a few more

4

carrots too—I always liked the dash of color they added to my slaw.

Cole slaw was one of those dishes that you really couldn't make ahead, because it would get all mushy and slimy. So I had to wait until Saturday morning to do that. It happened that my kitchen window had a great view of Marjorie's back yard, so I could watch her trotting around and hanging streamers and what looked like old Japanese lanterns and such. She'd begged a couple of the neighborhood teenagers to help her set up the grill and rake up the dead grass and what leaves had already fallen. I wondered if she was bribing them with a couple of cans of beer, since she knew they were underage.

I had to hunt down my grandmother's slaw recipe. The kitchen wasn't as neat as I'd once kept it, but I just couldn't be bothered these days. I didn't do a lot of fancy cooking anyway, mostly things I'd been making most of my life and didn't need to use a recipe for. I'd known my grandmother only in her later years—she'd come over from Germany after World War Two, married and had my mother a few years later. Only the one child, so we didn't have bunches of aunts and uncles and cousins to hang out with on holidays—or to pawn off grandma on some schedule.

She'd been a nasty woman. She never lost her accent, no surprise, and she bullied my mother. Nothing her daughter did was ever right. I envied my friends who had cheerful, smiling grannies who smelled like flowery perfume, and who would arrive with candy and hand-knit sweaters and cover their darling grand-babies with sloppy kisses. My grandmother wore shabby dark clothes and smelled of mothballs. The few times we'd traveled to her home, a row house in New Jersey, it had looked—and smelled—a lot like her. Dreary, musty, dark. And she was a pretty bad cook, which I could tell even as a child. Why had I kept her cole slaw recipe? I really wasn't sure, except that it was one of the few dishes of hers that I could eat without gagging, and it was easy to make. Kind of twisted that the only recipe of hers I had was the one I disliked least.

000

NOIR AT THE SALAD BAR

The news said the weekend weather would be nice, and it was. No way was Marjorie's little get-together going to be rained out. At least I could get it over with on Saturday. Early that morning I pulled out Gramma's stained recipe, written on a yellowed index card. Cabbage, carrots, mayo, ketchup and a dash of Worcestershire sauce. Plus a little of this and that. After I ate my breakfast I started shredding the cabbage. I chopped the carrots pretty fine, because my teeth weren't up to crunching chunks of them. I even threw in some interesting ones I'd gotten at the farmers' market—who knew there were red carrots and yellow carrots and other colors too? Made the mix kind of pretty. I dumped everything into an old chipped china bowl and mixed it all together with my hands—nobody was going to know anyway, right?—and added the final seasoning. Then I stuck it in the fridge and put a plate on top. Had to let it sit for a while to let the flavors blend together right, or so Gramma always said, but I knew you shouldn't let anything with mayo sit out and get too warm. It could make people sick.

Come three o'clock I put on my newest jeans and a clean shirt, combed my hair, put my slaw into a nicer bowl, and marched across my lawn to Marjorie's house. There were already a few people gathered there, holding cans of beer or soft drinks, chatting. I recognized most of them, although newcomers were beginning to buy into our block as the rest of us got older and moved away. I set my dish down on the table under a shady tree, turned back to the people and got ready to make nice. I could play the game. "Hey, Fred, your lawn's been looking really good this summer." *And I know you've been watering in secret, in spite of the town's drought regulations.* "Alice, love the color you painted your shutters— really spruces up the place." *Did you have to go with pink?* "Did you get a new car, Bobby? I'm thinking I should be looking for something a little newer." *Yeah, just as soon as I win the lottery.* I mingled. I smiled until my face hurt. I waited for the eating to start. Marjorie and a couple of guys were fussing around the grill. How hard was it to start a fire? There was a stack of raw hamburgers and some hot dogs on a platter, waiting for the cooking crew to decide the grill was ready. I found myself a plastic chair in the shade and sat down to watch.

6

No kids here—I guess once they hit their teens they wouldn't want to hang with a bunch of old fogeys like us. There were a couple of dogs, and some people threw Frisbees to entertain them. Finally Marjorie declared the fire was ready, and one guy appointed himself Griller in Chief and started laying out the meat on the grate over the coals (Marjorie had never bothered to get herself a propane grill). There was a pattern to eating at events like these, I'd learned: pick your meat first, stick it on your paper plate, and then fill in the rest with the side dishes. Find a seat, hoping you didn't drop the whole mess, and pig out. Repeat.

I waited until the first rush was over to go fill my plate. Marjorie was still hovering near the meat, in case it would burst into flames without warning. I helped myself to a greyish hamburger and a selection of salads, and made sure to take a heap of Gramma's slaw. Marjorie followed me. "I'm so glad you could make it, Nancy! Isn't it a perfect day? And it's great to see so many of the neighbors. We used to do this every year, didn't we? I can't believe how quickly time has passed."

When she finally paused to breathe, I finally said something. "Good idea you had, to get people together like this. And the weather cooperated. Did you try my cole slaw?"

"Oh, no, not yet."

"You should—it's my grandmother's old German recipe."

Marjorie dutifully added some to her plate and took a forkful. "Mmm, interesting. It's got kind of an unusual flavor. What is it?"

"Celery seed. Gramma always used that." It tasted kind of bitter, I knew—but Gramma had always been bitter.

"And are these things carrots? They're all different colors," Marjorie went on, dutifully taking another bite.

"Yes, I got some at the farmers' market last week. Makes the dish look kind of interesting, doesn't it?"

"I've seen the red and yellow ones, but I didn't know there was a white kind," she said, looking puzzled as she poked at a small chunk of carrot.

"Oh, that's one I grew myself, in the back yard. It wasn't hard. I bet you could grow them too." But I was pretty sure she wouldn't get the chance.

7

Marjorie gave me a kind of pained look, then took her plate and wandered off toward an empty chair. I took my own plate back to where I had been sitting, and sat and watched the crowd.

It took only a few minutes. The early birds had taken plenty of food and wolfed it down, so they were affected first. Some turned pale and clutched their mid-section. One vomited into a bush at the back of Marjorie's lot. As I sat there I took another bite of Gramma's slaw, savoring its tangy flavor as I watched more of Marjorie's guests flee the scene, no doubt looking for a bathroom—fast.

Marjorie looked at me from across the lawn, and then lurched unsteadily toward me. "What did you do?" she hissed, panting and struggling to breathe.

"Me?" I asked, trying to sound innocent.

"Yes, you. How did you make the neighbors sick? Because only the people who ate that slaw of yours are sick."

"Wild carrot," I said. "In the cole slaw."

"What?" She looked bewildered.

"It's also called hemlock. It's poisonous."

"I've got to call 911," she said. But her legs wouldn't hold her, and she sat down with a thud on the lawn in front of my chair.

"Won't make much difference," I told her.

"Why?" she gasped.

"Because nobody'll get here fast enough to help you. I timed it when I fed it to Harold. He always liked Gramma's cole slaw. You might last a little longer than he did."

"What? You killed Harold?"

"Yup. I did."

"Why try to kill me?" Marjorie's face had turned an interesting pale green color.

"I figured you deserved it, after what you and Harold did. Yeah, I knew all about it. Maybe he wasn't much of a man, but he was mine."

I looked over her head to see one guest writhing on the lawn in what looked like a seizure. "The stuff acts pretty fast. Some of these people will probably be okay, but it's kind of a crap shoot."

"Somebody will know it was you," Marjorie panted.

I shrugged. "Doesn't matter. I'll be dead too."

"What?"

"You heard me. I ate enough to kill myself."

"Why'd you wait so long?" Marjorie whispered.

"I kind of enjoyed making you miserable. First your husband dumps you, and once you got used to that, I took out Harold, in case you had your eye on him. But now I'm out of money, the house is falling down, and my kids hate me. It's not worth living anymore, but I thought I'd take you with me. Too bad I won't be around to see if the cops figure out what happened. I hope you have a good time in Hell, Marjorie."

She couldn't hear me anymore.

Sheila Connolly, Anthony and Agatha Award–nominated and *New York Times* bestselling mystery author, writes series set in Philadelphia, rural Massachusetts, and Ireland, as well as a paranormal romance series. She will introduce a new mystery series set in Maryland in 2018. Her short stories have appeared in multiple anthologies. She lives in Massachusetts with her husband and three cats.

NOIR AT THE SALAD BAR

HUMBLE PIE

BY SHAWN REILLY SIMMONS

Ivy always gave me that look. Her tight, prissy little lip twist, the laugh I could see right behind her eyes. I smiled back like I always do and stepped up to her judging table to set down my pie.

"Same kind as last year," Ivy said with a small shake of her head.

"I love mincemeat pie, especially near to the holidays." I smiled again.

"Well, good luck to you then, Sissy. This might finally be your year."

Sissy. She was always calling me that, even though she knew damn well I was married now and should be called Mrs. Cecilia Burns, if she wanted to be proper.

Ivy's eyes opened wide and she fussed at her orange polka-dotted scarf when she saw Jeanne Brody walking up with a latticed-topped, deep dish apple. She just about toppled her chair over backwards jerking up like that from her seat, reaching across the table to take the pie from Jeanne, acting all friendly and whatnot. I heard Ivy call Jeanne a dirty bitch once in the bathroom back in school, just because her daddy owned the junk yard and repair shop. Ivy didn't know I heard her, I had my feet propped up on the toilet like I used to do so I could hear what those girls were saying when they thought no one was around.

I guess Ivy thinks Jeanne's all right now since she's rich on account of her husband owning the one and only car dealership in town.

Owned.

It's Jeanne's now. Her husband fell over one day on the lot a year or so back. Right in front of a couple he'd just taken for a test drive in a brand new Buick Riviera. I heard he clutched his chest and called out for Jeanne. He was romantic like that.

"Jeanne, you just have to come to our next fundraiser," Ivy said through her smile, still tugging at her scarf in that anxious way of hers. "We're raising money to buy a new nativity scene for the square."

"So I've heard," said Jeanne. She folded her hands in front of her, showing off her expensive leather gloves.

"I like your scarf," I interrupted.

Jeanne and Ivy both looked at me.

Ivy smirked and tilted her head, then turned back to Jeanne. Jeanne squinted at me like I had a toe growing between my eyes.

"Like I was saying, the little Christ baby from our old nativity...the paint's all worn away. It's not right, having him sit out there all chip-faced and decrepit. It goes against God."

"How are you doing, Cecelia?"

Jeanne Brody had asked me a question.

"Fine, thanks. And you?"

"I'm all right. And how is Mr. Burns?"

I beamed and reached up a hand to straighten my hat. "We're both just fine, thanks for asking."

"Glad to hear it," Jeanne said. "I do see your husband from time to time, always out and about in his tow truck. Sometimes he pulls old trade-ins to the lot that don't run anymore."

"He's on the road all the time," I said, tripping over my words. "We'd have two or three babies by now if he could just be home more often."

"Yes, I'm sure that's true," Jeanne said wistfully. "Just remember life's little blessings come along right when they're supposed to."

I nodded and smiled, like I always do. The children at the next table rubbed sticky paint onto maple leaves and pressed them onto construction paper.

"I just remembered," Jeanne said, acting all surprised. "Ivy, weren't you and Marvin king and queen of the Fall Fest back in the day?"

"Oh...yes, we were," Ivy said, acting like she couldn't quite remember. "But that was so long ago."

"Yes, I suppose we've all gotten a lot older. Well, you ladies enjoy the season," Jeanne said in her grand way. She waved to someone in the crowd and drifted off.

NOIR AT THE SALAD BAR

I turned back to Ivy. Her eyes burned into the back of Jeanne's cashmere coat. She had that same look on her face that she did back in school. But this time she was too afraid to call Jeanne a bitch out loud in public now that we were all grownups. A surprise bubble of laughter rolled up my chest and I coughed into my fist to keep it down.

I sat on a cold metal folding chair and watched the rest of the Fall Fest pies come in. I knew mine was different. It would be the one they'd all be talking about after. When it came time for judging, Ivy and her friends hovered over the gingham table cloth, all official and whatnot in their frilly aprons. They tasted little bits of pie from plastic forks, acting out for all of us like they didn't ever take big bites of anything. Then they joked about getting fat and watching their waistlines, like judging a pie contest was the last thing they wanted to be doing. I watched especially close when Ivy tasted mine.

I pressed my own hand to my narrow side. It was almost done hurting from that last time. Marvin was good about leaving the marks under my clothes so when I was out and about in town no one could see my black and blues. I could keep my head up and look everyone in the eye that way. I slipped my hand in my pocket and felt the folded piece of paper, smooth at the edges from all those times I folded and refolded it, ever since I found it last week on laundry day.

"We have a winner," Ivy shouted. She stuck the big blue ribbon on the table in front of Jeanne's apple pie. Some people tried to clap through their gloves while balancing flimsy cups of cider in their hands. They sounded like that hurt bird I found in the yard that time, flapping its wings for no reason, just because it thought it should. I knew that bird would never fly again.

Jeanne made her way to the table and took a flowery bow, thanking all of the judges one by one. She took an extra long time to thank Ivy, holding both her hands with her own and pumping them up and down. They looked like a couple of overdressed milk maids churning a pot of butter.

Then Jeanne turned and smiled right at me before she wandered off in the crowd, ribbon in hand.

I heard a few sirens that night, but they were too far off for me to place what part of town. I was in my usual chair at the kitchen table, the radio playing John Coltrane low from the counter. Marvin didn't have a taste for music that he said white people had nothing to do with, so I always kept an eye out for the headlights so I could turn it off quick. Just to keep him from shouting about it.

I ate my pie slowly, one bite of mincemeat, then a bite of apple, taking sips of black coffee in between. The letter I found written in that prissy tight handwriting lay open on the table. I'd read it maybe a hundred times. Ivy still made those little curly-cue shapes on her Ys, like she hadn't grown up at all. I bid on both pies after the contest. Had to pay a lot more for Jeanne's than mine, of course.

The headlights skidded across the windows and I looked up, my heartbeat slowing to a thud. I folded Ivy's note and put it in my apron pocket. My legs tingled when I stood up and went to shut off the radio. The clock told me I'd been sitting there for over an hour. I'd eaten almost half of both pies.

The kitchen door rattled open.

"They're gone," Jeanne said, her cheeks flushed. She pulled her hat off and let her hair spill down over her shoulders.

"Gone?" I asked.

"They're dead," Jeanne said. "Brake failure out on the new two lane highway, headlong collision with a big wheeler. Marvin's tow truck was parked at the edge of the Fall Fest lot. Just took one snip."

"What about the truck driver? Is he all right?" I asked.

Jeanne barked a laugh and pulled off her gloves. Her fingers black with grease. "He'll live. It's all perfect."

Jeanne put her hands on my cheeks and pulled me close. She kissed me that way I like, gentle at first, then more grown up, her tongue sliding up against mine. I kissed her back, like I always do.

"I got you something," she said when we came up for air.

"What?"

She pulled Ivy's orange polka-dotted scarf from her coat pocket and handed it to me.

"How did you get this?"

13

"Ivy gave it to me when I promised to come to the next fundraiser." Jeanne laughed so hard she lost her breath. I smiled and kissed her again. Like I always do.

Shawn Reilly Simmons is the author of the Red Carpet Catering Mysteries, which are inspired by her experiences as an on-set movie caterer, and of several short stories appearing in various crime fiction anthologies. She serves on the Board of Malice Domestic, is a member of Sisters in Crime, Mystery Writers of America, and the Crime Writers' Association in the UK. Shawn is a founding member of the Dames of Detection, and is editor/co-publisher at Level Best Books. www.ShawnReillySimmons.com

SMOKED

BY MICHAEL BRACKEN

When Beau James raised the twin service bay doors of the converted Conoco station at eleven a.m. Tuesday morning, he had already been smoking brisket and ribs for more than eight hours, just as he had six days a week since opening Quarryville Smokehouse twelve years earlier. Rain or shine, Tuesday through Sunday, he served a two-meat menu, offering a single side and no dessert, and closing when he had no brisket, ribs, or coleslaw remaining.

Beau worked the indirect-heat pit alone, not allowing anyone to learn his technique for preparing fall-off-the-bone beef ribs and moist brisket with dark peppery crust, and four days a week he also worked the counter alone. He only hired help—his girlfriend's teenaged daughter Amanda—on the weekends when business typically doubled. The Quarryville Smokehouse lunch plate consisted of a choice between chopped brisket, sliced brisket, or beef ribs, accompanied by a scoop of coleslaw, four bread-and-butter pickle slices, a slice of sweet onion, two slices of Mrs Baird's Bread, and a twelve-ounce can of Dr Pepper. He offered no sauce and had been known to refuse service to anyone who requested it.

That Tuesday morning, he wore his graying black hair in a ponytail that hung below his shoulders, and a red paisley bandanna covered the expanding bald spot on the crown of his head. He had on an untucked black T-shirt that covered the tattoo on his left upper arm, faded blue jeans, and well-worn black harness motorcycle boots, a clothing selection that never varied and simplified dressing in the dark. He had gained a few pounds since opening the smokehouse, but at six foot two, he remained slender.

Like most mornings, Tommy Baldwin was sitting at one of the picnic tables beneath the canopy that had once sheltered the gasoline pumps. He had retired from Shell Oil after a lifetime spent as a roustabout, was living comfortably on his pension, and had nothing better to do each morning than read, eat barbecue, and visit with Beau. As the service bay doors rolled up, Tommy stood and grabbed the popular state-named magazine he had been reading. He walked through the six picnic tables arranged in the service bays and into the former Conoco station's showroom, which had been transformed into the smokehouse's order and pickup counter.

"The usual?" Beau asked of the grizzled retiree.

Instead of answering, Tommy tossed the open magazine on the counter. "Have you seen this?"

Beau wasn't much of a reader, so he hadn't. He picked up the magazine and found himself reading a review of Quarryville Smokehouse, a review that referred to his place as "the best-kept secret in West Texas, certain to be a serious contender in the forthcoming round-up of the fifty best barbecue joints in the Lone Star State." Next to the review were a photograph of the chopped brisket lunch plate and another of him working behind the counter—a photograph for which he had not posed.

"Jesus H." He threw the magazine down and glared at Tommy. "When did you get this?"

"This morning's mail."

Beau swore again. He had been relocated to Quarryville thirteen years earlier so no one could find him. Without asking again if Tommy wanted his usual order, Beau scooped chopped brisket into a Styrofoam three-compartment takeout container, added coleslaw and accessories, and shoved the container across the counter, not realizing he'd gone heavy on the brisket, light on the coleslaw, and had completely forgotten the pickles. He slammed a cold can of Dr Pepper on the other side of the still-open magazine.

Tommy slid back exact change. "I thought you'd like the publicity, maybe get more business. You can't be making much from this place."

"I get by." Beau glared at his most reliable customer. "That's all I ever wanted."

"What about that girl of yours? You want to take care of Bethany, don't you? Her and her daughter?"

"What do they have to do with it?"

16

"I see the way she looks at you," Tommy said. "I've never had anybody look at me the way Bethany looks at you. I've seen you look at her the same way."

"So?"

"You can't live for yourself, Beau. You have to live for the people you love," Tommy explained. "I thought I could help, so about a year ago I sent a letter to the editor, telling her about your barbecue."

Beau stabbed at the magazine article with his forefinger. "This is your fault?"

"I suppose so." Tommy glanced at the magazine and the open Styrofoam container next to it. "You forgot my pickles."

"Fuck your pickles." Beau didn't bother with the serving spoon. He reached into the pickle jar, grabbed a handful of bread-and-butter pickle slices, and threw them on top of Tommy's chopped brisket lunch plate, flinging juice across the counter, the magazine, and Tommy.

The retiree shook his head, tucked the magazine under his arm, and carried his lunch to one of the picnic tables outside, where he adjusted the holster hidden at the small of his back and set aside most of the pickles before he began eating.

The lunch rush, such as it was, kept Beau busy for the next few hours. After he sold the last order of ribs, put the cash and checks—he didn't accept credit or debit cards—in the office safe, and shut everything down, he saw Tommy still reading his magazine. He rolled down the service bay doors, carried two cold cans of Dr Pepper outside, and settled onto the picnic table bench opposite Tommy. "Don't you ever go home?"

Tommy looked up. "There's nothing there for me."

Beau put one Dr Pepper in front of Tommy and opened the other. After a long draw from the can, he said, "About earlier."

"Sorry for the surprise," Tommy replied. "I didn't think a little publicity would be a problem."

"You have no idea the world of hurt that's about to crash down on me," Beau said. He drained the last of the Dr Pepper. "There's no way you could know."

Beau had been one of the United States Marshals Service's easiest Witness Security Program relocations, a man without

17

baggage. He had no family and no desire to drag any of several random female companions with him into a new life. The San Antonio office had recommended Quarryville, a dried-out scab of a town in West Texas that had once shipped granite east to Dallas. After the quarry closed in the early 1950s, the town began a long, slow slide into oblivion, and few people lived there by choice. With the U.S. Marshals Service's assistance and money from the Harley-Davidson he'd sold before disappearing into his new identity, Beau purchased and renovated a foreclosed home. On his own he later purchased the abandoned Conoco station he could see from his front window and turned it into Quarryville Smokehouse.

He mentioned none of this to Tommy as they sat in the afternoon heat watching traffic pass the smokehouse on the two-lane state highway. When they finished their drinks, Tommy excused himself to use the men's room around the back, leaving behind the magazine he'd been reading all morning.

Beau spun the magazine around, thumbed through the pages until he found the article about his smokehouse, and read it again. Had it not been for the accompanying photo capturing his face in three-quarter profile, nothing about the article would have bothered him. In fact, everything the author wrote was quite complimentary.

ooo

Beau lived on the other side of the railroad tracks that paralleled the state highway bisecting Quarryville, on a street that also paralleled the tracks, at the leading edge of a neighborhood of single-family homes constructed for quarry employees during the town's heyday. He waited until he was safely inside the living room of his two-bedroom bungalow before using his cellphone to call a phone number he had memorized years earlier.

A no-nonsense female voice answered. "United States Marshals Service."

"I want to talk to William Secrist."

"He retired nine months ago," said the voice. "May I help you?"

Beau paced in front of the gun cabinet containing his and

Bethany's deer rifles. "This is Beau James. Secrist was my case officer."

"I'm his replacement, Deputy Marshal Sara Arquette. How may I help?"

"I've been outted," Beau said. He told her about the magazine article and accompanying photo.

"I should visit some day to see if your 'cue is as good as the writer says."

"You read the article?"

"I picked up a copy of the magazine yesterday."

"So everybody's seen it?"

"Not everybody," she said. "They don't read Texas magazines in Ohio."

Beau stopped pacing and stood at the front window, staring at his smokehouse and the other businesses on the far side of the railroad tracks and state highway. The storefronts along Main Street that weren't boarded up might as well have been. Only a pawnshop, the ubiquitous Dairy Queen, and a Texaco that still offered full service showed signs of life. "All it takes is one."

"What do you expect us to do?"

"Your job," Beau yelled into the phone. "Protect me. Relocate me. Express some concern for my health and well-being!"

"I'll reach out to the Columbus office and see if there's been any chatter about you," she said. "I'll let you know."

"You do that!" He could have slammed the receiver down if he'd phoned from the landline at the smokehouse. Instead, he jabbed his finger against the disconnect button of his cellphone so hard he almost knocked it from his hand.

ooo

Beau ate barbecue for lunch every day and relied on his girlfriend to prepare dinner. That evening Bethany made deer stew, using meat from a white-tailed buck she'd killed the previous season. Beau had never hunted until he dated Bethany and, after many meals prepared using the game she brought home, he had learned to appreciate her marksmanship.

19

Bethany's teenaged daughter Amanda had plans with one of her friends, so Beau and Bethany dined without her. They were nearly finished when Bethany said, "You've been quiet all evening. Is something wrong?"

Beau looked up from his last spoonful of stew. Bethany had not changed when she'd returned home from the veterinary clinic, and still wore her blue scrubs. Six years his junior, she had the figure of a younger woman, but a lifetime in the Texas sun had weathered her. She wore her highlighted golden-brown hair cut in a stacked bob—short in the back, but almost shoulder length in the front—and her pale blue eyes searched his for an answer to her question.

"I got some bad news today," Beau said. "I may have to leave you."

Stunned, Bethany asked, "Why?"

"Some people never forget the past, the rest of us try not to remember it," Beau explained, "and something I did a long time ago caught up to me today."

"You can't do this to me." Bethany dropped her spoon and leaned forward. Her hair had been tucked behind her ears as she ate and one lock fell free to swing against her cheek. "You can't do this to Amanda. Her father walked out on us when she was three. You promised us you would never—"

"It's for your own good."

"I don't believe you," Bethany said. "Where will you go?"

"I don't know."

"When are you leaving?"

"I don't know. It could be soon."

"What about the smokehouse?"

He shrugged.

"Don't you care about anything?"

"You," he said, "and Amanda."

"You can't care all that much if you're willing to walk away from us."

"It's because I care about you that I have to leave."

Bethany snorted with disgust, folded her arms under her breasts, and glared at Beau. "That's the worst line of crap I've ever heard. You don't know where you're going or when you're

20

leaving, but you're doing it because you care about us?"

"I've done some bad things," Beau said. "The people I did them with might be coming for me."

"I thought we didn't have any secrets," Bethany said with equal parts anger and dismay. "Apparently, I was wrong."

Beau did not know when—or even if—the U.S. Marshals Service would relocate him. "I'll say goodbye before I leave. If anything happens before I do, you call this number and ask for Sara Arquette."

As Beau recited the number, Bethany grabbed her smartphone to enter it into her contact list. He snatched the phone from her hands. "Don't put it in your phone. Don't write it down. Memorize it."

ooo

At two a.m. Wednesday morning, as he was dressing for the day and Bethany lightly snored on her side of the bed with her back to him, Beau heard the distinctive *potato-potato-potato* rumble of a lone Harley-Davidson motorcycle cruising along the state highway that bisected Quarryville. He kept a sawed-off double-barrel shotgun under the smokehouse's front counter, but he had grown complacent over the years and had long ago stopped carrying personal protection. The fading sound of the motorcycle haunted Beau until he unlocked the gun cabinet in the living room, removed and loaded his 9mm Glock, and tucked it into a worn leather holster at the small of his back. Then he relocked the gun cabinet and walked across the street, the train tracks, and the highway to the smokehouse, where he fired up the indirect-heat pit and prepped the brisket and ribs he would serve for lunch later that day.

Alone in the dark, in the fenced area beside the converted Conoco station where Beau smoked his meat away from the prying eyes of customers and competitors—though, until the magazine article had appeared, he had never considered the possibility of competitors—Beau contemplated his actions during the coming days. He had more baggage than the first time he had been relocated, and he wondered how easy it would be to walk away

21

this time.

Quarryville was a two-day ride from Columbus, a distance not much different than that from Columbus to North Dakota, a ride he had made several times with the Lords of Ohio to attend the annual Sturgis Motorcycle Rally. He likely had only a few days to decide where he wanted to go and who he wanted to be before the U.S. Marshals Service came for him. He was considering the Pacific Northwest when he finally rolled up the service bay doors to find Tommy sitting at one of the picnic tables outside.

Tommy rose, tucked the magazine he'd been reading into his back pocket, and headed inside. He placed his usual order and added, "You aren't planning to throw pickles at me this morning, are you?"

"I should charge you extra for them," Beau said as he filled a Styrofoam three-compartment takeout container with Tommy's lunch order.

"Fat chance you could collect it."

Beau slid a cold can of Dr Pepper across the counter and Tommy slid back exact change.

There were no other customers in the smokehouse and none approaching as far as Beau could see. "Yesterday you said there was nothing for you at home," he said, "but why do you keep coming here?"

"When I retired, I came home to care for my mother because she was all I had in the world," Tommy said. "She died a couple of years later, and I planted her in the Methodist cemetery, next to my father. I was spending every afternoon in The Watering Hole, drowning my sorry ass in cheap beer before you opened this place."

"You chose brisket over beer?"

"You're better company than a bottle of Lone Star," Tommy said.

"What about your old friends, the people you grew up with?"

"The few that didn't move away are dead or as good as," Tommy said. "These days, you're the closest thing to a friend I've got."

Unsure how to respond, Beau stared across the counter at

22

his customer.

"I never hear you talk about your people."

"There's nothing to talk about," Beau said. "They're gone."

"That's a damned shame," Tommy said. "Good thing you found Bethany. When I had to put my mother's cat to sleep a couple of years ago, your Bethany held my hand. That's a good woman you have there. Worth fighting for, don't you think?"

Without waiting for a response, Tommy picked up his lunch and carried it outside. A lone biker drifted by on the highway, the *potato-potato-potato* sound echoing into the former showroom until the door swung closed. Beau stiffened.

ϙϙϙ

Beau waited until he was in the privacy of his own home that afternoon before dialing the number he had memorized all those years earlier. After identifying himself to Deputy Marshal Arquette, Beau asked, "Have you heard anything?"

"Nothing," Arquette replied.

"Are you planning to relocate me?"

"Not at this time."

"I have people now."

"That complicates things."

"You have no idea."

"I'll be away from the office tomorrow and Friday," she said, "but my calls will be forwarded to my cell. Let me know if anything changes."

"Yeah," Beau said. "I'll call when I'm dead."

He stabbed the phone's disconnect switch with his finger and began pacing the living room. His first thought the previous day had been to abandon this life just as he had abandoned his previous life, but Bethany and Tommy had made him realize he had more to lose and nothing he wanted to leave behind.

He was sitting at the kitchen table nursing a bottle of Dos Equis when Bethany returned home from the veterinary clinic. He reached into the refrigerator behind him and brought out a second bottle. As he held it out to her, he said, "I'm sorry about last night."

"You should be." Bethany took the bottle and settled onto a chair on the other side of the table.

During preparation for relocation, William Secrist and other deputy marshals had promised that no one who followed their instructions had ever been hurt or killed while in the Witness Security Program under the protection of the U.S. Marshals Service. One of those rules was to never, ever divulge his prior identity, not even to a lover who entered his life after relocation. Too many relationships turn sour, and a spiteful ex who revealed his identity would endanger his life. Beau knew he had to risk that possibility.

"You know who I am," Beau said, "not who I was. I'm not that man anymore."

"Does this have something to do with your tattoo?"

Tattooed on Beau's left upper arm, usually covered by his shirt sleeve, was a skull with a crown of thorns and the phrase *Vengeance is Mine* written in Old English script in a ribbon below the skull.

He nodded. "I was an enforcer for the Lords of Ohio."

She shook her head.

"Hell's Angels. Banditos," he said. "Like them, but a much smaller organization."

"Organization?" Bethany said. "You mean gang? You're in a motorcycle gang?"

"I was, a long time ago. I'm not now."

"So, how do you quit? Do you just mail in a resignation letter?"

"I wish it were that easy." He told her about his arrest and the deal he'd made to roll over on his fellow Lords of Ohio. "The Feds had me dead to rights," he said. "I was facing life in prison with no possibility of parole."

Bethany listened without interruption.

"The Feds dropped all charges in return for my turning state's evidence, and they put me in the Witness Security Program, relocating me here when all the trials ended," Beau explained. "Eighteen members of the Lords of Ohio went to prison because of my testimony. Chainsaw Roberts must be out by now."

Chainsaw had not been convicted of any of the murders

Beau had witnessed in his previous life, the evidence too circumstantial despite Beau's testimony, and had gone away for ten years on a combination of lesser charges. Beau told Bethany the big man used a chainsaw for easy disposal of bodies while leaving behind copious amounts of physical reminders attesting to the deceased's violent end to discourage the deceased's friends and family from pursuing matters further.

"Sweet Jesus," Bethany said under her breath. She opened her bottle of Dos Equis and downed half of it before she spoke again. "So you were just going to walk out on us?"

He told her about the magazine article and how he thought the photograph outted him.

"I thought if I left, you and Amanda would be safe." Beau didn't mention that the U.S. Marshals Service had not yet committed to relocating him. "I realized today that if I walk away, I leave behind everyone and everything I've ever loved. I couldn't leave without you knowing why."

"No," Bethany said. "You're staying. We'll get through this. Somehow, we'll get through this."

Amanda, a young woman who resembled photographs of Bethany at the same age, opened the back door and stepped into the kitchen. Her presence ended their conversation.

000

Tommy ordered his usual lunch on Thursday. As he paid, he said, "You didn't exist until you moved here, and you barely exist now."

"How's that?" Beau asked.

"I spent some time on the internet yesterday. You're not on social media, don't have an email address I can find, and I've seen your cellphone. All it does is make calls."

"You have a problem with that?"

"A man has a right to privacy," Tommy said. "But your reaction to the magazine article got me to thinking."

"About?"

"About why a man might be hiding. About why a man might have no past to speak of," Tommy said. "I worked in the oil fields with men like you. Quiet men. Just wanted the world to

25

leave them alone."

"And?"

"Some were good men," he said. "Some weren't."

"And what do you think I am?"

Tommy smiled. "I haven't decided."

He took his food outside, and Beau watched Tommy through the front window until a pair of tellers from Quarryville Bank & Trust interrupted his contemplative observation with an order for seven lunch plates to go.

ѻѻѻ

The rest of Beau's day was uneventful. Dinner that evening consisted of the last of the deer stew, and Bethany joined him in bed that night for a physical reminder of what he risked losing.

Friday was different from Thursday only because Beau received his weekly meat delivery at ten a.m. and dinner that night came from the Dairy Queen because Bethany was too tired to cook.

Saturday brought a slew of unfamiliar faces to the smokehouse counter, people who had seen the magazine article and had ventured out of their way to experience Quarryville Smokehouse's limited menu. The phone also rang more than usual, with people phoning for directions or asking questions. Amanda answered most of the calls.

Just before two p.m., after they had sold out of ribs but still had brisket and coleslaw, Amanda picked up the ringing phone, listened for a moment, and then said, "There's no one here by that name."

After she hung up, Beau asked, "What was that about?"

"Some guy wanted to speak to 'Stick.'"

Beau looked out the window, saw nothing unusual, and then told his girlfriend's daughter, "You should head home."

"But you still have brisket."

"Not much," he said. "I can handle the last few sales."

Amanda removed her apron, hung it by the office door, and was on her smartphone to one of her friends before she stepped outside. She turned back just long enough to wave her fingers before sashaying down the street toward the Dairy Queen where her best friend had yet to master the art of making dip cones.

Beau watched her walk away, glanced at Tommy sitting at one of the picnic tables outside, his nose buried in yet another magazine, and examined the other remaining customers—a young couple outside making goo-goo eyes at one another over a single lunch order of chopped brisket, and a somewhat older couple wrangling two young children at a table in the service bays.

ooo

Deputy Marshal Arquette had been in Midland Thursday and Friday and was returning to the San Antonio office when she decided to take a slight detour to check in on Beau James and taste his brisket. Her unmarked black SUV entered Quarryville from the north, avoiding the East-West state highway that bisected the town. In a rush, she parked behind the Quarryville Smokehouse, climbed out, and hurried into the women's restroom.

The veterinary clinic closed at two p.m. that day, and Bethany was almost home when she saw a dozen motorcycles pulling into the Quarryville Smokehouse parking lot. The colors affixed to the backs of the bikers' jackets matched the tattoo on Beau's arm.

As the bikers parked and silenced their motorcycles, Beau stepped out of the former showroom and suggested the couple with children clear out. They didn't hesitate. The couple at the outside table also wrapped up their things and slipped away. Tommy Baldwin closed the magazine he'd been reading and watched as the bikers dismounted. None of the bikers paid attention to him as he slid the pistol from the holster at the small of his back.

As Bethany pulled her pickup into the driveway at home, she retrieved her smartphone from her purse and dialed the number Beau had made her memorize.

The roar of the motorcycles brought Amanda and her friend out of the Dairy Queen, and they captured the scene with their smartphones.

Two of the bikers entered the showroom where Beau stood behind the counter. The others began overturning the tables in the

27

service bays and tearing apart the limited decorations.

Bethany ran into the home she shared with Beau and shoved her smartphone into her pocket before she unlocked the gun cabinet and retrieved her deer rifle. She loaded it as she ran back outside and braced her arm on the hood of her pickup. She peered through the scope at the two men inside the showroom with her boyfriend. Both were armed. Beau had one hand beneath the counter.

"Been a long time, Stick," Chainsaw said. "You've put on weight."

Though they were of similar height, Chainsaw weighed more than twice what Beau weighed, heavy muscle hidden beneath rolls of fat. He wore a sleeveless jean jacket revealing arms liberally decorated with violent tattoos, and a crown of thorns was tattooed on his bald head. A chainsaw hung from his left hand, a .38 from his right.

Beau replied, "Not long enough."

Chainsaw glanced around. "Looks like this here's your last supper."

The deputy marshal in the women's restroom looked down at her cellphone when it rang. A call was being forwarded from the office.

Chainsaw raised the .38 he carried in his right hand and aimed it at Beau.

Bethany had Chainsaw's head squarely in her crosshairs. When he pointed his revolver at Beau, she squeezed the trigger, hoping the window separating them would not deflect her shot.

Before Arquette could answer her phone, she heard gunfire through the concrete wall. Then she heard the roar of a shotgun.

At the sound of the first shot, the ten bikers tearing apart the seating area in the former service bays drew their weapons.

The sounds catapulted Arquette, her sidearm drawn, from the restroom and around the building into a firefight involving a gang of bikers hiding behind overturned picnic tables in the former service bays, Beau James behind the smokehouse's counter, and an old man hiding behind one of the pillars supporting the canopy outside. What she didn't see was the woman on the far side of the railroad tracks using a deer rifle to pick off bikers.

The bikers had superior firepower, including automatic weapons, but expecting no resistance they had trapped themselves in a box. The entire melee lasted less than ten minutes, and left the Quarryville Smokehouse riddled with bullet holes and every biker dead or dying. Sorting out the chain of events took much, much longer and involved the use of video provided by Amanda and her friend.

The coroner was unable to determine if Chainsaw was killed by the single shot to the head or by the dual shotgun blasts to the abdomen. Slugs retrieved from the other bodies also came from more than one weapon.

No charges were brought against Bethany or Tommy, and after intervention from the U.S. Marshals Service, the U.S. Attorney's office declined to pursue charges against Beau for possession of a sawed-off shotgun without proper tax-paid registration.

ooo

When the smoke cleared, Beau James refused the U.S. Marshals Service's offer to relocate him. He had survived being outted, and the Lords of Ohio had disbanded, the few remaining members in Columbus absorbed into the local Hell's Angels chapter.

At Bethany's insistence, Beau did not patch any of the bullet holes before reopening the smokehouse. A significant increase in business followed, not just from being named the ninth best barbeque joint in the Lone Star State, but also from the notorious reputation the smokehouse had gained from the shootout.

The smokehouse had been highly rated for the quality of its brisket and ribs, but lost points for the limited menu. So Beau added two sides—macaroni and cheese, made from Bethany's recipe, and potato salad made from Tommy's mother's recipe.

Business increased so much that Beau could no longer handle it all himself. Each morning at eleven, Tommy rolled up the service bay doors and worked behind the counter with him until closing. On weekends Amanda and two of her high school friends waited tables.

And at the end of every day Beau returned home to his new

wife Bethany. She still knew him only as Beau James, the man he was, and not the man he had been.

Michael Bracken, recipient of the Edward D. Hoch Memorial Golden Derringer Award for lifetime achievement, is author of several books, including *All White Girls,* and more than 1,200 short stories published in *Alfred Hitchcock's Mystery Magazine, Ellery Queen's Mystery Magazine, Espionage Magazine, Mike Shayne Mystery Magazine,* and many other anthologies and periodicals. He lives, writes, and eats barbecue in Texas.

CULINARY TALES WITH A BITE

MY LIFE IN KILLER RECIPES

BY LESLIE WHEELER

It all began with macadamia nuts. I'll never forget how thrilled I was to have my yummy recipe for white chocolate chunk macadamia nut cookies included in *What's Cooking at Hillcrest Elementary School* on the very same page as Mrs. Frederick Sillerton's Krisp Kringles. True, I may have copied most, okay, all of the recipe from *Betty Crocker's Junior Cookbook*. But I wasn't alone. I'd noticed a recipe very much like Mrs. Sillerton's on a package of Nestles semi-sweet chocolate bits.

My lack of originality didn't stop Ricky Harrison, a fifth-grade classmate on whom I had a huge crush, from inviting himself over for a sampling. Fortunately, my mom was there to take him to the Emergency Room when he broke out in hives, vomited and fainted. I felt bad he got sick, but I would have felt much worse if he hadn't told me I was too fat to be his girlfriend just before he went into anaphylactic shock. It was an important learning experience for both of us. Ricky learned he was allergic to tree nuts like macadamias. I learned that certain foods could be lethal.

Fast forward from the nineteen-fifties to the early sixties, and I still believed the way to a man's heart was through his stomach. So did most of my classmates at Whately Prep for Girls. By then, we'd moved on from Betty Crocker to Julia Child. We were convinced we needed to get good grades so we could get into good colleges, where we'd find good husbands. We were equally convinced we had to master the art of French cooking as a sure-fire way of landing such hubbies. Since our private school didn't offer Home Ec., we started holding cooking sessions at each other's houses. It soon became apparent that while I could whip up a first-rate batch of cookies, my soufflés were a total flop. Instead of rising, they remained flat as pancakes. This was embarrassing enough without Ginny Collins, my arch rival at Whately, spreading

31

the word far and wide until people at school started calling me Flopsy.

What to do? An opportunity presented itself one afternoon when I and several other girls were trying out Julia Child's recipe for chocolate soufflés at Ginny's house. We'd reached the point in the recipe where it was time to fold stiffly-beaten egg whites into the chocolate egg yolk mixture when a carload of boys drove past, honking and waving. All the girls except me ran out of the house to get a better view and wave back. The boys circled the block three times, long enough for me to add a dash of Drano to Ginny's chocolate mixture and join the others outside without anyone being the wiser.

Ginny's soufflé came out of the oven so perfectly puffed and luscious looking the girls couldn't wait to taste it. But after a spoonful, they gagged and spat it out. "What did you put in this?" one girl demanded. "It's positively noxious."

"I didn't do a thing," Ginny protested. "It was tampered with, and one of you is responsible." She turned on us accusingly. One by one the girls denied it. When Ginny got to me, I said, "Not I…Noxy." The others picked up the nickname, and Ginny fled the kitchen in tears. I was never called Flopsy again.

Fast forward to the seventies, and instead of doing what was expected of me, I dropped out of college to join a commune in the wilds of Montana. It was headed by a charismatic man with piercing blue eyes, and long black flowing hair named Power Zenith. His real name, as I later found out, was Dwayne Yerkel. In the beginning commune life was fun. Everyone was friendly, we shared everything, and I liked living off the land. A farmer let us use a corner of one of his fields to plant crops, and we supplemented our diet by foraging in the woods. But after several months, things changed for the worse. The farmer kicked us off his land when some of our members were caught stealing his chickens and eggs, and we retreated into the mountains. Power Zenith went from being a benevolent despot to an outright tyrant. His word was law, and anyone who disobeyed him was punished. As his rule became more and more repressive, I began to look for a way out. But while it had been easy to join the commune, it was hard to leave, because no one was allowed to go anywhere without Power Z's permission.

I decided I had to put him out of commission long enough to make my escape. I couldn't do it with macadamia nut cookies or a Drano-laced chocolate soufflé. What I could do was draw upon the knowledge of wild plants I'd gained while foraging. Having learned that various wildflowers were edible, I'd delighted my fellow commune members and Power Z himself with my blossom stir fries and tempuras.

With his blessing, I went on a foraging trip. I returned with a veritable cornucopia of poison: buttercups, tall mountain larkspur, milkvetch, nightshade, spurge, and both mountain and meadow death camas. To prevent anyone from recognizing these as toxic plants, I covered them in batter and made one of my tantalizing tempuras. I arranged the crispy pieces of deep-fried flowers in our huge communal wok around a bowl of soy sauce. I briefly considered adding a dash of fuel oil to the sauce, but decided it would be overkill.

Power Z always ate first. When I presented him with my pièce de résistance, he beamed with pleasure. "You've outdone yourself," he said before digging in. I kowtowed my way out of the knot of followers surrounding him. Then I turned and ran. As I raced down the mountain, I could hear Power Z's awful retching and ghastly screams.

It took a while to get my life back on track after the commune fiasco. I finished college, married Mr. Right and had two children. By the mid-eighties, I was living in the Boston suburbs with every material comfort I could imagine. But I wasn't happy. There was too much pressure to be perfect: perfect wife, perfect mom, perfect housekeeper, perfect hostess, and perfect cook.

It was a time of intense competitive cooking, whether this involved preparing a gourmet meal for two, throwing a lavish dinner party for dozens of people, or baking the best-ever cookies for your child's school's PTA fund raiser. At first, I tried to meet these impossibly high culinary standards, but it was hard. My kids greeted the eggplant ratatouille and oatmeal soup I prepared for Sunday breakfast with gagging noises, and my husband was less than appreciative of my efforts. He'd say things like "Your braised rabbit with Chartreuse is decent, but not spectacular like Lily Gordon's." He made invidious comparisons like this so often that I began to wonder if he had roving eyes as well as a roving palate.

Then one day a ghost from my gastronomic past walked back into my life when Ricky Harrison and his wife Louise moved into our suburban cul de sac. It fell to me to host the welcome-to-our-neighborhood party, a potluck in which everyone contributed a dish. I made my signature seven-greens salad with homemade creamy raspberry vinaigrette dressing. Others brought dishes that were also straight from *The Silver Palate Cookbook*. Everything was going swimmingly until I turned to Louise Harrison, and said in a voice that could be heard throughout the room: "I suppose Ricky told you about the time I nearly killed him with my macadamia nut cookies." Why did I say that? The truth was I'd had it with striving for perfection.

A shocked silence followed. Finally, Louise recovered enough to say, "It was an accident, right?"

"Oh, yes. In those days, tree nut allergies weren't as well-known as they are today."

"I hope there aren't nuts in any of the dishes here." Louise glanced anxiously at the buffet table.

"Not in my salad." I paused, frowning. "Although now that I think of it, I may have used macadamia nut oil in the salad dressing. The bottle was right next to the bottle of olive oil on the counter."

My words cast a pall over the occasion. The Harrisons never darkened my doorstep again, and other neighbors began to regard me with suspicion—an attitude I encouraged by committing small and not-so-small acts of culinary sabotage. I undercooked meat and poultry, overcooked vegetables until they were limp and lifeless, and used salt in recipes that called for sugar, and vice-versa. Before long, people started turning down dinner invitations, the PTA stopped asking me to bake cookies for them, and my husband brought home take-out meals. After one final disastrous dinner party, during which I secretly released a cockroach I'd trapped at a greasy spoon and brought home, my husband turned to me and said, "Margie, I get the feeling you're not happy in your domestic role."

Ya think?

"Why don't we hire a housekeeper, you go out to work, and I'll run my financial advisory business from a home office?"

"Fine," I said, little dreaming he'd spend a good portion of his time at home canoodling with our next-door neighbor's Swedish au pair.

Six months later, we split up. He got the house and kids, and I used the hefty settlement I received to buy a condo in Cambridge close to Tout Pour La Table, the upscale kitchenware shop where I worked as a sales assistant. There, my knowledge of everything from spatulas to sauté pans served me well. I rose from sales assistant to assistant manager to general manager. I threw myself into the job. I showed up first thing in the morning and was often the last to leave at night.

One night I was working late, arranging the window display to give it a Christmassy look, when a rap on the glass caught my attention. I looked up to see George Olson, a big, jolly Santa Claus of a man, who frequented the shop in search of hard-to-find gadgets like Microplane grater-zesters. "So you're still here," he said with a smile. "I won't bother you with my question about Zwilling versus Wüsthof kitchen knives. But if you're ready to call it a night, why don't we have dinner together?"

At this point, you may be wondering if he'd use dinner to hit on me. Wrong. Although George did take me to a very nice restaurant, he was the perfect gentleman throughout. And the more we talked, the more I realized how much we had in common despite a twenty-year difference in age. We had such a good time that we started having dinner almost every night.

Soon we were spending weekends together as well. A widower and retired history professor at Harvard, George lived in a rambling Victorian in the Avon Hill neighborhood of Cambridge. We went for long walks, played with his two rescue dogs, curled up in his library with our books, and shopped for and prepared all our meals. Working side by side with George in the kitchen, I never felt the competitive pressure I'd felt during my marriage. If one of us made a mistake, we laughed it off and continued on.

Seven months later, I sold my condo and moved in with George. After another seven months, we married. I'd worried marriage might change things between us, but it only made them better. I'd never been so happy.

George's health issues did bring some changes in our lives, however. He suffered two heart attacks, and after the second one, his doctor put him on a strict low-fat, low-cholesterol diet. This was hard for George, because he loved red meat and rich desserts. A diagnosis of stage four pancreatic cancer several years later was another blow. But even in this, George managed to find a silver lining. "If I'm going to die of cancer, anyway, does that mean I can stop worrying about my cholesterol?" he asked his doctor.

After his doctor gave him the green light, George turned to me and said, "Let's go home and have a meal to end all meals. I want jumbo shrimp with cocktail sauce, Caesar salad heavy on the dressing, croutons, cheese and anchovies, filet mignon with Béarnaise sauce, asparagus with Hollandaise sauce, baked potatoes stuffed with bacon bits and cream cheese and..." Here George paused and half-closed his eyes, as if imagining the treats that awaited him.

"Dessert?" I prodded.

George cocked his head at me and winked. "Surprise me."

I was more than happy to oblige. Declaring the kitchen off limits, I set out to prepare what some have called the Big Mac of desserts, which also happened to be George's all-time favorite: chocolate lava cake. And not just any lava cake. A man with George's gargantuan appetite deserved better than that. I not only quadrupled the recipe, but poured the batter into one big mold instead of those silly little custard cups you're supposed to use. This made it trickier to get the cake out of the pan, but the extra effort was worth it. Topped with chocolate sauce and generous dollops of vanilla ice cream, my giant lava cake was an epicure's dream: mouth-watering walls of dark chocolate surrounding a warm, gooey center. Loving hands had made it, and a loving palate consumed it.

Our feast was indeed a meal to end all meals—for George, that is. He went to bed with a full stomach and a satisfied smile, and died sometime during the night. I missed him terribly, but took comfort in the knowledge he'd died happy.

George had grown children. Because his son was a prosperous lawyer, and his daughter married to a wealthy man, he decided they no longer needed financial help from him. So he left everything to me.

This did not sit well with his greedy offspring. His daughter cornered me in tears, claiming she couldn't afford yet another pair of Manolo Blahnik shoes—she already had a closetful of these and other pricey brands—so couldn't I give her a chunk of the inheritance she was sure her father had meant for her? The son was even worse. He'd barely walked in the door when he shot me a strange look. "Didn't I hear that you have some incurable disease, Margie?"

"No, where did you hear that?"

"Well, even if that's not the case, you should plan ahead." Without skipping a beat he went on to suggest that he set up a battery of trusts, whereby the money I'd inherited from his father and anything else I cared to bequeath would go to him and his sister upon my death. He also pushed for a living will, a health care proxy, and various powers of attorney, all of which I should entrust solely to him.

I told him I'd think about it.

And think I have, long and hard—but not about trusts or proxies or powers of attorney. Instead, my mind has strayed in another direction—to special recipes. My predatory stepson fanatically pursues the Paleo Diet, while his sister is an insufferably smug hyper-vegan. Surely there is something that will tempt even their picky palates.

Hmm. A tall order for sure, but I feel up to it.

The author of three Miranda Lewis "living history" mysteries, **Leslie Wheeler**'s short stories and essays have appeared in various anthologies, including Level Best Books' New England Crime series, *Day of the Dark, Stories of the Eclipse*, and *Dead in Good Company, A Celebration of Mount Auburn Cemetery*. When she's not writing, Leslie enjoys whipping up tasty, but non-lethal, meals.

GRAB-N-GO

BY A.B. POLOMSKI

Everyone was surprised when Margaret Laboy died. The whole grocery and half the town was affected by her death, especially me, since in a way, it was my fault. I can only be grateful that there weren't more casualties.

Margie's problem was a weak heart. She was on a slew of medications, enough so she needed an anti-nausea pill to keep the whole lot down. That was no secret. She talked about how her ex-husband, a pharmacist, managed her meds, doling them out in little plastic compartments for different times of the day. Not every divorce is as amicable, but Margie was practical and when she lost Albert to a gay man, she moved forward with a sizeable bank account and no hard feelings.

Financially, Margie was set for several lifetimes and would never have to work another minute of her life, but she had a dream, which took shape when she met our produce manager, Johnny Andrews. Johnny was full of charm and fine manners. It was understandable how Margie, a northerner with an almost undetectable facelift and a matronly bosom, would be drawn to Johnny, good looking in a southern bad boy way and twenty years her junior. Well, the wealthy do have their privileges.

As produce manager, our Johnny was a picture of dedication. He never failed to choose the ripest pears, the sweetest grapes and the most luscious cherries for Margie.

Margie complained about the pears not being organically grown, the grapes being trucked in from Mexico, which meant they were regularly doused in banned pesticides, and forget about the cherries. Chilean and genetically modified, she'd put money on it. Margie was the exceedingly picky type.

After their nuptials, I'm not sure if it was Johnny who put the bug in his new bride's ear or if it was Margie herself who thought of the bright idea to add out-of-season organic raspberries, goat cheese and designer lettuce to the inventory of a store that sold plain working people their toilet paper, spring bulbs, and olive loaf, but by then Margie owned the place lock, stock and barrel.

Within a week, the dingy yet welcoming Grab-n-Go was transformed it into a kind of Whole Foods for folks who didn't consider sugar poison. Plentiful Pleasures, Margie called it. Not as catchy as Grab-n-Go and a bit sexual if you asked some of the patrons, most of them elderly and on fixed incomes, though there were more and more people from New York and Connecticut moving into the new developments.

We sold Coke, Pepsi and Sprite, sweet tea and marshmallows that weren't vegan, though Margie was in favor of phasing out that stuff and bringing in more wholesome products. Cage-free eggs were non-negotiable on account of how hens were treated by "industrial farming." Almost everyone kept at least a couple of hens that produced enough eggs with sunflower yellow yolks to take your breath away if you've never seen a real egg before. Margie introduced quail eggs which had people scratching their heads at the high price of luxury.

Amazingly enough, Plentiful Pleasures was usually mobbed. Folks came by for their pound of bologna and to ogle the rest, including a nice selection of magazines with the latest hairstyles, organic gardening advice, and celebrity chef recipes.

Until Margie, we'd been satisfied with spotty bananas, wizened oranges, and overripe peaches.

After Margie bought the store, I went from head cashier, which was hell on my manicure, to produce manager, which was worse on account of the ever-present Margie. She never stopped grousing about the avocados not being piled up right or the red peppers looking less perky than she liked. She spoke with her lips paralyzed in a smile if customers were around. On the rare occasions she couldn't find anything wrong, she told me not to stand like a fly waiting to be swatted.

When the old Grab-n-Go crowd didn't snap up the rainbow carrots and passion fruit, Margie decided that she needed a more refined customer base. She got a bunch of us to drop off flyers in the swankiest new developments, inviting people to a grand re-opening of Plentiful Pleasures.

A week before the big she-bang, Margie had me hire some local high school kids who would work cheap. Not one of those kids knew any more about produce than I did.

Margie herself came up with the menu. I suggested a recipe for a caramelized shallot tart I'd found in a glossy food magazine. At first Margie turned up her nose, the automatic way she did whenever I made a suggestion, but then I told her it made sense to move those expensive shallots before they got much softer. Margie dressed me down for over ordering, but didn't suggest I seek advice from our former produce manager, Johnny, now store manager. Did she know Johnny and I had been an item before she sailed into town? I didn't know the answer to that, but I suspected to the point of deep certainty that my days at Plentiful Pleasures were numbered. Margie planned on having me fired, and it would be Johnny's job to let me go. I could see it so clearly, it was like a painting.

The Plentiful Pleasures luncheon soirée started out nice as you please. Once things got going after everyone had a glass or two of prosecco, an Italian sparkling wine, it was my job to dish up the tart. It was quite popular, I guess on account of some of the other menu items. The *boletus en croute*, actually mushrooms on toast with cooked onions, ham, and cream, weren't bad. The raw oysters, purportedly aphrodisiacal, fit in with the suspected theme of Plentiful Pleasures, but were daunting given the warm day. Ditto for the salmon roe *gravlax*.

I kept the slices of tart thin, except for Margie's, who was introducing herself as Mrs. Anders with the adoring and impossibly handsome Johnny at her side. He was not in his apricot-colored apron and checked-red shirt like the rest of us. No, Johnny wore a tuxedo and Margie a white dress with pink roses that set off her figure. She came back for seconds twice and I was happy to oblige.

Around five o'clock a few people started getting violently sick to their stomachs. The store was a mess, I can tell you. First thing I did was call 9-1-1.

Margie, who said she didn't feel sick at all, insisted on hanging around to smooth things over for the few press people who had arrived late and hadn't gotten ill.

NOIR AT THE SALAD BAR

She stayed in hyper-hostess mode right up until the moment she dropped, about an hour after the last ambulances left. Folks figured she'd had a heart attack on account of all the excitement and stress of having her soirée ruined. The police rushed her to Mercy General, but we all knew it was too late.

When the coroner ruled out heart trouble, the sheriff asked for an analysis of Margie's stomach contents. Johnny agreed, suggesting it might have been a bad oyster that killed his unfortunate wife. The sheriff found it suspicious that Johnny had been one of the lucky few who hadn't fallen ill. Johnny explained he wasn't into fancy food, something the sheriff could relate to given his own penchant for mac and cheese and frozen pizza, both drenched in gravy and hot sauce.

It was later determined that Margie keeled over from kidney failure caused by colchicine, a poison found in some crocus bulb varieties.

The sheriff came by to look things over and to question everyone, including the teenagers hired to work in the kitchen. He ended up figuring that some bulk crocus bulbs got mixed into the shallot bin by mistake. Both are small and brown with papery skins. They look remarkably alike, especially to the untrained eye.

I was pretty emotional. No one blamed me, of course, probably because Margie had told anyone who would listen that I wasn't up to speed in the produce department. If she hadn't gone toes up, Margie would have called my stupidity a health hazard and fired me herself.

The kicker is Margie wouldn't have died if it weren't for her anti-nausea pill. She'd taken it faithfully and never upchucked like the rest of us.

I felt real bad about what happened.

The whole store and half the town showed up for the funeral. There were tons of flowers, lots of rare varieties I'd never seen outside a magazine.

After the service, we all watched handsome Johnny, former store manager, bravely climb into his brand new candy-apple red Jaguar.

I went back to work the next day, but it wasn't the same without Johnny. I put in my resignation and cleaned out my locker.

CULINARY TALES WITH A BITE

First thing I did was pull out a copy of *Gardener's World* with a special pull-out section on common poisonous plants. Only three crocus varieties are extremely toxic.

I didn't worry about anyone finding me with the magazine before I tucked it back into the magazine rack. My knowing that certain varieties of crocus bulbs are highly toxic wouldn't have amounted to much. The produce section wasn't my responsibility when the spring bulbs were delivered. Ordering all that stuff had still been Johnny's job.

On my way out, I picked up two bottles of expensive sunscreen, paid for them and didn't hang around to say goodbye. I was going to see the world with a young widower waiting for me in the parking lot in a hot little candy-apple red Jag, engine idling.

A.B. Polomski lives and works in New Jersey. She has over twenty Solve-it-Yourself Mysteries published in *Woman's World*. When not writing, A. B. works as a mediator for the county court system.

NOIR AT THE SALAD BAR

THE LOBSTER TANK

BY E.A. AYMAR

Maxwell Stevens can't help overhearing the conversation next to him. Not that he minds the distraction. He needs something to keep him occupied while he waits in Red Lobster's bar for the person he's going to kill.

"They make me sad," the woman next to him is saying. "All shoved into that tank with bands around their claws."

"They need to be tied up like that," her companion—Max assumes he's her husband—explains. "Makes it easier for the staff to pick them up."

"I guess."

Max drinks down the rest of his Guinness, swivels in his stool toward the couple. They're older, maybe twenty years past his thirty-five, white and doughy, and they both wear glasses. They look oddly similar, maybe related. Max wonders if he's made the wrong assumption about their relationship.

"Their claws are bound," Max tells them, "because otherwise they'd crush each other. Crush, kill, then eat each other."

The woman frowns.

"Well, I don't think that's true," she says. "Lobsters live together in the ocean, and they don't attack each other there."

"It's because living in a tank makes them crabby."

The couple stares blankly at him.

"But, seriously," Max says. "They do attack each other in the ocean."

"I'm sure I can just look this up." Her husband reaches into his pocket and pulls out his phone.

"Don't bother." Max stands. "I know I'm right."

Neither the man nor the woman respond. They're staring into his phone.

Max grabs the phone from the man and turns it off. He gives it back. "I said don't bother."

"Excuse me?"

Max feels the stares from around the bar. He curses himself for being so unprofessional, for letting a few drinks and nerves affect his judgment.

But Max can't bring himself to apologize, so he turns and leaves the restaurant. Limps out into the parking lot, into the cold Virginia snow. Looks up into a blue-black evening sky and breathes deeply. He tries to calm down, tries to let go, tries to get sober. Tries to do nothing but concentrate on the people heading into the restaurant as he climbs inside his van.

ooo

She was a brunette with an uncertain smile, sitting on a stone wall in front of a beach, one leg pulled up, arms wrapped around her raised knee. It was a pretty photograph until you looked closer. Max has spent the past week staring at the photo and he's memorized the tiny details. The crumbling stones, the stains on her jeans, the silver chain circling her dangling ankle, the exhaustion around her eyes. The way her smile is forced.

Max puts the picture down, turns his attention back to the restaurant's front door. His eyes are half-drawn, but he's weary, not tired. Something's eating away at him, like piranhas tearing at his side.

Sadness.

Max doesn't understand where it's coming from. Emotions don't affect him, not the way they do other people. Not as a kid, when his shithead dad punched him while his mother watched, too scared to help. Not outside a bar in Baltimore, when a man who'd welched on a bet died with Max's hands around his neck. And not after jail, when he was put in touch with men who hired him to do bad things.

Max did those things. He had no problem doing what other people wouldn't.

But that ease is slipping away. He can almost feel it, like blood leaking from a wound.

It has something to do with Liz. Max figures their relationship hadn't meant much to her. It had only lasted a couple of years, when they were both in their early twenties, and ended

45

abruptly after his arrest. She was married when he was released a decade later. Max wasn't surprised that she'd found someone else or had turned respectable. Liz had always felt like a dream—just out of reach, soon to be gone.

But he showed up at her house once a month after he was out of prison, parked down the street, and watched her through the tinted windows of his van. Sometimes Max thought about walking over to her, seeing the surprise on her face. He wondered what would happen next, wondered if she'd clutch her kids, hurry inside. Not that Max would do anything with a married woman— he honored the marriage contract—but he thought about it.

He thought about it a lot.

And then there had been the year when his bosses sent him to Mexico, the year that ended with bullets in his leg. He knew something was off when he returned to Maryland last month, when he saw Liz's husband alone with their boys, walking heavy. The kids were older now, awkwardly tall, with unkempt hair and loose clothes. Then Max noticed the paper yellow ribbon on the window, and realized what must have happened.

He didn't know he was crying until his shirt was wet.

Sudden raps on the passenger window.

Max can't believe he was caught off guard, even if his hand's over his .380 by the time whoever's knocking has stopped.

It's Max's client, James Belle.

Max moves his hand away from the gun, unlocks the door.

James slides inside. "What are you doing?"

Max doesn't like him. James is blond, beefy, too confident; reminds Max of the fraternity rapist in every single Lifetime movie Liz made him watch. Then again, Max couldn't recall a client he'd liked.

"Oh," Max said. "Nothing. How about you?"

"Karen's already in the kitchen!"

Max had been too distracted to do as much research as he normally did for a job. "She works here?"

"She's the chef."

Max scratches his arm. "Red Lobster calls them chefs?"

"Someone has to prepare the food."

"Red Lobster calls it food?"

"She's a good cook," James says. Max is surprised he's defending her. He wonders if James is here because he's changed his mind.

That's happened a few times.

"Listen," James says. "I told you to do it here because Karen's expecting me. She thinks I'm buying her dinner for our anniversary."

"You're taking her to Red Lobster? For her anniversary? For food she already cooked?"

James glances out the passenger window. "I'm sleeping with my coworker and paying you to kill my wife so she doesn't divorce me and take everything. Pretty sure I'm out of the running for husband of the year."

"You didn't tell me you're sleeping with your coworker."

An annoyed look crosses James's face. "Stop making me feel guilty. You're a hit man. You've met worse."

He's right. Max can easily think of a dozen people worse than James. Some who had hired him, some he'd put down.

But this feels different.

Something's felt different ever since Max learned Liz died.

James raps the dashboard with his knuckle. "Are you going to kill her or not?"

"I said I'd do it. I honor my agreements."

"So what are you waiting for? Go put a bullet in her."

Max looks at him.

Max steps outside the van a few minutes later. He limps toward the restaurant, grabs the lobster claw-shaped door handle, walks into the bar. Doesn't see the old couple anymore. He flags down a waiter, tells them he needs to talk to Karen Belle.

"Our chef?"

Max grins, makes quotation marks with his fingers. "Yes. Your *chef*."

The waiter frowns. "She's really busy right now."

"Tell her it's about her husband."

Karen walks out a few minutes later, just as the bartender brings Max a ginger ale. It takes Max a moment to recognize her; the photo must have been taken years earlier. A couple of white

47

hairs shine, pulled back and buried in brown strands. And Karen's heavier, her face rounder, eyes tired.

Max watches the waiter point to him. Karen looks at Max for a few seconds, then ambles over. She sits on the bar stool next to his.

"Who are you?" Her voice has a little roughness to it, like she grew up in a tough neighborhood and carries its memories with her.

"My name's Max."

"How do you know James?"

Max takes a sip of the ginger ale. Too sweet for his taste. "He owes me money."

Karen doesn't seem surprised. "And you're trying to find him?"

"I found him. He didn't have it on him."

"Where is he?"

"Outside."

"Is he coming inside?"

Max shakes his head. He's surprised he hasn't lied to her. He usually does during these conversations. Usually doesn't even think about it.

"What does he owe you money for?"

"He paid me to kill you."

Karen's eyes widen. Her hand drops to the bar.

Max quickly covers her hand with his. "It sucks, I know. Don't scream."

"He...is this some kind of joke?"

"It's no joke."

Karen looks around the bar, stares at the bartender. Max squeezes her hand, brings her attention back to him.

"Look down."

She looks down, sees his hand inside his jacket pocket.

"I can shoot you and be out the door in seconds. No one can help you in time."

Karen's hand shakes under his.

"Please don't."

Her voice cracks when she speaks. Max has heard it before, the dryness in someone's throat that comes with terror.

"Wipe your tears. Don't let anyone see you crying."

Karen uses her free hand to lift her apron, presses it briefly against her eyes.

"Why'd he do this?"

"Because he's an asshole."

"Are you going to kill me?"

"No." Max lets go of her hand. "I've decided to become a different person. A better person. Don't you feel lucky?"

Relief comes over Karen's expression, even though she's clearly scared.

"Did you kill James?" she asks. "Is that why he's not coming in?"

"He's out in my van, in the back. Alive."

Her mouth opens, stays that way for a few seconds.

"Why didn't you kill him?"

"Told you, I've changed. I'm walking away, leaving this life behind."

Max notices the change in himself as he speaks. That sadness seems pushed back. Those angry fish scatter.

Karen is staring at him.

"You don't seem that upset about James," he observes.

Karen blinks. Then she bites her lip, slowly lifts the bottom of her shirt. Shows Max the bruises on her stomach.

"We have problems."

Max isn't surprised. He remembers that forced smile in her photo.

"Every single thing I've told you is true," he says, "except for one thing. I don't have my gun with me. It's wedged behind the tank at the front of the restaurant."

He takes his hand out of his pocket, gives her a napkin holding the keys to his van. Karen takes it, uncomprehending.

"James is unconscious, but he's probably waking up soon. His wrists and ankles are duct-taped, and so is his mouth. But he can get out of that. So you'd better hurry."

"I don't…"

"The police won't believe you if you tell them what he hired me to do. And he'll try and kill you again. I've seen it happen. People who want violence are like bad gamblers. They keep throwing in until they lose."

Understanding finally breaks through.

"I can't."

Max shrugs. "If I were you, I'd take that gun. But keep it in the napkin so your prints don't get on it. Then go to the van in the back of the lot and open the rear door. It's facing away from the street, and nothing's behind it but a vacant lot. Aim at his chest, pull the trigger, drop the gun, and get the hell away. The cops will think I did it. But I'll be gone."

"This is insane."

"James is also sleeping with his coworker. Just something to remember."

Karen's eyes are red, anxious. "I can't do this."

Max stands, touches her knee.

"Only thing you can do."

He limps out of the restaurant and back into the night. Looks up into the sky at the falling snow high in the dark heavens. The snow seems to slow until it pauses, frozen like a picture, a thousand flakes poised, like light breaking through from some other world.

And then it starts falling again.

E.A. Aymar's latest novel is *You're As Good As Dead*. He writes a monthly column for the Washington Independent Review of Books, and is Managing Editor of The Thrill Begins (for ITW). Aymar is also involved in a collaboration with DJ Alkimist, a NY and DC-based DJ, where his stories are set to her music. Visit www.eaalkimist.com for more information.

CULINARY TALES WITH A BITE

A MURDER IN MONTREUX

BY MICHAEL ALLAN MALLORY

Inspector Graf struggled to focus on the body. It was too early in the day to look at dead people. Luckily, for the moment his job was to stay out of the way of the forensic photographer who circled around the man on the beach. Graf let his gaze wander beyond the crime scene to the picturesque waters of Lake Geneva and the snow-capped French Alps on the other side. It was a much more uplifting sight.

Movement drew his attention back to the beach. An energetic man with a pointed chin had disengaged from the cluster of police and was walking toward him. Dressed in the same blue and navy of the Montreux Gendarmerie, Officer Durig marched across the sand to join Graf. A little too fresh-faced and eager for the inspector, Durig jutted his chin toward a distinguished figure in a gray suit approaching from the *Quai des Fleur,* the lakeside promenade of flowers.

"Is that him?" Durig asked.

Graf nodded. "That's him."

Detective Chief Inspector Alec Blanchard, the most well-known and respected member of the Geneva Cantonal Police, made his way down the steps to the small spit of beach.

Graf made introductions to the grinning young officer. "Durig was the first on the scene," he added afterward.

"An honor to meet you, sir." Durig pumped the chief inspector's arm as if he were drawing water from a well. It was all Graf could do to keep from kicking the overzealous officer in the rear. It pleased Graf to notice a hint of bemusement tugging at the corner of Blanchard's lips. The chief was a good sport and was known for taking a genuine interest in all members of his team. After a few questions about Durig's time on the job, Blanchard turned toward the crime scene.

"What do we have?" he asked in a voice as smooth as cream.

Graf summarized. "Deceased white male. Aged sixty. Name's Michel Dafflon, a local fruit merchant. Shot through the heart. Robbery does not appear to be a motive. He had fifty Swiss francs in his pocket."

"Who found the body?"

With a nod Graf indicated a young woman sitting on a wooden bench by the walkway of flowers, the alpine cityscape of Montreux looming behind her in the distance.

"The American woman?" Blanchard said without missing a beat.

"Yes." Graf nodded. The chief knew she was American the same way he did, from her neon green tank top and beet red Nike athletic shoes. Americans did tend to stick out like the proverbial sore thumb in Europe. "Her name is Cindy Johnson," Graf went on. "She's on holiday. She was out walking this morning when she found the body."

Blanchard turned to Durig. "Did she see anything?"

The officer seemed startled at being addressed directly by the chief inspector when Graf, his superior, stood right there. He recovered quickly, snapping to attention. "Mrs. Johnson didn't see anything or anyone," Durig reported. "The beach was empty by the time she got here."

"Which was when?"

"Seven forty." Durig stood proud as if he'd just given the correct answer to a pop quiz.

Too eager to please, Graf decided, a go getter. A little too ambitious for Graf to deal with before lunch.

Durig waited for the next question. It didn't come. Blanchard whirled about to examine the beach. The photographer was gone and the other officers stood along the perimeter. He made a wide circle around the body, stepping carefully to avoid disturbing the multiple sets of footprints in the sand. He stopped to view the murder victim. Dressed in navy pajamas and slippers, he had the rough cheeks of a hard working man who had little time to care for himself. A Gallic nose rose prominently above a brush mustache. Blanchard straightened suddenly at a realization. "I know this man. What did you say his name was?"

"Michel Dafflon, a fruit seller," Graf said.

"Yes, that's it." Blanchard's gaze shifted to the *Quai des Fleur*, beyond the orange and yellow poppies, colorful tulips and daisies to the storefronts on the other side of the walkway. His eyes narrowed on a whitewashed building with a green awning. "I've been to his shop. Sorry, the name didn't register earlier. I'm still waking up. Didn't sleep well last night." The chief swung round to appraise the dead man once more, then extended an arm toward a fuzzy walnut-like object coated in sand near the body. "That probably explains this."

"What is it?" Durig couldn't quite make it out.

Blanchard stared at the object. "A plum pit. Fresh. Hasn't been here long. A few hours. Possibly left by the killer."

"We'll bag it. And we'll take dental stone casts of the footprints."

The chief grunted approval. "The damp sand is ideal."

"Agreed. A few of the impressions are near perfect. You can see Dafflon's tracks paralleling the other set in front of his, the killer's. The footprints turned to face Dafflon. Probably when the suspect shot him. Our American friend's tracks got close but she had the presence of mind to keep her distance."

"Good thinking."

"The other set belongs to Officer Durig."

The young officer blanched. "I had to see if Dafflon was alive or dead," he said defensively.

Graf shot him a censorious look for interrupting.

Blanchard squatted on his haunches to inspect the footprints. "The killer was barefoot. And missing a toe," he said surprised.

Graf had wondered if the chief would notice that detail. He shouldn't have doubted him. The chief inspector didn't miss much. Studying one footprint in particular, his expression grew more and more disturbed. Over the years Graf had learned much from his mentor, how to listen for the meaning behind the spoken word and to not take anything for granted. Among the Swiss police, Blanchard was renowned for his passion for getting at the truth,

53

and his doggedness at sifting through minutia for the one meaningful element that could turn a case around. For that reason Graf was not surprised to see the chief transfixed by a sandy footprint, though he did seem to linger on it longer than expected.

After a dozen seconds, Durig leaned closer to Graf. "What's he doing?"

Graf shrugged. He didn't know and it bothered him that he didn't know. What had the chief seen he hadn't?

Finally, Blanchard rose to his full height, brushing off the sand from the bottom edge of his suit coat. "I'll want to see those footprint casts."

"Right." Graf nodded.

"Anything else?" Blanchard looked between the two men.

"Dafflon's shop."

With one graceful sweep of his arm, Blanchard motioned for Graf to lead the way.

The interior of Dafflon's shop was an array of neat rows of green plastic fruit racks tilted on wooden stands. The three policemen stood in an aisle in the center of the store surrounded by strawberries, pears, pomegranates, mangoes, and a host of other succulent delights.

Graf said, "There was a break in. Durig located the source of the intrusion. He can explain." The inspector could have finished the summary but he knew the chief liked to get his information firsthand whenever possible.

Once again all eyes trained on the young officer, who looked slightly unnerved at being under the spotlight. Durig cleared his throat and straightened his tunic. "There's a broken window in the back. As far as we can tell nothing valuable was taken. No cash. Nothing was vandalized. It seems the only thing disturbed was this rack."

The rack in question was beside them. Unlike the neat rows of fruit in the adjacent racks, the contents here were in disarray.

"There's also this," Durig added, pointing to a purple object under the stand, which stood out like a blight against the otherwise immaculate floor.

"*Plums*," Blanchard said in an undertone. "The intruder stole plums." He considered the fruit silently for a moment before continuing. "They're a favorite of mine, plums. My wife used to make a wonderful *Zwetschgenkuchen*."

Graf also enjoyed the plum tart; yet its key ingredient seemed a bizarre motive for burglary, let alone murder. "You see how peculiar the crime is, sir. Nothing of value was taken. The thief, it seems, broke in to steal fruit." He shook his head. Graf had few expectations of the Universe, though he did expect it to make sense. He suspected the chief felt the same as Blanchard contemplated the rack of plums with a taciturn expression.

Graf felt it prudent to interrupt. "The proprietor lived upstairs. Most likely Dafflon heard something and came down to investigate. By then the intruder had left by the front door and was headed to the beach. Dafflon followed and confronted him."

"Seems probable," the chief agreed.

"We're certain that's what happened."

"You seem very confident."

"We have a witness."

"A witness?"

"A kind of witness," Graf equivocated. "An old man who lives in the apartment next door. Hard to explain. He's waiting outside."

ϱϱϱ

The sun had risen above the Alpine peaks by the time they stepped outside. A tourist boat from Geneva was cruising on the lake, a large red and white Swiss flag waving from the stern mast. On the walkway of flowers, the three policemen stood by an elderly man with a stooped posture. His gangly frame was clad in simple clothes of gray and white. Wispy hair fluttered in the light breeze as ancient, uncertain eyes regarded them from behind thick spectacles.

Inspector Graf got the old man's attention. "Monsieur Lecomte, this is Chief Inspector Blanchard. He's in charge of the investigation."

"*Bonjour*," the chief greeted pleasantly.

"*Bonjour*," the old man said in a voice as dry as dust.

55

Graf spoke his next words with care. "Monsieur Lecomte, would you tell the chief what you told Officer Durig?"

"Everything?" Wispy eyebrows rose incredulously.

"Just the part after you heard the disturbance, after it awakened you."

"I can do that."

Except he didn't. An awkward silence followed in which the old man smiled blankly at the others. In the end, Graf felt compelled to move things along.

"You heard shouting." Graf rotated his hand to fan the witness's memory.

"I did," Lecomte agreed. "It came from outside, on the promenade. A loud and angry voice. It woke me out of a sound sleep. My apartment is there." He extended a bony finger toward a row of windows on the upper level of the building behind them. "My bed is near that first window."

"The shouting woke you," Graf reminded, hoping to keep the aged witness talking before he ran out of energy or forgot what he was going to say. "What happened next?"

"I sat up and put on my spectacles. Can't see a thing without them."

Another lengthy pause.

"And then?" Graf coaxed with a hint of impatience.

"What d'you expect? I went to the window to see who was making all the noise. It was Dafflon. He was shouting at someone on the beach."

"You knew M. Dafflon?" Chief Inspector Blanchard interjected.

"*Oui.* I was a regular customer. It was definitely his voice. No doubt about it."

"Did you see his face?"

"I didn't. But it was Dafflon."

"What time was this?"

"Two thirty."

"What happened next?"

"Dafflon shouted at the man."

"Did you hear what he said?"

The old man shook his head. "My hearing isn't what it used to be. I couldn't make out the words. Dafflon was angry, that's all I know. The man on the beach ignored him, which made him angrier. He ran down after him."

Blanchard asked pointedly. "This other man, did you get a good look at him?"

"*Non.* It was dark and he was too far away."

"Of course. Are there any general impressions you have that might help our investigation?"

Lecomte's mouth twisted as he dredged the depths of his memory. "There was something familiar about him. Can't say what exactly." Rheumy eyes narrowed behind the spectacles onto Durig. "Come to think of it, the other person reminded me of this young man."

Blanchard and Graf turned toward the startled officer.

"Me?" Durig blinked. "You must be mistaken! You're so nearsighted. How could you tell in the dark?"

Durig went silent when Blanchard touched his arm. "Monsieur Lecomte," the chief addressed the witness, "as my officer points out it was dark. You had a very brief look at the man from your window. Why do you think Officer Durig reminds you of him?"

. Lecomte adjusted his glasses, studying Durig up and down. "Nothing in particular. He just looks familiar."

Durig threw up his hands. "Maybe I look familiar because I patrol this neighborhood. You've probably seen me a dozen times."

The old man gave an indifferent shrug.

"What about the shooting?" Blanchard pressed.

Graf braced himself. He knew what was coming but wasn't going to forewarn the chief.

"Shooting?" Lecomte pooh-poohed. "I saw no shooting."

"You didn't?"

Graf leaned in and spoke softly in Blanchard's ear. "Monsieur Lecomte went to the bathroom."

"The bathroom?"

The elderly witness heard the comment and nodded. "*Oui.* After the shouting stopped, I saw Dafflon run after the man on the beach. I lost interest and went to the bathroom, then to bed."

"So you missed the actual shooting entirely." Blanchard cracked a smile.

The old man grinned back at the chief's kind face. The chief had an ingratiating manner that disarmed people. It was a trait Graf tried to emulate but while it came naturally for the chief, his second-in-command struggled at it.

"Thank you for your time, Monsieur Lecomte," Blanchard said, bringing the interview to a close. The witness bobbed his head and trundled along the *Quai des Fleur*, where he blended in with the tourists.

Blanchard looked to Graf. "What about Dafflon's family?"

"He was married. His wife's away in Schaffhausen visiting her sister. I've already sent a message to her. I'll follow up to see if she can tell us anything."

"She was away last night then?"

"For the last two days."

Blanchard nodded. "Good work, both of you." He sighed heavily. "Go back to the team. I'll join you in a little while."

A short time later, while supervising the crime scene team, Inspector Graf looked back at the walkway of flowers. Tourists and locals strolled along the floral promenade, taking in the mountains and cityscape, some curious at the police presence on the beach below. The chief stood at a scenic overlook, his hands resting on the metal guard railing, gazing across the tranquil turquoise waters, lost in thought. Graf could only wonder what was on Blanchard's mind. Graf had seen that faraway look before. Except this time it was different. The chief looked troubled. Was it something in the evidence? Graf's eyes narrowed. What had Blanchard seen that he hadn't?

000

Graf returned to the station the next afternoon, weary from a long day working on two other cases that had taken him to Lausanne and around Geneva. He'd barely walked to his desk when he saw the note from Blanchard, a simple missive written in the chief's fluid hand: *Please see me at your earliest convenience.*

Graf wasted no time. He didn't even bother to hang up his coat, instead tossing it across the seat of his chair.

Blanchard's office was a tidy space of orderly file cabinets, neatly stacked papers and pencil holders, all in proper alignment. The chief inspector sat behind his desk, engrossed in filling out a report. On the wall behind him was a large poster of the Grand Canyon, which always amused Graf. They worked in the shadow of the French Alps. Perhaps their constant proximity had inured the chief inspector to their grandeur, for his choice of art was a massive hole in the earth, the antithesis of mountains. A conscious choice? The juxtaposition was noteworthy. Graf wondered if the contrast satisfied Blanchard's need for balance.

The chief was fully absorbed at his task and was unaware of Graf's presence, so he rapped his knuckles against the door jam.

"You wanted to see me, sir?"

"Ah, Laurent, please sit down." Blanchard offered a warm, familiar smile. He waited for his second-in-command to get comfortable, then drew in a heavy breath as one about to take on an unpleasant task. That put Graf's guard up. Something was about to happen.

"I've reviewed the Dafflon evidence," said the chief. "I'm convinced the facts support one and only one conclusion. I've looked at different interpretations but the same answer keeps coming back."

A chill wriggled up Graf's chest. Something was wrong. His eyes locked onto the chief's. "What conclusion?"

Blanchard held Graf's gaze. "I know who killed Dafflon."

"Who?"

The chief's face clouded. "Me."

Graf gaped at him in confusion. "I don't understand."

A somber Blanchard met his eyes, and in those eyes Graf saw bewilderment and anguish.

"Believe me, Laurent, I don't understand myself. But the evidence is clear. I must have shot Michel Dafflon." He leaned forward. "I don't remember doing it, have no recollection of being there, yet it must have been me."

"Sir, there must be some mistake—" Graf protested but was cut off by Blanchard's raised hand.

"Thank you for your loyalty." The chief looked back with gratitude. "Please, let me finish. The footprints in the sand, you noticed the killer was missing a toe on his left foot. I'm missing a toe on my left foot. Same toe. Same foot. That's why I was eager to see the casts of the impressions. I wanted to verify them myself. There is no doubt. Those footprints on the beach are mine."

The chief sighed. "It does explain something strange I noticed the morning of the murder. I woke up and found grains of sand on the carpet by my front door. It made no sense. Now I know I must have walked out in the middle of the night. To the beach."

"And you have no memory of this?"

"No."

"I don't follow. Like sleepwalking?"

"I think so."

Graf would have none of it. "It's a setup, sir. Someone is making it look like you killed Dafflon."

"Laurent, it was my gun. Ballistics confirmed the bullet that killed Dafflon came from my gun. My footprints. My gun. It was me."

"How can this be?" Graf stared back, confused.

With a heavy heart, Blanchard elaborated. "When I was a boy, I used to sleepwalk all the time. Not every night but often, several times a month. I'd leave our house and wander the neighborhood and beyond. My parents took me to doctors. They could do nothing. It finally stopped when I went to University. Haven't done it for twenty years. I thought it'd stopped for good. I guess not...."

Graf waited. In the back of his mind lurked a desperate hope that this was a cruel joke, part of some elaborate scheme to unmask the killer. Blanchard, he realized with heartrending dread, was actually confessing to Dafflon's murder. Graf slumped in his chair.

"I've not been sleeping well," the chief went on. "I might've told you that already. Since Gina-Maria died last year, it's been a challenge. We were married for twenty-seven years.

The girls are grown and gone. I'm alone. Still adjusting. Perhaps that triggered the sleepwalking again."

"If you say so, sir. Yet, why kill Dafflon? I don't see the connection."

"Plums. It must be the plums."

Graf shook his head uncomprehendingly.

"I love plums," the chief explained. "They may be my favorite fruit. I've been to Dafflon's shop before. I must've had a craving and went there. I broke in. He caught me and I...I killed him." Blanchard shuttered his eyes and breathed a few silent, measured breaths. When his eyes opened again there was a sadness there Graf had never seen. From his drawer, the chief removed his badge and sidearm, placed them on the desk and slid them forward. "You must charge me with murder, Laurent. I've written my statement as best as I can imagine it, since I don't have a direct memory of the crime." He patted the sheet of paper on the desk.

Graf was beside himself. "This is insane. From what you tell me there are mitigating circumstances."

Blanchard's china-blue eyes regarded him with open appreciation. "Perhaps," he said wistfully. "That's for a court to decide. I spent the better part of thirty years bringing killers to justice. Everyone is accountable. Even me. You have to arrest me."

"Sir..."

"You must."

"Yes, sir."

"Perhaps the court will show me some mercy."

Graf bowed his head, feeling he'd just lost part of himself. When his eyes came up, the chief was looking around the familiar surroundings one last time.

"I'm ready, Laurent," he said, rallying a supportive smile for the benefit of his number two.

Graf took it to heart. Chief Inspector Blanchard always did the right thing, even now at his worst moment. About to be taken into custody, he displayed remarkable composure and integrity. Graf had a bitter task to perform but he couldn't have been more proud of his mentor.

Michael Allan Mallory is the co-author of two novels featuring mystery's first zoologist sleuth. His short stories have appeared in numerous collections. Most recently, the crime anthology *Cooked to Death: Tales of Crime and Cookery*, for which he served as co-editor, was listed as one of the best books for adults of 2016 by the St. Paul Pioneer Press.

CONSUMING PASSION

BY MARTIN EDWARDS

"Dining in Hall tonight, Roger?" the Domestic Bursar brayed. "I've been meaning to talk to you about the College's latest fund-raising..."

Roger Finn shook his head. "Sorry, Henry, but I'm just on my way to the Turl Gate. Honoured guest of Piers Carberry."

"Lucky fellow. Writing a review, eh? The Master and I sampled his salmon with fire and ice a few weeks ago. A culinary delight. Pity that I needed to re-mortgage to pay my share of the bill."

Roger smiled. "No review, this is pleasure, not business." Stretching a point, to say the least, but never mind. "Just a social get together. Piers and I were students together, you know. He's a Trinity man."

The Domestic Bursar tugged at his beard. "Ah, well, nobody's perfect."

Roger laughed. "Certainly not Piers Carberry."

With a wave, he strode through the porter's lodge and through the vast oak doors into Broad Street. Rain was slanting down in the November darkness, but he hadn't bothered with an umbrella. He was staying at the Master's Lodgings overnight, and the Turl Gate was only a minute away.

The restaurant was closed, as usual on a Monday, but he walked in to the hotel, and the attractive Iraqi woman at reception said Piers would be with him shortly, and would he like to take a seat?

Like everything else in the Turl Gate, the distressed leather armchairs were the last word in luxury, with the chance to admire the receptionist's glossy black hair and almond eyes an added bonus. A bronze plaque announced that a twirling gate had once been set in the old city wall. In the sixteenth century, it gave its name to Turl Gate Street, later modified to Turl Street. Well, well, you never stopped learning in Oxford. Twenty-five years in and around the city, and he'd never heard that story. But he didn't doubt it. Piers always did his homework.

He and Piers made an odd couple. One tall and fair with an Old Harrovian's languid self-assurance, the other short and dark with a burning intensity of purpose that had driven him all the way from an under-achieving Nottingham comprehensive to Trinity College. The two of them had met over a bread and cheese lunch in St John's after joining the students' Broadcasting Society and, as if to defy expectations among their college cronies, become inseparable. When Roger started going out with a pretty girl from LMH called Sonia, they'd introduced Piers to her younger sister Lois, and the two weddings took place on a beach in Antigua on the very same day.

"Roger." Piers marched out into the lobby. His handshake was as firm as ever. "You're looking fit."

Pity Roger couldn't say the same about him. The designer stubble was simply a long-term affectation, part of the image of a moody celebrity chef, but Piers' small eyes were bloodshot, and new furrows hatched his brow. A lot of water had flowed under the bridge since that scorching Antiguan afternoon. Was this evening a mistake? Roger didn't think so. He needed to talk to Piers, and when the invitation came, he hadn't hesitated to say yes.

"Shall we go through?" Piers nodded to a door opposite reception. The hotel was a boutique with a dozen rooms, and the restaurant was famously intimate—that is, tiny and claustrophobic. Both were crammed into a tall, skinny building, but lack of space was compensated for by exclusivity. There was always a waiting list for rooms and tables.

"I like your receptionist," Roger said as they took their seats at a candle-lit table.

"Amira?" Piers raised his eyebrows. "Your eye for a pretty face has never deserted you."

"Nor yours."

As they small-talked, Roger pictured Lois in his mind. She had been even more beautiful than Sonia, though her temperament was fragile, and her death from an overdose of sleeping pills a not totally unforeseeable tragedy. Five years after her suicide, Roger had introduced Piers to his second wife. He'd cast Nora Verlaine as the voluptuous heroine in a costume drama he was making for the BBC. Ratings were indifferent, but his match-making enjoyed greater success. Within a week of their first date, Piers and Nora were living together. Within ten, they were married. This time the wedding was a lavish affair in a Scottish castle. Finn's companion that day was a weather girl, one in a long line of dalliances on either side of his divorce from Sonia. He couldn't even remember the kid's name. Kelly, Kelsey, Kylie. Something like that.

"So how is life?" Piers asked as the Indian waiter, immaculately tailored in white jacket and trousers, poured a second glass of Dom Pérignon. The waiter was a slim, shy boy called Gautam, and Roger was sure Piers fancied him. Not many people knew Piers was interested in handsome young men as well as gorgeous women. According to Sonia, Lois had discovered the truth, and was utterly incapable of handling it. Yet Piers was adept at keeping his private life private. As far as the media were concerned, he was a man who had it all. Rich, supremely talented, one half of a glamorous celebrity couple.

"Couldn't be better. Enjoying a bit of downtime right now. Last month I finished filming a six-part series about East End gangsters. Low-budget, but a pretty good script."

"Not written by you, then?"

In those long ago Broadcasting Society days, they'd both loved writing. As two bright and ambitious undergraduates, they had always been rivals, as well as friends. After university, they'd graduated far beyond bread and cheese. Both developed a taste for fine food. Piers channelled his creativity into establishing a British equivalent to *haute cuisine*, while Roger dabbled in low-budget art house movies before making serious money in mainstream television. As Piers was finding fame as a gourmet chef in Chelsea, Roger developed a sideline of writing restaurant reviews for a downmarket Sunday newspaper. *Consuming Passion*, his column was called, and within weeks his scathing wit earned him half a dozen sworn enemies, and a new contract so absurdly lucrative that he was almost embarrassed to sign.

Roger pretended to narrow his eyes. "Be careful. I may decide it's time I reviewed the Turl Gate Restaurant."

"You'll be even more impressed than you were in Chelsea," Piers said as the Indian boy serving their steaks warned them that the plates were hot. *"The most perfect example of British beef you can find, at any price, in any place. Forget about the French, this Englishman wins my vote for the finest chef in Europe."*

"Wow," Roger said, miming applause. "Word perfect."

"You're my oldest, my most trusted friend. Your good opinion means a great deal to me. Though naturally, you spoke nothing less than the truth."

Roger watched Piers check out Gautam's trim backside as the waiter shimmied back to the kitchen. "Believe me, I was worried before I started eating. What the hell could I say if I hated it?"

"Lucky for me you have great taste," Piers said softly.

Roger had been careful to disclose in the review that he and Piers were friends, but to do anything but heap praise would have been a nonsense. The man was a genius, and he'd made enough money to sink it into this new hotel-cum-restaurant amidst the dreaming spires, catering for the great and the good. Not students, needless to say, other than those with parents who were millionaires.

"No," Roger said. "I loved it."

"You're too kind." Piers cut into his steak. "Speaking of love, are you still seeing that cute little Swedish blonde you introduced me to last time we met?"

Roger shook his head. "We've each moved on. So how are things with you and Nora?"

"Oh, you know what actors are like."

"Don't I just? Believe me, you're lucky with Nora, she's not as tough as most actors. So many of them are as hard as nails."

"You're so right." Piers shook his head. "But I wanted to ask your advice."

"Not in my capacity as a restaurant critic?"

"God, no, I'm confident you'll love every succulent mouthful." Piers leaned across the table. "Tell you the truth, I'm feeling a bit stressed."

Roger indicated their surroundings. "Must be hard work, keeping a place like this up to the mark. When you have a name for excellence...."

"It's not the business that's getting me down, Roger." Piers lowered his voice. "You see, I have an enemy."

Roger chewed thoughtfully. "To be honest, Piers, that's something we have in common. We both have enemies. People who want us to fail. It's the name of the game, when you make a few quid and have a high profile."

"But this seems very...personal."

"It's no fun, coming to terms with the idea that there are people out there who would like nothing better than to spit on your grave." Roger picked up his napkin and dabbed gravy from his mouth. "But you've said things about your fellow chefs that haven't endeared you to them. People demand honesty, but they don't like it when they get it. Believe me, I've ruffled plenty of feathers with *Consuming Passion*. I've even received death threats."

"Seriously?"

"Not a word of a lie. I once said a few harsh things about a little place in Notting Hill which turned out to be owned by a couple of Mafiosi, and then—"

"I need to remind myself," Piers broke in, "you're a storyteller. Brilliant at making things up. And what you love most of all is telling stories about yourself."

"Sorry." Roger was almost abashed. "You were telling me about this enemy..."

"Yes." Piers took another sip. "Marvellous vintage, 1988. Amazing, isn't it, how long it takes the finest Dom Pérignon to reach its peak?"

Roger raised his glass again. "I'm honoured. Now, do go on."

"I need your advice. There's nobody else I can ask. I want—"

"Hold on." Roger gestured with his fork towards the ceiling. Piers and Nora had a flat at the top of this building, as well as the place in Holland Park, and the villa outside Carcassonne. "Have you talked to Nora?"

"Only very briefly. She didn't understand."

"You surprise me. I mean, I know she can sometimes seem...well...a tad self-absorbed. But show me the actor who hasn't got an ego."

Piers shrugged. "You and I go back much longer than Nora and me. I've always trusted you."

"I'm flattered."

"Don't be." Piers put down his knife and fork, and leaned across the table. "I'm desperate, Roger. I'm facing ruin. The end of everything. The business, my marriage, a whole life's work."

Roger swallowed. "For God's sake, Piers, what is the matter? Is someone blackmailing you?"

It was perfectly possible. What if Piers had sacked some disgruntled young man who was threatening to run to the newspapers with stories about the master chef's unorthodox methods of rewarding his prettiest staff members?

"No, no. But..."

"But—what?" Roger savoured his last mouthful. "That was marvellous, Piers. You certainly haven't lost your touch."

"Thanks. I was about to say...I feel betrayed."

"Betrayed? By whom?"

"Ah." Piers smiled. "Trust the Balliol man not to forget his grammar even *in extremis*."

"Sorry, I don't understand."

"Don't you, Roger? Well, I understand perfectly." Piers clutched his knife as if it were a weapon. "And what I've learned is that you are the person who has betrayed me. Who is about to destroy everything I've worked for."

Roger threw his napkin on to the table. "What are you talking about?"

"About your affair with Nora." Piers sighed. "Don't embarrass us both with any denials, any of your imaginative excuses. I've seen the emails, checked her phone."

Roger took a breath. "Okay, okay. As a matter of fact, I was intending to come clean this evening. Over coffee and a liqueur, that was my plan. Trust me, Piers, I want this to be as civilised as possible."

"But how can we be civilised, given the circumstances? I've worshipped Nora from the day we met." Gautam appeared again, but Piers waved him away. "The boys are just a bit of fun. A bit of escapist fantasy, let's say. I love being married."

"But does Nora love being married to you?" Roger clenched his fist under the table. Time to shove Piers off the moral high ground. "Did Lois? Did you ever wonder why she killed herself?"

"Because you messed with her mind by screwing her, and then dumping her," Piers snapped. "Don't think I don't know that she was besotted with you. Though it did take me years to figure out the truth. I only realised you were my enemy when I saw the pattern repeating itself with Nora."

"This is different," Roger said. "Lois—that was a mistake on my part. Hands up, I admit it. I can't pretend I dealt with the situation well. But Nora and I want to be together for the rest of our lives."

"Don't tell me." A sardonic grin. "So this is another consuming passion?"

"Listen, Piers, there's no need to worry that she'll take you to the cleaners in divorce court. Or utter a word about your boyfriends. Like me, Nora wants things to be civilised."

"Too late for that, I told you."

"No need for bitterness, Piers. These things happen. They don't have to destroy our friendship."

Piers folded his napkin. "I think we'd better forego the desserts. Pity, I put a lot of time into their preparation. Like the meal as a whole."

"Of course it was magnificent."

Piers bowed. "You speak about our friendship, Roger, but will it survive your betrayal—or my act of vengeance?"

Roger stared at him.

Piers nodded at their dinner plates. They were clear except for a few streaks of gravy. "Nora was exceptionally tender, don't you agree? We both have excellent taste—in food, and women. And now we know the truth. It's not true what they say. Revenge really isn't a dish best served cold."

Martin Edwards has published eighteen novels, including the Lake District Mysteries. *The Golden Age of Murder* won the Edgar, Agatha, H.R.F. Keating and Macavity awards. He has edited thirty crime anthologies, and has won the CWA Short Story Dagger, the CWA Margery Allingham Prize, and the Poirot award. He is President of the Detection Club and Chair of the CWA.

"Consuming Passion" was originally published in the German anthology *Mit Schirme, Charme and Pistole* (2014) and subsequently in *Ellery Queen's Mystery Magazine* (2016), and has been reprinted here with the author's permission.

BASES LOOTED

BY JASON HALF

"Back to the skybox, Finn."

The moment before, the ballpark security guard had been standing to the side of the bleachers entrance, his earpiece buzzing dully, his head cocked to the left like a German shepherd listening to a dog whistle. Now he was standing in front of me, blocking the way.

"I've already been to the skybox. Now I need to get to the crowd and actually make some money." Instead of moving aside, he stepped toward me, forcing me to begin a retreat down the hallway.

"Skybox."

The guard switched from German shepherd to Australian cattle dog, herding me and my metal steamer full of franks and buns down the corridor.

Nearing the vendors' kitchen, I ran into Miguel Aronas, owner of Home Run Tacos, who also wore his food carrier from a strap across his shoulder. Inside were foil-wrapped burritos and paper boats of nachos, ready for sale. Outside was a frustrated Miguel, who was speaking excitedly in Spanish to a young guard just out of community college.

Miguel gave me a palms-up ¿Qué pasa? gesture. A glance into the tiny supply and prep kitchen showed me a busy and troubling sight. Two more security guards were working over the room, one yanking out drawers and pawing through cabinet shelves, another tossing out sleeves of stacked coffee cup lids in an effort to empty a cardboard box.

"Move," said my guard.

"Go on," squeaked Miguel's guard.

"Come on," I said to my colleague. "We're heading back to the skybox."

Four guards were already on the scene, and the park only had nine of them total. Not a good sign.

I found two more guards as soon as we entered the enclosed skybox deck. Like the kitchen crew, they were prodding and poking about the space, although with a bit more tact. This was likely in deference to the bigwigs assembled, five older men of varying waistlines and expressions of sour annoyance. They were here today to watch their teams compete in an exhibition game, but we were three innings in and no one was paying attention to the impressive view through the windows or the players on the field below.

Instead, they were studying the non-bigwigs who had already been rounded up and were involuntarily cooling their heels. If I wanted to know where my fellow vendors were, I needed to look no further.

Arranged, left to right, were Conner Beechum, a fussy little man who sold new-wave gourmet fare to ballpark customers wanting to chase a trend; Sue Gibson, an energetic and plain-speaking matron who, along with her cookies and brownies, had been a vendor icon for nearly two decades; and Karla DeNucci, an attractive single mom who sold Coca-Cola in commemorative plastic bottles. As it often does, my attention turned to Karla.

"Finn, what's going on?"

She had set her vendor's case on the floor, and was able to move to me unencumbered. My guard watched us warily.

"I don't know. Something's happened but they won't tell us."

Sue stepped toward the bigwigs, and I could tell before she spoke that she had no interest in playing maternal.

"Hey fellas, we can't stand around up here and watch your teams from the skybox, pleasant as that may be. We need to get out to the bleachers and earn *our* money." The implication was obvious, and I liked Sue even more then. "So if you don't mind—"

"Sit down," said my guard. "Everyone stays here."

"Hey. Hey." We all swiveled to look at the shortest and fattest bigwig, the well-fed and red-faced owner of the Topeka Peelers, who were currently at bat. He spoke to the guard. "Someone's missing. The loudmouth with the peanuts."

We looked at one another, and had to admit that he was right. Ray Rinaldi was not among us.

As if on cue, the loudmouth with the peanuts shuffled into the room, with park security manager Gabe Simmons pushing him along.

"You're not just violating my rights as a vendor," Ray was saying mid-monologue. "You're trampling on the rights of all those people out there. 'Buy me some peanuts and Cracker Jacks'. It's right there in the song!"

Simmons ignored him and turned to my guard.

"Rinaldi was already in the stands, E-Section. I want any men not assigned to the kitchen to start searching that area."

"Right away. Clear the attendants as well?"

Simmons hesitated for a second, but commerce won out. "No, leave them there. If anyone asks, say you're looking for a dropped wallet." The guard exited, taking two of his brethren with him and leaving the third to keep an eye on us.

"Please tell me, what's this about?" asked Miguel. I had slipped off my carrier and set it beside Karla's, but Miguel was still wearing his, the mounted circular logo of his odd little half-baseball, half-open-faced burrito grinning back at us from the front of the vending box.

Gabe Simmons looked about to reply—my guess is that it would've only been another "Sit down" or something similarly terse—but another bigwig, this one the owner of the Abilene Prairie Dogs, jumped in ahead of him.

"One of *them* has it," he said, staring at us accusingly. "Stands to reason, right? They're the only ones who have gone in and out of this room in the last ten minutes. Temptation was too great for one of them."

"I have no idea what you're talking about," said Sue, unwrapping a chocolate and cream cheese brownie. But I was starting to connect the dots, and I didn't like the picture forming.

"Well?" asked the Prairie Dogs' team manager, standing beside his boss in a show of bigwig solidarity. "Don't you think you should search them?"

"A search is already underway," said Simmons. "We'll get a report and go from there."

Ray Rinaldi had started pacing, which was a challenge considering the number of people in the room, the limited floor space, and the chips and peanuts tray he was swinging around with each turn he made.

"No one's touching me or my stock until you tell me what you're looking for."

"I can answer that." I stepped over to the opposite side of the room. The team owners started like spooked horses at my approach. "Easy, gentlemen. I just want to fill in my co-workers, since you're not planning to do so."

"Finn, get away from the table." Simmons gave the order in a low growl.

"The damage is already done, isn't it, folks?" I looked at my fellow vendors. "What do we have here?" I fanned the long table with an open palm, as if presenting merchandise on display. "Pennants, programs, trophies, a signed championship ball. So what's missing?"

The vendors stared at the table while the bigwigs stared at the vendors. "I didn't do nothin'," Ray muttered under his breath.

It was Karla who broke the silence.

"Finn, I don't know what was on that table. I just came in, put my drinks into that cooler, and left again." She gestured at a large ice-filled cooler sitting beside a food table that featured the wares of each vendor in the assembled group.

"We were all talkin' to each other, watchin' the game," said the fourth bigwig, a toothy Texan with a prairie twang and a suit that probably cost more than a season of hot dog sales. "Any one of 'em could'a grabbed it and ran."

"Just what are we talking about?" asked Conner Beechum, still seated and holding tight to his vending box, probably filled with bacon-wrapped garlic asparagus or ham-and-feta croquettes. The unusual circumstances seemed to have cracked even his fussy façade.

"¡*Ay, Dios mío!*" All eyes turned to Miguel, whose face had elongated into an expression of shock that was comical. But he spoke the next words with a hushed reverence: "The Double-A Independent Diamond Disc."

The Double-A Independent Diamond Disc indeed.

The next twenty minutes, spent in skybox limbo while the hallway, prep kitchen, bathrooms, storage closets, and most of the Section-E bleachers were searched, gave ample time for suspicions to grow and paranoia to flourish. Although we vendors hadn't yet been frisked and our cases dumped out and sorted through, we all knew that was around the corner. Outside, we were already losing food sales to the sellers who hadn't gotten caught up in this mess, and the prospect of an imminent search and seizure made no one happy. Mutiny flashed in the gimlet eyes of the bigwigs, and only Gabe Simmons and his desire for order had kept them in check.

I used the time to conduct a little research. Knowing that Karla was never without her cell phone, I asked her to look up details about the missing disc. I knew the basics: it was a valuable little circle of gold with soldered, tempered wiring under a plate meant to resemble a baseball diamond. At each base was a real diamond embedded into the frame, with a root-beer colored sapphire representing home plate. Five jewels, together worth a modest but significant five figures, out in the open and, until recently, on display in this room.

I had glanced at it when I had entered to set up the dogs and buns on the opposite table before the first inning, and I had openly studied it when I came back at the top of the third to replace the cool dogs with warmer ones. I had left the skybox just as Karla was entering, her drinks carrier leading the way.

Others must have gone in and out of this room while I was in the kitchen, switching out ketchup and relish pots and quick-steaming a new batch of buns for the customers in the stands. Third inning was the first decent break for everyone to get back, replenish the stock, and check on the bigwigs, and it must have been a regular French farce of entrances and exits in those ten minutes. But if, like me, an enterprising opportunist had taken note of the Diamond Disc during their first inning set-up, it wouldn't have taken very long to—

"Got it, Finn. Five-point-nine inches in diameter, four inset brilliant-cut diamonds and one champagne sapphire mounted and inlaid on bas-relief 18-karat yellow gold plating." Karla was reading from her phone screen, relaying the stats in a husky whisper. "Designed and created by Brooklyn gem setter Lorenzo

Tanni in 2010, commissioned by the American Association of Independent Professional Baseball Leagues. Currently on loan to the Topeka Peelers, last year's tournament winners."

A six-inch disc thinner than a dinner plate. And, unless stadium security dropped the proverbial ball, odds were good that the thing was less than a hundred yards from here, and probably a lot closer than that.

Simmons was in conference with the kitchen search committee, which had apparently returned empty-handed. Ray came up to Karla and me, tossing a bag of peanuts from one hand to the other in agitation.

"What're you looking at?"

Karla reflexively pulled her phone to her chest, but Ray had seen the small photo of the disc on the screen.

"None of your business," said Karla.

"It's *hurtin'* my business, stuck here while one of you's sitting on that trophy." Ray's expression changed as a new idea landed. It was never hard to track Ray Rinaldi's thought process, such as it was. "Hey. That kid of yours, she's been in and out of the hospital."

"Out now," Karla answered coldly, "and doing just fine. So nice of you to care."

Last year, Karla's daughter Samantha had gone through two surgeries to remove aggressively large lymph node cysts that could have caused problems as she grew older. I visited her after each surgery. Strong kid, just like her mother.

But Ray wouldn't let it go. "You must be racking up the doctor's bills. I'm just sayin'."

"You can stop saying it." Ray saw that I meant business. He sighed and changed the subject.

"Why didn't they just cater up here? That way we wouldn't be stuck in this mess."

That much was true. Normally, the park management hired the catering company under contract to provide food and drink for the skybox when bigwigs descended. It always worked out better that way, since the vendors weren't asked to serve two masters, hustling between skybox and stadium during a game. But occasionally someone would decide to give the V.I.P.s an old-fashioned beer-and-pretzels ballpark buffet, and then it was up to us luckless food merchants to make sure everyone was satisfied, for a nominal stipend.

I looked over at the bigwigs, who did not appear to like what Gabe Simmons was telling them. Had someone in that over-incomed semi-circle asked for us, knowing that vendors would be moving in and out of the room? Team owners could fall into debt with the same ease as us commoners.

But Simmons was on their side, literally. Standing in front of the bigwigs, the chief security guard turned to address us.

"Listen up. You're going to form a line and stand beside your food carriers. You won't move or touch anything during the search. Two guards are going to inspect your carriers, your food, and your person."

There was a general ruckus on my side, with everyone talking at once. Somehow, Miguel's rising tenor managed to be heard over the babble.

"What d'you mean, person? Which person?"

"He means a pat-down," Ray answered. "The rent-a-cops think they've got the right to frisk us."

"Unless you've managed to hire some female guards in the last five minutes, nobody's patting me anywhere," said Mama Sue.

"This is serious, and you don't have a choice. Ray, put your food down. Miguel, move back to your box."

More protests and grumbling, but I knew it could quickly become a lot less polite. Miguel and Karla were both looking at me.

"Go ahead. Let's get this over with."

Under Simmons's orders, the fresh-faced guard cleared away the food, serving trays, and cutlery spread out on one of the buffet tables. This gave the duo who had ransacked the kitchen some elbow room to hold their questionable search and seizure.

"Vollavent, we start with you." Before Conner Beechum could react, a guard had grabbed his linen-lined vendor's box and plunked it down on the table. Stenciled in fancy curling script on the front was the word—I thought it was a word—*Vol-au-vent*, which was the name of his upscale European fusion restaurant in the city's Arts district. Even though his fancy appetizers seemed like an incongruous addition to ballpark fare, the gamble had paid off. His chocolate and cream filled *crêpes* fetched five dollars a pancake and consistently outsold Mama Sue's Batter Up Brownies.

The second guard began to run his hands over Conner's slight figure, but the day's first official suspect was barely paying attention. Instead, he was frowning at the guard who had opened his vending basket and was rooting around inside.

"Hey, come on!" the restaurateur pleaded, breaking free from the pat-down and moving to the table. Simmons took a step forward and called for him to stop, but Conner ignored him.

"See! He's got somethin' to hide!" announced the Texan with glee.

"No, I'm trying to salvage my inventory." With that, he reached into the box and began to reorganize the contents. The guard flashed Simmons a *What now?* look, and the slow burn he got in reply didn't bode well for any of us.

"Now wait," I said, thinking that an appeal to common sense might be useful for all parties. "There's no reason why each vendor can't display their food and box to everyone here, a little on-demand show-and-tell to prove we didn't take the disc. But the guards don't need to paw through everything we still hope to sell. Our stock shouldn't suffer because of this."

"That's right," said Mama Sue. "I've got a hundred dollars' worth of brownies in that basket."

The red-faced, chubby bigwig wasn't having it. "You think we care about your brownies when there's a $15,000 trophy that's missing? And one of you has it."

"Or one of you." Ray Rinaldi looked defiantly at the bigwig, then pointed to the group. He turned to Simmons. "You're gonna search *them* when you get done with us, right?"

Now it was the bigwigs who babbled and complained. Simmons turned back to Conner.

"Vollavent!" The way he pronounced it, it sounded like *elephant*. "Unpack your box and show us the inside of the container."

With a guard on each side of him, Conner unpacked his food for sale, one neatly arranged stack of covered plates at a time. It was his gimmick to serve each *hors d'oeuvre* to the fan in the bleachers on a fancy plastic plate that was covered with a plastic grey lid, which he would remove with a flourish whenever proximity allowed.

At the table, he set out the first stack of plates. Even under these circumstances, the showman in him came through.

"Today, it's a parmesan, herb, and tomato mini-frittata wrapped in puff pastry," he announced, lifting the lid to reveal what looked like a bite-sized omelet with a pedigree. He lifted a second lid. "My most popular ballpark item. *Crêpe Parisienne* with chocolate mousse and Bavarian cream filling."

We all looked at the delicately wrapped pastry on the plate, dappled with powdered sugar, and damned if, just for a second, the thing didn't seem to sparkle.

Then the spell broke. The short bigwig tapped Simmons rudely on the shoulder.

"I'm not satisfied until we actually go through that food, and not just his, but everybody's! What about this? Whoever took the trophy could have taken out the jewels and thrown away the disc. And now those diamonds could be hiding anywhere, in one of those *crepes*—" This was pronounced *creeps.* "—or a bag of peanuts or a bottle of soda pop—" Ray and Karla reacted in turn. "—or anywhere! So you better get serious. I want the police called in, right now, the real police."

To his credit, Gabe Simmons didn't show it, but I knew him well enough to know that questioning his competency as a law official was not the way to go. After a beat, he spoke.

"One problem with that way of thinking. None of the vendors knew you would be traveling with the diamond disc today. If someone here is guilty, it was a crime of opportunity, not a premeditated one."

The bigwig looked confused.

"So what?"

"So, none of these people came to work with wire cutters or tin snips, and there's nothing sharper than a butter knife to be found in the service kitchen. Isn't that right, Finn?"

I was happy to catch the pitch. "Not only that, but the disc had been missing for fifteen minutes tops before you rounded us all up, meaning that a thief would have had to work fast to pry gems out of a frame designed by a professional jeweler. And he'd still have to get rid of the disc itself. And since that hasn't turned up yet, with or without the diamonds, it's a safe bet that your precious trophy is still in one piece."

"And I say everything should be searched," grumbled the bigwig. But he was overruled.

The next half hour was an odd hybrid of a cable-access food prep segment and mandatory customs inspection. Conner Beechum finished uncovering all his ready-to-go plates and then carefully moved each *crêpe* or quiche to one of two Tupperware containers, where it would wait to serve another day.

The packing up was thanks to a balding bigwig who had otherwise been quiet, but made the Sherlockian suggestion to uncover each plate, which was roughly the size of the AA Diamond Disc. How anyone could overlook a diamond-set gold medallion because it had a cream-filled pastry sitting on top of it was beyond me. But Conner complied, and finished with four precise stacks of plates and lids.

After the empty *Vol-au-vent* container was searched, it was Karla's turn. Because of the weight of lugging filled bottles of soda to thirsty attendees, Karla's carrier case was smaller by necessity, capable of stocking two dozen in six neat rows of four. She emptied the case onto the table.

"I still think those diamonds could have been pried off the disc," said the short, fat team owner, not giving up. "And that means she could've just dropped 'em in one of those bottles, put the top back on, and now they're hiding in plain sight."

Against my instinct, I held my tongue. Karla found hers.

"You can open these bottles," she said calmly, "and I will send you an invoice for goods purchased. Retail cost."

"You should open the ones still in there, too," said Ray Rinaldi, pointing to the ice-filled skybox cooler. "In case she made a bait and switch." He was just out of kicking distance, so I took a step closer.

"And the ice!" yelled the bigwig. "Diamonds could be hidden among those ice cubes! Guards, check that cooler!"

Simmons obviously disliked the order, but it needed to be done. Two security guards unloaded the soda bottles—along with an impressive mix of imported beers—then inspected handfuls of ice cubes before dropping them noisily into a bucket.

Meanwhile, Ray was reacting just as noisily to the demand that he empty the bags of peanuts and potato chips on his tray. When one guard sidestepped his protests and started to move the paper bags of peanuts, he squawked and grabbed his merchandise.

A disapproving trill of *tsks* came from Miguel. "It's only right, Ray. The jewels can be hiding among the peanuts just as easy as in the sodas, no?"

Ray glared at Miguel, who now wore the same smile as his baseball-taco mascot.

As much as Ray Rinaldi deserved to get the Deluxe Suspect treatment, I knew it wouldn't lead anywhere. There was also the fact that Sue, Miguel, and I were still waiting to be searched, and rules changed now would also apply to us.

I looked to Simmons, but spoke to the room.

"Gabe, the idea that someone popped out the diamonds and pocketed them or stuffed them into a nearby hot dog or *crêpe* doesn't hold up. Either with bases loaded or empty, that disc still has to be around."

"You said that before."

I nodded. "So here's a new thought. Have you looked *outside* the stadium, over the wall of E-section?" Ray barked a "Hey!" at me, but I ignored it.

The guard who had coordinated the stadium search reported.

"Thompson and I searched the grounds outside the stadium, just under the section."

"And how far out did you go? The thing's basically a Frisbee," said Simmons. The lack of immediate response was its own answer. "You and Thompson go out again. Take two others with you. It could've landed clear across the lot."

When the men left, the Texan bigwig started to cross to the door. Simmons stopped him.

"Where are you going?"

"I need to use the facilities. Or do I need your permission?" An executive restroom, much tonier than anything the average baseball fan used, was across the hall from the skybox.

"I'm going to have a guard accompany you."

The Texan glared. "I been doin' this solo for years." Simmons didn't blink.

"These are special circumstances." It took more glaring and staring, but the bigwig finally left with a chaperone.

On Simmons's order, the two remaining security officers took us in turn, first Miguel, who unpacked his tacos and paper boats of greasy tortilla chips, then handed a ladle to one of the guards, who skimmed around in the steel pot of melted cheese.

After the vending box was examined and the owner of Home Run Tacos given a brief but thorough pat-down, they moved on to me. Same process—a few extra minutes were devoted to draining and exploring the compartment that generated steam for the hot dogs in the tray above—and same results.

Mama Sue Gibson was last, and by that time the Texan had returned and the bigwigs were growing increasingly restless. After a deferential pat-down, the young guards barely touching the dessert seller's padded contours, they moved on to her shoulder-strapped picnic basket. Sue placed plastic-wrapped, oversized cookies and brownie bars onto the table.

I studied my fellow vendors. Karla was seated on the floor, texting on her phone, most likely trying to check in with Samantha. Miguel was listlessly stirring his quickly congealing potful of melted cheese. Conner appeared to be meditating among his stacks of lids and plates, sitting cross-legged beside his vending box.

I had expected to see Ray fidgeting with his bags of chips, but instead he was frowning at Miguel. At first, I figured he was still brooding over Miguel's suggestion to search his peanuts for hidden jewels, but then I followed the focus of his stare.

It didn't land on the owner of Home Run Tacos.

Instead, he was looking at the smiling baseball-taco insignia on the front of the vending case.

It was round and connected to the box with a few plate screws. And it was just over six inches in diameter.

At that moment, the duo assigned to the extended search returned. No sign of the disc outside. That was the last straw for the bigwigs.

"Enough! I'm calling in the police myself," said the V.I.P. who had made the demand earlier. He pulled out a cell phone.

Karla groaned. "No! We'll be stuck here the rest of the day."

The Texan stepped in. "Missy, we're talking about a $15,000 piece of memorabilia here."

She pointed to the bigwigs. "And when are *they* gonna get frisked? Who's to say one of them didn't pinch their own trinket?"

Voices were rising, but this time Ray's broke above the chorus.

"There. There! Behind the baseball face! I'll bet you anything." Ray stepped toward the taco carrier, and Simmons followed, more from precaution than agreement.

With the promise of a revelation at hand, the energy in the room changed as all eyes fell on the goofy grin of Miguel's mascot. Miguel, by contrast, looked thoroughly confused.

"Taquito? What about Taquito?" Ray was already running his fingers along the plate's base in excitement.

"Anybody got a screwdriver?"

Simmons was practically slapping Ray's hand away from the case. "I'm telling you," Ray continued. "It's behind this face. I'm thinking, how do you hide a disc like that so you could still get it out of the park? Answer: you hide it behind something else. It came to me like a flash. Hurry up!"

Like a flash.

A chocolate and Bavarian cream-filled *crêpe*, shining for just a second.

I looked over at Conner Beechum, still seated, watching the show underway. Four neat stacks of plates and lids all right, but one stack of lids was tilting slightly, halfway up.

I stepped over to Simmons, dropped my voice to a whisper, and redirected him from Mexican fare to French cuisine.

Now it was time to call the police.

000

Later, over beers with Karla at The Dugout, I made my case for the mix of impulse and opportunity that led to the theft. The trophy was there on the table, the bigwigs were watching the game, and it was easy enough for Conner to slip the diamond disc onto a plate and cover it with a lid when he was in the skybox setting out his food.

His luck held when he discovered that the circular disc would fit snugly into the tapered top of a lid, which allowed him to remove the lid during the search, hold it as if it were empty, and place it in the stack with the others. But the gold medallion had thrown a glint of reflected light onto the plate below when it was uncovered.

"Look here, Finn," said Karla, holding up her cell phone. On display was an image of a little round pastry with a filled center. "That's a *vol-au-vent*. Even his restaurant's named after a food that has a hidden compartment." She lowered the phone and looked at me. "I never knew that his place was in trouble. His food sold well at the ballpark, and I just assumed..." She opted for a sip of beer and left the sentence unfinished.

"The fact that he still needed to sell his stuff here made me wonder. Selling a novelty pancake to curious ball fans is one thing, but overhead on an expensive restaurant is something else."

Karla looked down at the bar counter. "Did the bigwigs offer you any reward for helping them recover their precious trophy?"

I smiled. Karla knew the answer before she asked the question, so she smiled too.

"Ah, well. I'm not in this for the money."

"Then why on earth do we do it, Finn?"

I leaned closer and slipped into a lazy Texan drawl.

"You know me, darlin'. It's all for the love of the game."

Jason Half is a classic crime fiction fan who teaches English, Theatre, and Film courses at multiple colleges in southern Ohio. His story "The Widow Cleans House" appeared in a recent issue of *Alfred Hitchcock's Mystery Magazine*. Jason maintains a tribute website to prolific British mystery author Gladys Mitchell at www.gladysmitchell.com.

NOIR AT THE SALAD BAR
DEATH AT THE HANDS OF LE FEE VERTE

BY VERENA ROSE

New Orleans 1900

Huitres en coquille a la Rockefeller (Oysters Rockefeller) was the
rage of the city and it had only been a year since Jules Alciatore
created the dish to replace escargot on the menu at Antoine's.
Louisiana oysters were plentiful and French snails were not but he
never expected the dish to become the newest culinary sensation of
New Orleans.

ooo

"Justine, make plans for dinner at Antoine's tonight. I want
to go and you will accompany me," said Amelie Pichot in that
demanding tone of hers.

"But, Aunt Mellie I am not feeling well and would rather
not venture out," said Justine Pichot.

"Nonsense. You always have an excuse but tonight you
will go, no ifs, ands or buts."

"As you wish," sighed Justine as she left the drawing room
to go rest, leaving her aunt to continue performing her morning
ritual of re-writing her will. Justine wondered who had displeased
her enough to be written out—it was her aunt's way of control—
threats of being disinherited. Well, soon she would be free.

ooo

Jules Alciatore entered the kitchen of Antoine's in a state of
agitation. "Chef, chef. Amelie Pichot has arrived for her dinner
reservation and she is demanding to speak with you."

"Me, M. Jules. Why would she wish to speak with me?"
asked Etienne Blanche.

86

"She did not tell me. She walked in, was seated and immediately demanded to see you."

Chef Etienne was nervous because a command from Mme. Pichot was never a good thing. He walked into the main dining room wringing his hands.

As he approached the table he bowed and said, "You wished to speak with me, Mme. Pichot?"

"Indeed I do. I'm here tonight to enjoy some of those Huitres en coquille a la Rockefeller and I want to make sure you prepare them properly. The last time I was here they were not prepared to my satisfaction," she said with distain in her voice.

"But Mme. Pichot, I prepare them exactly as M. Jules' recipe dictates. I do not vary any of the ingredients—ever. In fact since it is a closely held secret. M. Jules makes the sauce and I only finish the preparation for service.

Shaking her head, Amelie Pichot said, "Well, obviously someone did something differently because they didn't taste right to me."

Jules Alciatore had just walked up and heard Mme. Pichot's comment. In answer to her he said, "The only thing that would vary in the recipe is the oysters. Sometimes they are more salty, depending on the day.

"We shall see," said Amelie Pichot imperiously. "I have been a patron of Antoine's for many years so I expect nothing but the very best."

Seeing that Mme. Pichot was in a very unforgiving mood, Jules Alciatore sent his best waiter to her table. Eduard St. Denys had worked at Antoine's since he was a boy of thirteen, starting as kitchen help and working his way up to head waiter. Now patrons vied for his service and some wouldn't grace the restaurant with their presence unless he was available to wait on them.

ꝙꝙꝙ

"Mme. Pichot, Mlle. Pichot, how are you this fine evening?" asked Eduard St. Denys, bowing to the two ladies seated at the best table in the restaurant.

"We shall see, young man. It will all depend on the quality of the food and, of course, the service I receive as to whether I consider it a fine evening, or not," answered Mme. Pichot.

"Yes, Eduard, it is a very fine evening" said Justine Pichot, smiling warmly in spite of the glare she received from her aunt.

"Ladies, what may I serve you?"

"For starters we'll have the Huitres en coquille a la Rockefeller and then, I think tonight, we'll have the Chateaubriand." Not giving her niece a chance to speak, Mme. Pichot took charge of the ordering as she did in all things related to her family.

With their meal completed, apparently to the satisfaction of the Pichot family matriarch, Justine Pichot excused herself from the table to visit the Ladies Lounge. On her way she heard, "Psst, Justine." Turning, she saw Eduard rushing toward her.

"Justine, we must talk."

"Not now, Eduard. She'll get suspicious if I'm gone too long."

"Then meet me tomorrow in Jackson Square. I'll be there at noon. You do want to be free of her, don't you?"

ooo

Heading toward the stairs, Amelie Pichot turned to her niece and said, "Justine, I am going to retire for the evening. After such a heavy meal I am feeling quite unwell, in fact, a bit light headed."

"Oh, I'm so sorry, Aunt. Is there anything you wish me to get for you?"

"No, but let Leonie know that I do not wish to be disturbed until eleven. I have sent word to your brother to be here at one. There is much I wish to discuss with him."

"Gerard is coming tomorrow? I will be so pleased to see him. It has been such a long time."

"I rather doubt he'll be in the mood to visit with you after I get finished with him. I'll be informing him that he'll no longer receive an allowance from me and if he doesn't prove to me he can be responsible, I'll be cutting him off entirely."

Amelia Pichot turned to proceed up the stairs but was stopped by her niece's voice. Trembling with anger, Justine responded, "You'd do that to the only relative besides me who does anything for you? You really are the most unreasonable person I know."

"Have a care, my dear, or you'll be next. And another thing, make sure that cat of yours doesn't get into my room."

QQQ

The next morning around eleven, Justine Pichot was sitting in the library reading with her cat, Petit Papillon, on her lap. Her plan was to leave the house to meet Eduard before her Aunt came down. All of the sudden she heard Leonie screaming, "Mlle. Justine! Please. Come at once!"

Petit started and jumped down. Justine dropped her book and ran up the stairs, calling out, "What is it, Leonie?"

"It is your aunt. She's at the bottom of the back stairs and she won't wake up."

Justine followed the maid and saw that, indeed, her aunt was lying at the bottom of the stairs with her head at an odd angle. She went down but couldn't bring herself to touch her aunt's body. Turning to Leonie she said, "Please have Giles send for Dr. Moreau. Tell him it is an emergency."

"Yes, mademoiselle. At once."

QQQ

Dr. Moreau arrived within the hour and after examining Mme. Pichot's body went to the library to speak with Mlle. Justine and her brother Gerard.

Bowing his head, Dr. Moreau addressed the siblings. "First I must express my deepest condolences for your great loss. Your aunt was a formidable woman. It's hard to believe she's gone."

Composing herself, Justine asked, "What happened? She seemed fine last night when we came home from Antoine's. I thought she over indulged, especially the Huitres en coquille a la Rockefeller but she wouldn't hear a word about it."

"How many oysters did she eat?" asked the doctor, showing some concern.

"As is her habit, she ordered for everyone, not just herself. Last night she asked that three orders be brought to the table, two for her and one for me, even though I told her I didn't want any. I was not feeling well during the day so I didn't think such a rich dish would be good for my stomach. Never allowing waste, she consumed the whole of the three orders."

Gerard jumped up and faced his sister. "You let her eat that many oysters at one time? How could you be so irresponsible? You know she has a bad heart as well as other health issues and Huitres en coquille a la Rockefeller contains absinthe."

"I didn't *let* her do anything. She always does just as she pleases with no regard for the concerns of others. I told her it wasn't good for her to eat so many but she merely tut tutted and continued eating."

After allowing the siblings to vent their frustrations, Dr. Moreau sat down to explain his findings. "It looks like your aunt died from the fall. She has a broken neck. Certainly she could have experienced a stroke in the night and tried to get help, which may account for her being at the bottom of the stairs. However, the amount of oysters and absinthe she consumed concerns me greatly. For someone her age the amount from so many could have caused her to awake with hallucinations. But there is one worrisome item—one side of her face is covered in scratches."

"Are you saying that someone attacked her?" asked Gerard in disbelief.

"I can't say for sure, M. Pichot. But I believe we must send for the police. In matters such as these we are required to report our concerns."

000

"M. Pichot, Mlle. Pichot, I am Captain Henri Soniat of the New Orleans Police Department. Dr. Moreau's message indicated that he has some concerns about your aunt's death. I understand that she was found at the bottom of the back stairs but that she also has many scratches on her face."

"Captain, that is correct, but my sister and I don't think anything untoward occurred. Our aunt went out for dinner last evening and over indulged in oysters laced with absinthe. We've all heard stories about the effects of absinthe. They even call it *le fee verte*. And in someone of her age, she became unwell, tried to go for help and fell," explained Gerard Pichot, hoping that would be the end of the discussion.

"That's all very well, M. Pichot, but how do you explain the scratches? I am calling for an examination to be done before I can report this as an accidental death. I will have your Aunt removed and as soon as her body can be released for burial I will let you know."

ooo

Justine realized she had missed her appointment to meet Eduard in Jackson Square. Worried what he would think, she dashed off a note and asked Leonie to have it delivered immediately.

Eduard St. Denys had just started his shift at Antoine's when a messenger arrived. M. Jules handed him a sealed lavender envelop and said, "this just arrived for you."

He knew immediately who the note was from and opening it he read:

Dearest Eduard,
I am so sorry but I could not leave the house. Aunt Amelie died in the night and the police are investigating it as suspicious. Please come when you can. She's no longer here to refuse you.

Love,
Justine

ooo

While waiting for the completion of the medical examination of Mme. Pichot, Captain Soniat did some further investigation of the family. He discovered that Amelie Pichot was well regarded in New Orleans society but considered to be a ruthless

91

businesswoman and an unbendable tyrant to her family. She held the purse-strings and never let them forget it.

In questioning the servants he learned that her niece, Justine Pichot, who cared for her, was not allowed gentlemen callers. However, he also learned that she and a distant cousin, a waiter at Antoine's, Eduard St. Denys, were apparently meeting without the aunt's knowledge. Gerard Pichot, her nephew, was an accomplished writer but could not support himself on his royalties. Needing the allowance his aunt provided put him at her mercy. In fact, the day before her death he had been summoned to a meeting for the next day. His aunt, who didn't approve of his not being gainfully employed, had been changing her will again. Speculation was that he was to be given an ultimatum.

Three suspects, thought Henri Soniat.

Rushing into his office, a courier handed him an envelope and said, "This is the report you were expecting from the medical examiner. He said if you have any questions he'll be in his office for another hour or so."

"Thank you. Let him know I appreciate his doing this so quickly."

Opening the envelope, he read that Mme. Amelie Pichot died as the result of a broken neck. However, an analysis of the contents of her stomach showed that there were amounts of absinthe sufficient to have caused hallucinations. Based on the scratches on her face, possibly inflicted by an animal, it appears she struggled to get out of bed. If she had been hallucinating, she may have perceived the animal to be larger and more of a threat than it actually was. Additionally, there are signs that all of these factors contributed to her need to escape her room and go for help.

He saw no overt evidence of foul play, but given her age and the contributing factors to her death, it could not be ruled out.

000

Rushing into the parlor, Eduard St. Denys said, "Justine, I came as soon as I could. How did this happen? I know she's impossible, but no one would deliberately hurt her, would they?"

Just as she was about to answer, Leonie came in to announce the arrival of Captain Soniat who strode in right behind her.

"Mlle. Pichot, I've come to ask a few more questions."

"Of course, Captain Soniat. But first, please let me introduce my cousin, Eduard St. Denys."

"Excellent, monsieur. You have saved me a trip. By the way, mademoiselle, where is your brother?"

"He went home last night but should be here shortly. Do you wish to wait to ask your questions when he gets here?"

"No, I can begin without him. First, is there an animal in the house?"

Looking confused, Justine answered, "yes, my cat, Petite Papillon. Why do you ask?"

"Your aunt had serious scratches on her face that the medical examiner believed came from an animal," answered Captain Soniat.

"Oh no, Petite must have snuck into Aunt Mellie's room. She hated the cat but sometimes when an animal senses you dislike them, they bother you that much more."

"And how many Huitres en coquille a la Rockefeller did you say your aunt consumed?"

"She ate the entire three orders, so a total of eighteen," said Justine, shaking her head.

"That would be a large amount even for a man. And she ate an entrée besides?"

"Yes, we shared the Chateaubriand which, as you know, is prepared for two. And as I was not feeling well she ate the greater portion of that."

"M. St. Denys, you are a waiter at Antoine's, is that correct?"

"Yes, Captain, I am."

"And you waited on Mme. Pichot?"

"I did."

"And is it also true that you and Mlle. Pichot have been seeing each other secretly?"

Startled, Justine arose from her chair and started pacing the room. Before Eduard could answer she said, "Yes, Captain, it's true. Aunt Mellie forbade me to see Eduard. You see, he's from a poor branch of the family and she was convinced that he was only interested in her money, not me."

"So you and Eduard had ample reason for wanting your aunt out of the way. Maybe you influenced her to order a large number of oysters, knowing she wouldn't let them go to waste if you didn't eat your portion. And maybe Eduard, before serving the oysters, laced them with additional absinthe, enough to cause hallucinations that sent her running frantically from her room."

"I may not have liked her and she definitely came between Justine and me being able to marry, but I've done quite well at Antoine's and we were planning to take my savings and leave the city very soon," said Eduard indignantly.

"Captain Soniat, please believe that neither Eduard nor I had anything to do with Aunt Mellie's death," Justine pleaded.

Just then Gerard Pichot came in. "What is going on here?"

Standing up, Captain Soniat said, "I have received the medical examiner's report and I had a few more questions to ask. I wanted to share the results with you in person."

ooo

Captain Henri Soniat had no choice but to rule the death of Mme. Amelie Pichot an accident. He had three viable suspects but there was nothing conclusive to prove that one or all of them had a hand in her demise.

Going over the statements and the facts, it appeared that Mme. Pichot consumed a very large meal including an abundance of oysters laced with absinthe, then returned home and went to bed. It is believed that sometime during the night she was awakened, possibly by her niece's cat. It is also believed that the effects of the absinthe caused her to hallucinate and possibly believed the small cat was a larger, more deadly animal. The scratches on her face prove that she attempted to remove the cat from her bed and fought with it. Having lost her sense of reality, she ran from her room and tragically fell head-long down the stairs breaking her neck and dying instantly.

After filing his report, he sent a note to the Pichot residence letting her niece and nephew know that they could proceed with their aunt's funeral.

However, he still couldn't help feeling that he'd missed something, and the perfect murder had just occurred. It wasn't every day that you get a case where the possible crime has been aided and abetted by the family pet.

New Orleans Times Picayune – September 5, 1900

ESTEEMED NEW ORLEANS CREOLE FAMILY LOSES MATRIARCH

Local family matriarch, Amelie Justine Pichot died suddenly on Tuesday at her home on the Rue St. Ann. She was the daughter of the late Bernard August Pichot and Clotilde Amelie St. Denys Pichot. She became her parents' heir when she was predeceased by her two brothers, August and St. Denys. Both were tragically lost at the Battle of Antietam fighting in the Hays Brigade under Brigadier General Harry T. Hays.

Mme. Pichot was born on November 28, 1825 and upon her death was in her 75th year. During the War of Northern Aggression she worked tirelessly for the cause and even spent a night in the City Jail during the occupation of General Benjamin Butler. After the war she devoted her energies and wealth to many New Orleans charitable organizations.

Mme. Pichot is survived by Gerard Pichot, Justine Pichot her great-nephew and great-niece and many more distant family relations.

Funeral services will be provided by Jacob Schoen and Son and interment will be in the family crypt in the Lafayette Cemetery.

Verena Rose is the Agatha Award nominated co-editor of *Not Everyone's Cup of Tea, An Interesting and Entertaining History of Malice Domestic's First 25 Years* and the Managing Editor of the new series of Malice Domestic anthologies, including *Malice Domestic 11: Murder Most Conventional*, the recently released *Malice Domestic 12: Mystery Most Historical*, and the upcoming *Malice Domestic 13: Mystery Most Geographical* all published by Wildside Press.

In addition to her editorial duties Verena also serves as the Chair of Malice Domestic, is one of the founding members of the Dames of Detection, and a co-owner/editor/publisher at Level Best Books. When not indulging her passion for mysteries she works full-time as a tax accountant. She lives in Olney, MD with her four cats, Jasper, Alice, Matty & Missy.

CULINARY TALES WITH A BITE

BLACK COFFEE IN BED

BY SHARON DAYNARD

There are worse things in life than dying. Cooking is one of them.

The only kitchen appliances I use on a daily basis are the microwave and an overpriced grind and brew coffeemaker. I haven't a clue if the stove is gas or electric, or if the dishwasher even works. I wouldn't know a Kenmore from a Thermador. I don't subscribe to food magazines, watch the Home and Garden Channel, or care whether the chicken in the cacciatore I pick up at Geppetto's Ristorante is free range or caged.

The one meal I do cook is breakfast—black coffee in bed. I've perfected the art of dropping a handful of whole roasted beans into the hopper, pressing a few buttons and pouring the coffee into two mugs before heading back to bed.

I imagine I come from a long line of women whose lives revolved around a stove, a vacuum, and a darning needle. My mother and grandmother were house-proud and my older sister Margaret makes Martha Stewart look like a slouch. Margaret cooks, cleans and crafts like nobody's business. She has a passion for cutting coupons and scrapbooking and she lives for the opportunity to make every other item at a bake sale look like something I'd attempted under the influence of pain meds and alcohol.

Granted we share the same gene pool, but I've never felt compelled to purchase, let alone wear, matching oven mitts and aprons, sensible shoes, or white cotton granny panties. Margaret and I are a respectable thirteen months apart. Sometimes it feels more like thirteen years. Margaret has always been a Margaret. Never a Maggie, a Margie or a Peg. My parents went the same parochial route naming me Beatrice, but I had the common sense to demand being called Bebe when I was old enough to form a sentence.

As kids, Margaret and I shared a bedroom. My half looked like that of any other teenage girl forced to attend catholic school—posters of the Backstreet Boys, Ryan Phillippe and Leonardo tacked to the walls, Newports and Trojans shoved under the mattress, and a bottle of Jack tucked in the back of the closet. Margaret's half looked like an eighty-year-old nun had sublet it on sabbatical. Neat as a pin, my mother called it, everything in its place and a place for everything. A white eyelet comforter on her bed, crocheted doilies on her dresser top and the boxed set of Julia Child's *Mastering the Art of French Cooking* on her nightstand.

While Margaret was off winning blue ribbons for her peach chutney and pineapple rhubarb pies at 4-H competitions and state fairs, I was busy giving the neighborhood boys blue balls until I lost my virginity at fifteen to the pizza delivery guy on a dare. I imagine Margaret waited until her wedding night and even then gave it up reluctantly.

For all our differences, we're still family. I'm godmother to her youngest and she's rescued me from strange motel rooms after I've woken up naked and alone with no memory of how I got there. Of course, the ride home wouldn't be complete without one of her lectures on the virtues of self-worth and dignity. It wasn't an easy decision on my part to ruin Margaret, but it beat the alternative.

Margaret graduated magna cum laude with a degree in Classic Civilizations from Wellesley and took a job at the Peabody Essex Museum. After the kids came along she started a catering business out of her house and offered private cooking lessons. She's been married to the same guy for the last fifteen years. Walt's a senior auditor with the IRS. They live in a rambling Cape Code style house on a kid-safe street in a family-friendly neighborhood in the burbs—well outside the influence of Boston. Their kids attend prep school, play chess, soccer, and lacrosse and, no surprise, are honor students.

Me, I majored in partying at UMass Amherst and barely squeaked by with enough credits to earn a degree in Business. I jumped from job to job and eventually ended up owning a high-end consignment shop in Beacon Hill and a thrift shop in Dorchester. The junk's the same, the only difference is the price tag. I've married a bad boy, a momma's boy, and am currently joined in holy matrimony to a guy just bad enough to make his mother light a candle for him at Sunday Mass.

I'll be the first to tell you the old adage 'the third times a charm' doesn't apply to marriage. Derrick and I have drifted in and out of trial separations for the better part of the last two years. There've been bouts of infidelity on both our parts, lying and jerking each other around with promises neither of us has a prayer of keeping. On those rare occasions when the planets align, we're perfect for each other. For the last three months we've been giving couples counseling a try. We've even considered renewing our vows, taking a second honeymoon and making a fresh go of it. My decision to murder Derrick became a whole lot easier knowing he was screwing Margaret.

In a lot of ways I wished I had what Margaret has. Stability. Walt might not be every women's dream, but he's committed to their marriage, he worships the ground she walks on, and he's reliable—off to work every Monday through Friday at seven-fifteen and home at quarter after six, a change of clothes and parked at the dinner table at six-thirty, the *Wheel of Fortune* at seven, *Jeopardy* at seven-thirty, then a bit of mindless TV and to bed by half past nine.

Derrick's a junior partner at a quasi-prestigious Boston law firm. His schedule is about as predictable as the New England weather. We're living beyond our means in a Back Bay brownstone, but that will change once Derrick makes senior partner or his mother is reunited with her late husband. Much to my aggravation, Derrick has clients to the house three or four times a month for cocktails and dinner. I used to think it was his not-so-subtle jab at my shortcomings in the kitchen. I was wrong.

After several failed attempts at playing Suzie Homemaker, Margaret stepped in and saved me. She planned the menus with Derrick, prepared them in our kitchen, and served them to our guests. Derrick received a friends and family discount, Margaret picked up a new client or two every now and then, and all I had to do was make clever conversation. It was a win-win solution until Derrick got a little too involved with the meal.

NOIR AT THE SALAD BAR

It started out with him coming home early to help Margaret prep. Playing sous chef escalated to other role-playing games. I might never have found out if I hadn't come home one afternoon to see what was so friggin' fascinating about deveining shrimp. The kitchen was empty except for one of Margaret's heated banquet carts filled with fully cooked trays of that night's meal. Our bedroom, however, was abuzz with the sounds of afternoon sex. I'd almost convinced myself anything but sex was taking place on the other side of our closed bedroom door when I heard the nightstand drawer open followed by the familiar hum of one of my toys and Margaret's squeal.

Derrick and any other woman I could have shrugged off after I evened the score with a random guy or two. But prim and proper, holier-than-thou Margaret? I could have worked my way through every varsity and junior varsity team at Boston College and still never come close to being even. I thought about cluing Walt in on their little tryst, but I knew it would destroy him and the kids. Margaret was perfect in their eyes.

So I sat through one client dinner after another and family get-together after family get-together, waiting for inspiration. Who would have guessed it'd come in the form of an ad for an estate sale in Hyannis Port. Knowing an affluent address doesn't always translate to the quality of the possessions being liquidated, I read the recently departed's obituary and Googled her name before taking a seventy-five mile drive on a treasure hunt that could just as easily prove to be a fool's errand.

Truth be told, I'll take a tag sale at a hoarder's hellhole over an estate sale any day, but the late Ginette Harcourt Carlisle sounded too good to pass up. Author, philanthropist, and avid world traveler, Ginette passed away at the age of eighty-seven from complications related to surgery. She was survived by three children, five grandchildren, and eight great-grandchildren. Her husband, Douglas Carlisle predeceased her by forty-eight years. It was Ginette's world traveler status that caught my attention. *Tchotchkes* were a staple of my business and a woman Ginette's age probably collected a few mementos from every trip she took abroad. A trunk-load of the stuff could keep me well into the black during leaner sales quarters.

Unlike my track record with husbands, I have a knack for making that one special find that makes up in spades for the rest of the crap I buy. I've been in the business long enough that I know to pat down the lining in fur coats, suit jacks and overcoats, pry paintings and mirrors from their frames, and knock on every inch of a chest of drawers, armoire, and credenza. I've found everything from cash and jewelry to stock certificates and bearer bonds. And I know my way around a yard sale. I've picked up Waterford stemware for twenty-five cents, a solid-gold shoehorn for two dollars and a stack of vintage movie posters from the thirties and forties for twenty-five bucks.

As it turned out, Ginette wasn't a fan of *tchotchkes*, but it was worth the trip between a pair of Tiffany lamps and an antique William and Mary blanket chest crammed with memorabilia from every democratic candidate for president that had held a fundraiser in Massachusetts from Harry Truman to Hillary Clinton. I hit pay dirt with what I found in the false bottom of Ginette's blanket chest.

At first glance it looked like any other set of rosary beads, but I couldn't take my eyes of it. The cheap silver cross was unremarkable and one of the beads was missing, making it worthless. Still, the beads were gorgeous—deep ruby red with a single black dot and a luster that rivaled the finest porcelain. Oddly enough the beads weren't ceramic but some sort of a bean. My first guess was raw coffee beans that had been sealed with a high gloss lacquer. But the more I looked at them, the more they resembled some sort of pea.

Google Goggles identified them as seeds from the *Abrus precatorius* plant. More commonly known as rosary peas, the bright red seeds are traditionally used as ornamental beads for rosaries. The seeds contain abrin—one of the most potent toxins known to man. I ended my Google search there and headed to the library.

Native to India, the rosary pea is more deadly than ricin. A single seed, if chewed and ingested, could prove fatal. Unlike ricin, abrin works slowly. The peas could also be ground into a fine powder and inhaled or dissolved in liquid and injected into the bloodstream. Symptoms of abrin poisoning include severe nausea, vomiting, abdominal pain, and dehydration along with kidney, liver, and spleen failure commencing within one to three days after exposure. With no known cure, death typically occurs three to four days later. And if that wasn't enough to make a girl swoon, after metabolizing, the toxin was no longer detectable in the body. Fate had handed me the perfect poison, all I had to do was figure out how and when to use it.

It was a shame Derrick wasn't into snorting coke or mainlining heroin. I considered stopping by the brownstone the next time Margaret and Derrick were busy in my bedroom and stirring a rosary pea into whatever she'd be serving. Once back at the consignment shop I'd call to say I'd have to miss dinner to work on the inventory. But what good would that do? The outer shell of the pea is so hard anyone who bit down on one would spit it out. Swallowed intact, it would pass harmlessly through the digestive tract. And if by some miracle, the shell softened enough for someone to chew and swallowed the pea, there was no way to guarantee that someone would be Derrick. The real kicker would be if Margaret decided to partake in the meal and dropped dead.

I had bigger plans for Margaret.

ooo

Days stretched to weeks and weeks to months as I pretended not to notice the playful glances between my husband and my sister while I held my tongue and made pleasant chitchat with Derrick's clients. What I really wanted to talk about was how Derrick and Margaret banged out the meal we were enjoying.

If an Academy Award existed for Best Actress in the category of Clueless Wife, I'd have been a shoo-in. I served Derrick my idea of breakfast in bed every morning—a mug of black coffee. I snuggled up to him, spooned and porn-star faked it. Couples counseling was my idea, along with the renewal of vows. No big surprise Derrick wanted Margaret to cater the reception.

As a distraction from Derrick and Margaret I started researching Ginette Harcourt Carlisle. I read everything I could about the woman—where she was born, where she went to school, her engagement and wedding to Douglas, their children, and her favorite charities. Ginette stood out in every photograph. She wasn't just gorgeous; she was Grace Kelly gorgeous with pale blonde hair, alabaster skin, and bottle-green eyes. What also stood out was her absent smile in every photograph taken with Douglas. I didn't have to be a genius to figure out theirs was a marriage of convenience. Even their wedding announcement read like a corporate merger.

When I exhausted resources on Ginette, I delved into Douglas's life and death. From what little information I could find in archived newspapers, Douglas Carlisle wasn't exactly a catch. He'd had a few run-ins with the law, but nothing his father's money couldn't buy him out of. There were rumors of gambling problems and other women, but nothing I could substantiate. The circumstances surrounding his death couldn't have been more vague.

After returning from a vacation in London in the fall of 1969, both Ginette and Douglas were bedridden with the Hong Kong Flu. Ginette recovered within a few days. Douglas's symptoms worsened and he was admitted to a Boston hospital where he later died of complications. Ginette never married again. She chaired a number of charities and scholarships in his name and let his memory quietly fade away.

One of the newspaper write-ups on his funeral included a graveside, black and white photograph of the who's who of mourners including politicians, celebrities and Hyannis Port residents. Bolstered by the priest officiating over the burial, Ginette placed a single rose on the casket using her right hand. A set of rosary beads dangled from her left hand. It was impossible to tell the color of the beads, but after spotting a gap where one was missing, I'd have bet every dollar I had they were bright red with a single black dot.

ooo

Derrick awoke on Thanksgiving morning feeling a bit under the weather. Maybe it was the long afternoon he'd put in the day before at Margaret's, helping her prep for the dinner at her house. Maybe it was the five rosary peas I dropped in the hopper of our coffeemaker along with a handful of coffee beans two days earlier. Five peas were probably overkill, after all Ginette managed to kill her husband with only one. Still, the peas were forty-eight years older and I couldn't let Derrick off with just a tummy ache and a case of the shits. I'd suggested to Derrick he might want to stay in bed and rest instead of heading to Margaret's, but he insisted he was fine; nothing a cup of coffee couldn't cure.

Thanksgiving was Margaret's favorite holiday. Unlike Christmas, where gift-giving diluted the true meaning of the day, Thanksgiving was still all about the meal. Between the tablescapes, the handmade decorations, the foolish poems she wrote and the twenty or so of her closest friends and neighbors she always invited, Thanksgiving at Margaret's was hell. But for the first time in my adult life I couldn't wait to enjoy a home-cooked meal.

000

Margaret greeted us at the door with an annoying "Gobble-gobble." She offered Derrick a peck on the cheek and me a roll of her eyes when I held up my contributions to the meal—a bottle of Jack and a quart of store-bought pumpkin pie ice cream. I wasn't sure what offended her more, the alcohol or ice cream that contained artificial flavors and coloring. With an exaggerated sigh, Margaret pointed to the kitchen.

The ice cream, like everything else I've ever brought to a holiday dinner at Margaret's, would never make it to the table. If she hadn't given me an eye roll I would have tossed it in the trash. Instead, I removed the lid and deposited the container upside-down on the kitchen counter. With a little luck, Margaret wouldn't notice my culinary faux pas until the ice cream thawed and left behind a pumpkiny-orange puddle.

As amusing as that was to me, I was more interested in the thirty-two ounce Mason jar in the refrigerator filled with Margaret's signature blue cheese vinaigrette. I'd never found anything special about it, but it was the only salad dressing Margaret allowed at her table. If you didn't like blue cheese or, God forbid, were allergic to it or anything else she prepared, you were still going to eat it. And you were going to like it. Margaret was a bitch about things like that.

I reached deep into my purse and retrieved a small plastic container of what was destined to be the real star of the meal. I'm sure Margaret knew the technical name, but it's the watery pink liquid that collected inside the cavity of a raw turkey. I'd gone out of my way and made a special trip to the grocery the day before for a small, fresh turkey breast filled with the disgusting stuff.

I poured it into the vinaigrette, gave the jar a shake and returned it to the fridge. And like everyone else that day, I drizzled the blue cheese dressing on my salad and ate it without making a peep. I even asked for seconds. After all, how would it look if I were the only person who didn't come down with food poisoning?

We'd barely made it through coffee and dessert when Derrick excused himself from the table for some fresh air. I followed him outside to check his forehead for a fever. He insisted he was fine, just feeling a bit claustrophobic in the crowded dining room. When we headed back inside I handed Derrick a highball glass filled with Jack and cubes and poured myself one. I kept feeding them to him until it was time to leave, knowing Margaret would never let a guest who had been drinking behind the wheel of a car.

QQQ

By the time Derrick and I, along with Margaret and her family, checked into the ER at Saints Memorial Hospital the following evening, it was already overwhelmed with thirteen cases of what appeared to be food poisoning—nausea, vomiting, abdominal cramps and diarrhea. Everyone had one thing in common, Thanksgiving dinner at Margaret's. As if food poisoning wasn't enough, poor Margaret developed an acute case of mortification.

One of the quirky things about food poisoning is that there were twenty-five of us gathered at Margaret's table and only nineteen of us needed medical attention. The other six either toughed it out, couldn't make it out of their bathroom to call for help or never developed more than a case of indigestion. And because food poisoning affects people differently, not everyone recovers along the same time frame and with the same treatment. Take Derrick and me for example. One drip bag of saline to treat dehydration and I was good as new. Derrick on the other hand didn't respond to treatment. He got worse. And why wouldn't he? He was being treated for food poisoning, not abrin poisoning. Salmonella bacteria were detected in his stool, blood, and urine. They could have run a hundred lab tests and abrin would never have been detected.

It's been three days since Derrick was admitted to the ICU. Last rites have been read and his last wishes will be carried out in accordance to his living will. Through it all I've kept a stiff upper lip, offering him smiles, pats on the hand, reassuring words and promises he'll be up and about soon.

I think poor Margaret is taking it the hardest. She still can't understand how it happened. She still insists she roasted the two twenty-eight pound fresh turkeys to perfection, timing it at exactly five hours in a three hundred twenty-five degree oven. She told the nursing staff and anyone else who'd listen the meat thermometer registered one-eighty in the thighs and one sixty-five in the breasts and she prepared the stuffing in a casserole dish to avoid salmonella and other bacteria from finding their way into the food. She couldn't imagine one turkey let alone both being undercooked. And yet all nineteen of us tested positive for salmonella.

It's a mystery to me too, considering how obsessed Margaret is when it comes to avoiding cross contamination, keeping a germfree workstation and scrubbing her hands a full twenty seconds under hot water with antibacterial soap. I swore the color drained from her face when I asked if she used two carving sets and separate cutting boards for the turkeys. It was oversights like that that ended careers. I don't imagine she'll ever get another catering job or client asking for private cooking lessons. The local media's had a field day reporting what they call "The Thanksgiving Day Massacre." A bit over the top, but that's how stories get picked up and go viral.

Ginette Harcourt Carlisle took the secret of how she murdered her husband to her grave. Derrick will be taking mine. I'll make sure he's buried with my rosary beads in his hands in eternal prayer.

Sharon Daynard has crossed paths with a serial killer, testified before grand juries, and taken lie detector tests. Her short stories have appeared in magazines and anthologies. Her 51-word short story "Widow's Peak" received a Derringer nomination for Best Flash of 2004. She is member of the New England chapter of Sisters in Crime and a SinC Guppy. www.sadaynard.com

NOIR AT THE SALAD BAR

THE CASE OF THE APERTURED APICULTURIST

BY LARRY LEFKOWITZ

One Sunday evening early in September, I received one of Holmes' laconic wires:

Come at once if convenient—if inconvenient, come all the same.

An avid follower of crime reports in the press, Holmes had not missed the following brief item contained in the *Globe:*

Woman killed by bees

The shocking death of Dame Elizabeth Bixley, amateur apiculturist, whose perforated body was found two days ago in her apiary. The coroner has determined that it was an Act of God.

"I seriously doubt it," remarked Holmes. "I work with bees and have become something of an expert. There are a number of puzzling elements, even in the terse account presented by the *Globe.*

"Such as?" I said.

"Such as why wasn't Dame Bixley wearing protective clothing and a veil? And why did the bees, if it really was bees, attack her? And why was the coroner's jury verdict rendered so quickly? If we hurry I can get a look at the body before burial. I'll wire Inspector Lestrade, who probably has more influence than I thereabouts."

There was a gleam in Holmes' eyes and a suppressed excitement in his manner which convinced me that his hand was upon a clue, though I could not imagine where he had found it. "Mark my word, Watson, this case will have England buzzing."

ΩΩΩ

Armed with Lestrade's carte blanche, we traveled by coach to Haximer and by foot to Addersworth, the estate of the late Dame

Bixley. The scene of the crime was a high, dingy, narrow-chested house, prim, formal, and solid, like the century which gave it birth and the recluse who had inhabited it.

The undertaker was about to begin his work (on the premises as Dame Bixley had specified that she be buried in her garden among the primroses) when Holmes put a hand on his shoulder. "Just a brief look, if you please." The man at first seemed irritated, but glancing at Holmes, who wore his traveling tweeds complete with his old deerstalker, the man's jaw dropped.

"Not Sherlock Holmes!" he exclaimed. Holmes bowed, and then introduced me. The man stepped aside. "Be my guests, gentlemen."

Holmes bent over the body and scrutinized the perforations, first by the naked eye and then by magnifying glass. "Not bee-stings. Unless I miss my mark these perforations were made by an instrument other than a bee's stinger."

"How can you be so sure?" I asked.

"I have been something of an expert on perforation since 'The Adventure of the Black Peter.'"

"But a bee sting and a harpoon perforation are quite different."

"Same principle, Watson. Besides, I have been stung once or twice by bees. No, Watson, these marks were probably made by needles—and needles of a special type. This is of enormous importance," he added, making a note upon his shirt cuff.

"A hypodermic needle," I suggested, my medical profession coming to the fore.

Holmes looked up, his face wearing an amused smile at this brilliant departure of mine.

"My dear fellow," said he, "it was one of the first solutions which occurred to me, but I was soon able to dismiss it."

I was about to inquire as to what type of needle he had in mind, but I knew from experience that Holmes did not like to be pressed for information and that he would make it known at what he deemed to be the proper moment. What he did vouchsafe me was that according to the coroner's report Dame Bixley was a recluse who shared her estate with a small retinue indeed, since it consisted exclusively of an elderly servant in her employ for many years. Because she was crushed by the death of her employer and in addition being taciturn, suspicious, and ungracious by nature, it took some time before Holmes' pleasant manner and frank acceptance of all that she said thawed her into a corresponding amiability. He reported to me that the servant had confirmed his belief that Dame Bixley was more than the amateur apiculturalist reported in the paper. She had had considerable commercial success with her honey, to which she added ingredients of her own. A man had even tried to buy her out; he wanted to learn her recipes and mass produce the honey, but Dame Bixley would have none of it. She had no known enemies and was popular in the surrounding area, not for her company, which she did not disperse, but for her honey, which she did—for a good price. No hostess wanted to lack her honey for their cakes, which helped insure a successful affair.

Holmes concluded that the servant was above suspicion, even when I subsequently came to him with what I thought might be important information concerning her.

"What sort of information?"

"She is a prolific knitter."

"Not a crime, Watson."

"The needles, Holmes. She leaves her knitting needles scattered all over the place."

"Go on."

"Well, you said that the perforations on the deceased were made by a special type of needle. I thought—"

"I see where you are heading, Watson, but it won't do. Those were not the type of needles I had in mind."

The type of needles he had in mind remained there, for Holmes still declined to reveal their nature.

"What now, Holmes?" I said, as I so often did when I did not know what now.

"This man who tried to buy her out seems to be our only lead at the present time. The servant believes that he lived in the nearby town of Horsham and that his last name began with the letter 'R'."

"That doesn't give you much to go on."

"That doesn't give *you* much to go on, Watson. I want you to go to Horsham and see what you can discover."

"But—"

"You also know that he likes honey."

ǫǫǫ

I began my inquiries as to a gentleman whose last name began with the letter 'R' and who liked honey in a local public house.

"That could only be Riggles—although he isn't exactly a gentleman," I was told. "He produces confections including honey, but his honey doesn't compare with that of Dame Bixley's. A pity she is no longer in the business."

Riggles & Sons Confections was a low brick building situated on the outskirts of the town. It looked as if it had once been a stables which had been expanded. I chanced upon a bearded workman in a soiled smock who was unable to tell me where Mr. Riggles' office was. A second man, wearing a cleaner smock, pointed the way. I knocked on the door.

It was opened by a middle-aged man with a high, bald forehead and a huge grizzled mustache. His face was gaunt and scored with deep savage lines.

"What can I do for you?" he asked sourly, in contrast to the sweetness of the business he was in. "I see you are not from around here," he added.

"I wish to ask you a few questions."

"Ah, do you now. Very good of you, indeed. I thought you came to place an order."

"No, I simply wished to ask you about your relationship to Dame Bixley."

At the mention of her name, he scowled and became enraged, as if I had put a bee in his bonnet. Grabbing a bar on his desk of the type used for mixing sweeteners in a giant vat, he advanced toward me.

"I don't like investigators snooping about—professional or amateur. You are about to pay dearly for meddling in my business." He raised the bar, and I pictured my senseless body being poured into one of his vats. But just then the dirty-smocked gentleman whom I had seen previously rushed in and gave Mr. Riggles a very professional left hook to the eye. The bar fell harmlessly to the floor.

"Sir," I began, "I wish to thank you—"

"Oh come outside, Watson. You can thank me later."

"Holmes!" I cried, "Holmes! I never recognized you!"

"I'm not surprised, Watson, you rarely do. If not the costume and beard, the left hook should have told you something."

"Appreciation of your boxing prowess was lost in the excitement of the moment," I told him.

ꝘꝘꝘ

We were soon dashing along the smooth, white country road in the dogcart on the return to our temporary residence in an isolated inn.

"So we know nothing about Riggles," I said.

"Good of you, Watson, to include me in your lack of knowledge. But I found out what I wished to learn about Riggles— in addition to the fact that he has no sons."

"But the name 'Riggles & Sons'…"

"Riggles has a daughter, married, lives abroad. The 'Sons' in the name is to make an impression. But the important fact which I discovered is that he suffers from a painful ailment involving the nerves of the arm."

"If I had known that fact, I could have introduced myself as a doctor."

"Riggles has a doctor of his own choosing. His typist was a valuable source of information."

"You were at Riggles' premises a considerable time ahead of me, I see."

"Yes, Watson, it was for the best. I couldn't let you in on to what I was about. And I needed you to keep Riggles occupied while I completed talking to his typist."

"But what is the significance, Holmes, of the nerve pains in Riggles' arm?"

"The significance is that he receives treatment by acupuncture."

"Acupuncture? The Chinese needle treatment?"

112

"One for you, Watson," said Holmes.

"Not the needles you have been keeping a se…you referred to as a key factor in the case."

"You exceed yourself, Watson. The coroner's report indicated that Dame Bixby probably died from an allergic reaction to bee stings. I believe that the allergic reaction was a subtle poison introduced by—"

"The acupuncture needles!"

"Elementary, my dear Watson."

"So the perforations you saw were made by those needles."

"Yes, Watson. At first I did not recognize them. But when I learned that Riggles received treatment for nerve pains, I suddenly thought of acupuncture, having learned the rudiments of the art from the head lama during my visit to Tibet. I conjectured that perhaps Riggles' special doctor also used that method of treatment."

"And Riggles' acupuncturist is the murderer."

"A very real possibility, Watson. The typist gave me his name. A Dr. Barclay. A criminal who is capable of such a cunning method is worthy of a prominent place in your chronicles. An opponent with whom I shall be proud to do business with. In fact we both shall—tomorrow."

000

On the morrow Holmes was keen-eyed and restless, as when on the scent. "Bring your service revolver with you, Watson, this could be dangerous."

"Don't you want to call in the local police, Holmes?"

"When I have spun the web they may take the bees, but not before."

At the doctor's office later that day, Holmes sent our cards in. They were specially prepared for such use. One was of Grantley Thomas, agent, and the other of Jonathan Witherspoon, clerk.

"Which one of you is the patient—or are you both?" asked Dr. Barclay, looking from one to the other of us with suspicion.

"I'm the patient," said Holmes. "This is my companion who is here to give me moral, and if need be physical, support. I am weak at the sight of blood, especially if it is my own. I understand you are proficient in the art of acupuncture."

Dr. Barclay eyed him malevolently. "Who recommended me to you?"

"Mr. Riggles."

The man relaxed. "Ah, very good. You can't be too careful. I practice acupuncture somewhat covertly—the authorities haven't accepted it yet as alternative treatment. What is the nature of your ailment?"

"Pains in the leg," said Holmes. "I suffered a wound in the second Afghan war. A Jezail bullet."

I kept a straight face only with difficulty.

"Sit down, Mr. Thomas," instructed the doctor.

Holmes did so.

The doctor took a needle out of a drawer and approached Holmes.

Holmes put out a hand. "Do you mind if I examine the needle first? I would feel more confident."

With some impatience, Dr. Barclay assented.

Holmes took the needle, scrutinized it, then handed it to me. "Keep this for evidence, Watson," said Holmes laconically.

I did. The doctor was confused, but only momentarily. He lunged at the needle, but Holmes was quicker. All the demonical force of the man masked behind the previously listless manner burst forth in a paroxysm of energy. With a deft move, he dumped the doctor on the seat of his pants.

"In addition to learning something about acupuncture from the East, that part of the world supplied me with a certain knowledge of *baritsu*, the Japanese system of wrestling, which has, on the present occasion, been very useful," Holmes said. "Hold your revolver on him, Watson, while I have a look about."

Holmes proceeded with professional experience, opening cabinets and drawers until—"Aha!" He lifted a vial containing a yellow substance. "I think this will do it," he said, pocketing it.

"Look for something to truss him up with, Watson. His stethoscope will do for starters. We will turn him over to the local constabulary. They can pick up Riggles. The two planned the crime together after neither pain-relieving by the one nor threats by the other convinced the tight-lipped Dame to disclose her secret honey formula. Dr. Barclay was a silent partner in Riggles' business. I'm sure the locals will appreciate the credit for solving the crime. White Mason as a good chap and his career could do with a boost."

But when the local constabulary went to arrest Riggles, they were too late. He was dead. They had to call in exterminators to rid the office of the myriad bees swarming the place.

"Yes, Watson, anaphylactic shock."

"How did the bees get in, Holmes?"

"Maybe they were attracted by the honey-making. After our visit Riggles may have been too preoccupied to insure doors were closed." Holmes paused, and then said, "Or perhaps Dame Elizabeth Bixley took her revenge."

"From the grave, Holmes?"

Holmes did not respond to my question. His mind was engaged in another aspect of the case. Having picked up a jar of Bixley's Honey, he mused, "On the one hand it is said that Dame Bixley didn't write down her formula. On the other hand, discovering the same should not constitute an insurmountable obstacle to one versed in the art of laboratory investigation."

Larry Lefkowitz's stories, poetry and humor have been widely published. His humorous literary novel, "The Novel, Kunzman, the Novel!" is available as an e-book and in print from Lulu.com. and other distributors. Writers and readers with a deep interest in literature will especially enjoy the novel. Lefkowitz's humorous fantasy and science fiction collection, "Laughing into the Fourth Dimension" is available from Amazon books.

NOIR AT THE SALAD BAR

FAMILY BUSINESS

BY HARRIETTE SACKLER

Yetta Goldfarb knew she was an ordinary woman. Her five foot frame was as plump as a muffin, and her unruly brown hair framed a homely face that only a mother could love. But Yetta never dwelled on what the good Lord, in his infinite wisdom, had chosen to deny her. Instead, she was thankful for all that she had been given. And, to tell the truth, that wasn't much.

Before she left the old country, Yetta's parents had arranged her marriage to a young man from the same village. They wanted their daughter to be protected from the dangers of a long Atlantic steerage crossing and the beginning of life in a new land. They knew that Yetta didn't have much to offer and feared that she might spend her days as a lonely spinster.

Jake was a neighbor's son who, like Yetta, possessed a kind heart, but not much else. They were certain that he would treat their daughter kindly, and though it was unlikely the pair would enjoy any kind of easy life, they would have each other. And that was a blessing.

ରରର

Life amidst the teeming tenements of New York City's Lower East Side was not an easy one. The couple found a small apartment on Hester Street and began the slow and painful process of building a life in this strange and foreign place. Jake, a belt maker by trade, found employment in a small factory close by, but his wages barely provided for the couple's necessities. But they felt blessed. After all, in this year of 1898, the city was overrun with those fleeing the shores of their homelands in order to seek a new life in America. There were far too many who were unable to secure work or a dwelling, no matter how meager.

116

It was not long before Yetta realized that if she and Jake were to ever move ahead, they needed to increase their earnings. They both looked forward to the day when Hashem, the good Lord, would permit them to start a family, but they needed to be able to provide for a child. It was up to Yetta to find a way.

So each day after her morning chores were completed, Yetta left the tenement and walked the streets of the neighborhood. She carefully observed her surroundings: the shops, the street vendors, the crowds of people going about their daily business. One detail made an impression on her. It seemed that most of the people she saw were eating as they hurried about the streets, as though they couldn't spare a moment to sit down for a meal. Rather, they grabbed a bite to eat as they went from place to place. Interesting, Yetta thought.

She began canvassing her neighbors.

"Good morning, Mrs. Schwartz. May I ask what morsel you are nibbling?"

"Ah, Mrs. Goldfarb, this is a sour pickle from the pickle vendor. So tasty and crisp. Just what I need before going back inside to do the laundry. After all, who has the time or money to sit down for a meal?"

"Mr. Levine, what is that you're eating with such pleasure, may I ask?"

"A sweet roll I purchased from the bakery shop on Delancey. It's still warm from the oven and costs only two cents. I can enjoy it while I deliver the garments I've completed to the factory boss."

Over and over Yetta surveyed both those she was acquainted with and strangers as well. Their responses were all similar. No one wanted to take the time to sit down for a morning or midday meal. They needed to tend to business or chores, or just couldn't afford the time or money to eat at their leisure. A plan was forming in Yetta's mind.

One evening as they shared a supper of cabbage soup, bread, and glasses of hot tea, Yetta looked at her husband and began to speak.

"Jake, I have an idea. You spend ten hours a day laboring at the factory and yet, no matter how hard you work, we can barely pay our rent and buy food. We deserve better, and I think I have a way that can make our lives easier."

"What?" Jake smiled. "Did a rich relative back home die and leave you money?"

"Ah, if we only had a rich relative!" Yetta jokingly replied. "No, we'll have to make our own way in this world. And I know I can help."

"So, what's this brilliant idea of yours, Yetta? To become a thief?"

"Of course not, Jakie. I want to go into business!"

"Oh you do, do you? And what kind of business did you have in mind?"

"I want to sell blintzes. You always tell me that the blintzes I prepare for you come straight from Heaven. So, why not sell them in the street? I could start off a little at a time, buy the ingredients from the money I make at first, until the business grows. I've spent days talking to people and watching what the food vendors have to offer. Everyone wants a nosh during the day, and I know my blintzes will be a special treat."

Jake was silent as he sipped his tea. Then he looked at his wife with a sparkle in his eye.

"Yetta, if this is what you'd like to do, you have my blessing. But, please, we can't risk losing what we have. Living on the streets is the worst nightmare I can imagine."

"I promise you, Jakie, if I fail, that will be the end. I would never risk our well-being. Ever."

000

The next day, Yetta purchased a large metal platter at a good price from a vendor on Delancey Street. Over time, she had saved a small amount of money, and she now used it to finance her new business. She bought flour, sugar, butter, and pot cheese to prepare a large batch of her blintzes. Jake fashioned a harness of sorts from several belts so that Yetta could carry the large tray filled with her delectable creations.

On her maiden voyage into the world of commerce, Yetta sold all of her blintzes within one hour. The golden pancakes stuffed with sweetened cheese left her customers swooning and demanding more.

"I have never tasted blintzes such as these!"

"Mrs. Goldfarb, you have magical hands to be able to create such delectable food."

"Please, Yetta, bring more to sell tomorrow. I'll purchase enough to feed my family."

The next day, Yetta prepared twice the number of blintzes and, again, they sold in a wink.

When Jake came home from the factory that evening, Yetta was dancing around their tiny apartment.

"Jakie, we're in business! Who knew? She showed him a jar filled with the coins she'd earned that day.

"Tomorrow, after I sell the blintzes I prepare in the morning, I'll go to purchase more ingredients. Cherries and apples, also. I'll make a variety for my customers."

Seeing his wife so excited and fulfilled made Jake a happy man.

000

In no time at all, Yetta's blintzes were the talk of the Lower East Side. She could barely keep up with the demand for the large variety of tastes she had to offer. Strawberry, blueberry, apricot, peach. Spinach, potato, onion, and carrot. They were all superb and true works of art. Those who were employed as cooks and housekeepers for the uptown rich would place orders for dinner parties. No matter what countries people had left to come and make their way in this new land, they made it a point to purchase a blintz or two from Yetta to be shared with families living in the surrounding tenements. And Yetta always made it a point to give treats to the children who roamed the streets and slept wherever they could find a place.

Over time the Goldfarb's prosperity grew. Jake left his job at the factory to sell blintzes while Yetta prepared the delicious money makers. They eventually rented a store with a large apartment on the upper floor. The store was fitted with a stove and icebox and a large workspace. A long counter ran the length of the shop so customers could enter the store and make their selections indoors.

The Goldfarb's apartment was luxurious compared to the one they had previously occupied. Aside from a parlor, it boasted a kitchen, three bedrooms, and, best of all, its own toilet and bathtub.

Yetta and Jake had managed to squirrel away money and were planning to bring their parents to America. Their expanding business required more hands, and both their mothers were skilled in the kitchen, and could help Yetta in a variety of ways. Their fathers would be invaluable to Jake in keeping up with maintenance, sales, and the other responsibilities of business ownership. And, most importantly, how wonderful to enable their aging parents to leave a country of pogroms and danger to live out their lives in this land of opportunity.

000

But just as quickly as prosperity was visited upon the Goldfarbs, it threatened to leave.

Yetta sat at the kitchen table crying her eyes out as Jake attempted in vain to console his bereft wife.

"After all the work we've done! And now, we could lose it."

"Yetta. Yetta. My dearest wife. You're putting the cart before the horse. We've lost nothing! A little competition may do us good."

The threat in question involved a new business that had just opened diagonally across from the Goldfarb's store. Bernstein's Bakery boasted all manner of breads and bakery confections, including an assortment of blintzes. Yetta was terrified they would lose business to the new bakery. She was afraid the notion of free enterprise that had benefitted her so much would now work against her. She just couldn't let that happen.

000

In a few weeks, the Goldfarbs noticed a slight drop in business but nothing that would indicate cause for concern. Yetta's blintzes enjoyed a firm following, and most of her patrons wouldn't dream of taking their business elsewhere. But, Yetta, remembering the terrible poverty of her childhood and the struggle to make a living in her new land, was unable to put aside her fear of failure and a return to a life of struggle.

Yetta became obsessed. So she developed a course of action that would ensure that Bernstein's would cease to be a threat. She would put them out of business, and no one would be the wiser.

ooo

Early one afternoon, after Yetta had completed her day's work, she took her shopping bag and left the apartment. Stopping downstairs in the shop, she told Jake she was going to the market. She was being truthful, but would not be purchasing anything she would be able to use. She hurriedly walked many blocks toward a neighborhood she had never visited before and hoped never to enter again. Mulberry Street was a dismal area filled with decrepit tenements that housed hoards of the Lower East Side's poorest inhabitants. While the Goldfarbs lived in an area inhabited mainly by Eastern European Jews, Mulberry gave shelter, such as it was, to many nationalities, including many of Italian heritage. It was a terribly dangerous neighborhood that housed desperate people and violent gangs. Yetta hoped she would be able to complete her task and return home as quickly as possible.

With great difficulty she asked directions from a street vendor selling dented and rusted pots and pans. Yetta used a combination of signs and a few words of English, and he ultimately understood her request and pointed to a storefront down the block. Yetta mumbled a prayer asking the Lord's forgiveness for what she was about to do for the sake of her family's well-being. She thought she would faint as she entered the store and was barely able to utter the name of the product she sought to purchase from the proprietor. In a matter of minutes, she had paid the requested coins and placed the container in her shopping bag. She fled as quickly as her legs would carry her, heading back to the security of her home.

As she hurried along, it suddenly dawned on Yetta that she could not possibly bring her purchase into her home. It would be a *schande*, a disgrace that would be unforgivable. She had to deliver it to the place it was meant to be. So before going home, she took a detour down the quiet alley behind Bernstein's Bakery. She knew that their storeroom was located at the very back of the establishment, just as the Goldfarb's was. When she reached the Bernstein's back door, she pressed her ear against the wood, and didn't hear a sound. She gently turned the doorknob and was cautiously grateful to find that the door was unlocked. Not daring to breathe or make the slightest sound, she entered the bakery, and found herself in the storeroom, which was lined with crates and cabinets. Yetta quickly opened a large cupboard and placed her package inside.

Breathing a sigh of relief, she went home.

ooo

There was only one person who knew the origin of the rumor that marked the demise of Bernstein's Bakery. But as soon as the accusation was uttered, it took on a life of its own. It was unimaginable that a seemingly pious man could so blatantly violate *kashrut*, the sacred dietary laws of the Jewish people, and thus cause his neighbors and customers to unknowingly commit a sin. But this is exactly what happened.

Yetta Goldfarb appeared to be particularly distressed the morning after her clandestine excursion to Mulberry Street. She was standing in front of her store, talking to Sadie Cohen, the wife of the man who owned the fruit and vegetable stand where Yetta bought most of the ingredients for the fillings of her blintzes.

"Yetta, what in the world is upsetting you so? Has the Tsar's army reached the shores of America?"

"Of course not Sadie," Yetta replied. "I heard some very disturbing news this morning and it is weighing on my mind."

"So, what news?" Sadie was the kind of woman who felt it was her mission in life to make others aware of the good and, particularly, the bad of life in this part of the city.

"A party who shall forever remain unnamed, told me that Saul Bernstein has taken measures to cut costs in his bakery. He has gone so far, may the Lord forgive my utterance, that he is using lard instead of butter! Can you imagine such a terrible violation of our law? Unspeakable!"

Sadie's face became pale so quickly that Yetta thought the woman was going to fall to the floor and die.

"This is the worst news I've heard since the Cossacks ordered us to abandon our homes and village," Sadie was able to utter as soon as she recovered her breath.

"And what of all the innocents who purchase their baked goods from Bernstein?" Yetta's eyes filled with tears as she contemplated this tragedy.

"Thank you for sharing this terrible news, Yetta. I will take it upon myself to spread the word of this travesty. Bernstein will be punished for what he has done to be sure!"

ooo

In a flash, the rumor took on a life of its own, just as Yetta knew it would. When Bernstein learned about the accusation being lodged against him, he angrily denied it. How could his friends, neighbors, and customers believe such a lie? Shame on them!

But the damage was done and his reputation was destroyed. In an attempt to salvage his credibility, he asked that the *beit din*, the three rabbis who served as the local rabbinical court, come to his establishment and certify that his bakery was operated according to the strict dietary laws passed down through the generations. Little did he know that this request would represent his complete undoing.

The rabbis came to Bernstein's Bakery and spent hours combing through the kitchen's ingredients, utensils, ovens, and cleaning procedures. It was during this arduous process that they came upon the damning evidence. For there, hidden in the rear of a cabinet, was a container of lard, rendered from the forbidden swine. No God-fearing Jew would ever contemplate consuming any product derived from the body of a pig. Upon this discovery, the rabbis declared that Bernstein had violated the sacred laws and that his bakery could no longer be patronized by any observant follower of the faith.

Bernstein knew that he had been the victim of a malicious plan to discredit and destroy his business. But it was too late. The damage was done. He closed his doors and prepared to move his family to another city where he was unknown.

ΩΩΩ

About a month after the Bernstein family had left the Lower East Side as Yetta was on her way to visit the fruit and vegetable vendor, she was stopped by one of the pillars of the community. Izzy Stein was the proud proprietor of the largest and most successful fabric and notions establishment in the entire city. Customers from far and wide came to purchase goods from his extraordinary selection. Izzy was expanding his inventory to include a large variety of yarns and knitting implements and had taken over the property that had housed Bernstein's Bakery to accommodate the new line. Stein's store would now occupy half the block directly across the street from Yetta's shop.

"Good morning to you," Stein greeted her, his large well-tailored frame towering over her.

"Hello, Izzy. I trust you are well and prospering."

"Oh, yes, thank the Lord. But there is something I'd like to discuss with you, Yetta. Can you accompany me to my office where we can talk privately over a glass of tea?"

Yetta couldn't imagine what Izzy could possibly want to talk to her about, unless he wanted to place an order for blintzes.

"Of course," responded Yetta. "Would now be a convenient time?"

ΩΩΩ

Izzy's office was spacious and beautifully decorated. Even though fabric samples were stacked on the tables lining the walls, the room was orderly and neat.

"Yetta, please sit down." Izzy gestured to one of two chairs facing his desk as he took his place behind the massive piece of furniture.

"You know, I recently traveled to Philadelphia to conduct business with one of my suppliers. And, who do you think I met as I hurried along the street?"

"I've no idea," Yetta said curiously.

"Saul Bernstein! You remember the Bernsteins, don't you, Yetta?"

Yetta felt her face flush as she answered Izzy's question. "Of course, I remember the Bernsteins. Who could forget the scandal they brought down upon our community?"

Izzy ignored her response.

"Saul and his family are living with his brother-in-law and working to establish a new business. They are having a difficult time since they lost everything when they were forced to leave their home and bakery here."

"Well, they certainly did a terrible thing and are suffering the consequences," Yetta replied indignantly.

"Now, Yetta, you and I both know that Saul did absolutely nothing wrong. He and his family were victims of another's evil intentions."

"I have no idea what you're talking about, Izzy."

"Please, don't play me for a fool, Yetta. You see, my office window faces the alley behind my establishment and also what used to be Bernstein's Bakery. I saw you head down the alley and enter the rear door of Bernstein's. And when you exited just moments later, it was even more puzzling. But only days later when the news of Bernstein's so-called transgression surfaced, I put two and two together. I haven't become a successful businessman without the gift of intelligence."

Yetta thought her head would burst and she would die on the spot.

"If you insist on pleading innocence in this matter, I will be forced to consult with the rabbis and place this matter in their hands. As I'm sure you know, if they find my accusations have merit, you will be fleeing our community in disgrace. But, if you admit to your actions, this matter can be resolved with no one the wiser."

Yetta knew she could not win this battle. Better to acknowledge her wrongdoing and come to an agreement with Izzy. If not, she could lose everything.

"Yes, I am guilty. I was so frightened of damage to my business because of the popularity of Bernstein's Bakery. I've made a terrible mistake and have caused a great deal of harm to an innocent family."

"I'm going to give you an opportunity to redeem yourself, Yetta. And here is how. I am going to calculate a payment which you will give to me on the first day of each month. I will then send the money anonymously to Bernstein. It will serve as compensation for the cost of closing their bakery here, moving to Philadelphia, and funds needed to reestablish themselves in a new place. If you do not follow my instructions, I will immediate go to the *beit din* and inform the court of your transgressions. You have a great deal to lose, Yetta."

A shamed Yetta knew she had no choice in the matter. Izzy meant what he said.

"I'll do what you say, Izzy. But, how long will I have to make this monthly payment?"

"As long as I require you to do so. As soon as I am assured that the Bernsteins have established a successful business in Philadelphia, I will inform you."

ooo

A chastised Yetta left Izzy's office, finally acknowledging that her greed and self-interest were her undoing. She had committed a grave sin and had to atone for her selfish actions. Even in her shame, she realized that a pathway to redemption had been offered by Izzy.

In the days and weeks and months that followed, Yetta never strayed from a righteous life. Her business flourished and she always made payments to Izzy on time. Jake would sometimes

126

look at his wife and wonder why she had become a nicer, less driven person. But he never asked.

If he had, Yetta would have told him that she had learned the hard way that the Lord worked in strange ways.

Harriette Sackler serves as Grants Chair of the Malice Domestic Board of Directors. She is a multi-published, two-time Agatha Award nominee for Best Short Story. As a principal of the Dames of Detection, Harriette is co-publisher and editor at Level Best Books. She is a member of Mystery Writers of America, Sisters in Crime, Sisters in Crime-Chesapeake Chapter, the Guppies, and the Crime Writers' Association. Harriette is the proud mom of two fabulous daughters and Nana to four grandbabies. She lives with her husband and two little Yorkies in the D.C. suburbs. Visit Harriette at www.harriettesackler.com

NOIR AT THE SALAD BAR

THE SANDMAN

BY JOHN M. FLOYD

A visibly weary Lily Russell slung a frayed towel over her left shoulder, reached behind her head to retie her blond ponytail, and resumed wiping down the already spotless countertop. "How's your pie?" she asked me, without turning.

"The crust is too hard," I said from my barstool.

She shot me a bored look that said *There's nothing wrong with that crust and you know it*. What she actually said, though, was, "Look around you, Jack—you see anybody else eating? This is a tavern, not a diner."

I stopped chewing. "Seriously?"

"And even though we both know this is not a diner, I still bring in a cherry pie once a week just for you. I ask you, why do I *do* it?"

"Because you secretly love me?"

She rolled her eyes but couldn't keep from smiling.

I took another bite, thought a moment, and said, "Run away with me, Lil. Earl wouldn't miss you."

Another customer motioned to her, a young dark-haired woman in a business suit sitting at the other end of the bar. Before heading in her direction Lily snapped the damp towel at me and said, "You're probably right—he wouldn't."

"I was kidding about the crust," I said, but she was already gone.

With practiced ease she snagged a bottle from beneath the counter without slowing down and poured the young woman another drink. I watched her idly, chewing my pie and rotating my beer glass on its coaster. I'd known Lily most of my life, even before she married Earl. My ex-wife once said that if you looked up "kindhearted" in the dictionary, you'd find Lily Russell's picture beside it.

The two women chatted for a minute, owner and customer, then Lily came back, stooping to replace the bottle on the way and moving to the beat of an old Johnny Cash song blaring from the jukebox on the other side of the room. The jukebox, I remembered, had been Earl's idea, as had the name of the bar: The Lily Pad.

Lily stopped in front of me, frowning as if in deep thought.

"What is it?" I asked.

"Nothing. Thinking about old times."

"You and me?"

She seemed to come out of her trance and smiled a little. "Not that old. I was thinking about the guy who used to come in here with you. Big fella, red hair."

I nodded. "A good friend."

"He died, right?"

"Heart attack," I said. "Two years ago."

"I remember he liked country-western. What was his name? Jerry something?"

I opened my mouth to reply, but she was already turning to answer a call for a beer. And as I watched her fetch it and pour, getting just the right head of foam on it, I found myself glad that I hadn't ordered another one myself. I would've thought I was imagining things. The patron who'd summoned Lily this time, you see—he looked even more tired than she did—was Cal Borelli. One of the most notorious crime bosses in the city. And that of course wasn't possible, because Borelli had just been murdered. I'd seen it four days ago on the news.

When she came back I caught her eye, nodded at the man she'd just served, and whispered, "Am I losing my mind? I thought Cal Borelli died the other day."

"He did."

"Then who's that?"

"His brother, Michael. From Chicago, he said."

I swallowed the last bite of my pie, chased it with a swallow of Budweiser, and watched the guy from the corner of my eye. They could've been twins. Maybe they *had* been. "What's he doing here?" I asked her.

"If you mean here in town, he came for the funeral. If you mean here in my bar..."

"That's what I mean."

"He says he's staying in a hotel not far away."

"That's odd, isn't it? I'd have thought he'd be with the grieving family."

"He told me Cal was a widower, no kids," she said. "Anyway, Michael Borelli's relatives and living quarters are none of my affair. I can use the business—he's been here the past three nights, comes in at nine, leaves around ten."

"You're not giving him any of my pie, are you?"

She grinned, but it quickly faded. I saw a cloud pass over her face. "I wouldn't get too used to that pie if I were you."

"What do you mean?"

Her expression had gone dead solemn. She looked like she might cry. After a long hesitation she said, "I might be closing soon, Jack. Earl and I might be leaving."

That got my attention. *Leaving?* "What's happened?"

She blew out a sigh, picked up my fork and empty dish, and wiped off the counter where they'd been. "I took out a loan—a big loan—to add the new room."

"So? It's paying off, right? More customers, more income."

"Not enough, though. And not fast enough."

"What are you saying, Lil?"

"I'm saying my…creditors, we'll call them…want their money. And I don't have it."

She had paused and turned to stare out one of the front windows into the night. Her towel was draped over her shoulder again, her chin up, her fists on her hips. I studied her profile; it was easy to see she'd once been beautiful.

"How much are we talking about?" I asked.

Her face softened, and for a second I thought she was going to kiss my cheek. "Too much for you to cover, Jackie boy. Too much for anybody."

"So what'll happen? Will you have to sell?"

"Sell isn't the right word," she said. "I'll sign the bar over to them. It's that, or…"

"Or what?"

She shook her head. "I've been told not to speak of all this."

"Tell me, Lil. Or what?"

She looked at me and I caught the gleam of tears in her eyes. "Let me put it this way. You remember Rudy Kelso, from down the street?" When I shook my head, she said, "Well, he and his wife ran into money problems with their store a while back. The bank wouldn't talk to him, so somebody told him about Warren Drecker—I know you remember *him*. Bottom line, Drecker and his son loaned Rudy the cash, at a sky-high interest rate of course, and Rudy had trouble paying it back."

"And?"

"He became an example," she said.

"They hurt him, you mean?"

Lily just stared at me, saying nothing.

"They *killed* him?" I said.

She dug a tissue out of her apron pocket and blew her nose. "No—the Dreckers don't kill people who can't pay on time. They give them another chance to pay, later."

"Later? After what?"

"They killed his wife."

For a moment I sat there, looking at her.

"Are you serious?"

"They're careful," she said. "It looked like an accident. But Doris Kelso is just as dead."

"You know this for a fact?"

"Yes. I just wish I'd known it before I borrowed from them myself."

I shook my head. "What about the police, Lil? Why didn't what's his name—Rudy—tell the cops?"

"Wouldn't do any good. I told you, it looked legit. There's no proof, not even any records of the loan. Besides, the Dreckers have some of the cops in their pockets."

"You *are* serious, aren't you."

"Think about it," she said. "If Rudy Kelso had filed a report, how would he have known who to go to? Mention this to the wrong detective, even the wrong commanding officer, Rudy gets killed just as quick as his wife did." She sighed. "And he has his daughters to think of."

"But…people know about this. About *them*. You said so yourself."

"Come on, Jack. How long you been retired now?"

"Too long?"

"I think so." She lowered her voice. "They *want* people to know, honey. Not many, but enough. That's how guys like Drecker stay in control."

A silence passed. Fatigue and worry darkened her face. She stuffed the Kleenex back into her pocket, stuck out her lower lip, and blew a strand of blond hair off her forehead. I just sat there, gazing past her shoulder at my confused reflection in the mirror behind the bar.

"So that's the story," she said. "This time next month, Earl and I might be headed to Mexico."

"Mexico?"

"It wouldn't take much to run one of those seaside cantinas. And at least both of us would be alive."

Another silence.

"This Warren Drecker," I said. "What does he look like?"

"Don't you know?"

"I've heard of him. Never seen him."

"Them," she corrected. "Him and his son Darryl. The son's even worse than the father. I'm told Darryl does the actual enforcing. They're always together—they even come in here sometimes."

"Tell me what they look like."

"If I had my phone I could show you. It's in the office, in my purse."

"What do you mean, show me?"

"I mean I took their picture." She tipped her head to the right. "They were sitting over there in the back corner booth last night around seven, where they always sit. They've told me to keep it reserved for them, and I do. Anyhow, they were there, talking, and I snapped their photo on my cell phone."

I felt myself blink. "Wasn't that a little risky?"

"I suppose I didn't think about it until afterward. Want me to go get it?"

I checked my watch. Almost nine-thirty. The glimmer of an idea had just entered my head.

"I have to leave," I said. "Could you send it to my phone?"

"The photo? I guess so. What do you want it for?"

I ignored that question. Instead I made sure she knew my number and asked, "When can you send it?"

"Soon as I walk back and get my purse out of my desk."

"Okay." I stood, still thinking hard, and laid several bills on the bar as always. Suddenly I realized she was staring at me.

"What are you going to do?" she asked me.

"Nothing. I'm just leaving. It's late."

Lily leaned forward, placed both palms flat on the bar, one on each side of my almost-empty glass, and made sure I was looking at her. "I know you, Jack. So you listen: Don't get involved in this. You understand me?"

"I understand."

"I mean it."

"Come on, Lil. What do you think I'd do? I don't even own a gun."

"Tell me you won't do anything crazy."

"I won't," I said.

Our eyes held for a long moment, then she seemed to relax. "All right."

"All right." I drained the last of my beer, set the glass down, and put my jacket on. "It'll all work out, Lil. You just gotta be a believer."

"A believer in what?"

I thought for a second. "Justice."

"Justice?"

"Fairness, then. Believing that good things happen to good people."

"That's a fantasy, Jack. Like the Bermuda Triangle. Or Bigfoot."

"No, it's not," I said.

She gave up and nodded. She really did look exhausted.

"Give Earl my best, okay?"

"I will," she said.

I turned to leave, then looked at her again. "And don't let him have any of my pie."

ooo

I went straight home. My apartment was only five blocks from The Lily Pad, but because of traffic on the cross streets the walk still took ten minutes.

As I was entering my front door, I heard a single *ding* on my phone. I dug it out of my pants pocket, knowing already what I'd find. It was the photo Lily had told me about, along with her text message: *Wouldn't my kids be proud of me, using this new technology?*

I studied the photo—a clear shot of two dark-eyed men in gray suits, one old, one young, seated in one of Lily's booths—and typed a note back saying I doubted this was the kind of picture kids send each other these days. Then I signed off. In fact I switched the phone to SILENT. I didn't want to hear anything more from anyone for a while, including Lily Russell. At least until I did what I planned to do.

My next stop was the bottom drawer of the desk in my living room. I rummaged around for several seconds before finding what I needed. When I did, I took it carefully from the drawer and stared at it in the lamplight, feeling it, turning it over and over in my hands. Remembering. Then I tucked it into my jacket pocket, switched off the light, and left the apartment.

ooo

Fifteen minutes later, when Michael Borelli left Lily's bar at five minutes after ten, I was waiting. I spotted him as he stepped out onto the sidewalk, followed him to a rented Lincoln parked at the curb a short distance away, and called his name as he beeped the remote to unlock the doors. He turned, instantly alert, to face me.

"We need to talk, Mr. Borelli."

"Do we know each other?" he asked, in a heavy accent.

"No." I took both hands from my pockets and held them up in plain view. "But you'll want to hear what I have to say."

He studied me awhile in the yellow glow of the streetlights. "Where?" he said.

I pointed to a coffeeshop on the corner, a block from Lily's, waited until he nodded, and walked in that direction. I heard him re-lock the car, heard his footsteps following me. It wasn't yet late, but there were no crowds on the sidewalk. And no one I recognized. Two minutes later we sat facing each other at a table in the back corner of the café. I couldn't help thinking of the Dreckers' corner booth, the one Lily kept on reserve.

A waitress came over and I waved her off. She glared at me, sighed, and left. I turned back to Michael Borelli.

"Who are you?" he asked.

I took a leather badge case from my pocket, flipped it open. On the right side was the still-shiny shield itself, and a badge number; on the left were the words J. SANDERFORD, DETECTIVE. There was no photo—none had been required, back then—and there was no red RETIRED stamp emblazoned across the lettering, as there should have been. That had been an administrative mistake, and I was happy to take advantage of it. I was also, of course, officially breaking the law, but that didn't bother me either. The law and justice were two different things.

Borelli gave it a look and nodded. "I suppose you know, Detective, that I am visiting in your city. That I have done nothing wrong."

"I do know that. I'm not here to question you—I'm here to tell you something."

He showed me both his hands as well, on the tabletop, and did a palms-up. "Speak."

We sat there a moment, looking at each other. The fluorescent glare of the coffeeshop revealed much more of his face than had the dimly-lit bar or the streetlights outside—and he didn't appear as hostile as I'd expected. More than anything he looked curious. Which was good.

"You know a man named Warren Drecker?" I asked him.

"I thought you were not going to ask me anything."

"I lied. I have two questions. But they're important. Do you know him?"

"No."

I took out my cell phone, paged to the photo Lily had sent me, and turned the phone so he could see it. "You recognize these two men?"

"No." Borelli looked up at me. "As I said, I do not live here."

"Just making sure," I said. I pointed to the picture. "The guy on the left is Warren Drecker, the other is his son Darryl." The wall of Lily's bar, and several prints and photographs, were visible above their heads. "You recognize the place this was taken?"

"That makes three questions."

"Please. Do you know the place?"

Borelli studied the details. "It looks like the tavern I was in tonight."

"And the previous two nights. Right?"

"That is correct. My hotel is nearby."

"Well, this photo was taken last night, Mr. Borelli. I'm told these two men left just before you arrived." Lie number one, I thought.

He studied me a moment. "It would seem you have been following me."

"No," I said. I pointed once more to the photo. "I've been following *them*."

I was almost surprised at how quickly and easily the second lie had rolled out.

He looked again at the picture. "Are you saying these men were in this bar the same three nights I was there?"

"At it, not in it. They've been waiting outside for you, in their car. Watching you come in and leave."

He seemed to think this over. I got the impression this knowledge didn't particularly worry him. It intrigued him.

"So these two men—this Drecker and his son—they have been following *me*."

"It would appear that way," I said.

"Do you know why?"

"I know we've had their phones tapped for a week." I wondered if my nose was growing longer. I should consider writing fiction, I thought.

"And?"

"And your brother's name has been mentioned."

For the first time Borelli's expression changed. Hardened. He said, his eyes narrowed and suddenly fierce, "Are you telling me these are the ones who killed Calvino?"

"We have no proof of that. The overheard conversations were brief. Guarded. But they'd had differences in the past, and..."

"And why else would they now be interested in me?"

"My thoughts exactly." I put the phone and badge wallet away, drew a long breath, and let it out. "I'm wondering if they think your brother might've told you things. Things that the Dreckers had rather no one else knew."

"He did not," Borelli said.

"That doesn't matter, if they think he did."

Borelli seemed to consider that. He stared down at his hands a moment; both had clenched into white-knuckled fists on the table. Finally he nodded as if making up his mind about something and looked up at me. "Do they know you are tailing them?"

"I'm not sure."

"If they do, you probably did me a good turn. Being here, watching. It has kept them from making a move."

"I'm not sure of that either. I'm just saying I don't want another murder."

"What *do* you want?" he asked.

I remembered my talk with Lily an hour ago. "I want justice." *Finally*, I thought, *a word of truth.*

"Define 'justice.'"

"I think justice happens when bad people, like good people"—I paused, choosing my words—"get what they deserve."

"In other words, you want this Warren Drecker..."

"Stopped," I said. "I want him stopped and off the streets. His son too."

"In custody, you mean?"

"I'm not sure custody is what they deserve." I hesitated just long enough, and added, "I know, although I can't prove it, that both these men are killers. The worst kind of killers." I shrugged. "You understand?"

Michael Borelli's hands had relaxed now—or at least were no longer fists. He seemed almost as calm as before. Except for his eyes.

"I believe I do," he said.

"I also want silence. No one must ever know we met, or talked."

"That is my desire as well."

I nodded again, heaved a giant sigh, and rose to my feet. "Thanks for your time, Mr. Borelli. I'm sorry about your loss."

He nodded also. "Thank you for your information."

"What information?"

Both of us smiled a little. As I turned to leave, Borelli said, "Sanderford?"

I looked down at him, waiting.

"Is this the kind of thing they teach now, at the police academy?"

I was no longer smiling.

"They should," I said.

ǫǫǫ

Two nights later I climbed onto my usual barstool, rubbed my eyes, and waved my usual greeting to Earl Russell, who was as usual hurrying back and forth from the bar to the back office. Within seconds, also as usual, Lily appeared with a Budweiser and a glass in hand. She scooted a coaster onto the countertop on front of me, pinned it in place with my glass, and poured. On the far side of the bar, someone had cranked up the jukebox. Willie Nelson was informing us that he was on the road again.

"You're looking chipper tonight," I said to her.

"I am. But I can't help feeling guilty about it."

"Guilty about what?"

"My good mood," she said. "You haven't seen the news?"

"What news?"

Lily leaned back against the mirror and folded her arms. "Warren and Darryl Drecker. They were found this afternoon. Shot in the head."

"They're both dead?"

"Bullets between the eyes'll do that, I'm told." She stroked her forehead absently, as if thinking about that, then said, "It's over, Jack. No threat, no debt." She barked a nervous laugh. "How's that for poetic?"

I thought that over. "No one else knew about your loan?"

"Just them and me. There was no written contract. They wanted it that way. And they always worked alone. Unbelievable, right?"

Before I could respond, a man several seats down from me held up an empty shotglass and Lily left on a refueling run. After a moment she came back, looking preoccupied. She tucked the bottle of bourbon away under the counter, stared at me and said, "Sanderford."

I looked up. "Excuse me?"

"I finally remembered your friend's name, the guy you used to come in here with. The policeman. Jerry Sanderford."

I nodded. "The Sandman, the other cops called him. He could put you to sleep, like in the song."

"Put you to sleep?"

"With his stories. His jokes, too." I paused, smiling a little. Recalling better times.

"You were roommates, right? After his wife died?"

My pleasant thoughts drained away. "After she was murdered," I said.

"Murdered? I didn't know that."

"He was working a case, threatened the wrong people. They burned his house down with his wife inside."

Lily's face went pale. "You mean—someone killed his wife to get to *him*? Who would do such a—"

She stopped in midsentence. I just looked at her, watched her eyes widen.

"Warren Drecker?" she said.

"It was never proven."

"But it was him. Wasn't it. Or Darryl."

"Jerry thought so," I said. "He and I were friends a long time—I did his taxes, advised him on financial matters and whatnot. And since my divorce I had too big an apartment anyway, for a retired CPA. Jerry had no family. He moved in with me not

139

long after his wife's funeral." I picked up my beer, but set it down again without drinking anything. "I miss him."

Lily still looked shaken. "I liked him too. But he left you with good memories."

I thought of Jerry's badge in its leather case, remembered him bringing it back to our apartment the day he retired. Tossing it into the bottom desk drawer in the living room.

"Among other things," I murmured.

"What?"

"Nothing."

She stood there a moment, brows furrowed in thought, then reached down and squeezed my hand. "Jack?"

"Yeah?"

"You promise you had nothing to do with this Drecker thing? You swear?"

"I'm an accountant, Lil, not a fighter. I told you, I don't even own a gun."

"Yeah, and I bet you never told a lie either."

I gave her a tiny smile. "Look at it this way. Why would I do anything to keep you here with that husband of yours? I'm the one who wants to run off with you."

It was, somehow, the right thing to say. I saw the lines of her frown smooth out and disappear. "Earl would miss me," she said.

She released my hand and left, probably to fetch me a slice of cherry pie. I picked up my Bud, and this time I took a sip. I found myself looking around at the bar, the gleaming thirty-foot mirror, the multicolored bottles, the row of tall stools, the old and homey section behind me, the ancient jukebox, the window facing the street, the cozy new addition off to the left. I sat there studying the room, the customers, the now-empty back corner booth the Dreckers had told Lily to keep on reserve for them. I sat there for a long, silent moment, thinking about life and death.

And justice.

John M. Floyd's work has appeared in more than 250 publications, including *Alfred Hitchcock's Mystery Magazine, Ellery Queen's Mystery Magazine, The Strand Magazine, The Saturday Evening Post, Mississippi Noir*, and *The Best American Mystery Stories*. John is also a three-time Derringer Award winner and an Edgar nominee. His sixth book, *Dreamland*, was released in 2016.

NOIR AT THE SALAD BAR
HARVEY HOUSE HOMICIDE

BY JOYCE ANN BROWN

"Carrie… Your customer said he's waiting for his pie."

Wenona Yazzie clutched her order pad to her white apron, let the door swing closed, and took two steps into the apparently deserted kitchen of the sparkling new, 1900 Harvey House of Dodge City.

"Carrie? Chef George?"

Caroline Putnam, the only other Harvey Girl on duty at eight forty-five that Sunday evening, had entered the kitchen to get a piece of apple pie for a customer who'd eaten dinner earlier and then read. He'd arrived on the last Santa Fe passenger train at seven.

Wenona heard a faint gurgle from the other side of the center work area and tiptoed around. What she saw would cause most young ladies of nineteen to scream and run, but Wenona was Navajo and had witnessed much in her short life. "Chef George?" she whispered as she bent toward their exceptional cook and mentor. The chef lay with a butcher knife embedded in his chest, blood spurting out.

She peeked up. Where was the killer? Where was Carrie? The normally-locked back door was ajar. She stepped over, looked out into the silent dark, pulled the door closed, and locked it.

In the dining area, the studious-looking young man wearing a three-piece black suit and spectacles sat waiting for his pie. He could be a professor or a reporter or a wealthy businessman with connections. She stood on shaky legs and pressed her eyes to stop the tears. The last thing Wenona wanted was for someone to broadcast this atrocity. Mr. Fred Harvey had hired her—a boarding-school-educated Native American girl—paid her a whopping $17.50 a month plus room, board, and gratuities, and provided her train ticket to this magnificent facility. She and her fellow waitresses needed the impeccable reputation of the Harvey House restaurants to continue.

142

Taking a deep breath and smoothing her ankle-length black skirt, Wenona cut through flaky crust, scooped an extra-large piece of thick, warm, sugar-and-cinnamon-topped apple pie onto a plate, and took it to Carrie's customer. "I'm very sorry for your wait. Your waitress became ill and was taken to her room. Please accept this pie, compliments of the house. Can I refresh your coffee?"

Wrapping flatware in linen napkins with shaky fingers, Wenona glanced at her customer. As soon as he finished eating, she swooped over to clear the table. "Sir," she said with a smile, "the restaurant closes at nine o'clock, but there are fine lodgings next door at the hotel."

The man, appearing preoccupied, bookmarked his page and stood. "Yes. Yes. Thank you for the good service. The pie was delicious. I hope the other young lady will be okay. Please divide the tip with her."

Wenona counted the money—the price of his chicken and dumplings dinner plus a nice tip even after she paid for the pie. She felt her heart swell for all the human kindness in the world that surely outweighed the bad, then hurried to lock the front door, pull the shades, and rush into the kitchen. Chef George's blood still oozed from the jagged holes in his chest where he must have been struck several times from the left. Carrie couldn't have done this. The rotund, yet strong chef would surely have been able to wrestle the knife away.

The questions were multiplying. Why would anyone want to kill jolly George? Did an assailant kidnap Carrie after she accidentally witnessed the murder, or was Carrie's body yet to be found? Another thought—did Carrie know the intruder and go with him willingly after he killed Chef George? How would anyone else get into the kitchen? The back door was always locked.

Carrie, an educated society girl from Philadelphia, became Wenona's friend soon after they met as part of the crew of manager, two chefs, and six waitresses at the debut of the Harvey House Restaurant in the railroad depot of this western Kansas town. Some of the other girls snubbed Wenona at first, but because of her friendship with the bright, classy Easterner and the wise guidance of Chef George, all of them eventually became chummy.

No matter that separation and loss had been common in her life, Wenona couldn't bear to lose both of her new friends.

It had been barely fifteen minutes since she discovered the body. Wenona's first impulse to run to the police and report the crime so Carrie could be rescued vied with her desire to protect the restaurant from scandal. Maybe both could be accomplished, but probably not by a Navajo Indian girl who had no connections in town beyond the Harvey House. She could easily be accused of the crime she needed to report. Locking the kitchen door from the outside and running the short distance to the small cottage where the restaurant manager lived with his wife, she hoped for the best.

"Why, he's in his dressing gown at this hour." Mrs. Gerson held the door open only far enough for Wenona to see her old-fashioned black leg o'mutton sleeves and buttoned bodice. "Can't this wait until morning?"

"I'm sorry. It's a restaurant emergency," Wenona said.

"What is it, Miss Yazzie?" Mr. Gerson, the manager of the Harvey House Restaurant and connected hotel, walked to the door shrugging on his suit coat. "Our young waitress wouldn't have come if it weren't necessary, my dear," he told his wife.

"It concerns Chef George." Wenona glanced at Mrs. Gerson, a nice person, but one who gossiped with most every other matron in Dodge City. "Please come back to the restaurant with me, sir."

ooo

It turned out Mr. Gerson, the police chief, and the Santa Fe Railway station master all agreed to keep the case quiet to preserve the reputation of the Harvey House. Only the families of Chef George and Caroline Putnam and the staff were notified. With Carrie missing, no one suggested that Wenona had played any part in the killing. No one informed her how the investigation was proceeding, either.

ooo

Wenona worked the following days with her mind only half on her job. Edith, the thirty-year-old "mother hen" of the waitresses, chided her several times for moving too slowly.

"Listen, I know you're sad, what with Carrie and Chef George gone, but the customers deserve good service," Edith said with a kind smile after Wenona left a customer waiting as his simmering plate of broiled chicken, mashed potatoes, and peas cooled while she filled water glasses with a faraway look on her face. "Chef Thomas is working twice as many hours, and we're all filling Carrie's spots. You've got to do your share. We've been promised replacements soon."

"I'm very sorry," Wenona said. "I'll do better."

And she was. And she did. But after her early shift ended, she changed clothes and went to Mr. Gerson's office. Welcomed into the small wallpapered room off the hotel lobby, Wenona perched on a straight-backed chair in front of the manager's oak desk.

"Sir," she said, "I know the police think Carrie murdered Chef George, but—"

"It's the only explanation. No one saw anyone else enter the kitchen. We've sent her description by telegram and a copy of the wanted poster to every depot and train on the Santa Fe line and beyond. We've also notified her parents. When we find Miss Putnam, she'll be given a chance to claim self defense." He paused with a frown. "But, tell me, if it was self defense, what reason would George have for attacking her, and why did she flee?"

Wenona examined the copy of the flyer she'd seen posted about town and that was being circulated on trains going east and west across the country. Carrie's petite figure was circled on an indistinct photo of the six Dodge City Harvey Girls posing in their uniforms.

She looked up at Mr. Gerson. "Someone could have entered the kitchen after Carrie without my knowledge. We had two or three customers finishing up, and I went to the pantry to gather fresh linens, fill salt and pepper shakers, and measure out ground coffee for the next morning's rush. When I returned to the dining room, the one remaining customer asked me about a piece of pie Carrie had promised to bring. I didn't see what happened to the other customers or if anyone else came in while I was gone."

"I think your pie customer would have said something." Mr. Gerson tapped the end of his pen on the desktop and stood—obvious dismissal. "I'll let you girls know when we find out anything. I know you were all fond of Chef George."

ooo

Despite working two exhausting shifts that day and explaining over and over to regular customers that Chef George's delectable fish almandine had been mistakenly prepared with no almonds by an overworked Chef Thomas, Wenona couldn't fall asleep that night. She thought about the pie customer. He had been absorbed in his book, underlining and making notes in the margins. Would he have noticed someone follow Carrie into the kitchen and thought it impolite to mention? If Carrie had taken ill, as Wenona told him, he might have assumed that whoever followed her had helped Carrie to her room. Or perhaps that he was a suitor pleading his case under the watchful eye of the chef.

At another thought, Wenona opened her sleepless eyes wider. Why hadn't their late customer gotten a room before nine o'clock that evening? Carrie had said she'd come from a wealthy family. Maybe he sent Carrie to the kitchen knowing an accomplice was waiting to kidnap her for ransom, and when Chef George intervened, he paid with his life. Pie Man might have given Wenona an extra tip to avert suspicion.

It was a mess. Wenona tossed and turned the rest of the night, waking sometimes with a vision of that black-suited customer with a kind smile and a handful of money and sometimes with fire-red eyes and a contorted sneer. She finally slept for a couple of hours after she determined she'd look for him and ask what he'd seen.

The next day, Wenona was scheduled for twelve hours, but she would get an hour and a half break in the afternoon to, as their guidelines specified, *rest, eat, or take a walk in the fresh air*. After the lunch rush, another waitress handed her a note from Mr. Gerson directing her to his office at break time. Had Carrie been found? Found alive? Or…? Wenona felt alternately queasy and elated.

In his office, Mr. Gerson handed her a telegram. "I thought you'd like to read the message we received from Miss Putnam's parents."

Philadelphia, Penn. 1898 22 July

CAROLINE HOME TO MARRY HER INTENDED -stop-

WILL NOT RETURN TO FULFILL CONTRACT -stop-

MR AND MRS EUGENE M PUTNAM

"The police in Philadelphia have been notified. They'll question Miss Putnam and have her sent back here for trial."

"I'm relieved she's safe," Wenona said as she handed the message back to her manager, "but this doesn't make sense, Mr. Gerson. Carrie told me in confidence that she left home to escape from an arranged betrothal to a dreadful man important to her father's business. She wouldn't suddenly decide to leave and kill George for trying to stop her. Maybe someone took her."

"It's up to the investigators to determine what happened, not you. If I learn anything else, I'll let you know."

Wenona worked until eight o'clock that evening because of an extra surge of customers from the last passenger train of the day. It was too late to look for Carrie's pie customer, and she was so tired that she practically fell asleep while changing out of her uniform.

000

Up at five the next morning, Wenona bathed and dressed for the breakfast shift. "Do you mind if we trade stations?" Wenona asked another waitress. "If you take Mike, the brakeman, I'll take that fellow by the window."

Mike was almost finished, and the customer she'd wanted to find had just walked in with his book and found a table. Her friend raised her eyebrows but nodded. They all knew Fred Harvey's rule about never sitting or having personal conversations with any of their customers. Despite the directive, pretty young Harvey Girls married patrons on a regular basis, causing Mr. Harvey the inconvenience of screening new hires.

Wenona was sure everyone could hear her heart beat at ten times its normal rate as she walked to the table by the window with the coffee carafe, a planted smile, and only an inkling of an idea how she'd question her customer. She told herself to be patient and deliver his breakfast before she proceeded. People seemed more cheerful after a tasty meal and full-bodied hot coffee.

"I trust you found a good room at the hotel," she said as she poured his coffee.

The man, who looked younger but just as intense in the bright sunlight from the window, cleared his throat and looked up from his book. "Indeed. Quite decent. Thank you for directing me there the other night, Miss..."

"Yazzie. I'm glad the room suits you, Mr...."

"Capp. Jacob Capp. I'm here to work at the new secondary school when it opens in September, and the hotel must serve as my lodgings for now." He gazed around at the crowd. "This restaurant may become my regular dining room. The aromas are mouthwatering. The café on the corner near the school serves hard biscuits and greasy gravy—difficult to digest, unless one is a cow hand."

The breakfast shift was hectic as usual during the east-bound passenger train's hour-long layover. While passengers and crew filed in for a reasonably-priced, steaming hot breakfast, workers refueled, loaded baggage, and welcomed new passengers. Chef Thomas took pride in cooking up his specialties at lightning speed so everyone could return before the "all aboard" signal. The efficient Harvey Girls kept up the pace with dignity and good humor. Wenona did her share with automatic pluckiness as her mind swirled through possible ways of questioning the gentleman whose smile and friendliness had shattered the demonic image of her nightmare.

As she delivered a plate of firm, moist eggs scrambled with green peppers and onions, a thick slice of ham, and two pieces of toasted bread, Wenona wore a radiant smile of goodwill. "I hope you enjoy *this* breakfast, Mr. Capp."

It wasn't until Jacob Capp had almost finished eating that Wenona ventured the first of her questions while she refreshed his coffee cup. "Do you mind if I ask you a question about the night you were here and—?"

"I remember. And I don't mind."

"Oh." Her cheeks grew hot as she registered his warm, brown eyes gazing into hers. She lowered her lids and swallowed. "After your waitress left to get your pie, did you notice anyone else go into the kitchen before I came out of the pantry?"

"No, I didn't."

Wenona couldn't help the sigh that escaped as she felt the weight of disappointment on her chest.

Jacob continued with a contemplative tone. "There were two other customers in the restaurant before I ordered the pie. I heard one leave with a hearty "Good night" to the waitress. That was when I realized I wanted some dessert before closing time. It took a minute or two to order, because when I looked for her, the waitress seemed to be contending with arguments from the other customer. I finally caught her attention, but, after I ordered, my studies demanded my attention until you returned. From my table in the back I didn't see how or when the difficult customer left."

"Can you describe him?"

"Well-groomed fellow, dark hair with an impeccable middle part, close shave, tweed jacket and vest, fedora on the table. He had a pocket watch I saw him consult a couple of times. I didn't watch him for long. Seemed nosy."

"But you would recognize him if you saw him again?"

"Yes, I believe so. Patrician nose and cold eyes.... Sorry. I just didn't like the way he seemed to be treating the young lady."

Wenona looked around and found the other waitresses frowning at her. "Mr. Capp, I need to go, but would you speak to the restaurant manager about this with me? The incident in the kitchen was more serious than a slight illness, and what you saw might be important."

"Of course. You can contact me at the hotel or at the school. And I'll be eating my meals here, at least until I get my own lodgings."

"Thank you."

She scrambled to work harder for the rest of her shift, only eight hours this day, and to avoid the questioning looks of her colleagues. At three o'clock, Wenona fled to her room, changed into a long, bell-shaped, wine-colored skirt, a pin-tucked white blouse with long, slim sleeves puffed at the shoulders, gloves, and a soft grey hat. She'd saved to buy a modern summer outfit and wanted to look presentable.

When she asked for Jacob Capp at the hotel, a haughty registration clerk told her Mr. Capp was out. Not wanting to wait in the lobby under the smug observation of the clerk, Wenona decided to walk to the new schoolhouse. On the dusty sidewalks and streets, she held her new skirt as high as she dared in order to keep it clean, a futile effort in the windswept prairie town. The door of the brick two-story school opened to her, but inside, the hallways and rooms looked deserted.

"Mr. Capp," Wenona called and flinched at the echo. She walked down the hallway, opening each door and peeking into the rooms, empty for now except for green chalkboards and aluminum flag holders on the walls. "Mr. Capp, are you here?" she called up the wide stairway at the end of the hall. She heard footsteps on the hard tiles moving toward the top of the stairway.

"Who is it?" a male voice shouted down.

"It's me, Miss Wenona Yazzie."

Jacob Capp appeared at the top of the stairway and smiled. "Miss Yazzie, hello. Do come up and let me show you what I've accomplished in the science room. I'm very excited to have had much of the equipment delivered. No furniture yet, but it'll be here before school starts."

"I...I don't know that I should," she said.

"It's okay. This is a public building, and besides, I'm the only one here today."

Wenona hesitated. There were rules for Harvey Girls and rules for young ladies, especially those of Indian heritage. She couldn't afford to ruin her reputation, or his. "Perhaps another time, when a female or a headmaster is here?"

Jacob's face fell. "Of course. I understand." He walked down the stairs. "How can I help you, Miss Yazzie?"

"As I told you this morning, I need you to tell my manager what you saw at the restaurant. It's urgent because they think my friend..." Wenona pressed her gloved hands against her chest. "Can I tell you something in confidence, Mr. Capp that you promise not to divulge to anyone in town?"

She didn't know why she trusted him after seeing him in her nightmares, but the way he treated her and the kind look in his mesmerizing eyes convinced her that he was the only one she could trust to help. She took a deep breath and told him the whole story.

"And after I read the telegram that proved she's alive, Mr. Gerson, the manager, said the Philadelphia police will send her back here to stand trial. The authorities all believe she was the only one who could have killed the chef. Will you tell them about the argument you saw—and the customer?"

"I'll tell them what I told you," Jacob said. "But I didn't see enough to implicate him. That man could have gone out through the front door when I wasn't paying attention."

"But you saw the customer before him leave. You would have noticed if another customer left that way."

"Miss Yazzie, has it occurred to you that your friend might be guilty?"

"Carrie stands perhaps an inch over five feet and weighs a little over a hundred pounds. Not only that, but she loved Chef George as much as I did. Also, I know she wouldn't have killed him in order to sneak away and go back to an engagement she took a job to avoid."

Twenty minutes later, Mr. Gerson listened to Jacob Capp's story. He looked skeptical. "An argument, you say? Did the customer sound threatening? It could have been that he was complaining about his food or his bill. He didn't try to stop her when you called her over to order pie, did he?"

"No. As I said, my observations weren't very keen because I was concentrating on the textbook and notes for lessons. I didn't see the man leave through the front door but could have missed—"

"Exactly. However, I'll tell the sheriff you were there that evening. He may want your testimony."

ooo

Thursday turned into another seventeen-hour day, minus a short break during which Wenona ate a good meal and rested her tired feet and legs. Jacob Capps had two meals at another waitress's station and smiled at her once from across the room. Her imagination went wild, creating visions of Carrie's situation that focused on Carrie being fed bread and water inside a grimy cage while being transported by railway back to Kansas. Wenona heard nothing more from Mr. Gerson and went to bed exhausted, only to again suffer nightmares and interrupted sleep punctuated by panic.

At seven o'clock in the morning, the night train pulled into the station but delayed releasing its well-rested, hungry passengers to partake of fluffy buttermilk pancakes, ham, eggs, flaky biscuits, and coffee at the Harvey House. Trying to serve all in a short time, the Harvey Girls, dressed in their impeccable long black shirtwaists and starched white aprons, dashed from table to table with grace and determination to return the continuing passengers to the train before departure time.

Wenona took a to-go order from a conductor for five of the famous double cheese sandwiches. "We had extra work at this stop," he told her, his words of complaint contradicted by the pride in his voice. "I helped guard a prisoner, and others were assigned to keep the passengers safe in their seats until the sheriff and his deputies arrived."

"Was it a dangerous desperado?"

152

"Ha. Not hardly. Just a skinny girl followed by three older people. It took time to set everything up like we was told, though. Now, we gotta eat our sandwiches on the train."

For the rest of the morning, Wenona worked while her stomach trembled and her mind raced. Would her friend have returned in the custody of three guards? Lawyers? Not familiar with rules regarding jail inmates, she pondered how she might be allowed to talk to Carrie. She wondered if Mr. Gerson would help her, but by noon she'd heard nothing from him and worried that after she brought Mr. Capps the day before, he thought she was interfering and was reneging on his promise to keep her informed.

Locals ate lunch before the one o'clock train came in, but at twelve, well-dressed strangers sat at one of Wenona's tables. Visiting someone in town and staying at the hotel, she guessed, until she reached their table with water and coffee carafes and got a good look at the wispy woman, an older version of Carrie. In the well-dressed man, she saw nothing of Carrie but the strawberry blond hair, graying at the temples.

"You must be Miss Putnam's parents," Wenona ventured as she filled glasses and cups. "I'm Miss Yazzie, her good friend, and I don't believe she's guilty."

Both parents looked startled, and it took a long moment and clearing of his throat for Mr. Putnam to respond. "Yes, yes. Thank you." He glanced around and spoke with quiet dismissal. "We'd rather not discuss this in public. You understand."

Wenona nodded and took their orders without another word about the subject. But later, as she refilled their cups, she whispered, "I have some evidence of your daughter's innocence that the investigators don't know."

"We don't need help from a—" Mr. Putnam started with a scowl on his face.

His wife stopped him with a hand on his sleeve. "We need all the help we can get." She turned to Wenona. "Everyone here seems to think she is guilty of this horrible crime. They're so convinced she killed the chef that they won't let us post bail. Please, Eugene, let's let this person—this friend—talk to our lawyer."

Late that afternoon, the Philadelphia lawyer and Carrie's parents met Wenona and Jacob at the jail. The sheriff gave them the privacy of his small sitting room with its plank table and stone fireplace. He pulled a bench in from the outer office for extra seating. It wasn't often he needed to provide space for a wealthy Eastern lawyer to conduct business.

As he ushered the tiny young prisoner into the room, the sheriff announced, "I'm assigning a deputy to guard this door," and then left when no one at the table gave him a glance.

Dismayed, despite the fancy clothing, at how small and haggard her friend looked, Wenona hugged her and told her she was a sight for sore eyes. The lawyer allowed Wenona to introduce Jacob, and invited him to tell what he'd seen the night of the murder.

Carrie nodded. "Yes, the man I argued with is my—*was* my intended. He came to convince me to go back home with him, but I refused."

"Did he follow you into the kitchen?" Wenona asked.

"Yes." She lowered her chin to her chest and spoke so that they could barely hear her. "When I went for the pie, he came in behind me, grabbed my shoulders, and tried to force me to listen. Chef George was cutting up a chicken for the next day and came toward us to intervene. I broke away from Richard and fled to George to protect me. But—but I ran into his arm, and the knife he held pierced through his apron. I panicked, and Richard caught me around the middle. He squeezed me so hard against him that I must have passed out. The next thing I knew he was carrying me down the street. He told me the chef was dead—that I had murdered Chef George."

Wenona looked around the table. Carrie's parents looked grim, and the lawyer was nodding in agreement as if they'd all heard this before. Jacob wore a slight frown.

"I don't think the weight of your body would drive a knife far enough into his chest to kill him, and why would he come toward you with a butcher knife pointed toward his own heart?" Wenona looked at Jacob.

"The laws of physics suggest that story would be improbable," Jacob confirmed.

154

"I don't remember anything after George grunted and I tried to help him. Richard says I went crazy and stabbed him several times."

Wenona watched Carrie put her hand to her forehead and rub her temples and had a sudden vision of the chef lying on the kitchen floor with the knife sticking out of his chest. "Carrie," she said and waited until her friend looked at her, "you are right-handed, aren't you?"

Carrie dropped her right hand to look at it, as if to bring the out-of-nowhere question into focus. "Yes."

"The person who killed Chef George must have been left-handed. The knife went into George's heart from his right side. The handle tilted to the right. In order to have enough force, a right-handed person facing him would have to stab the heart from George's left." She showed them what she meant by using a willing Jacob as a target for her index finger.

They looked at her. "My left-handed grandfather killed sheep for mutton," she explained.

The lawyer shuffled through black-and-white photos of the crime scene, photos the sheriff had handed him with pride for being up-to-date in crime investigation. "She's correct. To leave the knife in this position, Miss Putnam would have had to strike in an awkward, backward manner. I'm not saying it's impossible, but it wouldn't be a posture of strength."

"And there were several knifings, all from the same angle," Wenona said, "all from the front."

"Richard is left-handed, I believe," Mrs. Putnam said, wide-eyed.

"How did Richard convince you to return home with him?" Jacob asked Carrie.

"He didn't. I would have stayed to confess, but Richard made me take a sleeping draught and put me to bed in the room he had hired. The next morning, while I was groggy, he dressed me in travel attire he'd purchased, including a veiled hat, and we took the first train going east. With the drugs in my system, I didn't have the wits or the strength to fight. On the way home, he threatened to tell my parents that we had been intimate if I confessed to the killing. It wasn't true, but I knew people would believe him."

She sniffed. "I didn't have the energy to try to convince my parents, but I intended to come back and confess as soon as I could. Of course, Richard called off our engagement after the police found me."

"He kidnapped you, drugged you, and blackmailed you. It's clear he also killed the chef and placed the blame on you," Jacob pronounced.

Later that day, after a conversation with the lawyer, the sheriff looked at the crime scene photos again and agreed to charge Carrie's kidnapper with the crimes. Carrie finished her year's contract as a Harvey Girl and signed up for a second year while her erstwhile fiancé went to prison.

Joyce Ann Brown, the author of the *Psycho Cat and the Landlady Mystery* series set in Kansas City, was a librarian, a story teller, a landlady, and a Realtor before becoming a short story and novel writer. She also has two mischievous cats. Joyce spends her days writing (with a few breaks for tennis, walking, writing groups, and book clubs) so that Beth, the landlady in her mystery series, and Sylvester, the Psycho Cat, can solve heinous crimes.

Her books and stories have won awards in Kansas and Oklahoma, a Summer Indie Book Award in 2016, and was a Wishing Shelf Award finalist, 2017. Joyce's short stories and articles have been published in local and national publications, including the *Kansas City Star* and *Kings River Life Magazine*. She is a member of Sisters in Crime and several writers' groups in the Kansas City area. Read more about the author and her works at http://www.joyceannbrown.com.

TOGAS AND TOQUES

BY ALAN ORLOFF

Detective Steven Baker stared at the lifeless body sprawled on the floor. The deceased was male, about fifty years old, wearing sandals and a blood-red stained toga. He'd called himself Jacques Caesar.

Baker turned to his junior partner, Patrice Cook. "Cause of death?"

Cook shook her head. "Nothing definite. Witnesses say he sampled the sauce on the stove, started talking about how funny it tasted, then keeled over about thirty seconds later, bringing the whole pot down with him."

Baker touched his own shirt. "So on the toga, that's not…"

"Blood? Nope. Raspberry sauce. One of the chefs— Armand Forillo, the one who made the sauce—is convinced it's been poisoned."

"Oh?"

"Said he felt responsible for a guy getting killed tasting his sauce, so he went back over the ingredients. Detected something funky with the sugar he used. M.E. seems to agree, thinks it might be poisoned. It's being sent to the lab as we speak."

"Good," Baker said. "Ever seen *Caligula's Cooking Coliseum?*"

"No. I'm not into cooking shows."

Baker nodded to a man and a woman dressed like ancient Romans, standing off to one side, watching the medical examiner do his thing. "See those two, wearing the togas and toques?"

"Toques?" Cook asked.

"Chef's hats."

"Who are they?"

"The gladiators. In the Cooking Coliseum, two professional chefs compete to make the best meal. Then the Emperor judges the meals with a thumbs up or thumbs down. Winner gets twenty-five grand. Jacques Caesar was the flamboyant host."

Baker pointed to the other side of the set where an obese man dressed in a fancy purple toga trimmed with gold piping was perched on an elaborate throne atop a wide-based marble pedestal. He fiddled with his phone, seemingly unperturbed by the fatal incident. "That's Caligula himself."

"Caligula?"

"The infamous emperor prone to excess," Baker said.

Cook shrugged. "It's all Greek to me."

"Caesar's dead, so I guess we have to find our Brutus," Baker said. "First we need to determine if he was the intended subject. Who's in charge around here, anyway?"

"Showrunner's name is Lalique Robbins. She's in her office waiting for us."

"I'll question her. You find out who had access to the tainted sugar, and see if all of it was contaminated, or just that chef's. Be sure to separate the contestants, and keep them away from Caligula. We need to check everyone's story independently. Oh, and don't let anybody taste anything else."

ооо

Baker found Robbins's office located off a hallway adjacent to the large kitchen set. A shelf of cookbooks covered one wall, and a computer occupied half of a gray institutional desk. When Baker knocked on the open door, Robbins looked up from her computer. "Come in. Have a seat."

Baker lowered himself into a molded plastic chair, which was more uncomfortable than it looked. "I'm Detective Baker. Hell of a thing, huh?"

"You said it. Terrible. Of course, if we ever aired it, we'd kill in the ratings." As soon as she said it, her face contorted. "Oh God, sorry about that. Just slipped out."

Baker's eyes narrowed. People reacted to death differently. He soaked it all in, but tried not to let unusual reactions get in the way of the facts. "Any idea what happened?"

"Like I told your partner, Jacques tasted the sauce, then collapsed shortly thereafter. Everyone's saying poison." She arched an eyebrow.

"Anyone have a grudge against the victim?"

"Jacques? No. He was a bombastic sweet goof, but everybody loved him. Except for his three ex-wives, I guess." Her lips quivered. "I especially loved him because he got us great ratings. He and Caligula are—were—quite a pair. They carried the show, for sure. Without Jacques, though..." She shook her head somberly, eyes moist.

"Was it typical for him to go around tasting the food while it was being prepared?"

Robbins wiped her eyes. "Sorry. It's hard to believe he's gone."

"It's okay. Take your time."

She forced a smile. "I wouldn't say it was typical for him to taste someone's dish. But not totally out of left field. That's one of the things that made him a great performer. His unpredictability. Of course, it drove the camera operators crazy trying to anticipate his next move."

"If Jacques hadn't tasted the food, it would have gone to the judge next, right?"

"That's correct."

"So maybe Jacques wasn't the intended target. Maybe it was Caligula." Baker examined Robbins's face, looking for any telltale signs of guilt, but saw none.

"Maybe."

"He have any enemies?"

Robbins laughed. "The only person who *didn't* despise Caligula—real name Daniel Mossenberg—was Jacques. Daniel is just as bombastic, except that instead of being sweet like Jacques, he's sour. He grates on everyone's nerves."

"That doesn't pare things down," Baker said.

"Sorry, but it's the truth."

"Who had access to the sugar?"

"Anyone, really. The crew. The two competitors, Terri Kent and Armand Forillo. Jacques. Daniel. Me."

"We'll get statements from everybody. Any chance to review the tape?"

"I figured you'd want to see the footage, so I've got some cued up to the appropriate segment." She swiveled the computer monitor so they both could see, then clicked the mouse. "And...action."

Baker watched the screen as the camera focused on Jacques in close-up. He was just coming back from a commercial with a recap of the action. The contestants were tackling the final round—dessert. Gladiator One, Terri Kent, was making a bread pudding, while Gladiator Two, Armand Forillo, was constructing a raspberry almond tart. After a few lame jokes he milked too long, Jacques strolled from his spot next to Caligula's throne to Forillo's cooking station. He grabbed a wooden spoon from a container full of utensils and dipped it into a pot on Forillo's stove. Then licked it clean.

"Well, that's..." Jacques's stagey smile faded. "Ugh. That...that's just..." He stuck out his tongue a few times, trying to get the bad taste out of his mouth. "Something's not quite right with that sau-, sau-, sauce." Wild eyes gazed at Forillo, who stared back at him, then Jacques's eyes rolled back into his head. He dropped the spoon and stumbled against the stove, finally falling, grabbing the pot's handle as he tumbled to the ground. Red sauce spewed everywhere.

Forillo rushed to his aid, followed quickly by others. The camera captured the chaos, people screaming and running everywhere. Robbins could be heard in the background shouting, "Keep rolling." Another voice yelled, "Call 911."

Robbins clicked the mouse and the action on the screen froze. She tossed an embarrassed look at Baker. "About that 'keep rolling' order. I, uh, just wanted to make sure we had a visual record of everything that happened."

Baker stared at her for an extra beat. "Sure." He nodded at the screen. "Can you play it again, but this time rewind farther? Maybe we can get lucky and see something that will shed more light on what happened."

Robbins clicked around a bit, then settled back into her chair. "Raw footage, right from the beginning."

Baker saw Robbins from the back giving last minute instructions to the two competing gladiators. Then she stepped out of the frame, and the camera zoomed in on Jacques Caesar as he launched into the show's introduction. The competitors were spotlighted, followed by a flowery tribute to Caligula amid a trumpet fanfare fit for, well, an emperor.

"Hey, it's reality TV. It's supposed to be over-the-top," Robbins said, almost apologetically.

Baker watched as the show progressed but didn't spot anything suspicious. When the show broke for commercial, he leaned back.

"Keep watching," Robbins said. "We roll right through the breaks. Sometimes the competitors say outrageous things when they don't realize the cameras are on. We turn off their mics so they have the illusion of privacy, but we leave some of the other set mics on. We use whatever we can to put together an entertaining show for our viewers. Like I said, this is reality TV. It's just as much about the competitors themselves as it is about the cooking."

As soon as the break started, both competitors went straight for their phones. Terri Kent seemed to scroll through a few items, then stuffed the phone back into a pocket under her toga. Forillo, back to both the camera and to Kent, was talking on his. After a few moments, he hung up and stowed his phone, too.

For a while, nothing happened. Then, as if cued by someone else, Kent stalked over to Forillo, put her finger in his face, and said something. Forillo's nostrils flared, and he barked something back at Kent. One of the studio mics picked up a woman's voice saying, "I'll kill you."

"Wow, she's boiling mad." Robbins shook her head. "That would have made for great drama."

"I guess that qualifies as outrageous," Baker said. "We'll see what Ms. Kent has to say about that."

Baker watched the rest of the recorded show again, but nothing sprang out at him. When Robbins stopped the playback, she sighed. "Damn Jacques. If only he'd followed stage directions a little better, he'd still be alive." She sighed again, longer and louder. "Where am I going to find a suitable replacement? I mean, what fast-talking celebrity is going to want to play second fiddle to Caligula and parade around in a toga? I've got some mighty big sandals to fill."

Baker bit back a snarky comment. "Thanks, Ms. Robbins. I have just one more question. Don't most chefs, at least those worth their weight in salt, taste their food before serving it?"

Robbins nodded slowly. "Yes, they do."

"That's what I thought." Baker got up to leave. "That's what I thought."

000

In a quiet corner of the set, Baker conferred with Cook. "I watched the incident. It certainly looks like Caesar got poisoned by the sauce. But I don't think he was the intended target."

Cook nodded. "Then who? Caligula?"

"You might think so, since he's the one to judge the meal. But most chefs taste their food before serving it, so the intended victim could very well be Forillo." Baker pointed to one of the counter workstations where Terri Kent sat on a stool by herself. "Twenty-five grand is a big incentive. Why don't you take her and I'll question Forillo?"

"I'm on it," Cook said.

000

Baker borrowed Robbins's office to interrogate Forillo. The chef had removed his toque to reveal a nearly bald head, now glistening with perspiration. If they'd been in the studio, Baker might attribute the profuse sweating to the hot stage lights. Now, it was plainly nerves.

"Hell of a thing," Baker said.

"You're telling me?" Forillo wiped a red-checked kerchief over his head. "I can't believe my sauce killed him. If word gets out, it'll ruin my business."

"It wasn't your cooking. It was poison."

"Not everyone will make that distinction." Forillo frowned.

"Tell me what happened."

162

"The tart was in the oven, the sauce was reducing on the stove, and I was about to make some whipped cream to top things off when Jacques came over, hamming it up for the cameras. That's his shtick. He sampled the sauce, then started complaining about how it tasted. I tried to tune him out and concentrate on what I was doing, but the next thing I knew he was on the floor. I tried to help him, but..." Forillo closed his eyes for a second, as if reliving the moment. "After the initial hubbub subsided, I went over to examine the ingredients. The sugar wasn't quite right, I could tell."

"But you couldn't tell when you were making the sauce?"

"We have strict time limits, so I was in a hurry. Besides, I had no reason to suspect anything was wrong with the sugar. At a glance, it didn't look weird."

"Have any enemies who would like to see you dead?"

"Me? No." He played with the kerchief, folding and unfolding it. "You think someone was trying to kill me?"

"Chefs taste their food before serving. You're a likely target."

"I've been stewing on that, but...." He sighed. "I own a successful restaurant. I'm sure there are people who would like to see me fail. And I guess things would go downhill quickly if I died."

Especially for you, Baker thought.

"Unfortunately, I can't think of anyone specifically who's out to get me."

Baker nodded. "Who did you call during the break in the filming?"

"Huh? Nobody."

"The cameras were rolling, and you made a call."

"It was nothing." Forillo's head glistened again.

"Stop waffling. You're involved in a murder investigation. If you don't answer my questions, I'll think you're hiding something."

"I'm not hiding a thing. I called my sous chef, Jamal Weathers."

"Go on," Baker said.

"I wanted to ask him a question. About a dish. I wanted to know if he thought I should go with my signature raspberry almond tart, or with a new recipe, brown sugar brownies."

"What did he say?"

"Raspberry tart."

"Mind if I see your phone?"

Forillo rolled his eyes as he handed his phone to Baker. "Don't believe me?"

"Trust, but verify." Baker glanced at the phone and memorized Weathers's number. He handed the phone back to Forillo. "Do you have something against Caligula?"

"No."

"Have you ever met him before?"

"The restaurant scene in town is a tight circle. I've known Daniel for years. We both own restaurants that compete in the same space."

"And whose is more successful?"

Forillo smiled. "Depends on who you ask."

"I'm asking you."

His smile dimmed. "For a long time, everyone was chasing him. I think it's fair to say that in the last year or so, my restaurant has moved past his. New ideas beat stodgy ones when it comes to cutting edge dining. And Daniel is burnt out."

"What were you and Terri Kent arguing about?"

Forillo's head jerked back, involuntarily. "What?"

"During a break in the taping you exchanged words. She threatened you, right?"

Forillo hesitated. "No." He stared at Baker. "Not really."

"I think you're going to have to explain that."

Forillo exhaled. "Like I said, the restaurant scene is pretty small. Terri and I used to see each other. Years ago. Things didn't end well."

"Why does she want to kill you?"

"She doesn't. She just has a bit of a temper. And a long memory. A real long memory."

ooo

Back on the set, Baker huddled with Cook. "What did Kent say?"

"She's a salty one, but I don't like her for it. No motive."

"Twenty-five G's is a lot of dough."

"Peanuts to her. Kent is loaded. Married a Wall Street wheeler-dealer last year. Got a house in the Hamptons and one in the Keys and one somewhere in Europe. Says she was planning to donate her winnings to a food pantry. In fact, she's pretty steamed the competition got called off. She wanted to slice her opponent to shreds."

"Literally? That might explain her threat to kill Forillo."

"That threat was phony. Says Robbins knew about her history with Forillo and put her up to it. Egged her on to stir the pot. Kent didn't mince any words. Realized it was a half-baked idea, but she went along anyway, trying to throw Forillo off his game so she could win."

"That doesn't sound like a recipe for success."

Cook shook her head. "According to Kent, stuff like this happens all the time on this show. Typical reality TV B.S."

"That's our role, Cook. Sifting through the B.S.," Baker said. "Do me a favor. Call Forillo's sous chef. Maybe there's something brewing at the restaurant that Forillo doesn't know about. Or something he's holding back." He recited Weathers's number from memory. "I'll grill Caligula himself. Assuming the great emperor will grant me an audience."

ǫǫǫ

Baker summoned Caligula from his throne, and they walked across the set to Robbins's office. No longer on his high pedestal, Baker pegged Daniel Mossenberg at about five-six. He still wore that ridiculous gold-trimmed toga and laurel wreath on his head. His silly-looking sandals slapped on the tiled floor.

When they were seated, Baker cleared his throat. "Hell of a thing, huh?"

"Indeed." Mossenberg pursed his lips.

"What do you have against Chef Forillo?"

165

"What do I have against him?" Mossenberg's jowly face shaded. "He poisoned the food he was going to serve me. You should be asking him what he has against me!"

"Forillo has been questioned, of course. Now I'm questioning you. So back to the question: What do you have against Forillo?"

Mossenberg's features tightened, then he broke into a cold grin. "He's a supercilious twit. Thinks he's the next great chef. An innovator. A genius."

"And is he?"

"He's a copycat trend follower. Flavor of the week. Small fry. I'll squash him, and he'll be gone from the scene in a year." Mossenberg all but huffed.

"You own competing restaurants. I understand that his has eclipsed yours in terms of popularity."

Now Mossenberg did huff. "Hardly. I'll admit his place has gotten some attention lately, but as I said, it's a flash in the pan. The Gashouse Grill has been around for fifteen glorious years. Restaurants like his sprout like mushrooms after a long rain, ten every year. And fall by the wayside just as fast. We're still standing. When he's got a track record as long as mine, then he can crow." Mossenberg tilted his head back and puffed himself up, as if he were actually Caligula.

"So maybe you decided to kill him."

"Ridiculous. I don't like him, but if I went after everyone I didn't like, I'd be too busy to do anything else."

"If you don't like him, how can you be fair when judging his meal?"

Mossenberg looked down his nose at Baker. "I would never tarnish my integrity by letting personal feelings get in the way of my judging. Besides, I wouldn't have had to lie about his food being horrid, because I'm sure it would have *been* horrid. Bordering on inedible. At least this incident means my palate will be spared."

Baker could see why Mossenberg might be the intended target. "Who would want to harm you?"

Mossenberg snorted. "Anyone who isn't a friend or family member, I should think. I play hard and I play to win. I can't help it if people's feelings—or pocketbooks—get pinched in the process."

"A list of names would be nice."

He waved his hand dismissively. "That's your job. The first and last name on my list is Forillo."

Baker met with Lalique Robbins again in her office. "I notice you have multiple cameras on the set."

"That's right."

"But I only saw the feed from one. What's on the others?"

"Different angles, reaction shots, other footage. We edit it into one tight package. I showed you the footage from the camera shooting the incident."

"Can I see everything you shot?"

"That would take a long, long time. How about if I cue up stuff from camera two? That should be a good place to start. Give me a few minutes to get you set up."

Robbins futzed around, and when she was ready, she got up from her desk. "You can sit here and view it yourself. I've synched the footage from cameras one and two so you can watch them side-by-side." She showed him how to control the playback. "I'll be in the office next door trying to figure out how to replace the irreplaceable Caesar. Just holler if you have any questions."

Baker hit play and watched the footage from both cameras. The feed from camera one, which he'd already seen, was mostly focused on the competitors. The other camera featured Jacques Caesar as he cavorted on the set, but it also showed Caligula from time-to-time, getting his reaction to whatever the chefs—and Jacques—were doing. Baker didn't see anything noteworthy leading up to the poisoning.

Baker slowed the playback so he could watch the incident in slo-mo. He concentrated on camera two, the one shooting Caligula. Baker viewed the whole incident, then rewound and examined it again. Something caught his eye.

He watched it one more time, to confirm his suspicions.

Baker clicked the stop button and rose. He'd seen enough.

167

000

Baker caught up with Cook on the set. "Did you speak to Weathers?"

"He didn't answer his cell," Cook said. "But I called the restaurant and spoke to his assistant. Chatty fellow, too. Said there was a rumor that Weathers wanted to jump ship."

"And?"

"And Forillo wouldn't let him leave. Seems Weathers signed a non-compete clause preventing him from working for another restaurant in town for a year after he left."

"Interesting. Did this assistant say where Weathers wanted to go?"

"Nope, just that he was convinced some other restaurant owner was trying to poach him."

Baker smiled. *Et tu, Weathers?*

000

Ten minutes later, Baker called Mossenberg and Forillo to Robbins's office.

"More questions?" Mossenberg asked. "Is that really necessary? I've told you all—"

Baker held up his hand. "This won't take long."

Mossenberg slumped back in his chair, simmering.

Baker addressed Forillo. "I understand that your sous chef, Jamal Weathers, wants to leave."

Forillo squirmed in his seat. "That's right. He came to me about a month ago, asked to be released from his non-compete clause."

"And?"

"I told him he was too valuable to let loose."

"Did he say where he wanted to go?"

"No, he didn't," Forillo said. "He wasn't happy about my decision at first, but I think he's gotten over it. I'm a very generous and caring employer, you know."

Mossenberg snorted.

Forillo jutted his chin out. "I'm a better employer than you are, that's for sure!"

Mossenberg smirked at him. "Is that so? Then why did Weathers want to leave?" He paused, for effect. *One beat. Two beats.* "And come work for me?"

"What? That's ridiculous. Why would he want to work for someone like you?" Forillo made a face that looked like he'd just eaten a few bad oysters.

"Simple, really. Because you're a lousy chef, and I am a great one."

Forillo's face turned beet red.

"Calm down, everyone," Baker said. "I thought it might be illuminating if we watched the footage together. Maybe we can determine what really happened. I've cued it up to the incident."

Mossenberg and Forillo scowled at each other and grunted, then directed their attention to the monitor.

"Here we go." Baker started the playback.

The footage from camera two rolled. Focused on Mossenberg, it showed him watching the chefs as they prepared their desserts. Twenty seconds later, his eyes grew large and panic flashed across his doughy face. A moment later, he recovered.

Baker stopped the video. "You seemed upset there."

"Of course I was upset. Horrified. I was watching a man die!"

"Well, that would explain it," Baker said. "Hold on a sec, though." He clicked the mouse a few times and a split-screen image appeared on the monitor. "Let's watch the two feeds side-by-side." He hit play.

Camera one showed the incident; camera two showed Mossenberg's reaction.

Baker froze the action just as Mossenberg's face reflected his panic. "If you'll notice, on the feed from camera one, Jacques is just putting the spoon up to his mouth. He hasn't tasted the poisoned sauce yet." Baker turned to Mossenberg. "But as you can see, on camera two, you are clearly agitated about something."

Mossenberg blanched. "Well, I, uh. There must be some mistake. The two feeds are out of synch. Obviously."

Baker pointed to the time stamps in the upper right hand corner of each video frame. "Nope. Same exact time. You were panicked knowing what was *about* to happen. You knew the sauce was poisoned. Because you poisoned it. And an innocent man was about to taste it."

"You bastard!" Forillo shouted, leaping to his feet. "You pompous slimebag! You tried to kill me!"

Baker reached out and grabbed Forillo's forearm. "Please put a lid on it. He'll be dealt with. The judicial system doesn't look kindly on murderers."

Forillo sank into his chair, searing.

Mossenberg glanced at Forillo, then at Baker, then fixed his gaze at a spot on the wall over Baker's shoulder.

"Weathers was in on it wasn't he?" Baker asked Mossenberg. "When Forillo called him to ask which dessert to make, Weathers made sure he chose the one using the white sugar, didn't he?"

Mossenberg remained mum.

Baker continued. "Who would suspect mighty Caligula? In fact, you had a fall guy—gal, actually—lined up. Knowing that Robbins pitted Kent against Forillo to create bogus TV drama— and with their history—you figured that Kent would be a logical suspect in Forillo's death. And with Forillo out of the picture, you'd get rid of a competing restaurateur *and* get yourself a new sous chef. Two birds with one cleaver. Care to comment, *Emperor?*"

Mossenberg refused to meet Baker's eyes. "I want my lawyer."

"Sure, but it won't do you much good," Baker said. "You're toast."

Alan Orloff's debut mystery, DIAMONDS FOR THE DEAD, was an Agatha Award finalist. His seventh novel, RUNNING FROM THE PAST, was a winner in Amazon's Kindle Scout program. His short fiction has appeared in JEWISH NOIR, *Alfred Hitchcock Mystery Magazine*, CHESAPEAKE CRIMES: STORM WARNING, *Mystery Weekly*, 50 SHADES OF CABERNET, and WINDWARD: BEST NEW ENGLAND CRIME STORIES 2016. www.alanorloff.com

NOIR AT THE SALAD BAR

SLEEPING BEAUTY

BY GERALD ELIAS

It was almost exactly three years ago when Leonard and I lunched at Gregory's, the posh—some call it staid—eatery on Manhattan's Upper West Side. I had all but forgotten about the remarkable event that took place there that day, but once my memory was reawakened, which it had been—jarringly—just this afternoon, all the improbable details flooded back in. It was like the experience we've all had when, after years of random accumulation, we clean out a closet and unearth a dust-covered carton labeled *Snapshots*. You pry open the top, and after sorting through a few faded photos, that long-forgotten Caribbean vacation or Grandpa's eighty-fifth birthday celebration suddenly seems like yesterday. That's what happened to me today. Except it wasn't a celebration.

A symphony tour was the occasion that had brought us to New York three years ago. Eating a heavy dinner right before having to play an even heavier concert has always made me feel dangerously lethargic, so Leonard and I opted for a substantial midday meal instead. Leonard ordered Gregory's "world famous" trout almondine and I a salad niçoise; not as famous, perhaps, but very nicely done with fresh seared tuna, French string beans, new potatoes that actually had flavor, and anchovies that weren't overly salty. The restaurant's ambiance offered the intimate tinkling of high quality china and stemware, laid out on crisply laundered white linen tablecloths with polished silverware that had the proper amount of heft. The waiters, dressed in black trousers and white shirts, were always at the ready but never intrusive, the way waiters should be. Subdued, polite conversation blended with understated, piped-in selections of well-known light classical music: Strauss, Tchaikovsky, Pachelbel. The usual mix. As veteran symphony musicians, Leonard and I had performed all of it more times than we cared to, and reminisced over some of the more hilariously disastrous renditions we'd been involved in. From time to time, we couldn't help but laugh out loud and, as you may have experienced—say, at a wedding or, worse yet, a funeral—the more inappropriate the setting for laughter, the harder it is to hold it in. We tried our best to keep it under wraps, confident we hadn't disturbed any of the other patrons.

Sitting alone at the table behind Leonard was a gray-haired woman, her back to us. She was a bit disheveled, at least for Gregory's, dressed in a fur-trimmed, off-pink woolen suit that might have been expensive when it was new, but whose color was now decidedly faded. While Leonard was telling me yet another uproarious yarn, this one about a conductor's pants falling down in the middle of Beethoven's "Missa Solemnis," I noticed the woman buttering a piece of toast. Actually, I must only have become aware of that in retrospect, but that is what she must have been doing in order for what followed to have unfolded as it did.

Our waiter—young, trimly built, and I suppose darkly handsome in an Eastern European sort of way—having observed the woman's empty coffee cup, approached her with a silver carafe. As he began pouring, the woman became highly agitated, yelled something venomous at him, and raised her knife. I had never before experienced that oft-recorded sensation of watching an event take place in a split second that seemed to stand still in time. I knew without a doubt what was about to happen, but in that snapshot of a moment, which suddenly seemed to be one of exquisite silence, I was immobilized, powerless to prevent it from transpiring.

The woman plunged her knife into the waiter's arm. His cry broke my spell. Time began to move again and I was roused from my paralysis. Many of the patrons, Leonard and myself included, rushed to the waiter's aid. The woman, who had been so violent just a moment earlier, slumped back in her chair and closed her eyes in resignation until the police arrived. She offered no resistance when they escorted her from the premises. She looked neither to the left nor the right, gazing only straight ahead, not so much to avoid everyone's stares, but more as if she were unaware of anyone else's presence; as if her gaze was directed into time and not space. A physician among the patrons treated the waiter on the scene and declared the wound to be superficial. The restaurant returned to its equilibrium and, by the time Leonard and I demolished a shared dessert of Strawberries Romanoff, the singular incident we had so recently witnessed seemed almost to have never happened.

The next day, when I read the story in the *Times*, I was astounded by the headline: *Imogen Stansted Implicated in Restaurant Altercation.* My first thought was, could it be *the* Imogen Stansted? My second thought was, how many Imogen Stansteds could there be in this world? I had only to read the first sentence to confirm it was indeed *the* Imogen Stansted who several years before had precipitously resigned from her lofty position as prima ballerina of the Royal Ballet. Who, at the peak of her brilliant career, had inexplicably fled from celebrity on the world stage and entered into a life of seclusion. Still, could it be that the stout, slope-shouldered, elderly woman I saw the day before had, in a matter of just a few years, so aged from the lithe, athletic, poetic presence she once was?

A week later, the Times published a follow-up. Imogen Stansted, seeking to avoid the harsh glare of a trial, pleaded no contest to a lesser assault charge, though no explanation was ever provided for why she attacked the waiter. Her lawyer simply attributed it to "erratic behavior," for which Madam Stansted was "unconditionally remorseful." The judge suspended her sentence, the result of her previous spotless record, her former fame, and her reduced circumstances, but required her to seek counseling. With no scandal attached to the story, it soon faded from public view. And so, after three years, did my memory of it.

000

This morning we were again in the city for a pair of mid-week concerts at Carnegie. Our plan for a brisk walk around the Central Park reservoir was thwarted when it began to rain by the time we hit Fifty-Ninth Street. As I had left my umbrella in my hotel room, Leonard continued without me, and even though it was too early for lunch I ducked into one of those trendy farm-to-table cafés that requires you to sit with strangers on uncomfortable, faux rustic wooden benches. With a backdrop of Mozart's "Eine Kleine

Nachtmusik" on the café's speakers, I ordered a croque monsieur and cappuccino—no cocoa powder, thank you—and eyed the seating prospects. No familiar faces and no lovely young ladies with a space next to them. Roaming off-leash at one end of the café was a gaggle of obnoxiously entitled toddlers, enabled by see-no-evil, hear-no-evil parents. I carried my lunch to the opposite end, where there was a vacancy opposite a nicely dressed older woman absorbed in a bowl of lobster bisque. I had managed one leg over the bench when the woman looked up from her soup.

It was Imogen Stansted. I hadn't recognized her initially, partly because she actually looked younger than the previous time our paths had so briefly crossed three years earlier. Though my first instinct, that of self-preservation, was to retrieve my leg and flee, I tried not to betray my recognition of her. My ability to disguise my reaction obviously failed because Madam Stansted gave me a knowing smile. "I've seen that look often enough," she said. "Sit down. I'm not going to stab you."

I can say I was more than a bit relieved, not only by her words but also by her secure and confident demeanor. I apologized for my lack of courtesy, and little by little we engaged in pleasant and increasingly open conversation. I expressed admiration for her inspired dancing of the past, which clearly flattered her. When she found out that I was a professional musician, she mentioned a few names and it turned out we had some mutual friends. But then, my guard down, I made a bit of a faux pas when I blurted out that she looked much better than the last time I had seen her.

"And when was that?" she asked.

I confessed that I had been at the next table at Gregory's on the day of her attack and said that I felt almost as badly for her as for the poor waiter.

"That day was the nadir of my existence," she said. "And the days after, of course. The public humiliation was even worse than a jail sentence and I never thought I'd be able to show my face on the street again. But, out of that catastrophe I found out I had more friends than I thought, so there was a silver lining after all. And an expensive psychiatrist didn't hurt, either."

I wasn't sure how to respond. Should I apologize for having brought back the worst of bad memories, or congratulate her on her return to an existence which, if not the pinnacle of her glamorous career, at least—

"You want to know why I did it. Don't you?" she asked, mistaking the reason for my silence, which apparently had been longer than I thought.

"I wouldn't dream of asking," I said.

"But you still want to know. Everyone does."

"Yes. I suppose so."

"Well, I've never told anyone," she said, "because it's no one's business but mine. But fate seems to have brought us together twice now, and you're a musician, so maybe it was meant for me to finally tell someone."

I leaned forward.

"But first you must buy me a coffee," she said, almost coyly.

"My pleasure," I said. I was half-convinced her request was a ploy for her to vanish while I was gone, but when I returned she was sitting placidly, her hands folded on her lap. To my relief, though, the neighbors who had been within eavesdropping distance at our pretend farm table had departed.

Madam Stansted spun two spoonfuls of sugar into her cup with the delicacy of sand through an hour glass and stirred reflectively, as if the dark currents of her coffee would reveal hidden truths. Gazing into the cup, but not lifting it, she took a deep breath.

"When I was with the Royal Ballet," she began, "I had many dancing partners. One of them was Yuri Ivanov."

"Your collaborations were legendary," I said, as encouragement.

"Well, more than legendary," she replied, and looked up at some image unseeable to all but herself. "But I'll get to that a little later.

"As you know, male ballet dancers are often referred to as 'furniture movers' because, for all the world, one of their main tasks is to haul us ballerinas from point A to point B. Gracefully, if they're capable. I won't bore you with all the terminology, but for many of them that really is essentially the limit of their capability.

"Yuri was different. He was an amazing athlete and an amazing artist."

"His leaping was legendary," I said, not able to think of a different word than legendary again. But it was, in fact, legendary.

"Yes, yes, leaping, of course," she said dismissively. The swan-like hand gesture that accompanied her comment made it clear what a consummate artist she had been and how out of my depth I was. "That's what gives the audience its cheap thrills. But Yuri had a combination of grace and strength that was absolutely unique. And so dependable. I would have jumped off a cliff, knowing he would catch me at the bottom. Such a calming influence."

Again, her gaze went heavenward.

"Until I started working with Yuri I was a nervous wreck," she said, coming back to earth.

"One would never have known that from your stage presence," I said. "You were always so...regal." I had almost said legendary again.

"And that's as it should be. But you should have seen me in the wings. I would break down from the smallest flaw in my performance. I would throw up between numbers. I can't tell you how many times I had to have my makeup reapplied during intermissions because of the tears.

"A lot of ballet dancers are chain smokers," she said, changing direction. "Did you know that?"

"No," I said. "I'm astonished. You'd think they'd need to keep their lungs in shape. Is it to reduce stress?"

"More to keep the weight down. But for me it was weight *and* stress. I was sure I was losing my stamina. My nerve. I didn't think I'd last another year. Until I met Yuri."

Imogen Stansted paused in her narrative. Though I was sitting opposite her and she was looking right at me I had a feeling she didn't see me at all.

"When he put his hands around my waist to lift me," she finally resumed, "I felt weightless, as if I were flying. I could feel his fingers through my costume meld into my body, finding the perfect balance points. We breathed together. I felt like the two of us were a single being. It gave me a confidence I never had with another partner. He gave me such assurance that I *knew* I would not fail. Not with Yuri. I felt as if I could go on forever. With Yuri, I could fly.

"We soon became lovers," she said without reticence. "I'd had lovers before, of course, but nothing like this. I had never been so happy in my life, either onstage or off. I had never danced as well, nor had the reviews ever glowed more brightly.

"One night, our last night, here in New York, we performed *Sleeping Beauty*. I adore Tchaikovsky ballets, don't you?"

"I agree," I said, meaning it. "I think his ballets are his finest works."

"Yes," she replied. "They are so visual. So visceral. The audience screamed its head off after the waltz. You could hardly hear the orchestra. After the performance Yuri told me he had to meet with his manager and I should wait for him at the Essex—we had adjoining suites. As I was getting out of my costume, he kissed me on the neck. Here."

She touched a very precise spot just above her collarbone with a subtly dramatic index finger—the manicured nail, long, tapered, and red—where it remained, almost nostalgically, for several seconds.

"I was halfway back to the hotel when I realized I had left my purse in the rehearsal room. So I returned to the theater. The rehearsal room was locked. I went to the security desk where I found someone with a key to open it for me.

"He opened the door and turned on the lights, and there, against a pillar in the center of the room, were Yuri and a first-year girl from the corps de ballet. They were half-naked and rutting like farm animals. At first they tried to hide around the back of the pillar but, you see, the entire room was mirrored. So there was no hiding. I saw them from every angle, all at once."

How was I to respond to that? I had no idea, so I said nothing.

"Do you know what they did next?" she asked, looking me directly in the eye. But I knew she did not expect an answer, so I didn't offer one. I think I might have shaken my head.

"Protestations of innocence?" she continued. "No. Abject apologies? No. 'All a terrible misunderstanding?' No."

Madam Stansted finally took a sip of coffee.

"Cold," she said.

When I looked at her questioningly, she said, "The coffee."

She paused, as if waiting for some internal decision whether or not to continue.

"What they did was to laugh," she said, still looking right at me. "The two of them snickered. Like drooling, lascivious hyenas. In front of me and the security man.

"I shut the door and left the ballet world behind me. It was the end. I knew that immediately. Do you understand? There was no choice."

Imogen Stansted took a deep breath, picked up a spoon, toyed with her coffee, and put the spoon back down again with finality.

"So there you have it," she said to me. "I can't say that it makes me feel better, though it is somewhat of a relief to get it off my chest after all these years."

"And if I've been of any help in that regard," I said, "I feel very, very honored. And you can be assured I'll never mention this to anyone."

She brushed that notion aside with a flick of her articulate wrist. *Whatever*, it said.

"But, if you don't mind, I do need to ask you one question."

"Yes?" she asked. She seemed surprised, almost irritated. "Haven't I given you the blow by blow in sufficiently lurid detail?"

"Yes. Of course," I said. "But you haven't really explained why you stabbed the waiter in the arm."

She looked at me as if I were an absolute dolt.

"But you said you were a musician!" Stansted exclaimed. "I would have thought it would be perfectly clear to you!"

I apologized for still being in the dark.

"The music!" she said. "The music being played that moment at the restaurant was the waltz from *Sleeping Beauty*. And someone was laughing. Hideous, mocking laughter! It was intolerable. I was no longer in that restaurant. I was in the rehearsal room at the theater. When that waiter came to my table, I didn't

179

see a waiter. I saw Yuri. God forbid, I could have killed the poor boy had my aim been better. My psychiatrist told me the laughter must have been in my imagination—my memory of that horrid rehearsal room—triggered by the waltz. He said, "Why would anyone laugh at *Sleeping Beauty*?" Why, indeed? But it all seemed so real. So, so real. It was the laughter that made me do it."

At that moment I could have told Imogen Stansted that the laughter was by no means her fantasy. That is *was* real. I could have gone further and confessed that it was none other than me who had been laughing. That, in a real way, it was I who had spurred her to attack the waiter. That it was I who had caused her the pain and humiliation of the past three years. Yes, I could have confessed all those things.

"Music can make people do odd things," I said, lacking anything better. Was I a cad? I felt like one, but what was I to do?

She looked at me strangely. Maybe it was the way I said it. Or was it a sudden recognition of my critical role in her drama?

Imogen Stansted wrapped her exquisitely expressive fingers around the coffee spoon sitting on the wooden table. We both looked at her hand, then at each other. She released the spoon.

I hurriedly offered to pay her bill and mine.

"That won't be necessary," she said quietly. "You've already done quite enough for me."

She said, "*for* me." Did she mean, "*to* me"? Did she believe I had somehow helped her, or did I detect a cold undercurrent in her voice?

I shook her hand, thanked her for sharing her confidence, disentangled myself from the bench, and escaped into the street, where the rain had somewhat abated.

Gerald Elias, internationally acclaimed violinist and author, shines an eerie spotlight on the classical music world's shadowy corners with his award-winning Daniel Jacobus mystery series. In his unique audiobook, *Devil's Trill* (Alison Larkin Presents, 2017), Elias recorded his own musical clues. His short fiction and provocative essays have graced *Ellery Queen* to *Opera Magazine*, and have been included in several Level Best anthologies. https://geraldeliasmanofmystery.wordpress.com/

THE HEARTS OF MEN

BY KAREN CANTWELL

Briggs LeFoy had a thing for dill pickles. Tangy, crunchy, garlicky dill pickles.

And Junie Harken, well, she had a thing for Briggs LeFoy.

Everyone in Tucker Creek knew Junie made the best dill pickles in all of Swisher County. Not a soul knew she lusted after Briggs LeFoy.

The mantle clock in Junie's living room chimed twice as she scrubbed her swollen hands in the deep porcelain kitchen sink. She sang along with Frank Sinatra as he crooned her favorite song, "People Will Say We're in Love." The reception on her Zenith radio wasn't so good in the kitchen, but she enjoyed listening to music while she worked, so she tolerated the crackles.

After drying her hands, she stood a few moments in front of the fan. Brushing perspiration-drenched tendrils of hair from her face, she closed her eyes and thought of Briggs. He'd be by soon. Freshening up was in order. A quick, cool bath would do the trick.

Quick was the plan, only the water lulled Junie, floated her away to that paradise where even The Beast couldn't reach her. A rapping on the screen door brought her back to earth. "Mercy," she muttered, bruising a shin on her clumsy tumble from the tub. With a towel cinched in place, Junie pulled the bathroom door open a smidge. "Hello?"

"Uh, Miss Harken, ma'am," Brigg's sweet and juicy voice replied, "did I come at a bad time?"

"No, Briggs, it's all fine, honey. Come on in and sit. Just do me a favor and shut your eyes a minute. I'm finishing up a soak and not exactly dressed for company, if you get my meanin'."

"Uh, alright. Should I close my eyes now or before I sit?"

"You can sit first, silly."

She heard the chair creak. "You sittin'?" she asked, just to be sure.

"Yes, Miss Harken, ma'am."

"You call me Junie. I'm way too old to be called Miss no more. Your eyes closed now?"

"Yes, uh, Junie."

She scooted across the narrow hall to her bedroom. Junie adored her house, especially as she owned it outright, but the thing was about as big as a postage stamp. From her cracker box kitchen you could see into her bedroom, bathroom, and living room. The only thing you couldn't see from her kitchen was the cold cellar beneath. And the bedroom didn't even have a proper door, merely a curtain fashioned from some oriental silk fabric she'd bought from Ethel Wainwright for twenty cents when Ethel's grandmama passed last year. Ethel said she didn't want the fabric because it was Japanese, and she didn't want nothin' from no Japs around her house, no way, no how. Junie figured that was plain silliness. It coulda been Chinese for all they knew. Regardless, Japanese or Chinese, Junie thought it was real pretty so she sewed on some fringe and hung it on a rod.

"Okay, you can open your eyes now, Briggs." Junie wiggled and shimmied into her girdle. She stopped a moment to catch her breath and reassure her guest. "I won't be but a few minutes."

"You want I should bring those cucumbers in now?"

She harnessed her substantial bosom into a crisp, clean bra scented with lavender oil. "Don't worry about those cucumbers just yet. Tell you what, honey. Get yourself a glass. There's fresh lemonade in the icebox. Made it just for you." Junie checked her reflection in the mirror from one angle and then another. *These are the prettiest breasts in town,* she thought to herself, *or there ain't a cow in Texas.*

"Well, thank you," Briggs said. "Don't mind if I do."

Junie heard Briggs open the icebox. "You're bein' so kind, helpin' me out. Just my little way of payin' you back is all. Drink up." She had to wiggle and shimmy some more to fit the new dress over her head and down past her waist. Smoothing the fabric, she admired the red rose pattern before pinning her hair into a pretty bun, quickly curling wispy pieces with her finger, and letting them fall around her neck.

"What station is this you're listenin' to?" he asked.

Junie brushed on some rouge, then colored her lips with Jungle Red, brand new from Woolworth's. "It comes from Abilene. They play Tommy Dorsey, and Glenn Miller, and Frank Sinatra. I just love Frank Sinatra. His voice gives me goose pimples." She pulled back the oriental curtain with a touch of drama, like Rita Hayworth posing for a photo shoot. "In fact," she said, "you kinda remind me of Frank."

Slender, blue-eyed, luscious-lipped Briggs LeFoy stared at her, lemonade pitcher in one hand, pink glass in the other. "You goin' out somewhere, Miss Harken? I mean Junie?"

She slithered toward him, smiling. "Nah, just felt like dollin' up." She took the pitcher from his grip, brushing his hand most purposefully, and poured lemonade into the glass. "You're gonna love my lemonade. It's got a secret ingredient."

"What's that?" He sipped from the pink glass.

"It's a secret, I just told you. You're so funny, Briggs."

"I am?"

"Sit. Sit. You like that glass, Briggs?"

"Sure. It's pretty, I guess. Don't know much about glasses, except you drink out of 'em."

Junie pulled another kitchen chair close to Briggs and sat, crossing her legs. She shifted just enough so he could plainly see the flesh of her freshly-shaved calf. She desired to rub her bare foot all the way up Briggs' leg to his crotch where she'd feel his manliness grow solid like a log. Of course, she never moved that fast. *Baby steps, Junie*, she reminded herself. *Baby steps*. "I collected those glasses from laundry soap, can you believe it?"

Briggs nodded. "It's pretty funny what you can find in a box of soap these days."

"I got plates too." She reached for the pack of Camels in the middle of the table. "You want a smoke, honey?"

"Aw, I don't smoke. Never took to it."

She lit up, but courteously blew her smoke away from Briggs. "Seriously? You don't smoke? I thought all men smoked."

Briggs shrugged. "Just never took to it." He chugged the lemonade with the manners of a drunk chimpanzee.

The boy needed some work, Junie could see. But she had time. She had all the time in the world. She could train this one real good. "What kind of music do you like, sweetie?"

"Oh, I don't know. I like the simpler stuff, I guess. Ernest Tubb, Gene Autry." He stifled a burp. "If you want, I could go get those bushels now. You want 'em in here?"

"Not right now, I don't, Briggs." Smiling playfully, she clicked her fingernails and bounced her foot a little. "Can't you see I just like havin' your company?"

"Oh, okay." He set the glass on the table and played at appearing comfortable.

Resting the smoldering cigarette in the ashtray, Junie stood. "You know what my very favorite radio show is, Briggs?" She took a plate from the cupboard. "Every Sunday night I listen to *The Shadow*. You ever listen to that show?" She lifted three cookies from the cookie jar on the counter beside the sink and placed them on the plate. Sitting back down, she slid it in front of Briggs. "Snickerdoodles," she said.

He brightened at the offering, taking a cookie. "*The Shadow*, now that is a good show. I have to agree with you there." Crumbs dropped onto his lap as he bit down.

Lifting the cigarette, she recited the opening line with a low, growling voice. "Who knows what evil lurks in the hearts of men?" Her eyes widened and she slapped the table. "The Shadow knows!" She laughed, and took a drag, nice and slow.

"You do a fine impression," Briggs said, laughing some himself.

Growing quiet, Junie regarded Briggs as she picked a piece of tobacco from her tongue. "Why ain't you fightin' in the war, Briggs?"

"I'm Four-F—unfit. Asthma."

"That's too bad, ain't it?" She hoped her words came out sounding sympathetic, because they weren't truthful in the least. It wasn't too bad at all. She was happy as a clam at high tide that Briggs LeFoy had found his way to her kitchen door instead a marchin' through some swamp in the Pacific or shootin' up Nazis in France. "So what brings you travelin' through Tucker Creek?"

"On my way to Los Angeles. Hopin' to get a job at General Motors buildin' tanks. I want to do my duty in some way. Every man should."

"You said you're from McKinney?"

"In a manner of speakin'." Briggs paused, seeming to consider his next words carefully. "You seem like a kindly and understandin' lady—can I be truthful?"

"Briggs LeFoy, I wouldn't want you to be anything but truthful with me. You have no worries that I'd judge. What is it? You can tell Junie anythin'."

"It's just folks get kinda nervous when I say I move from place to place. Like I'm a crook or somethin'."

"But you ain't no crook, right?"

"No, ma'am."

"You got family?"

"A cousin or two in Arkansas, possibly."

Junie Harken felt like she'd just hit the pretty boy lottery. "How old are you, Briggs?"

"Nineteen in two days."

Lordy, he was a child. Well, that was no matter. Who cared if he was sixteen years her junior? Better that than marryin' some old geezer with a faulty appliance. Yes siree, Junie, she congratulated herself, you'll be a married woman in no time. No time at all.

Junie sat up straight and stamped out her cigarette in the ashtray. She pressed her hand against his thigh. "So, you want to see my pickles?"

000

Accessed from a concrete stairwell just outside the house, the cold cellar offered relief from the brutal July heat. Junie sighed. "Some days I wish I could just move down here."

"It's dark, ain't it?" asked Briggs, squinting.

"Dark as the devil's riding boots, as my mama used to say." Junie pushed the switch on her trusty Winchester flashlight. "No need for electricity since all I keep down here is my canned goods." She shone a beam of light on the wall nearest the cellar door. "There they are. Last year's batch. And two jars from the year before that. Those won't be as good." She handed Briggs the flashlight and selected a jar labeled 1942. She turned the lid until the seal popped. "I just had me some of these last week. Still pack a crunch. Here, try." She pressed an offering to his lips.

Recoiling from her advance, he took the dripping pickle in his hand and crunched it between his teeth.

He's a shy one, she thought, smiling to herself. She just wanted to eat him up. "Tasty, huh? You ever had a pickle as good as that one?"

"No, ma'am. She was right. You do make the best pickles."

"She?" Junie's voice cracked. She hoped Briggs hadn't been aware. "Who's this she you're talkin' about?"

"Do you know Eliza Chitwood?"

Did Junie know Eliza Chitwood? Little tramp. Half the teenage boys in Tucker Creek knew Eliza in the biblical sense. "I do," Junie said. "Nice girl. Well now, you polished that one off nicely, didn't you? Here, have another."

This time, Briggs intercepted Junie's sensual overture. She bristled. The Beast stirred. Screwing the lid back on, she tried to brush off her growing irritation and gave him the jar. "You can take this one back to the boardin' house with you." She tugged gently on his arm. "Come on back up, honey. You bring my bushels inside and I'll fix you some dinner. Got two pork chops ready to go."

Briggs dropped the flashlight and it clattered on the hard dirt floor. "I appreciate your generosity, Miss Harken, but I'm meetin' Eliza at the fairgrounds." When he lifted the flashlight from the damp floor its beam lit up the far corner opposite them. A short shelf. Five jars. "What you storin' over there?"

Miss Harken, Miss Harken. The name echoed in her ears. The Beast hated that name. Junie snatched the flashlight, casting the light back up the stairwell. "Pickled this and pickled that. I don't want to hold you up, honey, but why don't you come back tomorrow mornin' to help with the picklin'? I'll pay you for your time."

000

Picklin' day.

Junie was up before the cock crowed.

With her hair pinned back and her newly washed apron tied, she started in, cooking up a proper breakfast for Briggs. She needed to put some meat on that boy's bones—grow him into the man that would pleasure her in the manner she deserved. As the eggs sizzled on the stove, she imagined her plans for Briggs LeFoy. The sun was only a bare hint on the horizon when he banged on her screen door.

"What the heck are you knockin' for, Briggs? Don't we know each other better than that now?"

"Sure smells good, Junie," he said, removing his hat as he stepped in.

"Gotta have a big breakfast before we get to work. Get us through the day. There'll be no breaks once we get started. Hang your hat right there on the wall, honey." She pointed behind him.

She smiled at the sight of his hat hanging on her wall, like it belonged there. "You like grits?"

"Who don't like grits?"

"I met a man or two who didn't," she said, "but you're right. It's a crazy person who don't like grits with their eggs and bacon, am I right?"

They ate and they laughed. The day heated up until it was almost unbearable, but that didn't stop them. They boiled glass jars, readied cucumbers, washed dill, and measured vinegar and alum. Sometimes they listened to Frank Sinatra, and other times they listened to Ernest Tubb. The day was grand. When Junie's mantle clock chimed four times, they'd already placed the last pickle jar in the cellar and were relaxing in the kitchen, sipping icy cold glasses of lemonade.

Junie lit a cigarette and sized Briggs from the toes of his boots all the way to the small cowlick on the top of his wavy head of hair. Soon now. Soon she'd run her fingers through that hair while his hungry, eager hands groped her behind and his lips and tongue found the sweet spot on her neck.

"You ever think of stickin' around Tucker Creek, Briggs? You know, rather than movin' on?" She enjoyed a long drag.

He wiped his mouth, setting the empty glass back on the table. He gave a short nod. "Maybe."

Happily surprised, she blew smoke into the air above her. "Maybe? Really? You been thinkin' about that?"

"It's a nice place. I been thinkin' of lookin' for a more permanent job, some security. Hard to find in time o' war, especially in a small town like this. You know of anything?"

"I know for a fact they're hirin' at the mill."

"That's where you work, right?"

"I'll talk to the manager on Monday." She could tell she'd just made Briggs LeFoy very happy. He'd be so grateful in return. Feeling the warmth growing between them, she scooted her chair closer to his.

"Can I be so bold as to ask one more favor, Junie?"

Junie wanted Briggs in her bed. She fixated on his lips, imagining how they'd feel when she kissed them. "Honey, you can ask me any favor. I ain't likely to say no to you now."

"Could I have a couple of those fine red blossoms from your rose garden?"

Junie held her smile, but an ache set in her bones. "Of course you can. They struggle in this heat anyway. What you wantin' those roses for?"

"You promise you won't tell?"

"Cross my heart. Hope to die."

"They're for Eliza. She loves red roses."

Junie did hope to die. "Of course. What woman doesn't? Why the secret though?"

"She don't want her mama and daddy knowin' we're an item until I'm properly employed."

Junie nodded. An item. They were an item now. She cleared her throat. "You can take as many roses as you like. That Eliza, she's a lucky girl, now ain't she?" Junie stood, although her knees nearly buckled under her. "And I need to pay you for today, Briggs. Let me get my pocket book."

In her bedroom, with the silk curtain drawn to hide her agony, Junie grasped the edge of her dresser. She closed her eyes and took deep breaths, hoping to thwart The Beast.

"I can't thank you enough for all the kindness you've been showin' me, Junie!" Briggs called from the kitchen. "You truly are a friend to a man in need."

"Uh-huh!" she called back. "Don't think a thing of it." Deep breath. Deep breath.

But she'd been here before. Deep breaths never helped.

The Beast summoned.

"Oh, Briggs, honey?"

"Yeah?"

"I just realized, I think I left my apron in the cellar. Could you run down and get it for me? I'm likely to forget later if I don't fetch it right away."

"Glad to," he answered.

Junie heard the screen door slam.

Staring at the apron on her bed, she fought back tears as she lifted the mattress. She wrapped her fingers around The Beast: the familiar, bloodied steel pipe that was both savior and foe. And at the end of picklin' day, The Beast in hand, she followed Briggs LeFoy down the stairwell.

ρρρ

Junie Harken died alone in her home on a hot and blistering day in August 1965, just two days after pickling day, the town coroner estimated. Officers Cornish and Bruford entered her tiny house that day upon the request of the textile mill where she was employed. She'd missed several days of work, but hadn't called in sick.

Junie had no family to claim her body and the townspeople couldn't bring themselves to hold a funeral.

A common theme echoed as people talked of the circumstances surrounding Junie's demise: Her pickles were the best, but she always did seem a little odd.

She left behind a small but well-cared for house on two acres of land, an abundantly fertilized rose garden, an antique Zenith radio in working condition, a mantle clock that had been in her family for generations, a record player, and a cold cellar hiding thirteen jars of pickled human hearts.

There was a fourteenth jar as well. Not in the cold cellar.

For it seemed Junie played favorites. Somehow, one of those young men must have touched her more deeply than the others.

The record player was still on when Officers Cornish and Bruford pulled back the faded oriental curtain that served as Junie's bedroom door. The needle bounced endlessly against the center spindle. Lying in her bed, Junie Harken had departed this world listening to "They'll Say We're in Love" by Frank Sinatra. In her arms, she cradled a jar preserving the heart of the long-missing drifter, Briggs LeFoy.

Karen Cantwell enjoys writing both short stories and novels. Her stories have appeared in *Chesapeake Crimes: They Had it Comin'*, *Chesapeake Crimes: This Job is Murder*, and other short story anthologies. On the novel front, Karen loves to make people laugh with her Barbara Marr Murder Mystery series and Sophie Rhodes Ghostly Romance series. You can learn more about Karen and her works at www.KarenCantwell.com.

NOIR AT THE SALAD BAR

DEADLY DINNER

BY LD MASTERSON

I didn't take this job to kill anyone. Truth is I'm not much into violence. Don't even own a gun. I mostly just needed a job, and I'd done food prep before. A couple restaurants. Worked a school cafeteria once but I couldn't deal with those damn kids. This was my first nursing home. Pay wasn't great but they let me work the split shift so I got enough overtime, and the work was pretty basic...peeling and chopping. It's funny, I always hear about these fancy chefs, all guys, but every kitchen I ever worked, we guys got the prep work. The real cooking was done by the women.

I came in at four to start prepping for breakfast and lunch, then a three hour break and back at two to get ready for dinner. I just hung around during my break. The home was nicer than my one room apartment and who wants to be outside in the winter in Ohio.

But after a couple months I was looking for some fringe benefits. Spring Hill Home—which didn't have a spring and wasn't on a hill—was your basic senior-nursing home. Had some folks who weren't doing too bad and some who were just waiting around to die. More importantly, it had your Medicare patients and your full-pay types—the ones with plenty of money—and I'd pretty much figured out who was who. I could use my staff badge to wander around the place, see what I could pick up. The wealthy like their expensive trinkets, even in a place like this.

Then, I stumbled on a chance for a real score.

I was peeling potatoes, tossing the skinless spuds into a big pan for washing, and letting my mind wander. Peeling potatoes doesn't take a lot of brain power. The other prep cooks were chopping veggies and cutting up a mess of chickens. Marla, the head cook, was mixing some sort of batter when something beeped in her pocket. She pulled out a cell phone, muttered something under her breath, and pulled off her apron.

"You, Bixby," she said to me, "tell Mrs. Hendricks I'll be back in a couple." Then she hurried out of the kitchen without waiting for an answer.

It was the first time I'd been in the dietician's office. It was a dinky little thing off the kitchen where Hendricks matched the day's menu against each patient's special dietary needs and gave instructions on how to modify their meals. She was seated with her back to the door, so engrossed in what she was reading on her monitor she didn't hear me come in. Curious, I stood quiet and watched the screen. Some of the columns I understood, like low sodium meant no salt, but there were a couple other columns…big words. I mean big. Like supercalla-whatever big. And lots of numbers and letters. Then I saw a word I knew: Warfarin. That was a blood thinner. My old man used to take that for the clots in his legs. Got it. This wasn't just the diet info, it was the medications list. For everyone in the place.

I wasn't sure how yet, but I knew it was something I could use.

"Um, excuse me, Mrs. Hendricks." I shuffled my feet like I'd just come in. "Marla asked me to tell you she had to step out for a couple minutes but she'd be right back."

As soon as I spoke, she touched a key that replaced the image on her screen with a picture of a cat. Basic screen guard to keep people from seeing things they're not supposed to. I gave her my helpful, innocent smile. I've got a bit of a baby face even though I'm on the wrong side of thirty, and most times it brings out the mother instinct in older women.

"All right." She smiled back. "Thank you, Bixby."

Huh. I didn't think she knew my name. I nodded and started to back out the door then saw my opening. That wasn't a stock image on her screen; that was a personal photo. "What a beautiful cat." I took a half step forward like I couldn't take my eyes off the really ordinary looking orange cat in the picture. "Is he yours?"

Bullseye. She turned to the screen, beaming. "Why, yes. That's Sir Reginald."

I crossed the tiny room like I was drawn to the image. I mentioned having a cat when I was young—actually it was my sister's, I hated the thing—asked a few inane questions, and let her babble on about the wonders of the stupid cat while I scoped out her workspace and made some mental notes. There were a few more pictures of the cat in frames sitting on her desk. No husband, no kids. That could come in handy later on. I waited until she started to run out of breath.

"Does he get angry when you're late getting home?" I asked. "My Mickey used to sulk if he didn't get his dinner right on time."

"Oh, I'm hardly ever late. I leave here at seven every night, like clockwork. I can't keep Reggie waiting."

I waited a week, just to be safe. Sure enough, crazy cat lady left every night at seven to go home to Sir Reginald. The last of the kitchen crew left about eight, after clean-up. I slipped into the darkened kitchen at nine, moving by the glow from the parking lot lights and the almost full moon. I tested the door to Hendricks' office. As expected, it was locked, but a piece of cake to pick. It was darker in there so I got out my penlight. She'd turned off her computer so I powered it up and waited for the password prompt. This should be easy.

First I tried *SirReginald*. Nope.

How about just *Reginald*? Invalid.

Hmm. Maybe all lower case. No. Stupid. I typed in *Reggie*.

Bingo.

I started flipping through the list, focusing on the non-Medicare patients. Whoa, some of them were taking enough meds to choke a horse. And most of them were damned expensive. I'd hate to have to pay those bills. Of course, Medicare covered some drugs even for the full pays but that still was a lot of money down the drain. Which got me thinking…there was a hell of a lot of money being spent here just to keep some old fogies alive well past their time. Money someone else was waiting in line for—if the doctors and the home didn't get it all first. Maybe someone who was getting a little impatient. Someone who might like a little help sending Great-Aunt Tilly to her final reward. And be willing to pay for it.

I started working it out in my head. Like I said before, I didn't take this job looking to kill anyone. But if the price was right… Wouldn't be hard. Hell, you could smother one of these old biddies—did I mention there were way more women than men?—with a pillow when they were sleeping. And you weren't really taking a lot from them. They were pretty much done anyway. I heard stories around about ones that cried all the time because they wanted to die. But I wasn't doing any mercy killings. I was looking for a score.

The trick was not getting caught.

There were a lot of pieces to pull together. I needed an old girl with money and an impatient heir who didn't care how he got it. Then I find out what drugs she's on and which would be the easiest to give a lethal dose of without a lot of obvious symptoms. Easy enough to Google. Then I boost some from the pharmacy, and start adding a little extra to her food every day. Have to do it gradual enough so there wouldn't be some big reaction, but quick enough that her doctor wouldn't start ordering tests. Then bingo, she's dead and everyone's all "well, it was time" and "now she's at rest." And even if the doctor wants to double check or the coroner orders an autopsy, they're just going to find the drugs that were supposed to be there. Nothing suspicious here, folks.

I started spending my daytime off-hours in the "Hospitality Room," It was this big room with couches and easy chairs, and tables with regular chairs to sit around. There were two TV's, one at each end, supposedly so the sound from one wouldn't bother the people watching the other. Except there was always someone who forgot their hearing aid and had their set cranked up to full volume until someone complained and a staff person turned it down. There was a snack bar with coffee and tea and such. The walls were this soft green color with pretty pictures of flowers and trees. You could almost forget you were in a nursing home expect for the flat industrial carpet—for wheelchairs to roll on—and the railings all around the walls.

Most of the residents who weren't bedridden spent some of their day in there, doing activities or just looking for company. That worked for me. The bedridden ones were probably far enough along that whoever was waiting for their money wouldn't need my help.

I took turns sitting with the ladies, chatting them up, seeing what I could find out. This was another reason the women worked better for me. The men always wanted to talk about old war stories, sports, or politics. The women liked to talk about their families, even if it was just to complain they never visited. After a couple weeks, I had three likely candidates: Gertrude, Edith, and Margaret. All had money, just one or two heirs, and were taking meds I could work with. Time to meet the family.

Gertrude's heir was her only son, Henry. He visited once a month and stayed one hour. Obligation visit. Gert was a sour old thing, tall and rail thin with a stiffly-sprayed hairstyle several decades old. She spent most of her time complaining that Henry didn't come more often and bemoaning the fact that he hadn't become a doctor like she wanted but followed her ex-husband (the skirt-chasing drunk) into his computer business. Henry had never married, which was somehow her ex's fault, and never gave her the grandchildren she always wanted.

At the end of his next visit, I managed a conversation by the simple trick of lifting one of his gloves from his coat pocket and pretending he dropped it.

"You're Miss Gertrude's son, Henry, aren't you?"

He gave me a suspicious stare.

"I'm Al Bixby. I work here...in the kitchen. I like to talk with the ladies in my free time."

"Good lord, why?"

I gave a little snort of laughter. "Well, yes, some of them can be a bit...difficult?"

"That's one way to put it." He started to pull on the glove.

"And yet you're here faithfully, every month." I offered a smile I hoped was somewhere between sympathetic and conspiratorial. "Dutiful heir?"

If he was offended, he didn't show it. "Hardly. Just fulfilling a promise I made to my dad. He set up a trust fund before he died to pay for this place. Whatever's left when she dies goes to her church."

Damn. I wouldn't have minded helping the world be rid of Gertrude. The son said something else I didn't catch. My mind had already moved on to Edith.

Edith the weeper. Not about her granddaughter, she was wonderful. Came every week even though it was over an hour's drive. But she missed her Ernie...gone to his reward three years ago and all Miss Edith wanted was to join him. Well, I wasn't above helping her out, if the granddaughter was interested.

But it turned out to be Margaret.

Margaret was actually my favorite of the three. She was friendly, cheerful, and still had all her marbles. Kept in shape, too, as much as anyone can on a walker. Spry old girl. She had a great-niece, Daisy, who came to see her a couple times a day, and Daisy's husband George who showed up on Sunday afternoon every other week.

This was his week.

It wasn't hard to lure him away. I waited till he wandered over to the coffee machine. Margaret and Daisy, sitting at one of the tables, were chatting away and didn't seem to notice his absence.

"Couldn't take the hen talk, eh?"

He looked at me and ran his hand over his face. "For this I'm missing the game."

"That sucks." I stuck out my hand. "Al Bixby."

He took it. "George Marsh."

"I'd offer you a beer, George, but it's not allowed on the premises. I know, I work in the kitchen."

"That's okay, this will do." He gestured with the paper coffee cup.

"Come on, let's let the ladies gab." I steered him to an empty table in the corner. It wasn't difficult. Since I had the time, I started out with sports talk...the game he was missing. Then we got into business and how tough things were these days. Me working in some nursing home kitchen. Him struggling to keep his furniture business afloat.

"But Miss Margaret has money. I mean...I'm sorry, but she's in the east wing and Medicare doesn't pay for those rooms so I thought..."

His scowl was an ugly thing. "She has money. But she's not giving any of it to me. Not while she's still on this side of the grave."

Dear Lord, could he have made it any easier? "Oh, so you're in line to inherit? Well, that's something."

"Maybe. If I can keep the business going long enough."

I took a deep breath and blew it out slowly. This was it. Now or never. If I was reading him wrong, he might call the cops and that would be the end of this game real quick.

"What if you could hurry her along?"

He stared at me through narrowed eyes and I could hear him turning the words over in his mind.

"What do you mean?"

No, I hadn't read him wrong.

"Well, at her age, it's just a matter of time anyway. Hell, half the women in this place will come right out and tell you they're ready to go. It's just a matter of helping them along."

"And you help them along?"

I shook my head. "No. But I could."

"How?"

Another head shake. "Better you don't know. But I can tell you it won't be violent," just in case he's the squeamish type, "and it will take a couple weeks, maybe three, to avoid suspicion."

He took a swallow of coffee and looked across the room where his wife and her great-aunt were talking and laughing. Their laughter seemed to make the decision for him.

"How much?"

I like a man who gets right down to business.

"Forty percent. Forty percent of whatever you get. I'll even be generous and make that *after* funeral and legal expenses and taxes. Forty percent of the net inheritance."

"Bullshit. Ten."

I just stared at him.

"All right, twenty. But no higher."

Since twenty percent was the figure I was really looking for, I let the silence drag out another minute and nodded. "Okay. Twenty." Let him think he chewed me down, make him happy. "But you can't change your routine. Your wife still has to come every day like she's been doing, and you have to come visit on your usual Sunday."

He scowled and glanced at the ladies. I guess he was hoping he wouldn't have to face Miss Margaret again, but he sucked it up. "Yeah, sure, no problem."

We got up and I walked him back to their table.

"Alvin. I didn't know you were here. Daisy, you know Alvin." Miss Margaret is the only one who calls me by my given name. Insisted I tell her what it was. To be honest, I kind of like it. She flashed a bright smile and Daisy gave me a friendly nod. Part of me wishes it hadn't been Margaret. Oh, I wasn't backing out. Not on that kind of money. But I would miss her. A hell of a lot more than I would have missed Gertrude.

"Sit with us, Alvin." Margaret gestured to the chair beside her.

"I'm sorry, I can't. It's time for me to get back to work." I shook hands with George, sealing the deal. "Nice talking with you, Mr. Marsh."

That night, I was back in Mrs. Hendricks' office, taking a closer look at Margaret's medications, and Googling all the medical websites. I didn't understand a lot of what I was reading but most of the time there was a link to another site that would spell it out for me. I finally figured out that my best bet was to go with *hyperkalemia*, which is basically too much potassium in the blood. There were a couple meds on her list that would boost her potassium levels if she got too much of them, and the symptoms wouldn't be too obvious. She already had a heart condition so, with any luck at all, it should kick her into cardiac arrest. And that would be enough since the old girl conveniently had a Do Not Resuscitate order on file.

Obtaining what I needed was easy. The lock on the pharmacy was better than the dietician's office but still not much of a challenge. I'd been picking locks way too long. None of what I needed was high security stuff like the opioids, but I still only took enough for a couple days. Didn't want to set off any red flags.

The other thing I'd been doing the last couple weeks was studying the routine for setting up the meal trays. I knew who prepared which trays and when they were picked up and taken to the rooms. And I'd started helping out, moving the trays onto the insulated wheeled carts. Everyone was so grateful. "Why, thank you, Al." "It's good of you to help, Al." That was my window.

Breakfast, the first day. I had Margaret's daily dose, or overdose, tucked up my sleeve, all ground up in a little vial I swiped from the blood lab. I worked my way down to her tray. Oatmeal. Damn, the sight of it made this almost feel like a mercy killing after all.

Then it was done. The first dose. The beginning of the end for Miss Margaret.

Every day I followed the same routine. Did my prep work in the kitchen, helped with the trays, and visited with the ladies during my off hours. At the end of the first week, Edith the weeper got her wish and went to join her Ernie. It was a shame I hadn't been able to hit up her granddaughter first. Might have gotten an easy job out of it.

Sour old Gertrude took exception to something I said and started giving me the cold shoulder so I was spending more time with Margaret, watching for symptoms. There should be some weakness, numbness, muscle pain, *something* by now. I'd figured out that she wasn't the complaining type, which was good for me, so I made a point of asking how she was feeling and if anything was bothering her. She told me I was sweet to be concerned but she was just fine.

After the second week, George made his scheduled appearance. I was helping one of the residents with the TV, trying to find the war movie he was certain was on. He finally settled for college basketball. George sat with Daisy and Margaret for a while, but when he saw I was done with the TV he headed for the coffee machine, his stare telling me to meet him there.

He didn't waste time on pleasantries.

"What's going on?"

I knew what he meant but played dumb. "What do you mean?"

"I mean, what the hell is going on? We had a deal. She ain't dead. She ain't even sick."

"Calm down. I told you it could take three weeks. I have to go slow. So nobody gets suspicious." I reached for the coffee pot to pour us both a cup but he grabbed my wrist.

"I haven't got time. I've made some promises, based on that money coming. To the kind of people you don't break promises to."

Not good. And he was right, dear old Margaret wasn't showing any ill effects from the increased drugs. I eased my wrist out of his grasp, nodding my understanding.

"Okay, I'll speed up the timeline. Don't worry. I'll take care of it."

"You'd better. If this thing doesn't happen, I ain't taking the hit alone."

The next day I doubled the amount of medication in Margaret's food. I had to start seeing some results and soon. I spent most of my free time sitting with her, talking, playing cards, watching for symptoms. It's funny, I think we would have become friends if I hadn't been, you know, trying to kill her.

Another week went by. I was dreading Sunday. It wasn't George's week but I half-expected him to show up. To point out that his wife's great-aunt was still very much among the living. I thought about hiding out in the kitchen, but that would be a little obvious. When I got to the hospitality room, George wasn't there. Neither was Daisy.

Neither was Margaret.

I worked my way down the hall to the nursing station and made my inquiry.

"Oh, I'm sorry, I thought you knew."

Alleluia! All those drugs had finally kicked in. And about time. Well, rest in peace, Margaret, old girl.

"Her niece passed away. Margaret's helping with the arrangements."

I stood there staring, trying to process her words. "What?"

She shook her head. "I mean her great-niece. I'm sure you met her. She came to visit every day. Daisy Marsh."

"But…what happened? I didn't even know she was sick."

"Cardiac arrest. From what I heard, it was quite unexpected, although she *was* overweight and that's never healthy."

I thanked her and wandered back down the hall, trying to get my head around it.

Well, okay. Okay. This still works. Daisy's dead, so George is the sole heir. Those drugs have got to kick in on Margaret any time now. Maybe the shock of losing Daisy will get things moving in the right direction.

Margaret was gone four days. I worried that her body would have a chance to fight back, to overcome the effects of the extra meds. I needed her to get back here and eat the food I prepared for her. I needed her to get sick and show George some symptoms to keep him off my back. Hell, I needed her to drop dead like she was supposed to.

On Thursday, she was sitting in the hospitality room in her usual spot. She looked a little pale and tired. Good sign. One of the nurses was talking to her—offering condolences, I imagined—so I waited till she was alone then went over.

"Miss Margaret, may I sit with you?"

Her smile was not quite as bright as usual but every bit as warm. "Alvin. I've been hoping I'd see you today. Of course," She gestured toward the chair next to hers.

"I heard about Daisy," I said as I sat down. "I'm so sorry."

Her lips trembled. "Thank you. It was quite a shock. I'm going to miss her so much."

"I heard it was her heart. Had she been ill?"

"No. Not at all. Although she wasn't very fit. She hated exercise and she loved to eat. She even liked the food here."

I must have given something away in my expression because she quickly apologized.

"Oh, I'm sorry, Alvin. I shouldn't have said that. You work in the kitchen here, don't you?"

"No, that's okay. You don't like the food?"

"Well, I hardly ever eat it. It's one of the benefits of having money. I have almost all my meals smuggled in from my favorite restaurants. I'm sure my nurses know but as long as I am careful with my choices, they pretend not to notice."

"But your trays come back empty. We check...to make sure you're eating."

"Yes, dear. I just told you. Daisy enjoyed the food here. She would schedule her visits around meal times and eat whatever came from the kitchen. I shouldn't have let her, knowing she needed to lose weight, but I thought it was better than having her stop at some fast food place on the way home. At least the food here wouldn't hurt her."

I sat there, letting the meaning of her words sink in. Margaret hadn't been getting any of the extra drugs. Daisy had. And Daisy was dead.

"So, just a heart attack? No other causes?" Damn. Did they run tests? Was there an autopsy?

"That's what her doctor said. At least it was peaceful. She went in her sleep."

I didn't dare ask any more questions.

"Maybe I let her eat here," she went on, more to herself than to me, "because I knew George was always on her about her weight. At least here she could relax and enjoy her meal."

Her words brought me back with a start. "Oh. George. How's he taking the loss?"

All the warmth went out of her. "The only loss George Marsh is grieving is the chance to get his hands on my money."

I didn't have to fake my confusion. "But isn't George your sole heir now?"

"Hah. That man was never my heir."

"I don't understand. You told me Daisy was your only family. With her gone…"

"Daisy wouldn't have inherited a thing from me. She knew that. Not as long as she was married to George Marsh. Now if she had left him, I would have taken care of her. I loved Daisy. I would have set her up in a nice place, given her a monthly allowance, anything she needed. But I knew as long as she was married to George, any money she got from me would have gone straight to him, to be wasted on one of his shady business deals."

Say what? "Did he know?"

"Well, I certainly never told him. That man was mean as a snake. Lord knows how he would have treated my Daisy if he knew he was never going to get any money out of her. And as much as she loved him, I think she understood it, too."

I was screwed. Screwed. My grand plan for killing Margaret was a bust. And even if I succeeded, there'd be no payoff. Twenty percent of zero was zero. Plus there was George…and his angry friends.

"So, who *are* you leaving your money to?" Wrong question. "I'm sorry. That was out of line."

Her smile was coy, and a little mischievous. "Well, I guess you could say I have lots of heirs. I like setting up individual bequests for people I meet. It makes me feel good. Most of them aren't aware and it makes me happy knowing I'm leaving pleasant surprises behind when I go. When the time comes, everything that's left after those bequests will provide an endowment fund for scholarships at my alma mater, Denison University."

"Wow. That's…" That's gonna piss George off royally. Wasn't doing much for me either. "That's really beautiful, Miss Margaret."

She studied me for a long moment then leaned in, motioning me to do the same. "I don't usually do this, but I'm going to let you in on a secret. While I was taking care of Daisy's affairs, I saw my lawyer…and added a bequest for you."

I leaned back and gaped at her.

"Close your mouth, dear," she twinkled at me.

"But…why?"

"Because you're a nice man who makes time for an old lady." She patted my hand. "It's not a fortune but it will get you out of that kitchen and let you do something you want to do."

ooo

That night I walked to the corner bus stop, trying to get my head around the weird turn of events. Margaret hadn't named a figure, and I sure couldn't ask, but it was going to be more than I'd get from George, the non-heir. Now I was the one waiting for the old lady to die, which meant I couldn't kill her, even if I could find another way. Heirs have motive. But I could wait her out.

I was so lost in thought I didn't notice the figure that stepped out of the shadows until he said my name.

"Bixby."

Shit. George.

"What the hell did you do? You killed my wife."

204

"What do you mean? I heard she died of a heart attack."

"Don't give me that crap. You were supposed to kill Margaret and now Daisy's dead. You screwed up. Without Daisy, I'll get nothing."

Should I tell him? Sorry, George, you were always going to get nothing. Nah, better not.

"Man, I'm sorry, but it's not my fault. I didn't touch Daisy. I swear. I couldn't know she was going to have a heart attack." Or that Margaret was putting me in her will instead of him.

"I don't see it that way. This whole thing was your idea. You said you could deliver. I made promises. Now I'm going to be paying the price."

His hand came out of his coat pocket holding a small but deadly .38 revolver and he gave me a cold, mirthless smile. "And so are you."

I opened my mouth but nothing came out. I guess neither of us were inheriting from Miss Margaret. She was going to outlive us both.

LD Masterson lived on both coasts before becoming landlocked in Ohio. After twenty years managing computers for the American Red Cross, she now divides her time between writing and enjoying her grandchildren. Her short stories have been published in several anthologies and magazines and she's currently working on her second novel. Catch her at: http://ldmasterson-author.blogspot.com or http://ldmasterson.com.

NOIR AT THE SALAD BAR

CANDY

BY ISOBEL HORSBURGH

When I came out of the pantry, the kitchen was empty. It usually is. It was glaringly white and clean, the way I imagined an operating theatre would be, not that I'd ever got as far as an operating theatre. The only patch of colour was a green Waitrose bag on the counter. It leaned over a little, the contents spilling like a cartoon bag, a bag put down in a hurry. I was going to get a good look at that. All this money for a kitchen, and everything in it was so white: dove white tiles, snow white walls, ice white marble, with steel surfaces reflecting the pervasive whiteness. It was meant to make your eyes brim with envy. If this was her dream kitchen, her dreams were bleached-out. I wondered if she was afraid of dreaming in colour. I would have been if I was her.

The other kitchen in this house has the dog basket with the tatty knitted blanket, and the microwave, the one she never admits to using. There's a cosy rocking chair, and some chintzy mugs from Morrisons spattered with blowsy orange and yellow flowers. She liked to imply that she doesn't use mugs, only some version of the kind of wide, white cup you get in French cafés, or dinky Turkish cups, bone china with fiddly handles. Lots of colour in the second best kitchen, none of it off a mood board. This one, where I am right now, the show kitchen, has the gleaming copper pans, the bain marie, the sous-vide oven that don't get used very much. Two kitchens in this house, but not much cooking goes on in either of them, ever. She brings people into this kitchen sometimes to show them her Sabatier knives and block, but it's all unsullied. In all the time I've been hanging around in here, I've scarcely noticed her actually cooking anything. If her significant other, Charlie, treats himself to a midnight fry-up, he doesn't dare do it in here.

Let's get a look at this carrier bag, then. On the top, harissa, methi, tahini, she was going for the vowels all right. Haloumi. That last one sounded like someone calling home the pet werewolf.

Tabasco. Oh, and a pack of jalapenos. Ouch. I didn't like the look of the hot stuff. For someone who wears nude shoes and palest cashmere along with a discreet pearl choker, this taste for heat might seem a touch out of character, But Aurelia isn't as bland as she seems. You might not be able to pick her out when she stands against a neutral background, but there's reasons for that.

One thing you might notice, should you access the photo albums in which Aurelia featured during her youth, is how hard she is to find. That's because she has always looked exactly like everyone else. She'd learned that lesson when she turned up for her first day at primary school with the "wrong" pencil case. By the second day, she not only had the right pencil case, with the right boy band adorning it, but she'd gained kudos from the teachers by generously palming off her old pencil case, (one given away with cough medicine and featuring a boss-eyed koala), to another girl who didn't have one at all, while turning that person into a pariah among the other kids. (Every time the poor girl tried to jettison the wretched thing by leaving it behind the bins or on the bus to Darlo, it was retrieved and handed back to her, with a reminder that she should be grateful to Audrey, which was Aurelia's name in those days).

Aurelia was also adept at drawing attention, in the kindest way, to whoever was hanging about alone in a corner of the yard, and advertising their friendless state to the entire school. Aurelia was never friendless. She was never anyone's best mate, either. She always looked something like the most popular girl in the room, but not enough to inspire envy: not a rival, colours just that bit muted. She was a photocopy of a photocopy.

At University among new, privately-educated friends, she implied that she too had once had "a difficult relationship with food." I happen to know that as a girl, the only difficulty she'd ever had was opening her gob wide enough to stuff food in, but, she said, bravely, during girls' nights in confession-sessions:

"What doesn't kill you makes you stronger."

I have my own reasons for taking issue with this remark. What doesn't kill you is saving you for afters.

Post Uni, Aurelia chose to ascend via the world of PR. When she came across Charlie, a man who would have been

207

invisible in the reptile house, their matching tongues flickered. Chameleon love blossomed, spiky as the desert cactus.

"I would never dream of eating anything with a face." Ebony Waterfield, director of the environmental charity Glass Houses, told Aurelia this over a blue cheese and walnut salad at Crunchers, the premier vegetarian restaurant in Barnard Castle. Aurelia, who was planning to get herself taken on as Ebony's right hand woman, agreed wholeheartedly. She didn't mention that she fully intended to go home and nuke up a pack of pork sausages. She'd already had an organic box of veggies delivered. Most of it went in the compost bin, but the neighbours got to see the van parked outside and that was what mattered.

Having achieved her objective of becoming indispensible, she found herself at Ebony's side in the Ramshaw Hotel, smiling as her boss received a Golden Grasshopper Award for services to environmentalism and the community. She also managed to be in shot whenever Ebony appeared on the local news. The downside of all this made itself known in short order. When Aurelia next went into the deli for some prosciutto, she was greeted with:

"Saw you on the news last night." She had to pretend she was after goats' butter and capers. Thanks to social media, and Ebony's high profile locally, everyone, whether they'd met her or not, seemed to know that she didn't eat meat. If she tried to get anywhere near the carnivore's section in Waitrose, someone or other invariably popped up between her and the steaks, eyeing the contents of her basket.

"I must say, you're a great advert for that kind of diet, Mrs Roseberry. I'm a bit too fond of the old lamb chops myself, I'm afraid."

Her ability to blend in against any background seemed to have deserted her. She braved the more downmarket shops, hoping to remain incognito while stocking up on wild salmon. But even there she found herself having to pose for selfies in front of the pre-packed salad while people told her how much they admired her stance on animal cruelty. It was like living in a police state run by Paul McCartney's family.

She and Charlie had always eaten out a lot, but they found that the lettuce-leaf telegraph had been at work there too. If she intended to order *foie gras* in some favourite restaurant, she would find that the nearest tables were occupied by people who recognised her, all with their ears flapping. People watched her while she ate, as though she was the only vegetarian they'd ever come across. Even the waiters were herding her in the direction of the delicious meatless options that neither of them wanted. In order to eat meat or fish, they had to drive to ever more distant places, consuming their clandestine haddock and chips in the car on a cliff top, or smuggling contraband burgers into their own home and concealing the evidence at the bottom of the bin.

They only got a dog so that they could pretend that the meat they bought was for him. He was a rescue pug, Bingle, and if he'd really eaten all the meat they brought in, he'd have been the size of a Zeppelin. They never walked anywhere, either. It just wasn't something they did, exercising outside the gym. They belonged to an exclusive health club, and retreated to a spa now and then. Bingle, their alibi for steak mince, had to be walked, not only for his own sake, but because people had to know they had a dog, and a rescue dog at that. Ebony, particularly, had to believe that they were the kind of people who'd take in a waif. Bingle wasn't an obvious waif, he was a bit stout and grumpy, but it could have been living with Aurelia and Charlie that did that to him. His chubby little body and stumpy legs required exercise, and that was where I came in. It was where I went out, also, as it turned out.

I was taken on for dog walking and a little "light" housework. I think she liked the fact that I hadn't been to college. She needed someone to look down on. I didn't explain that I was on a gap year that had somehow extended to three years, so that when my mates were graduating with colossal debts, I was not so encumbered. I'd done a few things, waitressing and so on, enjoyed myself and was planning to travel once I'd saved up enough money. This job was intended to be a stopgap. I'm glad, knowing what I know now, that I packed so much into those three years.

Aurelia used to sometimes waft about in the house with a duster and some orange oil, but she didn't exactly break into a sweat. She did advise me to join a gym, (not theirs, obviously), where I could become better toned, while I hauled the floor polisher about. She stood over me as I scrubbed the bathroom tiles, eyeing my haunches, and generously offered me the incentive of some of her old clothes, if only I'd just make a teeny effort to lose the puppy fat. I wouldn't have worn her clothes even if I'd been able to squeeze into them. The bland colours would have rendered me invisible, which would have suited Aurelia. I wore my brightest shades when I was at her house, just to annoy her. I wrapped a scarlet bandana round my head, slipped into tangerine sweats, and made like Rosie the Riveter.

"Such a shame schools don't teach domestic science now, Candy. If only people would cook from scratch, the weight would just melt away." By people, she meant me. I could cook perfectly well, but she was of the opinion that, "They just don't bother to learn how, do they? All this processed trash." Aurelia and Charlie ate more ready meals than I did, but I wasn't supposed to notice that. I didn't generally get to do the shopping, in case I gave the game away about their dietary habits. Aurelia thought me something of a blabbermouth. To be fair, I was. I couldn't keep a secret to save my life.

I'd also noticed a charred meat smell outside sometimes, but many of the neighbours had barbecues, and she and Charlie put the aroma down to them. Portable barbie out there? Not very likely though, not under the noses of the neighbours. Aurelia wouldn't have admitted to owning a barbecue pit anyway. She thought they were very *déclassé*. The garden was large and leafy. I couldn't be sure what went on out there, behind the huge conservatory. Then I heard them arguing.

"It's not going to be deep enough, Charlie." My ears pricked up, from my place on the landing where I was toiling away. I turned off the Dyson and pretended to fiddle with the nozzle. Their voices rose from the hallway below.

"It'll be fine, Aurelia. It'll fit young Perky to a T."

"He'll be down there for days, Charlie. What if someone notices? You'll have to go deeper, that's all."

"Well, if you're not happy, you have a go with the spade. I've got to go to the charcuterie." (They called it that because they thought I didn't know any French.) "I'm picking up *la cochon*, shortly, dear heart."

That's le cochon, *you prat*, I thought. I'd heard them before now, eagerly discussing *saucisson, Jamón Serrano*, and *Bruxelles pate*, under the impression that I wouldn't know what they'd been scoffing on the quiet.

"Just don't let Little Miss Mouthy know. Not that she's ever been little, I suspect. God knows what the parents were like. She's the elephants' child, all right."

"Touch of the Bessie Bunters," agreed Charlie. "I mean, a girl should have some meat on her, but really, she's too much woman, that Candy. Or her backside is."

It would have served the puny lizard right if I'd sat on him with my magnificent arse. Withered little skink. I've always been toned, and I was fitter than a lot of skinny types. I'm a swimmer, and nobody's ever been able to say I was lazy. I demonstrated this to myself by crashing about with the vacuum, pounding the shaking floorboards with my massive limbs, and drowning out their shrill voices.

After a while, when I thought they'd gone, I peeked out of the blinds. There she was again, striding down to the end of the garden in the direction of the hot tub, behind which lay the pit Charlie'd been sweating over for days. He'd been digging away as if he was auditioning for *Time Team*, and carting barrow-loads of stones to line it. She didn't take a spade with her, but she did have what looked like a silver tape measure clutched in her manicured fingers.

I went and sat on their bed, thinking that I wasn't going to be able to stand this house much longer. I'm not a quitter, but this was Toxicity Towers. Bingle put his head round the door. He wasn't allowed upstairs, so I picked him up, gave him a cuddle and put him on the bed, where he could roll about and rub his snotty face on their Egyptian high thread count linen pillowcases. When I answered the phone on the landing shortly afterwards, I assumed Aurelia was still out there, calculating. It was her boss on the line. I quite liked Ebony. She was a kind soul and she took Aurelia at face value.

"Hi, Ebony" I said. "I think Aurelia's out in the garden, measuring the fire pit again, but I can take a message if you like. And Charlie's about to collect the suc..." I didn't get as far as

211

"uckling pig", before I found myself airborne. I know now I was out of it for about seven minutes, after I hit the oak-veneered floor, down below in the hall.

Lying flat out at the bottom of the stairs, I came round from my daze to find that they were having a big row about insurance. She was worried about their no-claims bonus, if they managed to convince people that I'd tripped over the dog. I could hear Bingle whimpering up on the landing.

"This is such a nuisance. No consideration, really, I knew she was going to be trouble when she turned up looking as if she'd been dressed in tablecloths thrown at her by a pack of colour-blind gypsies. Go and get a cushion, Charlie."

I tried to say that, though I appreciated that they were trying to help, I didn't think that they should try to move me until the paramedics arrived, just in case. She took no notice. Charlie came scurrying back into the hall, a ruched bolster of ice-mint satin clutched between his scaly paws.

"Not that one, Charlie, for heaven's sake. Do you know what that cost? Get one from the other kitchen." (They were a hundred and twenty five quid a pop and I knew this because I'd spotted them in one of the lifestyle magazines she had lying about, and I'd said what I thought of the sort of idiot who pays that for a cushion before I realised they were what she had on the chaise longue in the drawing room.)

Charlie scuttled off and came back, this time with something on which Bingle had been in the habit of lying and dribbling on. He handed the cushion to Aurelia.

"If we ever decide to sell this house, it's not going to look good, is it?" said Charlie. "People might think the stairs aren't safe. And nobody wants to live in houses with a sad story attached." (What sad story? Get some help!)

"Really, Charlie, you are a fool." No argument from me there, even if I'd been capable of speech at that moment. And then she came over to where I lay. She looked down at me and said:

"She was quite plump, wasn't she?"

I was processing that *was* because it hadn't quite hit home yet. I tried again to say something about needing the paramedics. I was beginning to realise that something else was badly wrong.

They weren't speaking their version of French, but had reverted to English. They didn't care if I could hear them or not.

"And the paperwork," Charlie wittered. "Awful fuss, that."

"Really, this has come at an awkward time. Ebony won't like us being in the press, not over something like this."

Then before I could express my growing misgivings about the situation, the cushion, with its whiff of Bingle, was placed on my face. Afterwards, she actually prodded me in the ribs with the toe of her flesh-coloured stiletto. I assume it was her way of checking for a pulse. I didn't feel it, of course, but I saw it from the outside of myself, which is where I was by then. You're supposed to see a tunnel and a white light, but what I saw was Aurelia pursing her pale-painted lips. She was going into list-making mode. No one could ever have accused her of not thinking on her Louboutin-shod feet. Bingle was howling.

"Let's prioritise. Go and shut that animal up." There was the sound of feet on the stairs, and a yelp. A door banged. Then Charlie clumped back down once more.

"We're going to have to put her on standby for now. Can you just sling her over your shoulder?" I think she'd seen too many misleading TV dramas, where they toss the deceased about like a Guy Fawkes effigy. Charlie, a relatively small man with an unappealingly formed backside, of which I got an eyeful when his chinos started to slide down during the ensuing struggle, couldn't lift me off the floor, to which I clung like a clump of chewing gum. And neither could she, when she unwillingly joined in. I would have been more than happy if either of them had slipped a disc trying. I flopped about in their arms, passively resisting as they heaved at my shoulders. Aurelia scowled down at me, her face perspiring, muttering something about agreeing with Jamie Oliver for once.

"I wish people would take responsibility for their own health. And if there's one thing that working for Glass Houses has taught me, it's that there's simply too much waste in this world."

In the end they rolled me into the duvet from the spare room and hauled me across the hall floor and out to the wheelbarrow. When, after an epic battle, they had hoiked me into it, and Charlie was hunched doubled up and wheezing from the effort, Aurelia was already flicking at a recipe app.

"Forget the butchers, Charlie. I'm popping to Waitrose for some bits and bobs. Maybe some apples?" Next thing, I'm on the way to the fire pit.

ooo

Reader, I was in there two days, with a Bramley crammed in my gob so I'd cook properly, and let's not talk about the other indignities. I will never be able to face paprika again. Two days in the earth, smouldering, in every sense of the word. What they were doing up above, I couldn't be sure, but it would involve thumbing through the high end recipe books that were rarely cracked in that house, and drooling. I just hoped the dog was all right. At last, I was brought up from my bed of hot coals in the deep, dark soil. Charlie's measuring was spot on. I was done to a crisp, my crackling luscious. After that, I hung in the pantry. Thinking.

You may have wondered how I know so much about young Audrey, seeing that I wasn't born for about half of her life. I did a bit of browsing while I had the chance. The info is available in those circs, to those willing to make use of it, and I've always been a bit of a reader. (*They* do have a spirit of fairness, over on that side. Blabbermouth I may well be, but I really can't say more on the subject.) The only books in this house are for show, coffee table books about lofts in New York.

It had taken all my strength of will to get out of that pantry. I needed to be on hand for the next stage. Only the thought of Bingle's little face kept me going. There they were, seated on either side of a candle-lit table, with an antique cloth of pure white linen. There was even a vase of Dartington Crystal, holding pale pink roses (no vulgar red for Aurelia.) When she lifted the first morsel to her lips, she hesitated.

"Go on," I urged from the sidelines, "Get stuck in!" She continued to examine what was speared to the end of the silver fork.

"Everything all right, dear heart?"

"I was just thinking...more asafoetida?"

It isn't your own life that flashes past at the crucial moment of transition, it's the lives of people who've been important to you, for good or ill. By the time Aurelia was patting her lips with a linen napkin, I knew all.

ooo

Let us fast forward to the vicinity of the deli counter in a well-known upmarket supplier of pretentious comestibles.

"Ebony! How lovely to see you!" Ebony looked a bit surprised to be greeted like that. Aurelia wasn't usually so effusive.

"I just popped in for some tofu,"

"That's nice. We're having Hawaiian pizza." Ebony, who had never eaten pizza in her life, gave a polite smile, and then remembered something.

"The pineapple one? I hadn't realised there was a veggie version of that..." Even tinned pineapple would have made her gag.

"Oh, no, this was one with ham. Lovely pink, juicy ham. Yummy." Ebony flinched. She'd no more use the word "yummy" than she'd eat ham. Aurelia wouldn't have either, under normal circumstances, but she was on the verge of discovering that the chameleon thing works from the inside out, so to speak. Two can play at that game.

"Aurelia, are you feeling all right? This isn't like you." She had a point. Anyone watching Aurelia's face at that moment would have seen her mouth opening and closing as though she was struggling to speak, and a wild look in her eyes. Luckily there was a mirror behind the counter, so even as her hand went to her own throat, I was able to bask in the full effects of the panic she was experiencing.

"To be honest, Ebony," she heard herself say, "I've always thought you were a sanctimonious drip. I've been eating every kind of sausage on the fly ever since we met, ha ha, I do dearly love a haggis, and I'd eat raw kittens if it wasn't for the fur sticking on the way down."

I'd have liked to have stayed to watch the fallout from this, but I had to get back to Charlie, whom I'd left unconscious on the kitchen floor. "Aurelia" had whacked him round the head with a big jar of fair trade coffee. When his lizard eyes blinked open, he was due to try shoplifting some fillet steak in Marks and Spencer. Poor little Bingle and I would enjoy that for our supper tonight. What fun the four of us were going to have together! Especially me.

Isobel Horsburgh lives on South Tyneside in North East England. She used to be a long-term carer, and is now a casual library assistant and a volunteer. Her work has appeared in *SpaceSquid*, *Devilfish Review*, *BlinkInk*, *Buzz And Roar*, *The Drabble*, *The Casket*, *Urban Fantasist*, *It's All Trumped Up*, *Phobos* and *Gathering Storm*.

PLAYING GAMES

BY ELAINE TOGNERI

Mai slammed the head of iceberg lettuce on the counter, flipped it over and unscrewed the core. She tore a handful of lettuce leaves off and dropped them into the sink. She could strip a head clean in one and a half minutes, a game she played to keep her mind off her empty belly, another game she played. How little could she eat and survive? At times black spots rimmed her vision and dared her to give up and fall.

"Hey, Lo Mein." Sly referred to Mai as Chinese menu dishes instead of her given name. "You don't have to rinse that. Just throw it in the bin. Nobody will know the difference." Sly spoke Vietnamese with a GI's accent.

Mai stopped and lifted the stainless steel container the sink concealed so Sly could see it. He nodded and she returned to stripping leaves, clenching her teeth. He'd cost her seconds on her record. Little did patrons at the Happy Chinese Super Buffet know vegetables and fruit weren't washed, crab legs had reached their expiration date weeks ago, and the cooks had never been to China. Most, like her, had been abducted in Vietnamese ports and tossed on ships to arrive in America as slaves.

Boiling water splattered and sizzled on the stovetop as crab legs cooked, releasing seafood musk into the kitchen. The odor crept into her nostrils and the seams of her clothing. It would grow stronger each day until her weekly shower and laundry load. She paused before picking up the next head of lettuce.

"Chop, chop," Sly said. The gray-haired man guarded the door, overseeing access to the kitchen. She didn't know his real name. He called himself Sly after Sylvester Stallone. He'd shown Mai a picture of the actor once. He looked like an older version if you ignored the dull eyes that only sparked when delivering four-fingered slaps that left plum stains on her skin for hours.

217

Julie, the woman who ran the operation with her husband, hustled into the galley and scooped crab legs from the steaming pot into one of the ubiquitous steel pans that Mai would help Chang wash later. Old Chang shuffled in with a plastic bag full of frozen crab legs. Julie exited through the swinging door back to the buffet, carrying a pan stacked high with the long red legs. Chang emptied his bag into the still-boiling water. Julie and her husband Tom were the only two allowed in the serving area, other than a couple of waitresses who met them at the door to carry food to the buffet.

For the last three years this was Mai's life. Six days a week, eighteen hours a day in the kitchen and nights in a narrow cot, exhausted and hungry. On days the restaurant closed, she spent her time cleaning herself and a bedroom shared by five other women. Tom called her a bag of bones that no man would want to sleep with. That's how she ended up in the kitchen and not the whorehouse. When the restaurant closed for the day, Tom would decide which dishes to save and which leftovers the slaves could eat. Mai avoided rice and meat, rolling shrimp in lettuce leaves stuffed with tomatoes and limiting herself to three. Days when no shrimp was available, she ate the same without. Those nights her stomach would complain. Chang had given up trying to get her to eat anything else. But once, he had given her a stale almond cookie that she still dreamed about. Mostly though her dreams were of Vietnam, chasing chickens down dusty streets, sailing on her father's small fishing boat, sitting beneath banyan trees with her cousin. Dao had come on the slave ship too, but Mai didn't know what happened to her.

Tom whacked the back of Mai's head. "We need tomatoes cut."

Mai did not cry out. She moved to the cutting board and stacked tomatoes from a box on the floor, ignoring the scurrying bugs she disturbed. "Knife?" she asked.

Sly stood and positioned himself between Tom and Mai. Tom opened a locked drawer and passed her a small knife. Mai focused on cutting thin, even slices. The knife fit her hand well and she imagined turning quickly and stabbing Sly in the eye. The best spot to keep him from chasing after her as she ran, where? Into the restaurant where fat Americans ate too much? Would they even look up from their plates? No one had ever responded to her silent calls for help. Still, as Tom and Sly mocked her skinny behind, she cut the center out of a tomato slice, cut two slices in half and the pulp out of them to fashion a rudimentary SOS, the help sign her father had taught her. Without a backward glance, she arranged other slices on top, enough to hide her handiwork and fill the bin.

"Soon as we're finished, I'm going to get my nails done," Sly said, stepping back and grinning.

Tom laughed, pushed Mai aside, and took the tray. He extended his palm for the knife.

She presented it blade first, just to get him used to that. Another game she played, a thousand tiny steps to freedom. Someday she would jam it into him and hit Sly over the head with a hot wok. In the meantime, she still harbored hope of a rescue that never came.

Hours later as she lay in the rickety cot, she tried to remember the scent of dusty air, freshly sprung leaves, and even the pile of chicken manure in their yard. All smelled better than the sweaty bodies around her and the vinegar of unwashed feet poking from beneath a sheet inches from her face.

At daylight, Mai and the others left the cramped bedroom and marched to a dark van. At the door, she stopped and turned to look for a tree, plants, even a long glimpse of the sky. She spied a woman's face watching them behind a window screen of another apartment. Mai almost cried out, but a hand gripped her elbow and pushed her into the van.

"Move it, Egg Noodle," Sly said.

When they returned that evening, Mai held her head up and strained her eyes to see if the woman watched them again. After a week of searching with no luck, Mai didn't bother anymore.

She settled on her makeshift bed in the darkness, eyes wet, crying for the first time this year. Holding her sobs in, she felt ashamed to have the others hear her weakness, especially the grandfatherly Chang who might sneak out of the men's bedroom to comfort her and risk a beating. She no longer remembered the face of her mother, her touch, her scent. Instead of gentle wind through banyan trees, her dreams were of endless clanging steel pans, knife chops on wood, and bright red sizzling crab legs. Night no longer any different from day. She wiped tears from her face and focused on counting breaths until she fell asleep.

Mai woke when the bedroom door burst open, loud voices shouted, and a streak of light shot across the room. She sat up, clutching the sheet over her underclothing. A man yelled something and the other women stood. She joined them, dropping the sheet and exposing the tightness of skin over her ribs and the contours of bones on her arms and shoulders.

"Are they starving you to death?" he asked in Vietnamese.

Mai didn't respond. He motioned toward her with a gun that resembled military issue in her country. "Get dressed," he ordered. Two other armed men passed by the open door.

Her hands trembled as she bent to reach beneath the cot. A cold circle of steel jammed into her back. She rose, revealing clothing neatly folded under the cot. The pressure disappeared and she bent again to retrieve a black t-shirt and pants. She donned both quickly and slipped on her shoes. The man ordered all the women out of the room and into a dark van. What would happen to her? Was a rival gang taking over? Where were Sly, Julie and Tom? Could the unknown be worse than her current life?

The van finally stopped and they were herded into a large building. They passed through a foyer with a sliding glass window built into a wall. Shiny linoleum lined a long hallway that they trooped along in separate file. No buffet, kitchen sink, or booths, so not a restaurant? They sent her into a small room mostly taken up by a table and cushioned chairs that actually had wheels on them.

A woman in a uniform said something in English.

The man who led her in replied and then announced in Vietnamese, "Please sit. I will translate for you." He asked Mai. "What is your name and where do you come from?"

"I am Mai from the village of Ho Nai in Vietnam."

"And how did you get here?"

Mai ducked her head. "My cousin was promised a job earning in one week what we earn all year. I loved her so much I couldn't bear to part so I traveled with her to the port. As we said goodbye at the ship, I cried. Her boss said I could come on the ship for a minute. But then they wouldn't let me off."

"So where did you get off the ship?"

"I don't know. I told them I wanted to go home, but they locked us in a container box. It was so dark and I was crying again. I passed out and when I woke up Dao was gone and I was put to work at the Happy Chinese Super Buffet."

"How old are you?"

"Sixteen."

"Can you write out your full name, your parent's names, and address in Vietnam?" he passed a pen and paper.

Mai had not written in the last three years. Her hand shook as she clutched the pen and scratched out her information. She returned everything to him and ducked her head again.

They brought her to a holding area and showed her to a cot. She lay down, trembling. What would happen to her? Was this a rescue? She closed her eyes, but couldn't sleep for worrying. Would her family still want her? What did they think had happened to her?

She drifted off and woke to the aroma of fried eggs.

"Want breakfast?" the man asked. "You'll have to join the others. I put you here alone for your safety overnight."

She nodded and followed him and the bag he carried to a larger room with tables where the other slaves sat. Chang patted the seat next to him and after taking a sandwich, she joined him. The bun smelled of fresh fried eggs and she took a large bite. Chang laughed. "So good to see you enjoy food," he said. Crumbs of egg and bread dropped from her lips. She covered her mouth to hide it. She didn't want a beating. No one seemed to notice. Wary, she took smaller bites. The sandwich churned in her stomach and she swallowed several times to keep the contents down. Too much playing games.

After a full day and night without being slapped or forced to work, she decided this must be a rescue. But the officials had explained they would be transported to a detention center until they could be deported to Vietnam. She would head for her village in hopes that her mother was still alive and to see if there was any news of her cousin.

"Mai?" the uniformed woman she'd met yesterday asked.

Mai stood and padded behind her to a small conference room. What was happening now? She could hardly breathe. The door opened and her cousin sat, waiting. The first thing Mai noticed were Dao's long red fingernails with white swirls adding to the decorative color. The white matched the form-fitting dress she wore and the red, her lipstick. She was beautiful.

"I have come for you," she said. "You don't have to go to detention. You can stay with me."

"How?" Was this possible? Her heart pattered faster.

"I have a job. You will get visa and work there, too."

"But what happened to you?" Mai asked.

"I thought you were dead so I ran away. Then I found this nail salon. People who spoke our language. They took me in and helped me with my paperwork."

"But I wasn't dead," Mai held back tears. Maybe dead would have been better.

"I tried to find out what happened to you, but I couldn't talk to the smugglers. I have been worrying about you for the last three years. When I saw the raid in the papers yesterday, I called right away."

Tears streamed down Mai's face. Her cousin had done well for herself while Mai worked as a slave. "Go back to Vietnam with me," Mai said. "See our mothers."

"That's not the life for me anymore," Dao replied. "I'm too old for marriage. I won't fit in. Besides, I owe people here for taking me in. I would be greatly honored if you would come and stay with me." Dao's eyes blinked and her smile edged into a frown.

Would Mai fit in back in Vietnam? Everyone would assume she wasn't a virgin anymore. There would be no marriage proposals. A lonely life. No more games. And if Mai left, Dao would be without kin in this strange country.

"It will be like home, but with Vietnamese-Americans," Dao said. "I run the shop. We have a Koi pond. We cook pho and fishcakes."

Mai'd heard enough comments from Sly to figure out nail salons were fronts for whorehouses. Even with Dao running the place, Mai had no illusions of what her new life would be like. Eighteen hours of soaking, filing, and polishing nails. Wet hands, smelly glue, playing a game of counting nail polish strokes for pudgy American ladies who thought beautiful nails would make them so. Or home to a life she lost the day she boarded that ship. Dao was right. She had changed. There was no going back. Mai made her decision.

On the way out, Mai stared up at the gray sky. Shut her eyes for a moment and breathed in stale air. She opened them to a world of concrete buildings, roads, and sidewalks.

Dao led her to the car.

Mai wasn't surprised when she saw Sly in the driver's seat. Game on.

Elaine Togneri has over thirty published short stories, including three mysteries to *Woman's World Magazine*. He story "Paparazzo" appears in the 2011 MWA Anthology, *The Rich and the Dead*. Elaine holds an MA in English from Rutgers University and is the founder of the Sister in Crime NJ Chapter. Visit her website at sites.google.com/site/elainetogneri.

NOIR AT THE SALAD BAR
WITH GREAT RELISH

BY JOHN R. CLARK

It had been seven years since I'd seen my family, an absence caused by a huge lapse in judgment. Combining a sketchy location, potent local rum, and cursing in a language I wasn't particularly fluent in had netted me a six year sentence in a really nasty Central American prison.

My Spanish was far better now and I hadn't had a drink since that ill-fated evening, so it hadn't been a complete waste. The tat, a get-out-of-jail present to myself, covering my left arm from wrist to shoulder, was pretty spiffy too. Did people in Simonton, Maine still say things like spiffy? I'd find out soon enough.

I looked downriver as I crossed into Maine from New Hampshire. Portsmouth hadn't changed much.

The honey manning the toll booth winked as she admired my arm. "Cool tat, where'd you get it?"

"A place called Fraijanes."

"I want one!" she hollered as I sped north.

I wasn't sure who would be at the homestead for Thanksgiving dinner tomorrow. Mom and my sister Louella were the only ones who knew I was on my way home, but they had been vague about how many other family members would make some sort of appearance.

Doing time in a Guatemalan prison wasn't like spending a week in the Simonton County Jail. I'd survived three knife fights and killed more tarantulas than I thought lived on the planet. Those weren't the worst experiences either. The lack of contact with blood kin had been the most difficult part for me and now I was hoping to make up for it.

I stopped at one of those fancy mini-malls because I didn't want to arrive empty handed after a long absence. Money wasn't an issue, thanks to a little work I'd performed for another guy in my cell block after my release. He was facing five more years and knew his lady friend was entertaining someone. Hey, I'm cool with discouraging extramarital hanky panky, particularly when it pays twenty big ones. I could still hear the screams of that naked parish priest as I hauled his butt through a cactus patch.

I looked around at the shops as I exited the truck. Cheese, imported beer, fancy-ass candy, cards and a smoke shop. It was going to be a breeze covering everyone who might be there tomorrow. Mom and Louella loved any kind of cheese that had fruit or a smoky flavor. Uncle Dupe, the family loudmouth and lawyer loved Cuban cigars. Brut and Bub, his sons and my partners in crime during my teen years, were beer drinkers. Prissy, my favorite cousin and Dupe's only daughter, was a sucker for anything dark and chocolate as were my other cousins Sammy-Jean and Miranda.

With my purchases safely stored behind the seat, I resumed my drive. Maine hadn't changed much in my absence. I could see a few more houses from the interstate, but there were still plenty of trees in late fall glory. I spotted several chevrons of geese flying south as I followed Route One through Bath and into Lincoln County.

The Metcalfs helped settle Simonton well before the Revolutionary War. My ancestors fled England because we were too merry at the wrong time. In addition to borrowing a few steeds from the landed gentry and potting more than our share of royal hares and stags, rumor has it that we were into Wicca before it even had a name.

What I remembered from growing up supported that. Maybe everyone liked to party around bonfires, but there were several occasions when I saw things and creatures that sure as hell didn't get written up in the *Simonton Gazette* under society news. I had no desire to say something like, "My grandfather swigged down this bottle of green stuff, sprouted huge bat wings and flew to Rye, NY for the weekend," during show and tell. Yes, it happened, but nobody else seemed to think it was a big deal.

Family gatherings became even more interesting when I was a teenager. My cousins and I played a game called, "freak out the new boyfriend/girlfriend." It was great sport, until word got out about Prissy's one and only boyfriend coming home sporting a pig's tail that didn't disappear until his mother took him to the Simonton Baptist Church for an exorcism. I hoped family functions were still as much fun.

I stopped where the long gravel driveway met the town road, wanting to savor the feeling of being home for the first time in ages. Our place hadn't changed much. I couldn't count how often remembering this view had sustained me while in prison. Twenty acres of blueberry fields wrapped around the north side of the cedar-shingled farmhouse before sloping to the edge of Simonton Pond. Across the water, Fairbanks Ridge rose to meet the western skyline. I'd been part of the Ridge Runners, kids who raised hell and tore up logging trails branching off the rutted county road running along the top of the ridge for almost fifteen miles. I got back in my truck.

I wasn't terribly surprised to find Lou standing on the front porch with two glasses of iced tea and a big grin. We'd always been able to sense where the other was and how we were doing. In fact, she was the one who told Mom that I had been incarcerated well before the state department bothered to send a form letter.

"Welcome home, big brother." She set the two glasses down and gave me a hug that said more than words ever could before admiring my arm. "Nice art. Probably a steal compared to what something that elaborate would cost in the states."

"You could say that. How's life?"

"Still a bitch, but I got her brother's phone number." Lou grew serious for a moment. "We got a big problem, though." She looked out at the blueberry fields and didn't need to elaborate.

"Greedy-guts up to his old tricks again?"

"Yup. Son of a bitch was supposed to handle the financial side of the berry operation since he has his own hundred acres. Mom thought everything was fine until the town sent her a certified letter with a tax lien going back three years. Turns out Uncle Dupe 'forgot' to apply the berry revenue to the property tax and if we don't come up with forty-five hundred dollars by the tenth of December, this place goes up for sale. Want to bet who's first in line to pony up that money and grab the farm?"

"Gee, that's a tough one. Does his first name begin with D?"

Lou nodded, not needing to say any more.

Uncle Dupe's given name was Abercrombie Fitzwallace Metcalf, but he had been called Dupe ever since he got the navy to send him to law school and then used his newfound expertise to get a medical discharge and a nice sixty percent disability pension. Nobody in Simonton was quite certain what the alleged malady was. The joke around town was that it was reverse-effect stress, inflicted by Dupe on his superiors and later on unsuspecting widows and orphans.

"The bastard stupid enough to show tomorrow?" I asked.

"Stupid, arrogant, no matter, he'll come if only to drool over the probability he'll have the house in a matter of months. Besides you being home gives him the perfect excuse to pretend he's glad to see you while making you squirm."

I laughed. "If he thinks he can upset me he's in for a disappointing time. Anything that fat-assed fool could dish out would be like listening to a bee fart on the other side of the blueberry field. Believe me, I had times down in Guatemala that would have had him messing his lawyer pants over and over. Maybe I should tell a couple stories tomorrow as a warm up for turkey and gravy."

Lou grinned back. "Better to save them for dessert. Bet they'd go good with mincemeat pie."

I put my gear in my old room before asking Mom what I could do to help.

"Well, it wouldn't hurt to bring in extra wood for the cook stove and we'd hoped to get the rest of the stuff out of the garden before a hard frost. Oh, and I don't suppose you'd be willing to see if the cousins remembered to leave the boat far enough up on the bank so we don't lose it next spring."

In the old days, I would have groaned at this list, but quite frankly I was pretty eager to rebuild a connection to the family property.

"Thanks Bo, that's plenty of wood."

I admired my handiwork and remembered all the times I had filled the old captain's chest that held firewood for the kitchen stove. Mom and I had always enjoyed the same routine. I'd whine or grumble, but fill it and she paid me by putting her hands on her hips, admiring the full box and thanking me with a mischievous twinkle in her gray eyes.

"I'll check the cove and then get to the garden."

There was a thin crust of ice where the old birch trees prevented late fall sunlight from hitting the sandy beach in Lou's Cove. If you looked at Simonton Pond on any map, the cove had no name. We had given it our own in honor of Lou when she nearly gave Mom a heart attack by swimming all the way out to the long bed of pickerel weed on her sixth birthday.

I could see evidence of my cousins everywhere. Beer cans and discarded Styrofoam containers littered the area between the sand and the neat line where mowing had clipped berry bushes following the August harvest. I shook my head. Brut and Bub weren't bad guys, just lazy and thoughtless. Given who their father was, I couldn't expect much. I was pleased to see that they had moved the boat to safety and left it upside down on cedar logs that had been placed just so in order to keep it above ground.

Pulling a plastic shopping bag out of my pocket, because I remembered my cousins' laziness from our younger days, I picked up their mess, including a buck twenty in can money when I hit the local redemption center.

As much as I whined about doing chores as a kid, I'd never protested when Mom or my late father sent me out to the garden. The connection with growing things was a private magic that charged my emotional batteries and fueled my creative impulses. When other guys were working on cars and computers in high school, I was poring over seed catalogs and reading horticultural magazines. They'd talked about sex, I responded by talking about Mendel and cross-pollination. There were some unexpected advantages. I was the only male member of the Simonton 4-H club and it felt like having my own harem.

I shook my head as I surveyed the mess. Rotting pumpkins that should have been harvested in early October lay half eaten by deer and birds. A row of cornstalks that would have looked nice by the mailbox post were bent and broken. Nightshade grew all over the fence where scarlet runner beans once flourished. If we could get the financial mess straightened out and I found work, I promised myself this garden would look like it had back before I foolishly accepted a job offer that was too far away and more than I could handle.

ooo

"Need anything?" I was getting edgy the next morning waiting for the gathering that would either be very interesting, a royal disaster, or maybe both.

"Can you pick up more butter? I think we're set for everything else. Make sure you're back in time to peel potatoes."

I rolled my eyes and Mom grinned before turning back to the pie crust she was rolling out. We both knew how much I disliked peeling anything except tires on a hot car. She also knew I'd be back in time to make sure everything got done.

Lou followed me to the door. "I know there was something else I was going to have you get, but I can't for the life of me think what it was," she said, her voice loud enough so Mom could hear. She gave me a conspiratorial wink before going back inside.

My sister had something planned. I thought about the possibilities, but gave up as a buck ran across the road ahead of me. This was the biggest day of all for Maine deer hunters. I'd hunted every fall with Brut and Bub when we were teenagers. Maybe next year I'd give it another go.

Ross' store was open until eleven-thirty to accommodate folks like me who needed last minute stuff. It was one of those places you can only find in small New England towns. If you poked around in the upper floors long enough, you might even find Judge Crater or Jimmy Hoffa with a price tag attached to a mummified ear.

Bub swore he bought a funky lamp there once that had a real genie in it. Brut and I blew him off until we saw him at the drive-in with the hottest babe we'd ever seen. Never saw her again, but it was three months before the shit-eating grin was gone from his face.

The twenty-something beauty behind the counter sized up my tat. "Looks like one of Central America's finest got hold of you."

"You think?"

229

"I know," she said. "I've been in love with body art since I was twelve. The internet has really opened up a lot of opportunities to see who's good and where they work. Bet you got that one in Guatemala."

I lay the butter and a copy of the *Simonton Gazette* on the counter. "You know your art. The one and only Jose Guzman spent three hours working on this beauty. If I'd had more time before leaving the country, I would have had him do the other arm."

I paid for my purchases after getting her phone number.

There were two cars in the dooryard by the time I got back. Lou was sitting on the front steps chatting with a guy who was holding a beer and laughing at something she was saying.

"Hi Brut."

"Hi yourself, cuz. How's life in the tropics?"

"Warm, dangerous. Great place for getting intimate with big ugly insects." I gave him an evil wink, remembering how he used to freak out whenever a blood sucker or water spider came near him when we were teenagers.

Brut shuddered and killed the rest of his beer. "Too cold out here. Later, cuz." He hurried through the front door.

Lou gave me a disapproving look. "Brut may be a dumbass, but he is just as upset at what his father's trying to pull as I am, probably more so because of how many times he's seen Dupe screw some poor soul out of their life savings."

"Maybe I should drag our esteemed uncle into the swamp and save the citizens of Simonton more grief."

"How about being patient and seeing how your first Thanksgiving in seven years turns out."

I shrugged, Lou had a point. If I acted like a bull in a china shop, chances were good I'd end up in hot water and Dupe would have another reason to squeeze Mom. I certainly didn't want that.

My introspective moment was interrupted by the arrival of Dupe and my cousin Prissy in a new Cadillac Eldorado. Despite having a complete jerk for a father, I'd always liked my oldest female cousin.

She was out of the car and in my arms before I could say a word. She kissed me and leaned back. "I've missed you something wicked, Bo."

230

"Aside from the penitentiary, you'd really like Guatemala, Pris. It's warm, the food is great and those lonely south of the border dudes really go for an American gal like you. Say, how's the boyfriend business these days?" The moment I mentioned boyfriends, I regretted it. Her face fell and she tensed up.

"Not so hot, Bo. Dad drives them off faster than a skunk at a church social. Heck, I even tried one of those online dating services, but his reputation soured even the few nibbles I got there. If you do get crazy enough to go back to the tropics, I'll carry your suitcase and pay my own way."

"It's a deal, sweetie," I said quietly enough so Dupe couldn't hear. Not that he seemed to be interested in me. He was surveying the house and the blueberry fields the way a vulture would admire a dead buffalo. The jerk was doing all he could to avoid drooling with anticipation. I took Prissy by the arm and escorted her inside so my disgust wouldn't boil over. Lou was right, I really needed to chill or I would be in mega hot water by sunset.

I busied myself peeling potatoes and a big turnip while Mom played reluctant hostess in the living room. Every other comment seemed to come from Dupe and either hinted at what he'd be doing once he owned our farm or how much money he'd squeezed from some other poor fool in Simonton. I got so desperate to ignore him I took a couple mini-marshmallows and used them as earplugs.

Mom had to nudge me in the ribs to get my attention when it was time to carve the turkey. I removed the gooey marshmallow remnants from my ears and tossed them into the compost pail under the sink.

Lou was last to the table and was about to sit when she gasped and had a stricken look on her face. "Oh hell and damnation. I just remembered what I was going to have Bo get at the store, fresh cranberries. Oh Uncle Dupe, I'm so sorry. I know that my cranberry relish is your favorite Thanksgiving dish."

I'll give my sister credit, she played the sorrowful niece bit perfectly. I didn't know where she was going with this, but I was curious as hell.

Dupe's greedy eyes bulged with outrage and I could see he was working himself into a verbal tirade.

Lou jumped up and patted his arm. "My sakes, I completely forgot. We have those wild cranberries growing out on the bean fence." Her face fell as she continued hesitantly, "Gee, Dupe, I dunno if they have enough flavor to be an acceptable substitute..." She let the question hang in the air like a perfectly placed streamer fly on the eddy down by Simonton Pond Dam.

Dupe was out of his chair before her mouth closed, gluttonous greed etched in every line of his face. "Get me a bowl, Lou. Now!"

Mom started to protest that there weren't any cranberries on the property.

"Do I smell burning stuffing?" I asked, running interference even though I wasn't sure where this was going.

My mother took the bait, rushing into the kitchen without saying another word while Lou handed Dupe a melamine bowl and fought to keep a straight face as he waddled toward the back door.

Five minutes later, Dupe was breathing down Lou's neck as she ran berries, orange slices and enough sugar to hide the bitter flavor through a food mill. She added a dash of lemon juice and spooned the mix into a fancy serving dish.

"That's more like it." Dupe grabbed the dish and headed for the table. Brut, Bub and Prissy hadn't caught on yet, but Mom looked torn as if she felt she should say something. Lou and I were biting our tongues so we wouldn't lose it. I knew whatever came next would be as much fun to watch as the midnight ride I'd given that horny priest back in Guatemala.

I'll give Dupe credit. He waited until Prissy said grace before dumping half the relish onto his plate. He didn't bother waiting until the other dishes were passed around before tucking into that heap of trouble sitting before him. The nightshade berries began releasing their poison almost immediately. Dupe's pupils dilated and he began sweating like it was a hundred degrees inside. His eyes began rolling and he started turning and looking wildly at everyone even while he continued scarfing down more relish. He gasped mightily and aspirated a mouthful, turning purple before spewing partly chewed relish all over Bub who turned white and fled out the front door, his brother following close behind. Dupe's eyes rolled back in his head and he pitched face first onto his plate.

There was a moment of stunned silence as we all waited. When it was clear that Abercrombie Fitzwallace Metcalf had departed this world, we looked at each other, wondering who would dare to speak first.

Prissy broke the silence. "I know this sounds terribly cruel, but maybe, just maybe, I can finally have a life."

Lou stood and went into the kitchen, returning in a moment with a tray of shot glasses and a dusty bottle of scotch. She poured some in each one and passed them around before sitting again. She raised her glass. "Hail Dupe, may your eternal reward fit your earthly crimes."

I thought that a bit cruel, but then again I had been away and in a much harsher environment for the past seven years. "What are we going to tell the sheriff?"

"The truth, with a teeny bit of embellishment," Lou said, pouring herself another shot. "Trust me, the sheriff won't be heartbroken to learn that Dupe is no longer with us. I bet he's spent more time than he could spare dealing with the unfortunates who got shafted by our late uncle. I'll do my flustered female routine and sob a bit. You can act shocked, while Mom and Prissy can burst into tears. I doubt Brut or Bub will surface until they're completely smashed. Frankly, I'll be surprised if either one of them remember what really happened. The look on their faces when he spewed food all over Bub was worth a million bucks," she said with great relish.

John R. Clark is a retired librarian from rural Maine. He uses his experiences as a recovering alcoholic and mental health professional, as well as numerous conversations with interesting library patrons, as inspiration for his short stories. When not writing, he reads avidly and reviews books and DVDs for journals and online blogs.

NOIR AT THE SALAD BAR

RAGBONES AND THE CASE OF THE CHRISTMAS GOOSE

BY RIMA PERLSTEIN RIEDEL

Did you know that Sherlock Holmes had a pet dog? His name was Ragbones. As one would expect of any dog who owned Sherlock Holmes, Ragbones was the smartest, toughest little scrapper you could ever meet! As a matter of fact, that's how Holmes met him—on a case.

This was no ordinary case and Rags, as he was nicknamed, was no ordinary dog. He figured prominently in "The Case of the Christmas Goose." The first time their paths crossed, the little fellow was fighting his way out of yet another scrap.

It was a cold, damp day in December. Sherlock Holmes had donned one of his favorite disguises and gone out in search of his latest quarry. Meanwhile, back at the office, he was about to receive a commission from a most unexpected quarter—the Baker Street Irregulars. Someone had snatched the boys' holiday goose. Jim, one of the younger boys was dispatched to 221B Baker Street, to present their problem to the Guvnor (as Holmes was called by the boys) and request that he take the case.

Jim was greeted at the door by Dr. Watson, Mrs. Hudson having gone to visit her ailing sister.

"Dr. Watson, is the Guvnor in? I got a very important case for 'im what involves the Baker Street Irregulars."

"You don't say?" Watson murmured, stroking his chin.

"I do say, sir!" Jim replied, nervously twirling his cap in his hands. Someone pinched our Christmas goose!" Upon hearing the boy's request, he immediately ushered him into the study.

"My, that does sound serious. Come right through, young man, and warm yourself by the fire. Mr. Holmes is out on a case, but I expect him back presently. Here, sit down and tell me what has happened, while I prepare a nice warm cup of cocoa as we await Mr. Holmes' return. Nasty night out there."

"Thank you, kindly, sir," the boy replied, sitting down gingerly. "It's like this—"

Hearing the door slam downstairs, Watson said, "Hold it young fella, here's Mr. Holmes now." Why don't you tell him your story? I'm sure he can help."

Holmes strode into the room, wearing one of his favorite disguises—that of a rag and bone man. On seeing his idol enter the study, Jim jumped up and reverently touched his hat to his head.

"I say, Watson, who do we have here? Why it's young Jim, one of my newest irregulars. Anything new to report on our present case, young Jim?"

"No, Mr. 'Olmes, I been sent on personal business."

"Really... and what would that be?"

"It's about that Christmas goose what you gave us. Someone's snatched it right from under our noses!"

"Come, boy, sit down and tell me all about it. Don't leave anything out."

Jim sat down again and told his story while Holmes listened intently.

"We was getting ready for our big 'oliday dinner, when all of a sudden we 'eard the most awful commotion coming from the alley. We left the bird and run out to see what were 'appening. Two big, mean dogs was pickin' on a little one, what were chewing on a bone bigger than hisself. They tried to take it from 'im, but the little scrapper put up quite a fight, though it were a losing battle. Well, we all grabbed some sticks and managed to chase them beasties away, but when we turned back, the little fella were gone—vanished into thin air! We tried to find 'im, 'cause 'e were all beat up. It were getting dark, so we finally gave up and headed back to the building. Well, bless me, if the goose hadn't vanished too! Someone done a scunner with our Christmas goose!"

"And you say the dog disappeared, too?"

"That it did, Guv...and 'im all bloody and bruised, poor little fella," he replied, shaking his head sadly. "We were that worried, we were."

"Curiouser and curiouser," Holmes murmured to himself. Then he turned to the boy and asked, "Was it a small black terrier with brown and white markings?"

Stunned, Jim answered, "That's right, sir. Ow'd you know that?"

"Elementary, my dear James. Look at your pant legs. Rough white tipped black hairs are sticking to them." Holmes rubbed his hands together as he continued.

"Gentlemen, I now know the identity of the culprit. We shall soon reclaim your Christmas goose. Come, Watson, Master Jim—the game's afoot and we have no time to lose! Even as we speak, the evidence is probably being torn to pieces. Jim, show me the exact place where you last saw the dog." Not bothering to change his costume, Holmes turned and rushed out of the room, Jim quickly following at his heels and Watson bringing up the rear.

ꝘꝘꝘ

Jim led the two men to the alley where the dog had disappeared. Holmes knelt down and picked up the bone that had been left behind when the dogs had run off. Next he and Watson accompanied Jim to the boys' home base. They were all sitting around, rubbing their grumbling stomachs and looking very unhappy as the three entered the building. It was made up of one large cavernous room with peeling paint, cracks and gouges in the walls—some so big that a small child could easily hide in them. Holmes studied the layout of the room. It was a cold, bare, square room, lit by a single candle and an ancient oil lamp. The only furniture was a long table made up of six wooden planks set on four large barrels. There were two long benches on either side. Two rough chairs, also made out of barrels sat in the corner of the room. They were half hidden by shadows. Holmes examined the table where the bird had been left, then took out his magnifying glass and thoroughly inspected the surrounding floor. While Holmes was conducting his inspection, the leader of the Irregulars, Tom, entered the room. Not wanting to interfere with the investigation, he watched in silent admiration, waiting for the chance to greet the great man. Finally, the Guvnor appeared to be done. Tom ambled over.

Energetically pumping the detective's hand by way of greeting, Tom asked, "Got any idea who did this Mr 'Olmes?"

"I do," Holmes replied. "The thief is right here in this room." Without another word, Holmes strode over to the farthest corner and moved a barrel aside. Crouched against the wall was a small ragged looking black terrier guarding the remnants of the holiday goose.

"Here's your culprit," Holmes announced. He reached in and grabbed the little dog by the scruff of its neck. The little scrapper snarled and struggled to escape while still keeping an iron grip on his prize. Holmes set the dog on the table, holding him down with one hand to prevent his escape.

Laughing, he said, "Well, we've got the thief and we've got the goods, but I'm afraid the latter is quite the worse for wear. Looks like he was in even greater need of that Christmas goose than you." Several of the boys groaned.

"Fear not, my intrepid troop." Holmes smiled. "I'll soon send another Goose your way—this one even bigger and better!"

The boys all cheered and surrounded Watson and Holmes, who still had his hand clamped firmly on the little thief.

Looking down at the mangy little dog and gently scratching his head, Holmes said, "That leaves us with one last problem. What do we do with this little scrapper? What do you fellows say to taking on a mascot?"

Tom answered for the boys. "I'd say that would be great, but we've barely got enough food for ourselves. Besides, I've just 'ad a brilliant idea, Mr. 'Olmes! The little scrapper seems to have taken to you. Look at him! He's right calmed down and already half asleep. I say we give 'im to you in appreciation for all your help. What do you think boys?" The boys all nodded in agreement.

Watching from the sidelines, Watson laughed. Clapping his friend on the back he said, "Well, Holmes, it looks like you've just inherited a dog."

Holmes smiled wryly and replied, "On the contrary, my dear friend—*we* have inherited one!"

With that, Holmes picked up the ragged little creature, stuffed it into the capacious folds of his coat and headed for the door. Turning back, he saluted the boys, then strode swiftly out of the building, followed by Dr. Watson.

The boys heard him say, "This little fellow is such a ragged little bag of bones, I think we'll call him Ragbones." The dog barked as if in agreement as the two men stepped into the street. Suddenly, blood curdling shrieks pierced the night. Growling fiercely, Ragbones struggled to escape. Finally breaking free from the confines of Holmes' coat, he launched himself to the ground and ran off into the foggy night.

Slapping his friend on the shoulder, Holmes sighed and said, "Well, my friend, it would appear that once again the game is afoot!"

Rima Perlstein Riedel has had essays and mini mysteries published in Scholastic Scope. She has also written a number of skits, one and two act plays for her multigenerational grant funded Manchester Youth/Senior Theater Troupe (MYST). "Ragbones" is inspired by her real life rescue dog named Patch. This story is dedicated to all dogs who have "rescued" their people!

CULINARY TALES WITH A BITE

FED UP

BY LOUISE TAYLOR

A whirlwind trip to Paris to sample the city's most celebrated restaurants!

Mindy Dithers was living the dream...*almost.* She was grappling with a question she imagined many women contemplated during the long dreary plod of a marriage: how to unload an annoying husband while hanging on to the cash and prizes? Oh, and without spending ten-to-twenty in the slammer.

The trip to Paris would be perfect if only Daryl wasn't part of the package. But like an overgrown tumor that couldn't be cut out, Daryl Dithers and Mindy were stuck together. To say he cramped her style was putting it mildly.

Dressed in a delicate pale pink twin-set, beige trousers, and a string of cultured pearls, no one would guess Mindy Dithers harboured such murderous thoughts.

Guess again! she thought darkly, wheeling her shopping cart through the famous Parisian food market and department store Le Bon Marché.

I should never, she mused for the thousandth time, *have pretended to be some prissy debutante just to capture Daryl. Why did I listen to Cindy? I should have just been myself!*

It was too late for that now, Mindy reflected, as she stopped to examine a wedge of goat cheese infused with lavender and rosemary. Her whole life was a sham. While she had hoped that she would be able to unveil her true self to Daryl, bit by bit, as the marriage progressed, she had actually become more deeply entrenched in the role of the pearl necklace, sweater-set-wearing little wife. Back in high school she used to beat up girls like her. She missed the irreverent, salty, survivor Mindy.

Pushing her cart toward the fresh fruit aisle, she realised she had lost Daryl somewhere back in the pasta section. Well, that figured.

NOIR AT THE SALAD BAR

It was perplexing. After years of yearning for little else, Mindy was astonished to discover that money and security weren't enough—not all by themselves. Back before she had them, she would have sworn on a double martini that they would fix her life once and for all.

"I need to get me a rich man!" How many times had she slurred that as she perched on a barstool after the evening hadn't panned out and she was going home alone...or with someone just as broke as her?

For the first few weeks of their marriage, back when Mindy needed rest with a capital R after years spent trying to hook a man who would take her far away from her trailer park past, the money and security *had* been enough. It was novel padding into an all-equipped kitchen in the morning, making coffee with one of those George Clooney machines, taking organic soy milk from a gleaming chrome refrigerator before passing into a large elegant living room to curl up with a magazine. Spending her days getting manis and pedis, highlighting her blonde hair until it crunched when her head hit the pillow.

She met Daryl in Miami after Cindy got them into a private club where Daryl and dozens of men just like him were attending a weekend conference on hedge-fund management. Cindy, a gold digger par excellence, could sniff out money faster than a hound picked up the scent of a wounded bear.

"You're starting to look used, honey," Cindy told Mindy that first morning in Miami, squinting at her in the bright sunshine as they sipped mimosas and picked at croissants. Cindy frequently gave Mindy unwanted reality checks.

"I'm just tired," Mindy replied, trying to keep the annoyance out of her voice. She couldn't afford to be offended. Cindy was picking up the tab.

"More 'n tired," Cindy drawled, draining her drink. "You're getting hard-like. You need to settle on one."

Mindy rolled her eyes. She was only thirty-one, and her driver's license gave her twenty-six. She had time.

"You have to be an asset to roll with me, babe," Cindy said bluntly, refreshing the gloss on her plumped up lips.

There was not much friendship lost between the two women. Mindy, blonde and charismatic, was an asset as long as she drew attention. Cindy, living on a dwindling bank loan she had forged a few documents to obtain, was in Miami for one thing only: to land a man with money. A husband, to be precise. The minute Mindy stopped aiding in this endeavour, Cindy would cut her loose without looking back.

After brunch, they returned to the tiny hotel room they were sharing to rest and prepare for their evening. Cindy rejected every last item in Mindy's suitcase.

"Too slutty."

"Too whorish."

"Too cheap."

She finally decked Mindy out in an outfit of her own: a demure knee-length lavender-colored dress paired with silvery kitten heels and fake pearls. She styled Mindy's hair and applied a modest amount of makeup.

"Are you eff-ing kidding me?" Mindy gazed at herself in the bathroom mirror. She felt like Samson shorn of his power. "I can't work in this getup!"

"This is what they like," Cindy explained patiently.

"I don't think they do!" Mindy had been with her share of moguls and they had all gone crazy for her tiny skirts and push-up bras.

"Yeah, when all's they want is action. To keep 'em, you got to trick 'em. Make them imagine you on their arm at the office party. At the college reunion. In their parent's freaking house on Thanksgiving!"

Cindy was right about the club. The conference was filled cheek by jowl with mostly male Wall Streeters and venture capitalists down from New York for the weekend. Mindy and Cindy caused a sensation. In their pastel outfits and shimmering jewellery they managed to project a heady mixture of virginal propriety and eager willingness for fun. It was the performance of a lifetime. Mindy looked at a gaggle of women at the bar—the hard, determined faces and tight, revealing clothing—she had to admit that without Cindy coaching her, she would probably have been amongst them. Picked up for the night then dumped. Again.

It was almost midnight when she met Daryl. Though he left her indifferent, with his pudgy weak face, it was clear that he was attracted to her, sending fuzzy navels to the table where she sat with Cindy, trying to look carefree and light as a feather. As Mindy raised her glass to him across the bar, Daryl finally got up and sauntered over.

Ten years her senior, he seemed to prove the old adage about all the good ones being taken. Prissy and petulant, he was one of those city bankers who liked talking about his work. Luckily, Cindy had read aloud the financial news section of the newspaper the night before, in hopes that they might sound slightly knowledgeable, and by some miracle Mindy was able to hold her own. Daryl actually thought she was educated. His favorite topic, however, turned out to be food, and here was an area where Mindy did possess some experience. As a child, she spent great swathes of time in her grandmother's kitchen whenever her mama was drying out or running wild with some man. Sitting at the table with her crayons, she watched her grandmother salt eggplant, chop basil and marinate artichokes and turnips. Daryl sat mesmerized while she described her grandmother's secrets from the kitchen. At the end of the evening, he asked to see her again. Within nine months they were married.

After the better part of a decade living on the edge—the thin, wobbly outer lip of the edge—Mindy was darn near wrung out. It was novel to have a man who didn't beat her or gamble away his earnings. As Cindy pointed out, Daryl represented what was missing in her life: comfort, respect…a bank account. Looking at it this way, Mindy had to concede that Daryl was okay, as far as husbands went. But all too soon she was wondering how far that actually was. When she complained to Cindy that he just wasn't attractive, Cindy took a logical approach: couldn't she say the same about plenty of other men she had been with? Cindy, who had landed a tech geek venture capitalist from California, had an unlimited supply of slogans to rally Mindy, her favorite being: Weren't all cats grey in the dark? Besides, with enough alcohol, just about anyone started to look good. Her advice when Mindy was ready to walk away? Drink more.

CULINARY TALES WITH A BITE

If Daryl wasn't much in bed, financially he performed splendidly. Enough for a six bedroom home in town and another small cottage on the beach. Mindy soon realized that Daryl couldn't have just one of anything. Besides two homes, there were two identical BMWs in the garage, two accounts at the bank, even two refrigerators in the kitchen for Christ's sake. When it came to food, he was particularly insecure, frequently eating two full meals in the evening. It was a little like living with Henry the Eighth. Although Mindy had watched her grandmother cook, she'd never done much of it herself. She began ordering elaborate take-out dinners with the spending money Daryl gave her, pretending she had cooked the meals herself. She hid the empty food containers, sneaking them into the neighbor's trash can after Daryl left for work.

Within months, Daryl morphed into the prototype of the bloated broker. With his manicured nails and solid gold cufflinks, he reeked of smarmy self-indulgence. His weak chin disappeared into folds of fat. No matter how much he earned or bought or ate, he could never get past the fear that there wouldn't be enough. While he never mentioned his childhood, at their wedding reception his elderly aunt Elda had given Mindy the lowdown, which involved a mentally ill mother, an errant father, and an empty fridge.

"That's why he chose a nice girl like you, dear," Aunt Elda smiled at Mindy through filmy eyes. "After his terribly precarious past, he wants someone who can give him stability. You know, security. One winter," Elda continued, leaning in until Mindy could see the crop of whiskers on her chin, "the poor little sausage couldn't even go to school because he had no shoes."

Well, that explains the hundred-odd pairs in his walk-in closet, Mindy thought, trying to work up empathy. Perhaps they may have bonded over their mutually squalid childhoods if Daryl had been a nicer person, but he was frequently so arrogantly unlikable that Mindy stayed isolated and mute. Besides, she had her own hardscrabble past to contend with. It was a dog-eat-dog world and she would rather eat than be eaten. They were a couple of fakes, but it didn't bring them closer. "Beggars can't be choosers," Cindy coldly reminded her during their furtive late night phone calls.

Their marriage got off to a bad start right away. Their honeymoon in Venice was supposed to be a celebration of love. And, in a way, it was. It celebrated Daryl's love for *la gastronomia italiana*. Night after night he gorged—the antipasti, the pasta, the fish or meat course, the cheese, the wines, the sweets—returning to their hotel room too satiated to make love. Mindy's silky night things went virtually unravished. The same could not be said for the dessert cart. Daryl scrupulously planned a circuit that included every Venetian restaurant any Trip Advisor fan had ever gushed over. They didn't see the inside of a single museum or church.

By the fourth night, the one dish that was making Mindy's mouth water was the swarthy young waiter holding the menu. Mindy might dress the part of the prim wife, she might convincingly act the part of the prim wife, but scratch the surface and you'd see how un-prim she could be.

If only Daryl over-indulged in women the way he did in everything else, she'd have a legitimate cause for divorce and be entitled to half of everything. Infidelity was one of the very few loopholes in the marital agreement Daryl had drawn up tighter than the skin on an Eskimo's drum. He was also paranoid, it turned out.

On bad days, she calculated that if she could hold out until she was, say, fifty, she would probably grow into a sedate life that revolved primarily around rich food. Cindy, who had read a few psychology books, told Mindy that she was addicted to adrenaline; she had post-traumatic stress that made her mistake danger for excitement. That may be well and true, but life with Daryl still sucked, aside from the money.

Mindy stumbled upon her idea the day Daryl's annual check-up concluded with a stern warning. Daryl, whose paranoia extended to anything medical, begged Mindy to accompany him to the exam his workplace required. The results were not good: his blood pressure was up and his cholesterol was off the charts. He was on his way to cardiac arrest, holding the distinct honor of being the worst patient Dr Carmellan had come across in Daryl's age group. Daryl hung his head as the physician declared that he would not be held responsible should anything happen if Daryl didn't change his habits.

And neither will I, Mindy thought, her eyes narrowing, *If I plan everything just right.*

The very next night she made *confit de canard*—one of Daryl's favorite dishes. Mindy had started experimenting in the kitchen out of boredom more than anything else. She found the old adage to be true: if you could read, you could cook. She followed the recipe faithfully, only going 'rogue' when it came to the vegetables. Instead of steaming them to contrast the fatty content of the duck as the recipe suggested, she sautéed them in the very grease the duck sweated out, along with a hefty portion of potatoes she marinated in rosemary and olive oil.

"Mindy," Daryl whined as he sat down to dinner, "you know I'm not supposed to!"

Despite his protest, she noted that he was already tucking his napkin into his collar.

"Duck is actually a lean meat," she assured him. "And Dr Carmellan said you need more vegetables." Grease dripped from the ladle as she spooned potatoes onto his plate.

For dessert, she prepared a rich sponge soaked in saffron-laced cane sugar, with mascarpone on the side.

The next morning, she surprised him with a smoothie.

"Dr Carmellan said you have to cut back," Mindy chirped, placing the tall chocolaty drink in front of him. She had gone straight from the doctor's office to a sports supply store, where she purchased weight-gain powder, hiding the box and accompanying cartons of cream behind some boxes in the garage. She told Daryl it was a high-protein drink designed specifically for weight loss.

"But I need a real breakfast—I can't work all morning on just a cup of chocolate milk," Daryl complained.

"Try it," Mindy urged, putting her arms around his thick girth. "Come on. Be a good boy. One taste and I'll make you scrambled eggs as a reward."

"With bacon?" Daryl pouted.

"One piece for every sip!"

Daryl managed to draw the shake out to fifteen sips.

A promise is a promise, Mindy thought gaily as she fried up the rashers of bacon. It was fun having a project! At over 1400 calories per drink, the daily shakes served with bacon and eggs followed by the rich lunches Daryl indulged in with his banker colleagues and the double-feature dinners he demanded in the evenings all worked their magic. Within weeks, he was waddling.

Mindy decided it was almost time to move into the next phase of her plan. In her sweetest, wifey-est voice, she suggested a vacation...a follow-up to their honeymoon in Venice.

Paris. The land of *crème fraiche* and *foie gras*. Wines and cheeses and truffles and sauces and *crème brulée*. Far from home, in a country where neither of them spoke the language. It was the perfect place to execute the next part of her plan. The final course, so to speak.

Although she had never been to Paris, even Mindy could see that the hotel staff pigeonholed them as "Ugly Americans." It was little wonder with Daryl snapping his fingers at the waiters, demanding butter for his bread and cola to accompany his *escargots à la Bourguignonne*. More than ever, Mindy was impatient to be free of him.

They had full champagne breakfasts followed by three-course luncheons. In the afternoon, while Daryl napped before they went to dinner, Mindy sat alone in a little café near their hotel, carefully thinking. It was a balmy afternoon when she proposed they walk from their hotel to Le Bon Marché to purchase some delicacies. They had reservations that evening for Lasserre—the culinary high point of the trip for Daryl, who had spent the morning poring over the restaurant's menu, dictionary in his lap. He was still dithering between the scallops served with pumpkin raviolis and the *filet de bœuf*.

"It's a little old-fashioned," he explained to Mindy as they strolled across the ornate Pont d'Alexandre. "It isn't one of those new, trendy restaurants. We won't find any chrome and mirrors in there."

Why did Daryl say everything with such obnoxious pedantry? He didn't speak, he lectured. It was one of many things she would not miss about him. Another, she reflected, as they passed an old beggar, was his smug, unquestioning belief that he

246

was entitled to live better than others. Daryl skirted the weathered old man as though he had the plague.

"Give him a euro," Mindy urged.

"No. It will only encourage him," Daryl retorted, as if they were talking about feeding a squirrel that had crept into the back yard.

"It's a veritable institution." Daryl was back on Lasserre. "The type of place the old money likes."

Which is exactly what we are not, Mindy thought, rolling her eyes. Still, as Cindy frequently said: nouveau riche was better than no riche at all.

Of course, being riche *all by myself is going to be best of all*, Mindy smiled to herself.

"I've heard the wine selection is exceptional," Daryl continued as he puffed along, pink with exertion. But Mindy had stopped listening. Her attention was diverted by a strapping member of the French armed forces who was striding toward them, a semi-automatic clasped in his strong, calloused hands. Daryl, sweat slicking his upper lip, droned on as Mindy and the soldier exchanged a glance just long enough for a jolt of lust to pass between them. It made her ache for her old way of life.

Not much longer now, she assured herself.

At Le Bon Marché, Mindy retraced her steps until she found Daryl gorging himself on pasta at the store's onsite café. They took a taxi back to the hotel and prepared for their dinner at Lasserre.

By the time the trip to Paris drew to a close, Daryl was florid with food and drink. Even his eyeballs were bulging. Walking onto the plane, Mindy took a deep breath. This was it.

As they left France behind them, Daryl sipped at a glass of champagne. While he rummaged in his bag for the sachet of Ladurée macaroons he had bought before boarding, Mindy carefully opened the precious vial of powder she had kept hidden in her handbag throughout the trip. Furtively, she added the contents to his glass, delicately mixing the drink. Retrieving his macaroons, Daryl settled back into his seat and picked up his glass.

"This champagne is bitter!" he said loudly. Her heart pounded at the words.

"Darling, we aren't in Lasserre now."

"But we are traveling first class," Daryl grumbled, as he drained his glass.

Yes, and this is your final trip, so you better enjoy it, Mindy thought. Biting her lip, she looked across him out the window to watch Paris disappear in a glitter of lights.

A night flight, the cabin lights were soon dimmed. The conditions were perfect: Daryl, gorging on champagne and macaroons, would be sedentary for hours. When the malaise struck, Mindy planned to lower his eye mask so he appeared to be sleeping. She willed herself to act as naturally as possible as the powder took effect. Within minutes he was out, his head tilted back, mouth open. His breathing soon slowed and his body slumped.

Somewhere over the Atlantic, Daryl passed into a coma. Upon landing, he was loaded directly into a stretcher and rushed to the hospital.

Who knew he would cling so tenaciously to life? While his brain was in a deep non-responsive state, his massive heart kept on pumping. He lingered longer than expected, forcing Mindy to assume yet another role—that of anxious, grieving spouse. She wasn't very good at it and occasionally caught Daryl's colleagues—who took it in turns visiting his hospital bed—glancing at her speculatively as she sat flipping through fashion magazines. She was planning on taking a cruise as soon as Daryl…well, after he was *gone*. The open sea might be breezy and she was choosing her wardrobe. If Daryl held out much longer, the rainy season would begin and she'd have to wait. In any case, she was going to make herself scarce the minute Daryl succumbed and the will was read.

Finally, on a clear blue Monday morning, Daryl gave up the fight. Mindy was having her hair done when the hospital phoned with the news.

"Oh, okay," Mindy said amid the hum of the hair dryer. "Do I need to come over to…to identify the body…or whatever?"

"It isn't a murder," the treating physician said drily, causing Mindy to tremble.

That night she felt surprisingly subdued. It's not that she regretted what she'd done. But she did feel sad for Daryl. He'd had a tough childhood. She decided to go to an out-of-the-way Italian restaurant Daryl had been fond of for her own private commemoration.

She had fought hard to keep her slender figure throughout her marriage, but tonight she would order a full meal—and finish up with a tiramisu.

She had done it. She had played the part for as long as needed and now she would be rich. Rich and free. No need to pretend to love someone. No more sleeping around to make ends meet. For the first time in her adult life, she could wear exactly what she wanted, without worrying about the impact it would have on any man. She'd stuck it out, and it would be worth it—two homes, two fat bank accounts, probably even life insurance—she hadn't been able to check. Daryl kept all his private papers locked away.

Mindy emptied out her wallet to pay for the meal. How long would it be before she got the money, she wondered. She was out of cash. The lawyers probably made some sort of widow's fund available right away. She should have thought to put some aside while she was waiting.

No matter—the house was stocked with food and drink. The cars were both filled with gas. She just needed to wait out this final step.

How soon could she contact Daryl's lawyer? Would tomorrow look callous and greedy?

She needn't have worried about it. Daryl's lawyer contacted her the next day.

"My sincere condolences," Mr. Wesley began. It was the same lawyer who had prepared the prenuptial Daryl insisted on.

"Thank you," Mindy tried to make her voice sound nasally—as though she'd been crying.

"You must be so proud of him," the lawyer continued, smooth as silk.

This comment threw her a little. Proud of...? That he was a banker? That he'd stuffed himself to death like a hog?

"I am," she conceded uncertainly.

"You know, he told me his story—his past," Mr Wesley continued.

"Ah, yes," Mindy said for something to say.

"He had such a difficult time," Mr Wesley said.

"Oh, he did," Mindy agreed softly, while her brain was screaming, *What are you talking about? Get to the point! How much did he leave me?*

"And you, too—so admirable!" Mr Wesley sounded like he was about to cry.

"Well, it is hard losing a husband—" Mindy agreed soberly.

"Many women wouldn't be so generous. But Daryl said you were a survivor. You were both survivors," Mr Wesley cut into her sentence.

"Okay…" She was lost. What were they talking about?

"I must say it's refreshing," the lawyer said. "In fact, it's the first time in my thirty years as an attorney that I've seen an entire estate left to charity. Every last penny. Now, that is commitment. Of course, Daryl told me about his past hardships. The winter without shoes, the empty fridge. The Children's Food Fund will be able to do so much good! What devotion! Why you, you and Daryl—you renew my faith in the human race."

Mindy was no longer listening. The shock was too much. She was buried beside Daryl a week later.

Louise Taylor is a copy editor for a scientific publication from 9-5. Evenings and weekends, she juggles family, housework, homework and mystery writing. Born in Colwyn Bay, Wales, Louise lived in England and California before settling in Paris, France. Her fiction has been published in Six Little Things. Her favorite guilty pleasure is the chestnut and cream-based mont-blanc.

BUENA VISTA SANDWICH CLUB

BY FRANK COLLIA

Emery breathed in the end of the day, the salt-laced breeze of beach dusk. She had made good bank that afternoon, riding a Zen groove between production and concession. She operated her food truck solo, unusual and not recommended, but she liked working alone. She needed it.

Hard work had never been a problem. If anything, it proved to be too much of a virtue in her other life. However, now, here, it felt liberating, gratifying, like an arbitrated penance. Even the act of wiping the dry-erase sandwich board beside her truck each evening, despite the menu never changing, had grown from task to ritual. Emery had found her place in the world and for that she would offer thanks.

She served one item: Cuban sandwiches. Two, if one counted bottled drinks: water and assorted Latin American sodas. Simplicity. Occasionally, she considered expanding to *café con leches*, but that would require an expensive espresso machine and a coworker to run it. That wouldn't do. Her business could swing the cost, but it would take too big a chunk out of her psychological bottom line.

Tucking the blank sandwich board under her arm, she took in the Gulf, the water appearing one with the beach in the fading winter light, a billowing shadow. In every sense, she had come a long way to get here. She did not know how long she could stay, but she'd be damned if she wouldn't appreciate every moment while it lasted.

She heard the footsteps before the voice, so she didn't jump, didn't overreact. Turning, she put on a smile. "I'm sorry?"

"I only just asked if you were still open, but..." The man standing before her pointed at the board under her arm.

He looked at least ten years older than her, maybe even mid-fifties, and close to an extra C-note on the scale. His stiff floral-print shirt and linen slacks marked him as a tourist trying to pass as a local, clothes picked off a mannequin in a department store's tropical display.

To Emery, he looked a lot like back home.

She shrugged, acknowledging the sandwich board answered his question. "I'm here every day."

"I know. I eat here all the time, it's just—"

"Funny, I'm pretty good with faces." She wanted back in the truck, but he stood between her and the door.

"Okay, I lied." He appeared to be playing at casualness. "I thought if I sounded like a regular you'd take some pity on me."

Emery played along for now. "Are you saying I should pity my regulars?"

"What? No." He snorted out a laugh. "I'm actually here visiting my niece."

"Your niece?"

"Yeah, and she couldn't stop raving about your food."

"So she's a regular?"

"I don't know about that, but she's eaten here and, like I said, loves it."

Emery shifted the board so that she could grip it with both hands if needed. "That's great to hear, but I know for a fact that my food tastes even better for lunch."

She chose to move toward the door. What happened next would be on him.

He moved to let her pass. "How about this: I give you double for one of your inferior—your words—dinner sandwiches?"

With a foot on the truck's step, she paused. Not because she cared about the money.

"I'll sweeten it some more," he said. "Double the price and a great review on this thing here." He tapped the phone attached to his belt. "As soon as my niece shows me how."

She looked him over for a moment, then stepped fully into the truck and closed the door behind her. "Let me check what I have left," she said, reappearing in the open service window.

"You don't know how much I appreciate it. I've been thinking about this all day."

252

Emery moved out of his view. She didn't have to check her supplies, just herself. She closed her eyes, pictured the beach, the sun, and wondered if the good memories stayed as vivid over time as the bad.

"Just give the press a couple minutes to warm up," she said, back in the window, back to smiling.

"That's alright. I don't need it pressed."

"What did you order?"

"What do you mean? A Cuban."

"Cubans are pressed. You just want a sandwich, find a Subway."

The man raised his hands, palms up. "My apologies. I should've known better."

"I'll give you a pass this once." Emery pulled in the napkin dispenser from the counter outside the window. "Where did you say you were from?"

The left side of the man's mouth curled. "Up north."

"What, like Santa?"

"Not that far, but you couldn't tell from all the snow."

"Not a worry here."

"No, this is beautiful. I can see why someone would set up shop here."

She didn't know if he was good or she was out of practice, but she couldn't quite read him. "Summers are tough."

"They're tough everywhere," he said, his tone flattening, now almost deliberately inscrutable. "But this, this I could get used to."

"You could move down. Be closer to your niece."

"I could." Despite his joviality, his eyes never left hers. "Maybe if this Cuban's as good as I hear."

"Why don't you go have a seat and I'll bring it over." She nodded to a bench on the other side of the sidewalk. She didn't expect him to accept the offer, but hoped he'd turn around reflexively to follow her gaze. At least long enough for her to see if he had a bulge in the back of his pants.

But he didn't budge. "I'm good."

"So's the press," she said. She moved out of view, maintaining visual contact with him via the mirror affixed to the side of the truck.

As if anticipating this, he turned and spoke to the mirror. "You mind talking me through it?"

"Through what?"

"Making it. The sandwich."

"Seriously?"

"What can I say? I have a little soft spot for food." He patted his belly and snorted another laugh. "Okay, a big soft spot."

Emery peaked around the window frame, hoping to catch a profile glimpse of the man, but he had already turned back to face her. *He's good* and *I'm rusty*, she thought. Then, *crap*.

"Well, okay," she began. "First, you start with the bread. Has to be Cuban. *Pan Cubano*. Nothing else counts."

"You sure like your rules."

"Everything worthwhile has rules."

"Glad you feel that way."

She let that slide. "Then you butter the press and place the two halves of the bread face down on it to soak up that buttery fat and get a good crisp going." She allowed the butter to sizzle, that heavenly aroma to start to swirl.

"When the bread's right," she continued, "you start layering. Start with ham, then the roast pork—"

"How long do you marinate the pork?"

"About twelve hours. Don't ask me my recipe because if I tell you..." She leaned back into view, but didn't finish her sentence.

He smiled. "Go on."

"Swiss, and only Swiss cheese, and then dill pickles sliced lengthwise. A long smear of yellow mustard on the top bread and you're good to go. More butter on the press, even more on top of the sandwich, then drop the top and seal in all that flavor."

While she waited, she didn't speak. She continued watching him in the mirror. He didn't move, didn't speak either. *A Cuban standoff*, she thought.

After three minutes, she sliced the sandwich diagonally, plated it with a handful of plantain chips, and passed it through the window. "Order up."

The man took the food, his eyes finally dropping from her, his expression turning lustful.

Emery cleared her throat. "Double, right?" *Money's still money*, she thought. "Twenty."

He handed her a crisp bill and didn't waste any more time before digging in. "Oh my god," he moaned. "That's the best thing I ever put in my mouth." A scrap of meat fell from his lips as he tried to laugh. "That didn't come out the way I wanted."

"I bet."

After swallowing his second big bite, he motioned to the writing on the side of the truck. *Buena Vista Sandwich Club.* "Funny, you don't look Cuban."

"What gave it away," she asked, "the red hair or the pasty skin?"

"You go to cooking school?"

"I took a few classes, yeah."

"Career change?"

She reinforced her customer service grin. She no longer needed him to turn around to know he was packing. Or why. The only uncertainty remaining was whether he would finish his sandwich first.

"Well, it suits you," he continued. "Real artistry to what you do."

"And what is it you do?"

"Me? Nothing special. Collections mostly."

She filled her lungs with sea air. How, she wondered, if time were linear could the past keep catching up to you? But, of course it could. After all, it had a head start.

"No one's around," he said.

He had caught her scoping beyond him. Sloppy. Worse, he was right. The deserted beach, the vacant parking lot. No one to hear. No witnesses. No one to get in the way of the inevitable.

Worse, but exactly how, she didn't know yet.

"I'm gonna come in now, okay, Emery? Gonna come in and talk."

She turned off the press, brushed off her workspace. Her stomach growled, matching the sound of the truck door opening and closing behind him. She hadn't eaten yet, had planned to stop for sushi.

"Don't bother trying to figure it out," he said behind his pulled .38. "You don't know who I am."

"But you know me?" She grew more relaxed the more smug he became. She liked when they got like this, when they strapped on their arrogance like blinders. When they were just where she wanted them.

"Know who you are. How much you're worth."

"Dead or alive?"

He snorted, this time without the trace of humor. "That's negotiable. I'd prefer alive."

She pointed to his gun. "Really?"

"Negotiating tool. Listen," he said. "Believe it or not, I am really down here visiting my niece. Then I see you and think—"

"It's fate?"

"I think it's a business opportunity."

"Me and you?"

"I asked around. You got some good word of mouth around here and from what I just tasted you're even better than I've heard."

"Thank you?"

"And I was serious. I always thought about getting into the food game. A little place of my own."

"Your own?"

He shrugged. "We'd be partners."

"See, I don't really work well with other people."

"I'm not going to work with you, honey. You're gonna work and I'm gonna get paid, let's say, what, seventy percent? That sound fair?"

"And you're positive no one else knows you're here right now?"

"No one."

"You swear?"

"What'd I say?"

"Just so we're clear..."

"What do you want, a notary—"

His gun dropped from his hand as the small chef's knife she had hidden in her apron shot into his throat. Just as swiftly, she pulled it out and covered the puncture with a dish towel before it could spout. Then, to free her hands for other tasks, she held the towel in place by reinserting the knife through the fabric.

For a second, she caught his eye, his frozen gape of shock and, if she had to guess, a little respect. *You don't bring a gun to a kitchen fight*, she thought as she jabbed a serrated knife she had used for the sandwich, into his gut and twisted. And to think she had worried about rustiness.

With a professional economy of movement, she grabbed a clear plastic tarp from beneath her workstation and spread it on the floor. Above her, he swayed, double-stuck, wheezing, no doubt second-guessing his negotiation tactics.

Emery stood, turned her short-lived business partner around, then bent over and chopped him sharply across the back of the knees. He buckled and she used his momentum to lower him onto the tarp. Standing over him, she reached down and removed the knife from his throat. It was evidence, of course, but also expensive to replace.

After wrapping his sizable frame as tight as she could, she stood, admiring the cleanliness of her work. She had worried she'd have to hose out the truck, which would have seriously cut into her sleep that night. But now she just had to dump the body and if the past few minutes had taught her anything it was that she still remembered a thing or two.

As for him claiming he didn't tell anyone about her, she believed him. Which meant she could stay a while longer. Which meant she had marinade to make. Meat to prep. Otherwise, it wouldn't be a Cuban.

Frank Collia lives near Tampa, FL, where he writes author bios in the third person when not searching for *el más sabroso* Cuban sandwich. His short fiction has been featured in *What Has Two Heads, Ten Eyes, and Terrifying Table Manners? I, Dark Tales from Elder Regions: New York,* and *Mental Ward: Experiments.* Tweet him @temporary_lull.

BEEF STEW

BY E L JOHNSON

"So this is how you express yourself," Mama said. "Why can't you be more like your brothers?"

I peered at the steaming bowl of meaty brown liquid I'd placed before her. She sniffed at it, her bulbous nose wrinkling.

"Smells funny," she said.

"It's good, I swear."

"That'd be the day!" she exclaimed. "See what I mean, Gorn? This is what I'm talking about. He doesn't raze villages, he doesn't crunch men's bones, he won't even swear! What am I supposed to do with him?"

I hung my head. This was not the first time my ineptitude as an ogre had been pointed out, but it was the first time she'd mentioned it to someone outside the family.

I looked at our guest. Across from Mama sat Gorn, clothed in the loincloth and ceremonial bone necklace that announced him as our clan's shaman. He stroked his long greying beard and looked strangely at the bowl of steaming liquid before him. He glanced at me and tentatively poked the bowl with a gnarled finger.

"It's hot!" he said.

"It's supposed to be," I said.

My brothers, Grunch and Sugblud exchanged looks. Grunch pounded his fist on the cave floor, making the misshapen rock bowls tremble. Hot liquid splashed out onto the ground.

I shot him a dirty look. "You're making a mess!"

"Good." He grinned, flashing rows of broken yellow teeth.

The shaman looked back at his steaming bowl. "And this is....food?"

"It looks like crap," Grunch said, sniffing it disdainfully.

"It's not even innards!" Sugblud complained.

"It's meat!" I said. "It's *beeefff stoo.*"

The others looked at me incredulously. *"Stoo?"* Mama repeated. "What is that?"

I walked to a corner of our cave, rummaging through the debris of broken bones, decaying animal pelts, and rocks until I found it. I held up the small square object and brushed off the dirt, flipping it open. I delicately turned the flimsy sheets, covered with a foreign language and curious images, until I found it. *Beeefff stoo*, the human had called it.

It was dirty and covered with grime but I held a treasure in my hands. I'd stolen it from our last foray into the nearby human village. I'd showed promise as an ogre until then, or so I'd thought.

Inordinately small for my kind, I'd gone with Grunch and Sugblud to prove my worth. I should have known better. Bigger and stronger than me, Sugblud had shoved me into the house where I sailed through a window with a shout.

Screams and cries sounded. I was not alone.

I opened my eyes and came face to face with a miniature pink two-legged creature. A human cub, most likely. It shrieked and dove under a raised platform on four legs, hiding behind the huddled form of its mother.

I got to my feet, shaking off glass and bits of their wall. My brothers' laughter in the distance mocked me.

The largest of the humans stood up. He was a male but made a poor defence, trembling like a leaf. He moved in front of the others and whipped out a wooden implement from atop the platform, wielding it at the ready.

My mouth curled in a smile. Surely he knew I could kill him where he stood. Yet the human did not move. Instead he said "Pleeezzz" over and over.

I stared at the male. This must be a special word. Maybe it was a battle cry!

I let out my best blood curdling roar in response, but it came out more like a cry of alarm.

Then the smell hit me. This did not have the sharp tang of fresh blood about it, nor the rancid stink as we ripped open fresh bowels. This was different. It smelled....good.

I looked around the room. There, hiding under the raised platform were the mother and her two cubs, shaking and mewling like rabbits. To my surprise, they did not eat on a cave floor like us. On top of the platform sat a pot of steaming brown liquid, surprisingly having survived my crash intact. I stared and inhaled the delicious scent. It had a rich, meaty, intoxicating flavor that wafted under my nose and made my mouth water.

I stared and pointed at the food. "What is that?"

Of course the beings didn't understand me, lacking the mental capabilities to understand Ogre.

I edged closer and pointed again at the intoxicating food. It smelled much better than animal bones and rotting carcasses. I could practically taste it. My fangs showed from my mouth as I salivated, licking my lips. The youngest cub screamed.

I ignored the humans and reached for the bubbling pot of food. It looked mysterious, tempting me with little floating squares of meat. I wanted it.

I dipped my finger into it. It burned! I shrieked and snatched my hand away, sucking on my burnt finger.

The male stared. He took a curved rounded object and dunked it into the pot, filling it with the steaming mixture. I watched as the human blew on it, then held it up to his mouth and tilted it, taking a sip. He held it out to me, his hands shaking. Precious brown liquid slopped over the sides and onto the messy floor. "Pleeezzzz. Beeefff *stoo*," he said.

I took the object and followed his example, blowing on its tantalizing contents. I blew too strongly and some flew out and hit the floor. Small chunks of meat floated in the liquid, along with other things I could not identify. What were these things? A different kind of meat? No, that wasn't right. These animals did not eat themselves.

I opened wide and upended the contents into my mouth. Rich meaty liquid poured down my gullet. It was wonderful. I swallowed and licked my lips. I wanted more. I drained the whole pot of the stuff, leaving when my brothers called for me.

I began going back after that. First a few weeks later, then once a week, and soon every other day. They grew used to me. It helped that I brought them rocks to rebuild the wall I'd broken. The male who fed me the meal at first was scared, but seeing I only wanted food, he taught me how they cut meat from the cow carcass and didn't eat it raw. He showed me strange human foods, called *kareotts* and *pohtayetoes*. Never had I paid such attention before.

It excited me, learning about human things like *par-slee* and *bee-fff*. One of the happiest days I'd had was when he gave me a funny looking square object. He called it a *buuk*. It was a wonderful square item, full of images of food. *Beeefff stoo* was my favorite.

Which brings me back to my predicament. Dinner. I'd meant it to be a surprise, a tantalising treat to show Mama and my brothers what a wonderful secret I'd discovered. Who would have thought that such weak pink animals could produce something that tasted so good?

I returned to the table, cradling the *buuk* in my pitifully small hands. Embarrassingly small by ogre standards, they were only slightly larger than what I'd need to turn the calf skins of the *buuk* to see the images. I smiled as I realized my hands weren't entirely useless after all.

I sat back down on the cave floor and glanced at their *stoos*, now growing cold. Mama daintily hooked a curved black fingernail around a piece of meat and put in mouth, swallowing it down. Her face was a mixture of horror and revulsion. "This meat is terrible!" she said.

My brothers laughed. "All right, good joke, Ogblud. Now where's dinner?" Grunch asked.

I swallowed. That was dinner. I hadn't killed any humans for their meal. To be honest, I'd never killed any before. I'd eaten them, but I didn't like the taste. Too stringy, too fatty and far too many bones. Mama was fond of telling us our father died from a human thigh bone stuck in his throat.

I said, "That is dinner."

Sugblud stroked his greasy beard and Grunch hunched over, flicking bits of meat out and sending them flying across the floor. They exchanged looks of dismay. "No humans?"

I shook my head. The shaman looked at me, his black eyes thoughtful. He bent down to the bowl and sniffed.

"I know this smell."

He did? I smiled triumphantly at my brothers. Here was proof that I was not inept, or a failure, just because I was smaller than other ogre males my size. I had made food that our clan's shaman knew!

The shaman glanced at Mama, then at me. "It is human food." He said scornfully and picked up the bowl, turning it upside down onto the floor. I watched as the beef *stoo* I had so carefully prepared dribbled and stained our cave floor.

"Ugh," my Mama said. "That smells disgusting. How could you?" she looked at me.

The others stared. "Ogblud," Sugblud began, "Did you make human food?"

I looked down at the precious *buuk* in my lap. Such a tiny treasure full of little secrets. What a waste.

Grunch reached over with his big hands and plucked it away, holding it in the air. "What's this?" he asked.

The others leaned in to see. "It's a human thing!" my mother declared. She looked at me, her face twisted in horror.

I met the disappointed eyes of Gorn. He knew. He cleared his throat and said "Ogblud, Mama Blud, come. We need to talk." He rose without waiting for a reply.

I gnawed my lip. My brothers snickered and began flicking bits of the *stoo* at each other, drenching each other in the savory broth.

"You've got it on you!"

"No you have!"

"Human!"

"You're the human!"

"You stink like one."

"You look like one."

"Take that back!" They ran at each other, punching and biting, sending all the *stoo* flying. If this wasn't such a common occurrence, I would have wept for the loss of my *stoo*. But I had something else to worry about now.

Mama led us out of the cave to sit on the rocky hillside at the cave mouth. Our cave stood over a treacherous cliff, with a steep drop below, hundreds of feet. You always knew it was an ogre abode because of the animal carcasses and bones left lying

263

around. We often dropped our eaten remains off the cliff. The rocky crags below were covered with shattered half-eaten bones and decaying carcasses. It stank, and I longed to clean my hands with more than animal blood, but it was home.

Shaman Gorn stiffly arranged himself on a rock, staring stubbornly into the setting sun. I sat beside him. Mama shoved me aside, sat down between us and said, "I should have known this would happen."

I looked at her. "What do you mean?"

She watched the sun finally sink below the horizon in a blazing sky of pink and blue. As the last warming rays disappeared, evening's cool wind wrapped itself around our necks with silky fingers, sending shivers down my spine.

"It's my fault," she said.

Gorn said, "I cannot believe you would do such a thing."

"What?" I said. "I'm sorry, I didn't mean to cause trouble, I just wanted to make a meal for everyone—"

"Shut your mouth, boy," he hissed. "Mama Blud, how dare you? How could you?"

She hung her head in shame.

"You know what our laws say," he said with finality, then wearily getting to his feet. He cracked his ancient knuckles, leaning on Mama's shoulder to steady himself. He looked down on her accusingly.

My fists curled.

The elderly shaman fixed me with an even glare, sending a chill through my bones. "You are a disgrace, Ogblud. We should have seen the signs sooner and your Mama should have done something."

"The signs?"

His black eyes shone with distaste. "You scorn proper ogre food, and you hesitate to kill for your meat. You are smaller than a child ogre half your age, but that would be of no consequence, if you truly showed ogre-like behavior. But tonight, you touch and you..." He looked at me in wonder. "You take human things and burn your meal, instead of eating raw like any true ogre. You will get no blood nutrients from overcooked meat."

"But I—"

He shook his head. "I had heard rumors, but I had to see it for myself." He spat. "There is only one cause for this behavior."

"What? What are you talking about?" I asked.

"Your mama, Ogblud. Our laws say she must be stoned to death. Or exiled."

"But why? She hasn't done anything wrong!" I said.

"It is the punishment for lying with a human."

What? But then that meant...

I sputtered, "You mean to say, Papa wasn't my...?"

Shaman Gorn and I looked at my mama. A beat passed, and a lone tear coursed down her green cheek.

"Mama?" I said.

She shook her head sadly. "He was a giant. I was lonely, and my husband had just died, and..."

"Save your excuses!" The shaman snapped. "I've heard enough. The clan elders will hear of this. This sick...abomination." he looked at me, but his eyes held no pity for what I was, or for what was to be my fate.

"I am not an abomination!" I cried.

He shot me a withering look. "Mama Blud, come with me."

"No! I won't let you hurt her!" I yelled. I was smaller than he, but younger and faster. I snarled at him, uttering a growl low in my throat. It surprised me.

Mama looked at me in surprise, but the shaman simply snorted. "You are no more than a halfling, boy. You are a hardly-formed ogre. The fact your mother admits to an unholy union with a giant just proves what anyone thinks when they look at you."

I gasped. Was this truly what our community thought of me? My brothers? Our neighbors? That I was deformed?

"I don't care. You're not going to hurt her." An ugly tone crept into my voice.

"She's coming with me." He turned to her, his long greasy beard dotted with beads of spit. "Come now or I'll be back with others. The clan warriors won't be so kind."

Mama swallowed. She got to her feet, taking my hand to help herself up. Her eyes were downcast. "Ogblud, tell your brothers I....I've left. Don't let them come after me. I don't want them to know until after I'm gone," she said tearfully.

265

"They won't. Any true ogre would be ashamed to have you as a mother. They will be more worried about their own social standing in the clan after a scandal like this. What ogre maid would want them now?" He shook his head. "You have brought shame and dishonor upon this clan, Mama Blud."

I shot to my feet. Mama would give herself up? Where was her fighting spirit we ogres are known for? My blood boiled, and the hairs on my arms stood up like small spines. Why did she not challenge the shaman and beat his bones to dust?

"No," I said.

The shaman's face twisted. "Enough. This cannot go on. It explains everything." His eyes raked me from my horned skull to my little toe claws. "Come with me now, slut." He took her roughly, pulling her away from me with greasy black claws.

I shoved her aside and grabbed him by the arm. "Don't you touch her. Leave us alone!"

The shaman spat, "Let me go, half-breed."

My teeth gnashed in frustration. My body trembled, and my vision filmed over with red. My world was blood-colored, and my sight narrowed to a single point in the shape of an elderly ogre with a greasy beard, bony legs like sticks, and a far too inflated sense of self-worth.

I cried out in rage. Before I knew what I was doing, I grabbed the shaman and hoisted him over my head.

Mama yelled, "Ogblud, no!" But it was as faint as a buzzing bee.

"Leave us alone!" And I threw him off the cliff. He sailed through the air, a shrieking bag of green bony limbs and greasy hair. His cry cut off with a sudden crack.

I fell to the ground, feeling the cold grass and rocks bite into my hands like little pinpricks of pain, bringing me to my senses. A cool wind slapped my face, and Mama stood beside me.

I'd killed an ogre. And I'd killed not just any ogre, but the shaman of our clan, the oldest and wisest of us all.

Mama whispered, "Ogblud, what have you done?"

I looked up at her.

"Mama, I didn't mean to..."

She wrapped me in a warm hug. "Stupid boy. Just when you start acting like a real ogre you land us in the muck. Now we're both as good as dead." She chuckled grimly.

It was true. While killing was encouraged, murdering our own kind was not. Unless it was in the arena and sanctioned by our elders, murdering another clan member was an instant death sentence. And I had killed, without a second thought. What was to become of me? What would happen to her?

I looked into her large black eyes. We were as good as dead. Unless...

"It doesn't have to be that way," I said. "He said the punishment was stoning, or exile. What if no one knew I was a half-breed? The only other ogre who knows is dead."

"You mean..."

I dashed back into the cave. My brothers sat on the ground, their fight forgotten. Grunch saw me and chucked a rock at my head. It hit me on the forehead and I crashed to the floor. Sugblud laughed as I picked myself up and scurried over to where the *buuk* lay.

I snatched it up, turned and ran, desperately trying to block out my brothers' jeers behind me. Once out of the cave, I hurried over to Mama.

"What are you doing?" she asked.

"No one has to know but us. And what Gorn said is right. I'm an embarrassment to you, Mama, I always have been. He spoke the truth. I'm too deformed to be a real ogre, so I must be something else."

"Oh Ogblud, you were never an embarrassment. Not to me."

I sniffed and wiped my nose. "It doesn't matter. No one must find out what happened."

"Ogblud, you don't have to go. We can keep going, no one will suspect."

I paused. She and my brothers were my only family. To leave her love and affection, even with its disappointments, was to shatter every familiarity I had ever known. I could stay in the cave, act like my brothers, take on the guise of a bloodthirsty ogre, pillaging and killing. I might grow to like it after a while. My brothers might even respect me in time. Would I leave them all behind?

"Someone might find out where Gorn had gone. It's too risky for me to stay. I have to go."

"No! Stay and we will face them together."

"It's only matter of time before it comes out. I've been an embarrassment to you so long, Mama, the least I can do is save you from a death sentence."

She brushed away tears with clawed hands. "You think I care about that? You could die out there."

"It's a risk I'll take."

I ran. I hurried down the rocky paths, trodden flat by our clawed feet. As I made my way through the darkness and down the hill, all I could think of was keeping the *buuk*, so I hugged it to my chest as I ran. My feet went out from under me and I fell, feeling the rocks and tough hillside dig into my skin, mixing with my tears at leaving her and the life I'd known.

A pale moon lit the night sky. Bones dug at my skin, and the stink of long decayed carcasses assailed my nose, making me want to gag. In the moonlight, the glassy black eyes of the shaman stared at me, seeing nothing.

I kicked away the bones at my feet and found my way among the huts and homes, drifting through the human village. I crept up on the house I'd come to know so well.

As I rapped delicately on the wall, the door opened and out peered the male I'd first met. Seeing me in my dirty state, holding the *buuk*, he looked at me.

I groaned. I didn't know what to say. What was their word for exiled and alone? I racked my brain and said the only words I knew.

"*Buuk. Bee-fff stoo. Pleeeezzzz.*"

He looked surprised. After a minute, he brought out a bowl of steaming meat and set it on the ground before me. I sniffed it hesitantly.

He pushed it toward me and said, "Bee-fff stoo. Dum—plingzz."

I watched him close the door, shutting me out into the darkness. I may be in exile, but I wasn't alone.

A Bostonian who's traded clam chowder for fish and chips, **E.L. Johnson** now writes thrillers in Britain. She is a member of the Hertford Writers' Circle, runs a book club in London and is lead singer of the gothic progressive metal band Orpheum. Her debut novel *The Inheritance Murders* will come out in autumn 2017, published by Sands Press.

NOIR AT THE SALAD BAR

ANTIPASTDEAD

BY LORRAINE SHARMA NELSON

Wiltshire County, The Cotswolds, U.K. 1970

Honoria Stanton-Cooper lifted her gaze to her friend sitting across the table, smiled shakily and keeled over into her antipasto.

Five hours later, Bridget Finlay sat at the card table in the Cooper Estate library, blinking at Detective Chief Inspector Molly "Mo" Marbury. "We both had the soup," she said, blowing her nose with what Marbury thought was a scrap of lace, but was in actuality a very ineffective handkerchief. "And we were talking about this afternoon's plans."

"We were all so excited to be here, you know? Honoria had planned to have us to her country estate for ages, but our schedules were in such conflict. Then finally, we all agreed on this week." She looked at Marbury. "Do you know, today, after lunch, we...we were all going fox-hunting? With a faux fox." Bridget's voice trembled, and she blinked back tears.

"Err...ahh...a faux fox?" Marbury said, glancing at her colleague. Detective Sergeant Poole returned her gaze, shrugged, then turned back to his notes, pen poised.

Bridget nodded. "We all agreed that chasing a sweet little fox with a pack of hounds was inhumane, so we decided to put a shaggy red wrap around one of Honoria's dogs—she has five hounds you see—and send him off, and then have the other dogs chase him. We were all so looking forward to it," she said, her voice breaking.

"Easy now, Miss Finlay," Marbury said. "We understand that the...sudden demise...of Miss Cooper was a great shock to you." She glanced around at the other guests seated around the fireplace in the ornate library, all in various stages of grief and shock. "And to your friends of course." Marbury offered what she hoped was a sympathetic smile. "Please do continue. You were saying you both had the soup...?"

Bridget nodded. "For the main course I had the ploughman's lunch, but Honoria fancied something a little more continental, so Poppy made her an antipasto plate." She shuddered. "How she could eat anything with anchovies in it is beyond me, but that is...was Honoria. So adventurous..." She choked, her voice breaking, and started to sob quietly into her scrap of linen.

Marbury waited until the tears subsided, then pushed on. "So Miss Cooper had the antipasto, did she?"

"Yes, but she barely ate anything though," Bridget said. "Just a few bites, it seemed like. And...and the next thing I knew, she...she just..." The woman hiccupped, and Marbury, alarmed that she was going to weep again, hastily concluded the initial interview.

As Bridget rose to her feet, she glanced at her friends. She leaned toward Marbury, dropping her voice to a whisper. "If I were you, Chief Inspector, I'd keep an eye on that one." She nodded toward a slender woman dressed in a very expensive-looking green dress gazing out the French doors.

"Oh," Marbury said, following her glance. "And why is that?"

"Because just before lunch, I overheard Honoria having it out with her in the morning room. Honoria accused her of stealing one of her design ideas, and she laughed. She told Honoria that she had more talent in her little toe than Honoria had in her whole body, and that she didn't need any of her tired, outdated ideas."

"I see," Marbury said, her eyes flicking between Bridget and the woman. "And just what is this young woman's name?"

Bridget grimaced. "I'm sure you've heard of her, Chief Inspector. She's Sheena Baker. *The* Sheena Baker, of SB Designs."

Marbury looked at her blankly. Bridget's finely-shaped brows drew together. "Don't tell me you don't know who she is? Everyone knows who she is."

Marbury glanced at Poole, who was frantically scribbling on his pad. He looked up briefly, shook his head, and turned back to his notes.

Bridget rolled her eyes. "Oh, for Heaven's sake. She's designed some of the queen's most admired hats." She crossed her arms and glared at Marbury. "Where have you been the last few years? Living under a rock?" Gone was the contrite, grieving woman from a few minutes ago.

"No, miss," Marbury said. "Been right here in Abington Grove, solving crimes. Now, if you please," she said, indicating the door. "I have other interviews to conduct."

ooo

Sheena Baker sat down on the newly-vacated chair, and crossed her long, shapely legs. "So, Inspector? Did Bridge tell you that I'm the culprit?"

"That's *Detective Chief* Inspector to you, miss," Poole said before Marbury could respond.

"Forgive me," Sheena said, her gaze darting between the two police officers. "I'm not used to seeing many female Chief Inspectors."

"*Detective* Chief Inspector," Poole muttered, his eyes on his notepad. "It *is* the Seventies, by the way."

Marbury cleared her throat. "Miss Baker, I understand you and Miss Cooper had a...ah...disagreement before lunch today?"

ooo

By the time the next guest was summoned, Marbury decided that this was the most privileged group of women she had ever interviewed in her entire career in law enforcement.

"You are Poppy Saint James?" she asked the woman seated across the table from her.

The petite woman nodded, her lower lip trembling. "It was I, wasn't it? I killed her." Tears filled her eyes, and she choked back a sob.

"Would you mind elaborating?"

Poppy sniffed delicately. "I'm the chef," she whispered. "I cooked the entire luncheon. In fact, I planned our entire weekend's menu. It...it was my idea to include antipasti dishes, since Honoria was so fond of them. Oh God...oh God..." She covered her face with her hands, sobbing quietly.

Marbury cleared her throat, hating this side of her job. "Miss Saint James?"

Poppy looked up through wet, spiked lashes. "I'm so sorry," she whispered. "It...it's just that no one's ever died from my cooking before."

"Now, now, Miss Saint James. There's no evidence pointing to your cooking. I'm sure it's delicious. You—"

"Do you know that I've catered parties for Bucky Starlight?" Poppy said.

Marbury's eyebrows shot up. "The rock star?"

Poppy nodded. "He's just one of many famous celebrities that I've cooked for. But now, when word gets out that Honoria died while eating a lunch I prepared, I'll be ruined."

"Don't worry," Marbury said. "No one will get wind of anything. I was told there's no phone service in the house, so there's no way for anyone to call out and pass on the tragic news."

Poppy brightened visibly. "Oh, I say, that *is* good news." Her face turned crimson as she realized what she'd said. She scrambled to her feet and clasped her hands in front of her. "I'm so dreadfully sorry. I didn't mean—"

"It's okay, Miss Saint James. You may return to your room. I ask only that you don't leave the premises, or talk to any strangers that may turn up at the front gates. Oh, and refrain from discussing our conversation with the others."

"Certainly, Chief Inspector," Poppy said, turning away. The relief at being dismissed was visible on her small, pinched face.

ooo

"Bit of a sticky wicket, what?" Poole said as they drove back to the station house.

Marbury sighed, leaning her head against the seat cushion. "Any one of them could have killed her, Poole. It's also entirely possible she died of natural causes. We'll know more when we get the coroner's report."

At the station, Marbury and Poole were discussing the interviews when the coroner's report arrived.

"Bloody hell," Marbury whispered after she'd pored over the file.

"What is it, Chief?" Poole said, leaning forward.

"It appears that Miss Honoria Stanton-Cooper was poisoned. Death occurred when her heart and respiratory muscles became paralyzed as a result of the poisonous plant, *aconitum*, also known as *wolfsbane*. Poor Miss Cooper." She set the file down and leaned back in her chair. "Since the only people in the house were two long-time servants and her six weekend guests, I think it's safe to say that she was murdered by someone she trusted."

"Let's not forget the groundskeeper and stable hand," Poole added. "That leaves a grand total of ten suspects."

Marbury sighed and glanced at the wall clock. "It's almost midnight, Poole. Go home, feed your cat, and get some sleep. Pick me up tomorrow morning at eight sharp. We need to finish the interviews and move on."

ooo

Marjorie Hemingsworth took a long drag on her cigarette and smiled at Marbury as she released the smoke from between scarlet lips. "You don't honestly consider me a suspect, do you, Chief Inspector?"

"Everyone on the Cooper Estate is a suspect for now, miss. Even a famous actress like yourself. Tell me, please, where were you when Miss Cooper—?"

"Shuffled off this mortal coil?" Marjorie supplied, a small smile tugging at her lips. "I was right there at the table, Chief Inspector. I saw my dear friend's head drop to her plate, and I jumped to my feet. As did all of us."

"So everyone was at the luncheon table?"

Marjorie shook her head, leaning forward to grind out the cigarette in the ashtray. "Not all of us. I believe Tina was still out riding, and Belinda was with the groundskeeper." She sat back, meeting Marbury's level gaze. "Anything else?"

Marbury stared at her for a moment, assessing, then slowly shook her head. "No. That'll be all for now, miss. Thank you for your time." She turned to Poole. "Please call Miss Crowder."

000

Tina Crowder glared at Marbury. "I don't appreciate being treated like a common suspect, Inspector. Do you know who I am?"

"A tennis player."

Tina's eyes narrowed as she leaned forward, her patrician, suntanned nose almost touching Marbury's pale, upturned one. "An international tennis *star*," Tina ground out, her voice dripping acid. "I've never lost a match, do you understand?"

"Of course, Miss Crowder. Now, tell me, please, at what time did you come in from your horseback riding?"

Tina sighed. "About twenty minutes or so after poor Honoria...died, I suppose."

"And can anyone vouch for that?"

Tina's face turned a delicate shade of pink. She fidgeted in her chair before responding, keeping her gaze averted. "The stable hand."

"The stable hand?"

"Yes, the stable hand," Tina snapped. "Is there a law against the stable hand accompanying a guest on a ride in the country?"

Marbury suppressed a smile. "Of course not, Miss Crowder. No doubt he can verify your story?"

"No doubt," Tina said, angry splotches of color now staining her smooth cheeks. "Are we done here? May I go now?"

"Certainly." Marbury stood up. "But please keep in mind that we may call on you again. And I want to remind you that this discussion remains private."

"Go to hell," Tina muttered, as she stormed out the door, slamming it behind her with so much force, one of the paintings fell off the wall.

000

"Is there a reason I'm being interviewed last, Chief Inspector?" Belinda Archer Beaumont said softly.

Marbury smiled. "Someone has be last, miss," she said.

"Mrs.," Belinda supplied, smiling back.

275

"Of course. Forgive me, Mrs. Beaumont. I momentarily forgot that you are the only married woman here."

"I very much doubt, Chief Inspector, that you *momentarily* forget anything."

Marbury inclined her head. "I shall take that as a compliment."

"Which is as I intended."

"Tell me, Mrs. Beaumont, are you and your husband happily married?"

Belinda's eyes widened slightly. "Is that really relevant to what's going on here?"

"Humor me, please."

She shrugged. "We're as happy as any married couple, I suppose."

"That's a very ambiguous answer. Could you please clarify?"

Belinda straightened in her chair, her face tightening slightly. "Very well. We're as happy as a couple can be when the husband is unfaithful. Is that what you wanted to hear, Chief Inspector?"

Marbury regarded her, unfazed by the woman's biting retort. "I'm sorry to hear that."

"Oh, come now, Chief Inspector. Don't tell me you didn't know about his sordid affair with that little stage actress last year? The one who was in that wildly popular West End play, *Of Woman Born?*"

Marbury leveled a gaze at her. "We've gotten a little off-track," she said. "Coming back to the matter at hand—"

"Of course. How may I help you?"

"Well, perhaps you can start by telling me where you were during the unfortunate event."

Belinda nodded, a slight frown marring her tanned forehead. "I was in the greenhouse with Alfie, the groundskeeper. We were discussing the flower arrangements for the dinner after the faux fox hunt."

She shook her head. "I'll never forget Maisie...the housemaid, you know...running down to the greenhouse, screaming that her mistress had passed out and—" Belinda stopped short, her eyes filling with tears. "Please forgive me," she said, her gaze seeking out Marbury's, who saw genuine regret there. "It's still so hard to fathom, you understand."

"I understand completely, Mrs. Beaumont." Marbury gazed at her thoughtfully. "Forgive me for asking this, but wouldn't the flowers be Miss Saint James' department? I mean, she is a chef, and I thought they handled all the details surrounding dinners and such."

Belinda shrugged, nonplussed. "That may be, but everyone knows I adore flowers. And I seem to have a knack for decorating with them." She cocked her head, smiling at Marbury. "Perhaps I'm in the wrong profession. Instead of raising thoroughbred horses, I should be in the decorating business. What do you think, Chief Inspector?"

"I'm hardly the right person to ask," Marbury said, smiling back. "That will be all for now. Please understand that we may have to call on you again."

After Belinda departed, closing the door softly behind her, Marbury turned to Poole. "What do you think so far?"

He shook his head. "I don't know, Chief. This is a tough case, this is."

"Well, let's go find the cook, Mrs. Dodson, and the housemaid. What was her name again? Maisie Crookhead?"

"Crookshank," Poole supplied, following her out.

000

"Well, that was a waste of time," Poole said as he steered the GT Cortina down the estate's winding driveway. "Never seen so much blubbering in my life."

"You can't blame them for being upset," Marbury said, leaning back and closing her eyes. "They've been with the family for years. Poor things."

000

Marbury was at her desk, poring over the Cooper file, when the coroner called to request her presence in his lab.

"I hope you have an early Christmas present for me, Nigel," Marbury said as she strode into the forensic lab located in the basement of the building.

Nigel Farnsworth looked up from his microscope, his wan, sallow face in dire need of sunshine. "I do indeed," he said. He turned toward his massive desk, strewn with papers, articles, journals, and the remains of a half-eaten sandwich. Even from where she stood, eight feet away, Marbury could smell the tuna.

"Ah, here we are." He plucked a paper from the giant pile on his desk. "We found a couple of hairs on the Deceased's tweed jacket, stuck to the underside of the collar."

Marbury scanned the report quickly. "Two red hairs?"

"Yes. I understand that two of your suspects are redheads?"

"They are indeed. Thanks Nigel. I owe you one," she said as she headed out of the lab.

ooo

"So, it's either Miss Saint James or Miss Crowder?" Poole asked, almost maneuvering the car into the hedgerow as a bus passed on the opposite side of the narrow, winding country road.

Marbury shrugged. "The evidence points to it." She glanced at Poole. "Who's left?"

"Just the stable hand and the gardener."

"You get their statements, please, Poole. I'm going to talk to our redheads again."

ooo

Tina Crowder's eyebrows lifted. "Am I a suspect, then?"

"It's to aid our ongoing investigation, Miss Crowder. No stone left unturned, that sort of thing. I'm sure your hairbrush has a few strands on it. Detective Sergeant Poole will accompany you to your room to retrieve them as soon as he...ah, here he is."

Tina stared at Marbury for a long moment. "Fine," she said finally, rising and giving Poole a cursory glance. "This way."

"Thank you," Marbury called out as Tina vacated the room followed by Poole.

278

Poppy Saint James blinked up at Marbury. "You...you need a lock of my hair?"

Marbury shook her head. "Not a lock, no. Just a few strands will do. Maybe from your hairbrush?"

"But why? What has my hair to do with Honoria's death?"

"It's just routine, miss," Poole said, striding forward and holding out a chair for the distraught woman. "I can accompany you to your room for the—"

"Oh, there's no need for that. I'll run up and be back in a jiffy," Poppy said, turning away and heading quickly out of the room.

When the door clicked shut behind her, Marbury turned to Poole, brows furrowed. "She didn't want you accompanying her, did she? When she comes back down, keep her busy. I think an examination of Miss Saint James' room is in order."

Poole nodded. "Yes, Chief."

"By the way, what did Alfie and Thomas have to say?"

He shrugged, a slight smile tugging at his lips. "Alfie's hopping mad and suspects all the guests of being in cahoots with each other. And Thomas," he hesitated, his cheeks turning scarlet. "He...uh...got very cozy with Miss Crowder on their rides, and said she picked wildflowers and such."

"Interesting. What if the *wolfsbane* was one of the plants she picked on their jaunts together? She could easily have added the herb to Miss Cooper's lunch before going riding yesterday. For the record, any of the suspects could have. It's hard to keep track of people, what with all the comings and goings in the kitchen."

Marbury grimaced as she surveyed Poppy's room. *What an unholy mess. I've seen cleaner pigsties.* She snapped on a pair of latex gloves and proceeded to meticulously search the entire place.

Nothing.

Just as she was about to give up, Marbury took a step back, and tripped over a high-heeled shoe. She righted herself before falling, and turned to shove it out of the way.

Marbury froze.

The shoe was flipped onto its side, and something was taped to the underside of the instep. Her heartbeat quickening, she bent to examine it more closely.

A pair of earrings. Diamonds, it looked like, taped down with a piece of cellophane tape. Marbury frowned. Why would she tape a pair of earrings to the sole of her shoe? Was she afraid someone would steal them, or…?

The thought sprang into Marbury's head with such conviction, she caught her breath.

They're stolen.

Poppy stole them from one of the other women, and Marbury didn't need to be Sherlock Holmes to guess who the rightful owner was.

Poppy stole the earrings from Honoria. Marbury was sure of it. That was why she didn't want Poole coming into her room. Poppy was a thief. Marbury frowned as she stared at the gems. But was she also a murderer? Did Honoria confront her, and did Poppy kill her rather than risk her reputation being ruined?

When Marbury walked back into the library, Poppy sprang to her feet.

"Are we done here, Chief Inspector? May I go now? I'm planning a roast venison dinner for tonight and—"

"Please sit down, Miss Saint James. I have one more question for you."

Poppy's eyes dropped to the plastic bag in Marbury's hand, and her face turned as white as the china tea service on the sideboard. She sank back down onto the chair, and covered her face with her hands.

Marbury set the bag down on the side table and waited.

A minute later, Poppy turned to face Marbury, tears spilling down her cheeks. "I didn't kill her," she whispered. "You must believe me, Chief Inspector. "I…I was going to pay her back for them, once things started picking up. I just needed the money to clear up some of the debt that's been piling up. I swear I would have paid her back every penny I got for them."

"Why didn't you just ask her for help?"

Poppy sniffed, rubbing at her nose. "I did. But she refused to help me. She said I still owed her eleven thousand pounds." Poppy leaned forward and clutched Marbury's arm. "You must understand, business has been so bad lately."

"So you killed her out of desperation."

"No. No I didn't. I may be a thief, but I'm not a murderer, Chief Inspector. I'm not." Poppy broke down again, sobbing quietly into her hands. "She was just so mad at me," she said, her voice muffled. "She wouldn't even listen when I tried to talk to her."

"You did owe her a great deal of money, Miss Saint James," Marbury said gently.

"No, not about the money." Poppy's face turned a bright cherry-red. "She was angry with me because I didn't approve of the man she was seeing. You see, right after she lent me the money, I found out about her relationship with him, and begged her to end the affair."

ooo

On the way back into town, Poole spoke up. "So Miss Saint James is the murderer, then?"

"It does seem the most plausible explanation, doesn't it?" Marbury responded. "After all, she's the chef. She fixed the antipasto plate for Miss Cooper so she could easily have added the herb to her plate. She has a working knowledge of horticulture and she'd know exactly what kinds of poisonous plants to look for. She stole the diamond earrings from Miss Cooper, plus owed her a further eleven thousand pounds. And she's a redhead. "

"But...?" He drawled the word out, a slight smile hovering on his lips.

Marbury looked at him, eyebrows raised.

Poole laughed. "You don't fool me, Chief. You're not buying it, are you?"

Marbury shook her head, sighing deeply. "It just feels too...pat, don't you think? Everything points to Miss Saint James. She's been practically gift-wrapped and handed to us on a silver platter..."

Her voice died away as she sank deep in thought. Poole remained silent beside her, concentrating on the road ahead. It had started to rain, and big fat drops spattered the windshield, making visibility difficult.

"Poole?" Marbury said after a few minutes. "What if someone overheard both women talking and found out that Miss Saint James owed Miss Cooper a large sum of money, and then came up with the perfect way to implicate her by placing those hairs on Miss Cooper's jacket?"

"But we don't know if those hairs belong to Miss Saint James," Poole said, swerving to avoid a pothole rapidly filling with water. "They could belong to Miss Crowder, which would place her back in the running as Suspect Number Two."

Marbury laughed, a short harsh sound that made Poole jerk in surprise. "My dear Poole," she said softly, "Miss Crowder was never out of the running."

ooo

"Well?" Marbury said, tapping her toes impatiently as she waited for Nigel's report. "Do they or don't they?"

"Yes, Mo. The hairs from the Deceased's jacket definitely match the hairs from Miss Saint James' hairbrush."

Marbury nodded. "I thought they might," she whispered. "Everything wrapped up with a nice, neat bow."

"What was that?" Nigel asked, leaning toward her.

"Nothing." She took a deep breath, fixing the tall, lanky man with a hard gaze. "You're absolutely sure? No mistake?"

He nodded. "Without a shadow of a doubt. You'll have my report on your desk first thing in the morning."

Back upstairs, Marbury relayed the information to Poole, and grabbed her coat and bag.

"Where are you off to, Chief?" Poole asked.

"The library."

282

Poole's eyebrows shot up, practically disappearing into his hairline. "The library?"

"Yes, Poole. It's a fascinating place. Houses all kinds of books that one can take home, for free. With no catch either, believe it or not. Oh, and pick me up at eight tomorrow morning."

ꝺꝺꝺ

At precisely eight forty-five the next morning, all the suspects were gathered in the library. And none of them looked happy to be there.

"I've asked you all here today," Marbury said, surveying the room, "because I've come to a conclusion. I know who murdered Miss Cooper."

Thunderous silence followed that statement. Marbury glanced around the room at the ashen faces staring back at her. "After interviewing each of you," she continued, "all the evidence pointed to one person in particular." Marbury refrained from glancing at Poppy. "In fact, this person had legitimate cause to kill her. His or her life would certainly be easier with Miss Cooper out of the way."

A sob from Poppy made Marbury rush on. "Nevertheless, when all the evidence was gathered, it seemed too pat. The suspect was all but handed to us gift-wrapped."

"Whatever are you talking about, Chief Inspector?" Sheena Baker asked, standing in front of the fireplace, her trademark platinum-blond hair swept up into its usual chignon.

"I'm talking about a frame-up, Miss Baker. I believe that the murderer set up Miss Saint James as the killer." Her gaze darted to the woman in question, whose face had drained of color at the mention of her name. "I believe the murderer overheard a private exchange between Miss Saint James and Miss Cooper, and realized that the topic of conversation would be a perfect catalyst for Miss Saint James to kill Miss Cooper, if she were so inclined."

Marbury smiled at Poppy in hopes of reassuring her. "She was not. Whatever Miss Saint James' shortcomings, committing murder is not one of them."

"But the rest of us are still under suspicion?" Bridget Finlay fidgeted with the fringe of her suede vest.

"For God's sake," Tina Crowder burst out, angry splotches of color appearing on her cheeks, "just get on with it!"

"Very well." Marbury turned to the beautiful woman sitting erect on a straight-backed chair, jaw clenched, lips pressed tightly together.

"Mrs. Belinda Archer Beaumont, you are under arrest for the murder of Honoria Stanton-Cooper."

Time froze. No one moved. It seemed to Marbury that everyone was holding their collective breath, waiting for something to happen.

Then Belinda's eyes flickered, and she slowly raised her gaze to Marbury. "How?" she said so softly Marbury barely caught the whispered word.

Marbury took a deep breath. "Your husband was having an affair with Honoria," she said softly. "Only this time he fell in love with the other woman, didn't he? He told you that he was leaving you for her. And you knew that a divorce would leave you penniless, thanks to the airtight prenuptial contract you signed when you married Patrice Beaumont."

"I couldn't let him leave," Belinda said, her voice soft, dreamy, as if she were talking to herself. "I would lose everything, you see?"

"So you knew something had to be done about Miss Cooper," Marbury said. "And when she invited a few of you—her closest friends—to spend a few days at her country estate, you saw your chance."

"I had to, don't you see?" Belinda said, her eyes sweeping the room. "He was going to leave me penniless. After all the years I've spent with him. After all the affairs I had to endure. All the humiliation—" Her voice broke, and she covered her face with her hands. "Oh dear God, I'm so sorry. I'm so, so sorry."

"You tried to frame Poppy?" Bridget's voice was tight with anger. "How could you?"

A muffled sound between a laugh and a choked sob came from Belinda. She dropped her hands from her tear-stained face. "It was easy," she said, her voice hoarse. "Dear little Poppy made it so easy. I heard Honoria accuse her of stealing a pair of diamond earrings, and then I found out that Poppy also owed her a great deal of money. All I had to do was find the perfect way to kill Honoria, a way which would lead back to Poppy." She laughed, a soft, broken sound that, under other circumstances, would have twisted Marbury's heart.

Quiet sobs and whispered denials filled the room as Marbury walked slowly over to Belinda and reached out a hand. "Mrs. Beaumont," she said, her voice laced with regret, "I have to ask you to accompany Detective Sergeant Poole and myself to the station, whereupon you will be formally charged with the murder of Miss Honoria Stanton-Cooper."

ooo

The sun slipped below the horizon as Marbury and Poole sat at a small table in the corner of the local pub, nursing large glasses of Guinness. Belinda Archer Beaumont had been formally charged with the murder of Honoria Stanton-Cooper. Fingerprints and mug shots had been taken. She sat now in a holding cell, awaiting the arrival of her lawyers, at which point the legal process would officially begin.

Poole leaned toward Marbury, talking over the din in the room. "Time to come clean, Chief. How did you know about the affair?"

Marbury smiled, settling back in her chair and stifling a yawn. "I told you, Poole. The library is a magical place. It contains the knowledge of the ages, all in one wonderful spot. Including," she said, smiling broadly, "a veritable treasure trove of gossip magazines."

Lorraine Sharma Nelson grew up globally, and as a child, escaped into the world of fiction-writing as a way to alleviate the stress of always being the new kid in school. With the publication of "ANTIPASTDEAD" in the *NOIR AT THE SALAD BAR* anthology, she is now published in sci-fi, horror, fantasy and mystery/c

A MURDER OF CROWS

BY MARA BUCK

"Me? I'm between jobs at the moment. After the incident I stopped writing my food column for *The Maine Palate*. I mean, where in hell do you go after something like that? Takes you to quite another place, an uncomfortable place at best. At the time, the whole state was upscaling like mad and Portland especially was making a national name for itself as a foodie destination, but, shit, after what happened? After that, for anybody with any sense at all, it was back to burgers and fries and looking over your shoulder. And maybe keeping a shotgun by the bed just in case. Screw that upscale junk. You never heard the story? That was the incident at The Game Café, one of those seasonal tony eateries on Casco Bay. Only open for that first summer, but they sure made a name for themselves in more ways than one. Everyone refers to it as "the incident" because nobody wants to discuss it any further, but some say it was murder and suicide along with one stupefying, horrendous accident—some say it was something else. I'm betting on the something else, myself…"

ᴑᴑᴑ

"Four-and-twenty. That's twenty-four, right?"

"Yes, John. That last one was pretty scrawny, so let's make it twenty-five."

"Top and bottom crusts, both? Or only top? Or I could use mashed potatoes instead of a top crust like a shepherd's pie?" The sous-chef was eager. This was a good gig. Mustn't blow it.

"Shepherd's pie? Hmmm, hadn't considered that. Terrific idea. Extends the rural theme. Should save us time and money both. John, my boy, you're a treasure. A real gem."

Maurice had been wrist-deep into working the **pâté brisée**, and, in an unexpected gesture of goodwill, the chef placed a floury

287

paternal hand on John's denim shoulder. Maybe the kid was right and they could cut corners with an old-fashioned Maine lard crust without all the extra work and expense for upscale French butter pastry. The handprint radiated a ghostly glow in the well-lit summer kitchen. The restaurant sat in a pretty spot with the kitchen window facing a thick stand of oak. A lone crow hid in the branches, peering in at the men. The crow was uncharacteristically silent.

The younger man beamed, flashing rat-like teeth behind cracked lips. John had a habit of chewing his bottom lip until he tasted blood. He found it soothing.

The hunters had plucked the birds before delivery. All part of the package. Those long glossy feathers had made their way to China where they'd been transformed into hat trims and toy crows tethered to long poles to be sold at the dollar stores throughout America. The feathers had flown around the globe and still returned a handsome profit. An ironic immortality for the crows.

That pile of plucked birds looked mighty pitiful to John. The heads and feet were already amputated, ground up for pet food he supposed, but Sweet Jesus those carcasses were scrawny. Maurice was right. It'd take at least twenty-five for a decent pie. Crows looked fierce as military commanders when they were strutting around in full-dress plumage, but lying naked in a pile of death, John felt sad for them. He never felt sad for chickens. But he'd heard tell that crows were some smart and helped each other out. John respected teamwork.

He hadn't been fond of his boss's idea to turn the restaurant into a game café, but he was saving up to buy Sheila a genuine diamond solitaire from the jewelry counter at the Walmart, and Maurice treated his help better than most. Still, he had to swallow back the bile when he began butchering the birds. Thank God the heads were gone.

Maurice's intuition had been right to change the focus of the restaurant. Portland had become a major foodie town and most diners had grown bored with artful smears of *foie gras* under a concert of micro-greens decorated by one lonely crab claw. Even the popularity of radicchio was waning. The millennials were the ones with the money and they craved the unique. Maurice was determined to oblige.

The economy being what it was and the environmentalists' priorities overcome by the complexities of climate change and tainted water, the hunting regulations had been relaxed. With the encroachment of the suburbs, deer had become pests, moose were a highway liability, and coyotes could be shot on sight twenty-four-seven. Gulls and crows were scavengers and joined the list of the pesky and the unwanted. Raccoons carried rabies, beavers and porcupines destroyed trees, and nobody wanted skunks around. Bears were dangerous and gobbled up too many blueberries, snakes were scary, and frankly it was all delicious and exotic and the gourmands were thrilled. A win-win all around.

John had grown up with deer hanging to bleed-out in the back shed and he'd skinned his fair share of rabbits and squirrels. He loved dogs, so he'd barfed the first time he'd carved up a coyote. After the third or fourth time, he got used to it. But those piles of dead crows still bothered hm. He'd seen a PBS special showing how smart the buggers were, how they solved problems and remembered people from years before, those who'd been good to them and those who hadn't, and he'd been mighty impressed. Crows mated for life. And he respected that too. After all, he expected he and Sheila would stay true for a lifetime after he proposed. Now here he was with a kitchen full of the dead anonymous critters to make into a gourmet feast for some rich folks at an exorbitant price and he wasn't happy with it. Not at all.

Actually the idea of the menu change hadn't been Maurice's, but his wife Lola's. Ever since Martha Stewart had been crowned queen of the kitchen, Maurice's missus had channeled the domestic diva's cooking energies, decorating skills, and empire-building into her own Maine versions. What Lola lacked in talent, she more than made up for in ambition. She banished the ubiquitous plastic lobster décor, dimmed the lights, and created a forest dining room filled with taxidermy. Bobcats, foxes, and raccoons peeked out from unexpected places and a rather moth-eaten black bear guarded the hall that led to the restrooms. Earthy, gamey, sexy, and just a touch wicked. Hot, hot, hot—it was featured in all the latest magazines.

Lola had always been a looker and she played her husband

and the restaurant's male customers with finesse. She considered it great fun to include Eartha Kitt's version of "Whatever Lola Wants" in the restaurant's musical play loop along with the undercurrent of forest sounds, and she would flounce around the dining room, flirt at the tables, humming along with Eartha, raising her eyebrows, and lowering her neckline. What the hell did that have to do with haute cuisine? Not a blessed thing, except Lola was able to persuade reluctant diners to "just try the Muskrat Ramble Terrine for me, honey. I think I know what men like." And, once plied with an overpriced pinot noir and Lola's cleavage, the gentlemen declared the smelly brown glop on their plates to be heavenly manna.

More often than not these flirtations evolved into short-lived affairs. The restaurant became quite the bed of intrigue. Maurice was very European about it all. He played his part as executive chef and Lola played hers as executive courtesan. A workable adult relationship. As Lola giggled to Maurice, "Darling, we're selling roadkill at filet mignon prices. That's the real game."

Yes, it started off as a lucrative summer. The weather was excellent, the game was plentiful, the tourists were eager, and the money poured in. But then the soufflé collapsed when The Game Café became the site of "the incident."

000

"We've got a pretty good idea who did this. Horrible business. Just hideous. I think the Chinese or one of those Asian places call this the death of a thousand cuts, like she was stabbed over and over until she finally died. None of these wounds seem to be fatal in themselves, but the shock and the loss of blood finally finished her. We'll know more after Doc Collins takes a look-see. Must have been done with one of those sharp chef's tools. Jonesy, bag this knife."

Detective Belford was a meat and potatoes man from way back and loathed the over-priced joints and pretentious clientele they lured into his jurisdiction. Snooty out-of-staters with their honking huge Hummers parking their fat asses anywhere they damn well pleased and then tying up the courtrooms with their lawyers beating the tickets. And this frigging woman, cheating on her husband with first one then another of them. Flaunting it for the world to see. Stupid bitch. Never cheat on a French chef who's that good with a knife. Belford sighed. Sometimes his job was almost too easy. "Round up the jealous bastard. Don't give him a chance to create an alibi. He'll be down at the morgue. No matter what she did, he's a sadistic prick to cut her up like that."

When they found Maurice, he was still hiccupping over Lola's bloody corpse stretched out on the coroner's table, ruined eye sockets staring upwards into the neon lights of heaven. She'd always been a pale woman, but now with the pallor of death, those hundreds of cuts gaped red like midget screaming mouths. He wiped his eyes on the sleeve of his white jacket. He was surprised to see the detectives so soon again. He'd only found the body a couple hours ago, crumpled on the small patio near the woods behind the kitchen. He'd called 911, and when the police arrived, he'd blubbered out the obvious. Yes, he'd just found her. No, he hadn't seen anyone else. No, he'd had his headphones on for a call and hadn't heard her screaming. They'd followed the ambulance to the morgue where he'd been with his wife for the last hour or so.

"You guys find anybody yet? Anything?" It seemed too early, but these people were professionals and maybe they knew of some lunatic who'd been butchering women like this. Some Charlie Manson type. Maurice willed himself not to start blubbering again. He and Lola had had their differences, but no one could believe it would have ever come to this...

"Only you, Chef. Only you. We found her blood on your knife and your DNA is still wedged deep in the handle." Detective Belford wasn't buying the grieving husband routine. Seen it all before. It's always the husband. Or the wife. Detective Belford was a wise man and had never married.

"But I loved her," Maurice wailed. "She was some great shot. We'd go hunting together. She really loved to shoot crows even though we bought most of the ones for the restaurant from the Harrison twins. She was the one who created the recipe for Blackbird Pie. Everybody loved it. She cut herself on that same knife just yesterday while she was butchering some of the birds. I didn't kill her! Don't know who would have. Oh God, so many punctures. All over her. So much blood. Why would anyone do this? It wasn't me, I tell you, dammit. I loved her."

"Maurice LaPierre, I'm arresting you for the murder of your wife, Lola LaPierre. Anything you say…" Belford yawned. He could use some sleep. And a weekend off. Maybe fishing at Moosehead Lake away from this fucking yuppie burg. But then, even Moosehead had been fast-tracking lately, catering to the upper-crust for quite some time. He sighed. He found himself sighing a lot these days. "Put the cuffs on him, Jonesy."

When they hustled Maurice into the patrol car, there was a tremendous squawking overhead. Crows everywhere. Belford looked up and caught some whitewash right in the eye.

000

With Maurice in jail and Lola deceased, John was left to muddle through on his own. He figured he'd serve up the remaining game in the freezer and then hang out a closed sign until Maurice was released. John couldn't believe his boss could have murdered his wife. Not like that! John bit his lip until the blood soothed him again. He'd ask Shelia to come by later for a private dinner after the customers had gone. He'd just bought the ring and he couldn't wait to pop the question. He pulled the small plastic box out of his pocket and opened it. A full three carat Cubic Zirconia set in genuine fourteen-carat plated gold. The Walmart jewelry associate had assured him no one could tell the difference between a quality CZ and a genuine diamond and he believed it. That stone sparkled better than any gem he'd ever seen. He took it to the kitchen window where it flashed like a beacon into the branches of the oak. Sheila would be tickled pink. He just knew it.

000

Meanwhile, back at the jail, although Belford had cautioned Jonesy that Maurice should be put on suicide watch due to the violent domestic nature of his crime, it was a Saturday night and the dopers and the drunks were puking in the halls, and Jonesy, not the most competent at the best of times, had his hands full and figured

Maurice was locked up snug. There were a couple haphazard bars on the window in his cell, but no screens, and nobody had ever cared since it was a deadly drop to the pavement below. Jonesy had confiscated the prisoner's shoelaces and belt, standard procedure, so he was shocked by the unresponsive body that greeted him at his midnight check.

Maurice had managed to wedge his head through the bars, perhaps to jump, perhaps only for fresh air, and somehow the window had dropped like a guillotine on the back of his neck, trapping him with enough pressure from the metal sill on his windpipe that, over time, he suffocated. The chef's face hung outside the window, frozen in an expression of alarm—his eyes bulging in terror, his mouth distorted in a grotesque silent scream. Jonsey peeked out through the bars from the adjoining cell at the seemingly disembodied head and shuddered. The face was a gargoyle on the side of the building.

Belford was not pleased. "On your record, Jonesy! On your record! This is such bullshit. What in hell happened?"

"Maybe he was trying to jump and got caught?" Jonesy was a chronic screw-up but even he knew this exceeded his worst. Dead prisoner. Holy crap!

"And what's this white all over his head? You touch him?" Belford put a gloved finger on the sticky mess puddling around Maurice's head. The windowsill and the bars were covered with it. "Bird shit! Jesus, who's supposed to be cleaning these cells?" He backed away from the body. "Get forensics in for pictures and tell the doc we've got another one. What a damned mess."

Belford would be postponing that fishing trip a while longer.

000

Sheila had never been inside The Game Café and John could tell she was properly impressed. Now that the customers had departed from the final seating of the evening and they had the place to themselves, he served her at a prime table and, under the watchful eyes of raccoons and squirrels, they dined on *venison bourguignon*, *soufflé crème du mallard*, and the remaining Blackbird Pie. For the big moment he'd chosen an inexpensive split of domestic bubbly and hoped Maurice wouldn't mind if he paid for the wine later from his upcoming salary.

"John, this is so elegant. So delicious. You're spoiling me." Sheila simpered at her boyfriend over her forkful of venison and, a true post-graduate student of Flirtation 101, actually batted her carefully-applied eyelashes. She was pretty and pert and deep down had never considered the scrawny cook worthy enough for more than a casual date, but she looked around at the crisp linen, the shining porcelain, the crystal glasses, and like Lola before her, she saw potential. "Do you think you'll be able to become head cook when they convict Maurice?" A little of the venison blood had caught in the corner of her mouth and gave her a feral look which John found captivating.

"That's executive chef, darling, and I can recreate the full menu, so I don't see why not. I don't know legally what happens to this place if Maurice is convicted, but maybe I could buy him out over time. He'll certainly need money for lawyers and all. And speaking of our future..." This was it. The time for the proposal. John's hands were trembling.

It was a warm summer night and the bugs were minimal. John had left the back window open to air out the cooking odors not captured by the range hood. He'd lit candles in all the sconces for the most romantic mood possible and the eyes of the stuffed creatures reflected the candlelight as if the foxes and the muskrats and the rabbits were joining in his special moment. The candle flames flickered in the draft from the window, giving the restaurant a homey quality, like an old-time movie. John had replaced the background musical loop with ambient canned "Songs For Lovers" rather than the usual forest sounds, but a low gurgle of tweets and caws and growls and rustles persisted, interspersing Barry White and the Righteous Brothers.

John reached into his pocket and brought out the tiny pink plastic box. He'd practiced opening it so the ring would face Sheila, so she'd get a full view of its dazzle. He'd considered getting down on one knee, but he thought the ring would be better showcased against the white linen tablecloth. John cleared his throat.

"Sheila, will you do me the honor of becoming my wife?" Not original, but the ring spoke for him. Sheila was mesmerized.

"Oh, John. This is gorgeous. So big! It must have cost a fortune!" She reached into the plastic box, slid the CZ onto her engagement finger. It fit to perfection. "Oh, honey, of course I'll marry you. We'll have such a wonderful life. We'll be a great team!" She angled her hand back and forth in the candlelight and the ring sparked like a Roman candle, ricocheting bursts of fire around the dining room. The forest sounds had amplified, but neither of them noticed. They looked deep into each other's eyes and toasted with champagne, so overcome with the emotion of the moment that they failed to feel that the drafts of air from the open window had increased, increased enough to blow the candle flames horizontal until they touched the fake greenery, which smoldered until it traced further flames up the walls, until those flames tickled the feet of the stuffed game and caught the long-dead pelts, until the smoke choked them, until it was too late.

000

"We'll assume for the moment that this guy's that cook John. Anybody know his last name? Anybody know if he had a girlfriend and who she might be? Might have been. My God, what a fucking gruesome mess. Why didn't someone call in the alarm sooner? Must've been burning for hours."

Belford was way past giving a shit. This case had turned the corner into seriously-weird and he contemplated shaking the mire of it off his shoes before he sank any deeper. He was experienced enough to realize that some things were better left undiscovered. He tucked his face into his shirt in a vain attempt to filter out the smell of burned flesh. The two bodies were still sitting at the table, but they were little more than skeletal remains. The cheap cutlery had melted into dark puddles, but the restaurant-quality china had withstood the heat. In the center of the collapsing table was a melted pool of pink plastic. "Jonesy, bag that pink stuff, will you? Jonesy?"

Jonesy was outside, retching under the oak off the back patio. What was left of the dining room was a horror show of

295

taxidermy armatures and skeletal remains backlit by the early morning light. Bits of hides and feathers and fur still floated on the updrafts from the fire and the deputy didn't want to consider that some of that hide might be the remains of the couple at the table, that those cooked bits of flesh might not be leftovers from the kitchen. He retched again and wondered if thirty was too early for retirement.

ọọọ

In his nest high in the oak behind The Game Café, the crow studied his reflection in the three-carat Cubic Zirconia. He missed his mate and would miss her for the rest of his long life, but the reflection gave him some consolation. Some of her feathers still clung to the nest, and he was finally able to sleep, more at peace than he had been since her death. She would have loved the ring.

Crows like shiny things.

Mara Buck writes, paints, and rants within a self-constructed hideaway in the Maine woods— she hopes to return to civilization soon. She's been published in many of the usual and unusual places with recent firsts for the F. Scott Fitzgerald Poetry Prize and the Binnacle Prize. She treasures crows among her closest friends and has never eaten a friend yet.

PETUNIA AT THE TIP TOP

BY JENNY DRUMMEY

Billy, the invisible regular, feels the electric sparks of danger in the diner where he is eating his Sunday special. An abstract menace, a wild-eyed man, enters holding a bulging beige tote bag. He grimaces and struggles to keep it over his shoulder.

The small diner, lined with six booths along the walls, has a counter that sits ten. Billy is in his regular spot, in the first booth to the right of the entrance, facing it, always attuned to how quickly the restaurant's atmosphere could change with each swing of the door.

Billy's spoon hovers between a sunken slice of lemon meringue pie and his mouth, still smudged with lipstick. He forgets the tart delight is on its way. He forgets the opened, drooling creamer containers scattered around his half-empty coffee cup, and the scratch of polyester against the back of his thigh and that his hairdo has started to collapse. He is proud of his hair, and stands up for it when he's in the club, happy to convince others that it is not a wig.

Billy used to be an innie. Now, sitting in the Tip Top diner, his shy navel protrudes below a belly shelf. While its permanent emergence was depressing, he was not dissuaded enough to avoid the late, luxurious lunches or the powdered sugar on his fingers.

But for this uncertain moment, when the frail, angry man stands so close to him, breathing heavily under the weight of his bag, none of these things are real.

000

Billy went by "Petunia" professionally, and this hidden part of his life—where he was draped in boas and roaring at tasteless jokes—was the happiest. Outside of the club, only his most intimate friends used the name, which was the truest word Billy knew. Even if they used it to scold him, he was grateful. To him it said, "I am."

But in all other public situations, Billy was guarded and craved anonymity. Sometimes it worked.

But when it did not, it was dangerous. He had lost money, dignity, and, one horrible night surrounded by dark figures with steel-toed boots, most of his upper teeth.

At the diner, he was not so much accepted as ignored. He longed for more from this place where he saw the same faces almost daily: Mr. Knowley, the diner's portly owner; Henry, the spry widower; the family with the fattest baby he had ever seen. If it were possible that he could be accepted outside of the club, he hoped it might be here.

Billy was fearful and lonely, but mostly he was kind.

Mr. Knowley, who was only ever polite to him, who served him white fish and fries and tomato soup and coffee, who smiled at him slightly even if he hadn't fully wiped his face clean of makeup (not something Billy expected anywhere else, where the slightest sight of him as a performer severed everything), in the full diner, said to the man holding the bag:

"Hello, son. What can I do for you?"

As though all the trembling figure would need was a packet or two of saltines and then he would be on his way.

Mr. Knowley was a quiet and careful man with dimples, dark skin and close-cropped hair. He wore a tie, even when he had to step in and work the fryer. Reluctantly, he hired and fired the erratic and dopey, the only applicants for Tip Top employment. There was surly Marcus, who, on an unscheduled break, discharged a weapon into a refrigerator door, shattering a twenty-gallon container full of cooking oil. And Missy, who left with a roll or two of unforgiving toilet paper after every shift, who hissed and spat when he asked for her loot before escorting her to the door for the last time.

Then there was Barry, who walked in to the diner on a sub-freezing February day in shorts and a t-shirt, looking for work. When asked to describe his strengths, he said, "My legs don't get cold." This did come in handy when loading stock into the walk-ins, where Barry ended up spending the majority of his time and where he eventually overdosed.

CULINARY TALES WITH A BITE

Mr. Knowley, like Billy, could feel trouble like a sudden drop in temperature on a dark forest path.

This day had begun fading into itself right from the start and Billy's thoughts flowed behind him in a long stream. Was it just this morning in the shower when Billy thought of his mother's shoes on the sidewalk when they emptied her apartment the first time she was evicted? How the pairs of them, so clean on the outside, but so filthy inside, were embarrassing and beautiful: Cracked heels, stretched straps, dirty footprints on soles, and rhinestones trembling, dangling by threads. Each pair was ruined in its own way.

Or perhaps it was only an hour ago, when the door to Beautiful Dreamers closed behind him and he floated gracefully out into the night, when piles of his mother's silver and red pumps rose up in his mind. No one needs all those shoes if they aren't going to take care of them, he thought.

But Billy's mom, Rose, could barely take care of herself. She believed in the healing power of mugwort and insisted that the mail carrier was throwing her outgoing mail in the garbage.

And just this morning, as Billy approached her front door with her morning biscuit, he saw an envelope addressed in a shaky scrawl to the Publisher's Clearing House under a bush.

She had been right all along.

If she was right about this, what other crazy shit was she right about? Was the house really full of bugs, even though Billy couldn't see them? Had his father truly been so good and kind before Billy was born? After years of sixty-hour weeks, had he just worked himself mean, as she always claimed?

As they ate breakfast, Rose told him there were horses in her youth that were still in her mind. There were sour cherries warm from the tree, and dive bombing blue jays, and a bend in the Thyme River where she spent most of her eighth year. In her dreams, it ran next to her sleeping face and poured itself dry when she woke up.

Billy always brought her food with a teal napkin, her favorite shade. It showed her lipstick especially well when she wiped the grease from her face. Her apartment's green wallpaper was occasionally visible behind piles of what she called her projects and what Billy teased her was her abundant nonsense.

Piles of tangled skeins speared through with crochet hooks and metal coat hangers. Single shoes soaked with perfume. An unkempt braid.

"It's a rat made of my mother-in-law's hair. After she had your father, she cut off her long hair. He was a puller. Also a pincher and a biter. He was a very mean baby."

"But he was always nice to me," she said. Rose chose to believe the easiest history.

"I am so glad you are here to help take care of me," she sighed.

She owed him everything, and vice versa.

ǫǫǫ

Melinda, that ditsy bitch who claims she is my social worker, said I could get help at the Wellness Center for all the parts of my neglected body. "Your cheeks are sunken, hon. You can't get no job with that skull face."

"You got to show us you can get on by yourself. Otherwise, you gotta go back." She meant to the hospital of maximum velocity, where I had just spent an unforgettable time. The corridors went on for miles and all I ever got in there was lost.

She tried to pat me on the head, but I put a stop to it. Swiftly.

She pretended to ignore me. Like everyone else.

But, I *was* tired of only eating pudding.

At the Wellness Center front desk, I waited for all the promises of the brochures, but Tony from intake was more interested in a lady named Lucy who he kept telling to quit it. She had brown teeth and smiled broadly.

He gave me a form. The questions I read on it were:

How are you supposed to learn anything in this noisy world?

300

What would you do if you cared?

Do you have any memories of your birth?

Why didn't they feed you?

Have you met the President and, if so, what was he wearing?

Who did this to you?

I tried to answer them all, but sometimes the words on the paper squirmed, curled up and rolled away and the questions changed. It took hours, but even then some of my responses were just silhouettes.

Okay, said Tony, when I finally turned them in. He only glanced at my answers. But they were the right ones. They told the whole story of how I was starved, and now was a young guy with an old guy's problems, how pieces of me had just dried up or fell out, how things hadn't been right for a million years.

He said, "Wait over there and someone will see you." But I am visible all the time. No one needs to see me. They need to help me. They need to listen.

I need help to carry my collection.

ooo

The cop across the street from the Tip Top diner doesn't yet know that there's anything amiss. No one does, except for Billy and the owner, who stands and calmly asks again:

"What can I do for you?"

The customers, many regulars, argue with the others at their tables, or argue silently with themselves. Ketchup is passed after multiple requests. The mother of the fattest baby tries to jiggle him on her knee, but she quickly tires and struggles to place his little bulk back into the stroller.

Henry the widower sits at the booth in the corner, his regular seat, where the floor is always gummy. It comforts him to stick to the ground a little. He doesn't want to fly off just yet. A half-drunk milkshake sits before him, the delicious goo commutes up the straw.

He carries his coins in his dead wife's change purse.

Alone is boring, he thinks.

He is especially curious, but is only ever an observer, watching through a frame. While he tries to engage, other diners smile and nod at him, but then dive back into their massive hamburgers, or fiddle intensely with a jangling, overloaded key ring.

The only one who speaks to him is Billy, but Henry has his suspicions. Billy has perfect eyebrows and an exaggerated smile.

Henry cannot imagine what someone like Billy would want from him.

A full minute passes, and the man with the heavy bag is still standing just inside the door.

Mr. Knowley takes a step toward him. This doesn't change anything.

ooo

There are twelve deliveries on Monday, thinks Frank R. Knowley. There's early morning dairy, right after there's bread. Fruit and veg mid morning and the flowers for the tables to last through Tuesday. Every month there's office supplies and the wandering eyes of the soda salesman, who is always asking if he can squeeze in one more tap. He'll say: It's grape this month that the kids love. I've seen it in *Concession Monthly*. I wouldn't lie to you.

Then there are two meats, one right after the other, beef and pork, then pressed pimento loaf. Napkins and straws and adding machine tape. It all comes on Monday.

Perhaps this fellow can help me with all of this. Most of the time, people just need a job, he thought. He could start right now. He could refill the sugars.

Mr. Knowley always hoped that someday, some lunatic would become employee of the month.

ooo

Billy felt happiest in the present tense of performance when he was Petunia, suspended in perfect seconds, full of blind love, without the need for sisters or night cream or a windfall in the form of piles of tights discovered tucked back behind the dresser drawer.

302

The best thing about performing is that everything is forgotten—it's only now. The band-aids over his nipples didn't rub. The snakes that were hidden under his bed in the dorm weren't writhing in his mind. His stomach, usually a rock tumbler, stopped and the lights made everyone look like friendly, people-shaped shapes.

He didn't have anything depending on him up there, not even a little dog.

Billy thinks: I owe women everything. They taught me how to be myself.

Billy thinks: Everyone should know the moment of hot life and nothing mattering and everything mattering. How music causes a bloat of happiness until buttons pop with joy.

Why not try kindness, so unexpected?

Billy puts down his fork. "Want to sit with me?" he asks, pointing to the seat across from him. The gnome with the bag stares at him, smirks.

ϙϙϙ

Henry watches the scene at the door and slurps up the last of his milkshake. He was careful as he finished not to make that rude sound that his wife so despised, even though she was no longer there to roll her eyes. They had been married for thirty-five years. In all of that time, his mustache had whitened. That was the only obvious change he could see.

When they first met, he and Georgina ate out of each other's hands.

Now he longed for the feeling of her fingers stroking behind his ears.

Now no one touches him.

What was in that scrawny fellow's bag? He strained to see it, sucking in his breath.

ϙϙϙ

Mr. Knowley, tired of waiting, waves frantically at the cop in the car across the street, who is immersed in a story on the radio about his elementary school burning to the ground.

With Mr. Knowley's sudden movement, the gnome comes alive and swings his bag, it hits Billy, *hard,* in the mouth. He swings again, and a streak of blood smears across his face. To Billy the bag feels full of stones.

Billy dives beneath the table as the man swings his bag again, just missing him. From the ground, he sees a tooth fly free from the bag, and the gnome scoop it up.

The room is silent, everyone too stunned to move.

"Teeth!" the gnome screams, swinging the bag around his head like a flail. "I need everyone's teeth! Who's first, you fuckers?" His face is red and snarling. From his bag, pliers appear. Kids start wailing.

Billy sticks his head out from under the table. The regulars he can see are white faced. Each one alone in their terror. There is no way to comfort one of them without comforting all of them.

In the corner, Henry shrinks, feeling the gnome's eyes on him. Was this how he would be touched after such a long time? By a madman who wished him harm? He could not blink. His eyes were dry.

Then Billy has a plan.

He stands up, wobbly.

"You can have mine."

The gnome is determined, poised, in control, unhinged. He is at Billy's side in a moment.

"Show me," he says and presses the pliers to Billy's cheek. Billy smiles slowly. They are straight, evenly spaced, perfect.

"Take a good look," Billy says. "Show me what's in the bag, and you can have them."

The gnome sighs and raps the pliers on the table distractedly.

"Fuck no."

My bag is full of little abstract mountains on a tumbling troubled landscape strewn with the husks of hearts.

I spent years extracting teeth from the skulls of butchered animals that I bought: fair, square.

None of them fit me.

000

"Open up," he grunts. Billy doesn't, but through a clenched jaw:

"Before you take them, tell me why."

"Because somebody took them from me."

He stomps on Billy's foot, who opens his mouth in pain, and then feels the pliers against his gums.

The gnome yanks.

He is confused when the plate comes away, wet and warm, and plops on the table, and so surprised that he loses his grip on the pliers and they fly across the room. The diner is full of wild, fear-powered laughter, overwhelming the gnome who is tackled by the cop who has finally raced in from across the street.

His breath is knocked out of him. The gnome sees no point to inhaling, but his body has other plans.

Then Billy, with his beaten face, faints.

000

Billy's on the ground, bleary, and his face feels sticky, torn and sore. Who knows when Petunia will come out again? He will probably scare his mother. He cannot tell if the bleeding is coming from inside his mouth and swallows, choking. He turns on his side and opens his mouth to let it drain.

The present advances then retreats like a wave.

Billy can feel the other diners gather around him, as though he is a clearing deep in a forest surrounded by dark trees. They encircle him, murmuring.

They speak in ways he cannot believe.

"It's okay, Petunia, the ambulance is on its way."

"Petunia, can we help you up? Can we get you some pie?"

"Your shoes are beautiful, Petunia." He looks down and sees piles of his mother's red and silver pumps around him.

"Petunia."

He is getting lost in the vast plane of the stage.

"Petunia."

Hearing his name fills him with gratitude, joy, light.

Jenny Drummey is a poet, painter, musician, parrot adoption coordinator, technical writer and author. Her novel, UNREQUITED, stars an adolescent who receives the distressing "scientific" prediction of a loveless life, and a mysterious recliner that gives its occupants refuge in an oasis of improved, immersive rememories. With "imagery highly crisp and nuanced…a singular excursion." (Amazon) Visit jennydrummey.com.

CULINARY TALES WITH A BITE

JANE DARROWFIELD, PROFESSIONAL BUSYBODY

BY BARBARA ROSS

The day that started Jane Darrowfield down the path to her second career, one as a professional busybody, was in all ways completely ordinary.

The afternoon was filled with the *burrr* and *thwack* of shuffling cards, and the pungent smell of lime meringues fresh from the oven. The four of them, Helen Graham, Irma Brittleson, Phyllis Goldstein, and Jane, had played cards every Monday for close to forty years. Their weekly bridge game had started as a respite from husbands and kids, then became a refuge from jobs and volunteer work. The previous year, when Jane had finally retired, and Irma, the group's oldest member, expressed concerns about driving at night, their meeting time had changed from evenings to afternoons.

The game rotated among their houses, sharing the burden and blessing of hospitality. They had started with store-bought cookies, hastily purchased. But over the years, as the demands of children and work had fallen away, cooking, and, in particular, eating, had moved to the fore. Their desire to feed each other well had become a friendly competition, to the point where Phyllis had suggested they call themselves, an "Eating Club where a Game of Bridge Sometimes Breaks Out." This was an exaggeration, but only a bit of one.

That afternoon, they were at Jane's solid, shingled house in West Cambridge, Massachusetts. The last hand was almost over when Helen Graham announced with uncharacteristic hesitation that her daughter Elizabeth was engaged.

"That's wonderful!" Phyllis called out, starting the chorus of good wishes. As a group they had married off most of their children, some of them more than once. Stevie Goldstein, quite memorably, more than twice. Elizabeth Graham, called Lizzie, was one of the few singles left. Her engagement should have been a happy event.

Or so it seemed, until Helen burst into noisy sobs.

"Oh, honey." Irma held out a cocktail napkin. "You're not losing a daughter, you're gaining a—"

"That's not it." Helen blew her nose and selected another napkin from the pile on the card table. "I think this man will make her terribly unhappy."

"Is he arrogant, rude, miserly?" Jane asked.

Helen wiped her eyes and shook her head, no.

"Is he impoverished, uneducated, inattentive to personal hygiene?" Irma prompted.

"Goodness, no!"

"Is he married? Gay? A practicing Satanist?" Phyllis suggested.

"Phyllis, you have *got* to stop watching daytime television," Jane admonished, not for the first time.

"Is he mean to her?" Irma asked in a quiet voice. "He doesn't…hurt her?"

"No. No. Not that I know of." Helen dried her eyes.

"Then what is it?" Jane patted her friend's hand.

Helen raised her head to face them, looking at each in turn. "When I look into his eyes, I see nothing looking back. It's like he's dead in there."

000

At home that evening, Jane fixed a bowl of her Andalusian gazpacho, put four tea sandwiches on a plate and sat at her kitchen island. The evening after she hosted bridge club was her favorite of the month. The leftovers were even better when one had the solitude to savor them.

But that night, the cold soup hardened the cold pit of fear in Jane's stomach. Helen's problem haunted her. Everyone agreed it was counterproductive for mothers to express doubts to their daughters about fiancés, particularly doubts that involved the expression "dead behind the eyes."

But what would happen, Jane worried, if he really was? Weren't these dead-eyed men the very ones who murdered their wives, so often when they were pregnant, disposed of their bodies, and blamed the disappearance on foreigners, hippies, or strangers in a van?

Jane liked Lizzie. She was a sweet girl, athletically pretty. While it sometimes seemed like she'd been working on her Ph.D. forever, Lizzie was the apple of her mother's eye, and Helen was Jane's closest friend.

Jane turned this over in her mind. It'd been thirteen months since she'd retired. In that time, she'd cleaned out her closets, basement, and garage. She'd organized her photographs chronologically, her spices alphabetically, and her recipes categorically. She'd traveled to Florence, Siena, and the Amalfi coast. She'd planted a hosta garden on the shady side of the house and written the names of each variety on little ceramic tags. These were the things she'd dreamed of doing all those years at work, and now they were done.

She'd stopped herself when she'd begun sticking acid-free cards to her most precious possessions, explaining what they were, where they had come from, and why they were important to her, so that when she was gone, her son wouldn't be left burdened and baffled, as her mother had left her. *Enough*, she had told herself. *You're not dead yet.* If actuarial tables were any guide, she had twenty more years.

So that evening, Jane decided to break an unwritten rule of forty years of friendship. The bridge club ladies, as their children called them, were good friends, supportive friends. They had taken turns driving Irma to chemo and held her head while she vomited afterwards. They'd made sure Phyllis had plenty of casseroles and companionship while her husband was dying. They'd held their bridge game at Helen's house for two whole years until her mother's Alzheimer's progressed to the point where she'd had to be moved to safer place.

They cared. They supported. But they didn't stick their noses into one another's business and try to change things. That's what their grandmothers and great aunts had done back in the small towns and urban neighborhoods where their parents had grown up. It wasn't what well-educated, modern women did.

It certainly wasn't anything Jane had ever been tempted to do. Until that moment, at her kitchen island, when she decided she must act.

ooo

If she was going to intervene, Jane's first order of business was to tell Helen. She wasn't going to do anything behind Helen's back.

It was a conversation better had in person, so at a little after nine the next morning, Jane walked along the curving sidewalk of her Cambridge neighborhood, headed toward the next block. The day promised to be a scorcher and almost every yard in their little enclave was in riotous bloom. As she walked, Jane thought about how happy she was to be here, in this strange island of almost suburban homes, a mere mile and a half from Harvard Square.

As Jane came up Helen's front walk, the door opened to reveal lanky, loose-jointed Hugh Graham, going off to his job as judge at Middlesex Superior Court.

"Jane, bright and early."

"Is your wife about?"

"In the kitchen."

"Congratulations on Lizzie's engagement. What do you think of him?"

Hugh shielded his eyes from the morning sun and looked down at Jane. "So you've heard the 'dead behind the eyes' theory. The truth is I don't like him much, but a father is suspicious of any man who takes his little girl, particularly his baby. Lizzie's almost thirty. I don't see what we can do to stop her, so I'm playing the role of supportive father of the bride."

Jane said good-bye to Hugh and found Helen in the Grahams' comfortable, French country kitchen. They sat at the table overlooking the small, beautifully cultivated yard with its tiny waterwheel and goldfish pond. It was a testament to how truly worried Helen was that she didn't protest when Jane explained what she wanted to do.

"How will you do it?" Helen asked.

Jane had thought the first part through. "I think I should meet him." Jane trusted Helen completely. Her friend was not one for hyperbole or drama. She and Hugh had successfully married off their two older children and through their engagements there had never been any discussion of dead eyes. Nonetheless, Jane thought if she was going to break up an engagement, she needed to confirm the problem for herself.

"What's this fiancé's name?"

"Philip Debenow."

"Where does he live?"

"In one of those big condo buildings on Memorial Drive, near Kendall Square."

"I could try to see him there. Is Lizzie likely to be with him?"

"Oh, no. She's kept her apartment. I get the impression they spend most of their time together at her place." Helen shrugged. "You know how things are. They're adults." By today's standards Helen had been a mere girl when she'd married and given up a place at Harvard Law School to go to work as a legal secretary and put Hugh through instead.

"I need to find someplace where I could easily run into him," Jane said. "Where does he work?"

"In the biology lab on Divinity Place. He does some kind of research. I don't understand it, though Lizzie has explained it to me. It has something to do with cows' eyeballs. Lots and lots of cows' eyeballs. He has them delivered by the crate."

"Good heavens."

"Wait a minute." Helen glanced across the room at the digital clock on her stove. "Lizzie told me she meets him at the Starbucks on Church Street at ten every morning for coffee. It's between their two offices. If you leave now, maybe you can catch them."

Jane noted her friend's eagerness, another confirmation of her desperation. She returned to her house and grabbed her bag. Weighing the impossibility and expense of parking in Harvard Square against the time and the heat of the day, Jane decided her best bet was to walk. Passing the magnificent mansions on Brattle Street, their gardens at a summer peak, strengthened her resolve.

Outside the Longfellow House, a gaggle of tourists waited for the first tour of the day. A young National Park Service guide tipped his Smokey Bear hat to Jane, revealing a sweaty head. As she walked, she plotted her next move.

Jane arrived at Starbucks with ten minutes to spare. She bought a latte and hovered behind the line of sleepy summer students and young mothers with strollers waiting for a seat.

A few minutes later, Lizzie Graham danced in and took her place in line. Watching her, Jane was struck by how pretty she was. Her blonde hair tumbled around her face like a Botticelli painting and she had the healthy body of the rower she was. By ten o'clock, Lizzie was almost to the front of the line when a man well into his forties walked in. He was darkly handsome with a white streak in his beard. Lizzie gave him a peck on his cheek.

"Lizzie!" Jane called. "What are you doing here?"

"Aunt Jane! How wonderful to run into you."

Jane walked deliberately into their orbit. She was a little surprised by Philip Debenow's age. Perhaps that was at the heart of Helen's objection. But Lizzie was almost thirty, as Hugh had reminded Jane that morning, so the difference wasn't impossibly great.

"Aunt Jane, I'd like you to meet my fiancé, Philip. Dr. Debenow."

Mrs. Darrowfield looked up and Philip Debenow looked down. Their eyes met. Jane had the sensation of swimming in great, dark pools of nothing at all. A chill ran up her spine.

ooo

"Now what will you do?" Helen used her fork to play with the piece of blueberry coffee cake on her plate until it collapsed into a pile of crumbs.

"If he has always been without a soul, there must be trouble in his wake. Friends betrayed. Girlfriends broken-hearted. Torture of small animals," Jane said.

"Stop."

"Have you met his parents?"

312

"They're both dead. You must have noticed he's a little older."

"Not so old that it isn't tragic to have lost them both," Jane said, thinking her own son's beard must have some gray in it by now. "Where is this Dr. Debenow from?"

"He grew up here, in Cambridge."

Back in her home office, Jane typed "Philip Debenow" into a search engine. Fortunately, it was an unusual name.

Philip Debenow ran in a lot of road races. And he gave a good many speeches about eyeballs, some with the most startling pictures of a cow's optic nerve, which looked like a lonely, windswept tree sitting on a hillock

A genealogy site offered up a birth certificate: Forty-six years ago, at Saint Elizabeth's Hospital in Brighton, Massachusetts, Philip Andrew Debenow. Father Robert. Mother Louise.

Jane checked the White Pages online. Philip Debenow didn't appear, but a Robert Debenow was listed on Hurley Street, East Cambridge.

ⓆⓆⓆ

Jane parked across the street from Robert Debenow's house. It was as far from Jane's own house as it could possibly be in her dense little city, almost four miles away. The lots were tiny, the houses close together, but even this urban neighborhood, so long home to artisans and factory workers, hadn't escaped gentrification. Several of the houses had been fashioned into gleaming contemporaries, to the point where it was impossible to imagine their original exteriors.

Robert Debenow's house had definitely not been gentrified. From its barely shingled roof to its peeling asbestos siding and sagging porches, it was the most run down house on the block.

Jane sat in the car until the heat got to her, sticking her to the seat. "No time like the present," she muttered. A push on the doorbell resulted in a scuffling sound, followed by the opening of bolts, at least three. The woman who stood in the dark hall,

313

blinking at Jane standing in the sunlight, was slight and stooped, dressed in a sleeveless housedress.

"Whaddya want?" she demanded.

"I'm wondering if you're related to Philip Debenow, who works at Harvard?"

"He's my son," said the apparently unlate Louise Debenow.

"Oh." *So we know at a minimum he's a liar.* "I'm a friend of his fiancée's and I'm only in town for a couple of days. I lost her phone number and address and neither of them are listed. I saw your husband's name in the phone book and I'm wondering if you can help me?" Jane was amazed at how easily it was to lie in a good cause.

"You're a friend of Gina's?"

Gina's? Now Jane was the one who was blinking. "A family friend," she amended. "Do you know how I can reach her?"

"I've never been to her place, but you can check his. She might be there." To this statement, Louise Debenow added a meaningful, "these young people," look.

"Thank you so much. You're a lifesaver. What is your son's address?"

"75 Cambridge Parkway. Apartment 10B."

ooo

Jane stood in the airless vestibule of 75 Cambridge Parkway, scanning the mailboxes. She had considered going straight to Helen's and reporting what she'd found, but decided she needed to be sure. She'd been hoping to find two names on the mailbox, easy proof, but the box for 10B was labeled "P. Debenow."

Jane was wondering what to do next when a woman with a small dog opened the inside door. The dog danced a tiny jig, like he might not make it to the street, and while the owner was distracted, Jane scurried into the building.

She found 10B with no trouble and put her ear to the door. No sound came from within. Jane hit the bell, which gave a satisfying pong, but it was followed by silence. She was about to give up when the elevator dinged and a young woman in running

314

CULINARY TALES WITH A BITE

clothes walked off, headed straight toward her. The woman's brown hair was pulled back and she was covered in a thin coat of perspiration, but you could tell she was gorgeous, in a darkly exotic way. Just the opposite of Lizzie Graham's blond farm girl look. A diamond ring sparkled on the woman's left hand.

"May I help you?"

"I'm considering buying a condo in the building." Jane had decided as she rode up the elevator this would be her cover story. "Do you like it here? Is this your unit?"

"My fiancé's actually," the woman said as she put her key in the lock at 10B. "I could never afford it. Are you considering buying the Carstairs' place?"

"Yes, I think that's their name."

"It's lovely. I've been in there. Of course, the units on that side don't have river views."

"Do you think I should wait until one with a river view opens up?"

"See for yourself." The young woman swung the door open and waved Jane inside.

The apartment was beautiful, in muted grays and beiges. The lines were clean, the decoration spare, but carefully chosen and placed. And, of course, through the windows of the open living and dining areas, there was a breathtaking view of the Charles River, with the Boston skyline beyond, the golden dome of the statehouse gleaming atop Beacon Hill.

"It's lovely," Jane said. "But these views must add a lot to the price. What does your fiancé do?"

It was the first intrusive question Jane had asked, but the pleasant, open woman who must be Gina didn't seem to mind. "He's a professor of biology at Harvard. He bought ten years ago, before the prices exploded."

"And you?"

The woman laughed. "I'm working on my doctorate in medieval philosophy." There was a sharp, vibrating sound. The woman took her cell phone out of the pocket in her arm band, looked at it, then placed it on the coffee table. "The building management is pretty good," she continued, "and the condo fees are reasonable. But as I said, I don't own the unit. My fiancé Philip could answer those types of questions. He'll be here any minute. He's just texted me from the garage."

Jane's heart lurched. "No, no. I've taken up too much of your time."

"Are you sure? Do you want to see the amenities? There's a gym and a pool, and a common roof deck. I have a pass key."

"No, thank you." Jane moved toward the door. "You've been too kind." She stuck out her hand. "Thank you so much for showing me the apartment."

The younger woman gave another one of her broad smiles. "I hope we can be neighbors. My name is Karen. Karen Albanese."

Jane scampered out to door, so distracted by Philip Debenow's imminent arrival, she could barely process what she'd heard. *Karen, not Gina. A third fiancée!*

The floor indicator lights above the elevators were both on L for lobby. Thank goodness. But before Jane could push the call button, the one on her left began to rise. Second floor, third. In no time it would be at the tenth. Jane's stomach rose with each movement of the light. Looking wildly around, she spotted an exit sign and ran for the stairway. When the elevator dinged, Jane peeked through the barely open fire door. Philip Debenow got off, walking casually toward his apartment, keys held out in front of him, his eyes as dead as a doll's.

ooo

Jane and Helen sat in the Graham kitchen, chewing on Helen's remarkable shortbread cookies along with what Jane had learned.

"You could have knocked me over with a feather," Jane said. "I checked the mailbox on the way out, just to be sure, and there it was, 'P. Debenow.'"

"Is there any chance this could be some terrible mix-up?"

Jane considered. "No. One extra fiancée is perhaps a mix up, but two is solid evidence." She reached down and rubbed her calf. When she'd tried to open the door to the ninth floor of Debenow's building, it had been locked and she'd had to climb all the way down to the lobby.

316

"I'll have to tell Lizzie." Helen didn't look happy at the prospect.

Jane had been pondering this eventuality ever since her meeting with Louise Debenow that morning. "Helen, I don't think you should. We don't want Lizzie to hate the messenger."

"But she has to know. What should we do?"

"I think I should have a talk with Dr. Debenow."

ooo

The next morning, at five minutes to ten, Jane planted herself firmly on the corner of Church and Palmer Street. She'd looked up the Harvard building where Philip Debenow worked, and she was certain he would approach from this direction for his daily coffee break with Lizzie. His eyes had so unnerved her, she wanted to confront him in public, not in his lab or the empty hallway of his apartment building. If the sequence from the previous day was their usual one, Lizzie was already safely inside Starbucks, waiting in line.

Sure enough, a few minutes later, Debenow walked into view. Jane stepped into his way. She was nervous, but this was about Lizzie, and ultimately about Helen, with whom Jane had been through so much. Jane squared her shoulders and spoke. "Dr. Debenow, I'm Jane Darrowfield. We met the other day."

Debenow stopped. His face betrayed nothing. Probably, Karen Albanese hadn't mentioned an encounter with an older condo purchaser. And probably, he hadn't spoken to his mother since Jane had been to see her. Probably.

"I met you with your fiancée," Jane continued. "For clarity, that would be Lizzie Graham, but I also know about Karen and Gina. Would you care to explain?"

Debenow's expression changed swiftly, like thunderheads rolling in. "No." He pushed past her, hitting her shoulder and spinning her around. "No, I would not."

Jane hurried after him. "Good. Because honestly, I don't like to have my time wasted." By then, they were across the street in front of Starbucks plate glass window. Now that she'd started, Jane had to see the conversation through. She touched Debenow's

317

arm to get his attention. "Here's what's going to happen. You're going to break it off with Lizzie. Today. Or I'm going to the police. I'm not sure what the crime is, but I'm sure there is one. Remember, Lizzie's father is a Superior Court judge who works daily with the police and prosecutors. They'll be interested in what I have to say."

"Shut your face, you stupid old busybody!" Debenow raised his hand. Jane braced for the blow.

"Philip! Aunt Jane!" Lizzie stood in the doorway of Starbucks, her pale skin nearly translucent.

"You haven't heard the last from me!" Debenow shouted. But then he turned and walked away briskly, and Jane thought they probably had.

ooo

Jane was late to bridge the next Monday, the victim of her dentist, whom she adored, but who couldn't keep on schedule if his life depended on it. It was clear when Jane entered Phyllis Goldstein's living room that Helen had told the whole story.

Lizzie had been crushed by the end of her engagement. But she was going to be crushed by Debenow at some point, and it was better done completely and cleanly, as soon as possible. She was home for a few weeks, in the house she grew up in, enjoying the ministrations of her sympathetic parents.

"How did he expect to get away with it, all of them living and working within two square miles of one another?" Irma Brittleson asked.

"Cambridge is a big city and a collection of small towns," Jane answered. "Harvard is too, for that matter. Lizzie and Karen probably passed each other hundreds of times, one sculling, the other running along the Charles. But if Debenow compartmentalized enough, took each one only certain places, never introduced them to colleagues, friends or his 'dead' parents, it could be done. It was done."

"But what was the end game?" Irma asked. "What was going to happen when one of them demanded a wedding or got pregnant?"

318

"He'd chop them up in little pieces and bury them in the garden," Phyllis said.

"Phyllis, we've told you to turn off the darn TV," Jane warned, but Helen said nothing. She had, after all, originally described Debenow as "dead behind the eyes."

Jane shuddered. Her mind wandered to the knot she had been trying to untie for the last few days. What, if anything, did she owe to Karen Albanese and the surnameless Gina? Helen had invited Jane to solve a family problem, but Karen and Gina hadn't asked her into their lives. Were Jane to say anything, would she be seen as an old lady buttinsky, or would the information she had be accepted and eventually valued?

"Jane was wonderful," Helen said. "She knew what to do. I don't know what would have happened to Lizzie without her."

Jane deflected the praise. "Any one of you would have done the same." But the truth was, while solving the problem of Philip Debenow, she'd felt more alive and useful than she had in months. It was invigorating to pull out the skills that had served her so well at work—breaking down a problem, researching, planning, taking action, bringing about a resolution. And most of all, understanding people, how to read and motivate them.

The bridge hands were dealt and the goodies passed. Jane's dentist had warned her not to eat or drink for an hour, so she took a piece of Phyllis's delicious quiche and put the plate aside. It would be even more pleasurable later.

The women moved on to other topics. But at the end of the game, as Jane walked to her car, Irma Brittleson called after her.

"Jane! Jane! I wouldn't normally ask, but after what you did for Helen, I wonder if you could help us. It's about my mother."

Barbara Ross is the author of the Maine Clambake Mysteries: *Clammed Up, Boiled Over, Musseled Out, Fogged Inn,* and *Iced Under. Stowed Away* will be released in December, 2017. Barbara's books have been nominated for multiple **Agatha Awards for Best Contemporary Novel,** and **RT Books Reviewer's Choice Awards**, as well as the **Maine Literary Award for Crime Fiction.**